UNDERCOVER
TARGET

OTHER BOOKS AND AUDIO BOOKS

BY FRANK HOLDAWAY

Undercover Saint

UNDERCOVER TARGET

a novel of suspense

FRANK HOLDAWAY

Covenant Communications, Inc.

Cover image: *Hikers Silhouetted at Dusk* © guvendemir, *Rifle Sight* © dvarg, courtsey of istockphoto.com.

Cover design copyright © 2016 by Covenant Communications, Inc.

Published by Covenant Communications, Inc.
American Fork, Utah

Printed in the United States of America
First Printing: August 2016

22 21 20 19 18 17 16   10 9 8 7 6 5 4 3 2 1

ISBN-13: 978-1-52440-058-3

This one's for Cory

Prologue
A CHANGING OF THE GUARD

PENG LOOKED DOWN THROUGH THE tiny holes he had drilled in the ceiling above the consultation room. The area between the supporting beams and the heating duct was barely sufficient for him to squeeze his small body into. He really didn't like confined spaces, but this was important. He slowed his breathing and lay still. He couldn't afford to be discovered. Not today.

The door opened. Mistress Wu entered, the two foreigners trailing her. Peng strained to get a better look at the American woman. At first, all he could see was her hair. Mountains of it. He had never seen hair like that anywhere before. Even in American pictures. Even in American movies. Even among the women of the evening in rough areas close to the docks. Peng wondered why anyone would want so much hair and what kind of woman would be under it. He wasn't sure he liked what it might say about her. He thought about pulling back from his hiding place, rushing to Jin's room, and fleeing with his sister before the transaction could take place. But then the woman turned toward Mistress Wu, and Peng could finally see her face.

He almost gasped but caught himself. The woman was beautiful. Extremely beautiful. As beautiful as anything he had ever seen in his life. But even at that, it wasn't her beauty that had caught him off guard—it was the light. It emanated from her face like a beacon, and kindness seemed to pour out of her eyes in a never-ending stream. Her eyes were nothing like his mother's, yet Peng could see in them the same thing that he had seen in his mother's when she had held his baby sister. It was as if this woman's eyes had the power to wrap a person in a blanket of safety and not let the pain that was the world enter in.

He felt relief flood into his limbs. But also a little sadness. He could fulfill his promise today. He could see Jin safely placed into a good home, and with his promise fulfilled, he could finalize his plans for getting Shi-Shi away from here before everything was taken from her. He began to think ahead, imagining traveling down the hallways and corridors of the orphanage to Shi-Shi's room, bypassing the doors and locks that would lead to the outside world and eventually to freedom.

Peng began to wriggle his way out of his hiding place when he realized he had almost forgotten to look at the man. What if Jin was going to a home like the one she had just come from? One where the mother was everything a mother should be but the home itself was tainted by a dominant and abusive male? He adjusted himself so he could see the man's face. He breathed another sigh of relief. The man's face was strong, and his eyes reflected intelligence and curiosity. No signs of cruelty like Peng's stepfather. No leering hunger like the guards. There was something else in them, too, that differed from most men's. A watchfulness. A keen attentiveness to the actions going on around him. He even looked up at the ceiling. For a moment, Peng held his breath, thinking he might have been spotted. But the man paused for only a moment before continuing to scan the room.

"So sorry," Mistress Wu said to the couple. "My Engrish not very good." This was interesting since Mistress Wu spoke flawless "Engrish" and insisted that all of the girls and boys in the orphanage master the language—including practicing the very difficult pronunciation of English L's and R's.

"I will call for the interpreter," she said, nodding to a man who was standing near the door. "Mister Seng," she said in Chinese, "go get Mae and the baby, and make sure you smile and bow as you leave the room. You look like a prison guard."

Mister Seng bowed. "I am a prison guard," he replied in his native tongue, smiling and nodding as he left the room. "But I know how to play my part."

Mistress Wu nodded to Mister Seng. The smile remained on her face, but there was ice in her glare. Peng stared at her fake smile and thought about Mister Seng's fake bow. He stared at the fake warm light in the fake reception room and felt the bile rising in his throat. He pushed back the sickness that permeated this place and reminded himself that he would leave here tonight and he would take Shi-Shi with him. Where they would go he did not know. But any place was better than here. He had only this one promise left to keep, and the woman and man were better than he could have hoped.

He eyed them once again. The man looked a bit anxious. He was studying Mistress Wu. There was a glint of suspicion that had not been there before. In a matter of seconds, something had changed. But what was it? Peng replayed the scene in his mind. Mistress Wu's polite instructions to Seng. Seng's apparently deferential response. Nothing to raise suspicion unless . . .

The man had understood what Mistress Wu and Mister Seng had said. He understood their language and could see right through the act. Peng's gut twisted inside him. His promise, his plans, his future were all in jeopardy. He had not cried since his real father had died when he was eight years old. Not when his mother had dropped him and his sister off at the orphanage doors, saying it was the only way to keep them safe; not when the guards had beaten him mercilessly; not even when word had come that the reason he no longer saw his mother walking by on the roads was because she had suffered a terrible accident. But he wanted to cry now. His hopes were placed in the two people below him, and Mistress Wu was ruining everything.

Before Peng's despair manifested itself, Mister Seng reentered the room, along with a female interpreter. She held something precious in her arms—Peng's baby sister. As if by some metaphysical connection, the baby's eyes seemed to look up through the ceiling and focus on Peng. She squealed with laughter, and Peng smiled despite the situation. Light flowed out of her, and Peng realized the baby and the foreign woman were alike in that way. They were perfect for each other. This match was meant to be. He was sure of it. But what would the man do?

The woman let go of the man's hand and rushed to the baby, excitement in her eyes. "She's beautiful. May I hold her?"

The interpreter handed the baby to the woman. "Certainly."

The baby squealed again as the woman took her and their light melted together. "Oh, Matt," the woman said, "isn't she perfect?"

The man cast his eyes around the room and then let them rest on his wife and the baby. His suspicion seemed to melt away as he saw the two of them together. "Perfect," he agreed, walking toward them. "Absolutely perfect."

"We want her," the woman said to Mistress Wu. "We want to take her today."

Peng let out the breath he hadn't known he was holding. He smiled down through the ceiling at his little sister. She would have a home after all. She had played her part well. The man wouldn't stop this, would he?

Mistress Wu spoke to the interpreter, and she indicated that the couple should sit down at the table while Mister Seng retrieved the paperwork. The woman handed the baby to the man, who seemed both awkward and overly careful, asking several times if he were holding her correctly. It reminded Peng of when he had first held Jin. The woman laughed and kissed the man on the cheek. They would be a good family for his sister. He could be at peace about his promise.

Mister Seng brought in a folder filled with papers and whispered something in Mistress Wu's ear. Mistress Wu changed her expression from smiling to distraught and said something sharp under her breath. Mister Seng shrugged and nodded to the folder.

"Is there a problem?" the foreign woman said.

The translator interpreted.

Mistress Wu nodded to the woman, who had taken the baby back from the man and was holding her nestled against her shoulder. She spoke to the interpreter in Mandarin. "I think the hook has been set. You know what to do." Peng wanted to scream at her through the ceiling. *The man can understand you, you fool.* She thought she was being clever, and she was going to ruin everything. The man called Matt stiffened at her words but didn't say anything.

"There seems to be an issue with this child," the interpreter said, pretending to translate Mistress Wu's words. "There is a stipulation in the contract for the adopting family."

"What kind of stipulation?" Matt asked.

"Apparently, the child has a brother. The contract stipulates that the family cannot be broken up."

"She has a brother?" the woman with the large hair asked. "How old? Where is he?"

Peng jerked and bumped his head on the ceiling. The noise was audible, but no one in the room seemed to notice, except Mister Seng, who looked up. Peng thought he saw the hint of a smile.

"The boy lives here at the orphanage," the translator said to the woman. "He is ten years old. He is little Anna's older brother. A good boy."

There were so many lies that Peng almost laughed. He was thirteen, not ten. His sister's name was Jin, not Anna. And he was definitely not a "good boy."

"And the cost would be the same?" the American man asked. "For us to take the brother too?"

Mistress Wu spoke, and the translator interpreted. "You must understand, there would be a paperwork fee for the boy as well. It is the law, and we cannot go around it."

Matt spoke directly to Mistress Wu. "Actually, I think the law might be very interested in your mode of operation here at this orphanage."

"Very well," Mistress Wu said, somehow remembering her English. "If you do not want the child, we will take her back now. There are other families who are anxiously waiting."

The woman with the hair pulled Jin closer to her bosom. "Matt, it's not about the money," she said. "She has a brother. They are family. We can't separate them."

"They've had this planned from the beginning," Matt said. "This whole thing with the paperwork is just an act. They wanted you to fall in love with the baby first, and then they would bring in the boy and ask for double."

"I know," the woman said. "And I'll bet Mistress Wu doesn't even need a translator. But I don't care. We can't leave this baby here, and we can't separate her from her brother."

Matt stared at his wife and the baby, and his stance seemed to relax just a bit. "I want to see the boy first."

"Very well," Mistress Wu said. "Mister Seng, please go get Andrew."

"Certainly, Mistress." Mister Seng stepped across the room in giant steps and opened the door.

No, no, no, Peng thought. He began to frantically inch his way out of the crawl space. What was he going to do? If he left now—found Shi-Shi and escaped into the country—he could be out of this place and gone forever. They would have no food, no shelter, and no friends, but it would be better than remaining here. He could take care of Shi-Shi. But who would take care of Jin? He had promised to see that his sister was placed with a good family. If he ran away, the shining woman and the clever man might also leave. Who would Jin be sold to then? Would they keep her until she was older and auction her off to one of the stinking fishermen with the leering eyes like they planned to do with Shi-Shi?

Peng emerged from the heating duct and stood still in the boiler room. Should he let Mister Seng find him or go to Shi-Shi and flee? He felt as if his feet were nailed to the floor, not willing to make a move in either direction. He frantically brushed the dust from his pants.

"Not a good way to make a first impression for your new parents." Mister Seng's voice was tempered and pleasant, as if he were speaking to someone over rice at the dinner table. Peng turned to run, and Mister Seng caught him by the neck. His grip was hard, and his fingers seemed to bite deep into Peng's spine. "I know you want to stay here with us, but there is a time when a boy must grow up. When he must become a man and accept responsibility." Peng struggled to free himself, but it was no use. Mister Seng dragged him through the hallway toward the room with the foreign couple. Toward the room with Jin. Away from Shi-Shi and away from freedom.

Mister Seng stopped before they entered the room and spoke in a low voice. "I would advise you to be on your best behavior."

Peng glared back defiantly.

Mister Seng shrugged. "Suit yourself. But know this. If your sister does not leave with these people today, I have secured another buyer. A man from a ship who would gladly take both a baby and a young girl for a very good price. So be careful of what you say."

Peng felt like his knees were giving out under him. Even if he and Jin left with the Americans, Shi-Shi would remain here. She was his friend. His only friend. They had arrived at the orphanage on the same day. She was just beginning to emerge from childhood to become a young woman, and although Peng had been in the orphanage only a few months, he knew that pretty young women did not last long. She would be sold soon for a high price—if the guards did not ruin her first. She had barely escaped so far, and that was with Peng watching out for her. His plans to protect her had been destroyed, and there was nothing he could do about it. Mister Seng opened the door and nudged Peng until he stepped inside.

The woman holding Jin rushed toward him, compassion in her eyes as she searched his face. "What is your name? Do you speak English?"

Peng could feel a warmth emanating from her. He longed to leave with these people, to get away from this place, and this longing brought him shame. He bowed his head and looked at the floor.

"Answer the nice lady," Mister Seng said to him, then turned to the woman. "He speaks English, but he is very quiet. He is a good boy. Very obedient." Mister Seng nudged Peng with his arm.

"My name is Peng," he said to the cold tile floor that seemed to mock him.

The woman bent down in front of him so she could look up into his face. "Would you like to come live with us in America? You and your sister, Anna."

"Her name is Jin," Peng said, his eyes lifting to meet the woman's. Mister Seng glared at him.

Mistress Wu laughed and waved a hand. "It is true. Her Chinese name is Jin. But we also give the children English names. She is a baby. You can choose whatever name you like."

"Her name is Jin," Peng said again, defiance in his eyes. "It is what our mother named her."

"Jin." The American woman nodded as she spoke. "That is a beautiful name. I think she should keep it." The woman winked at Peng, and he felt himself wanting to smile. He almost couldn't stop himself. He felt drawn to her. It was only by picturing Shi-Shi that he was not completely taken in by the woman's personality. He could not leave his friend here.

Peng turned to Matt. "We have another sister," he blurted out. "Her name is Shi-Shi. We cannot leave without her. Our mother would not want it. They want to sell her to the fishing boats." He said the words quickly before Mister Seng or Mistress Wu could stop him.

Mister Seng's face turned red, and he took a step toward Peng, then stopped himself.

The mask of pleasantness Mistress Wu wore on her face disappeared briefly and then returned as she composed herself.

Peng watched the foreign man's eyes and knew that he had seen everything.

"How old is Shi-Shi?" Matt asked Mistress Wu.

Mistress Wu stumbled on her words. "Shi-Shi is ten, but you do not understand. She is not their sister. This boy is infatuated with her. You know how young love can be."

Matt ignored Mistress Wu and spoke directly to Peng. "She is the same age as you?"

"I am thirteen," Peng said. "Shi-Shi is ten. She cannot stay here." Peng cast his gaze to Mister Seng, and he felt a burn coming into his cheeks. Matt watched him carefully and then nodded, seeming to understand.

"You told us Peng was ten," Matt said to Mistress Wu. "It appears that you have not been truthful with us. There are many stories of Chinese orphanages misrepresenting the ages of older children. I believe the regulatory agencies would be interested in knowing about this."

Mistress Wu laughed nervously. "Did I say ten? I meant thirteen. It was an honest mistake."

"An honest mistake that seems to have made it into the official paperwork," Matt said, pointing to the folder in front of him.

"Matt," the American woman whispered. "What are you doing?" He nodded to her as if saying, "Trust me."

"We'll take all three children," Matt said. "And we will take them today. Please go get Shi-Shi, Mister Seng."

Mister Seng raised his eyebrows in Mistress Wu's direction.

"But, sir, there is the matter of payment."

"We will pay you triple what we would have paid for the baby. And you know the market price for adopted older children is less than infants, so that is more than a fair deal."

"For older boys, maybe. But for young girls . . ." Mistress Wu seemed to catch herself midsentence.

"I don't think you want us looking into your market for young girls. Go get Shi-Shi now, and bring her paperwork. Otherwise we will leave and come back with the authorities."

Mistress Wu's smile disappeared. "You are a long way from home, Mr. Knight. A long way from ears that will listen to you."

"Do you think so, Mistress Wu? How do you think we came to find out about your orphanage here in the middle of nowhere? I have plenty of ears in high places that will listen to me. Believe me, you don't want to test that."

Mistress Wu did not replace her smile, but she did nod to Mister Seng. "Get the girl. Let's get these people out of here."

On his way out the door, Mister Seng turned to Peng and spoke in Mandarin. "It looks like you will have a new set of guards."

Matt turned to Mister Seng and said in a nearly perfect accent, "The term is *guardians*, Mister Seng. There is a difference. A big difference."

Chapter 1

ESCAPE

Two years later

"MATT, WAKE UP." HOPE SHOOK my shoulder, but I was already awake. Wide awake. I had awoken as soon as she had stirred and left the bed. Years of training will do that to you. Training I wished would work its way out of my system—especially at three o'clock on a Sunday morning when I had been intending to sleep in.

I could feel the anxiety in Hope's voice when she spoke. "He's gone," she said.

I groaned and sat up. "The locks?"

"Still locked."

"The alarm?"

"Still armed."

"And you're sure he's not anywhere in the house?"

"I checked everywhere. He's not here." I could see now that she held Jin, asleep, in her arms, the baby's head hidden in the curls of Hope's hair. The sight of them silhouetted in the light in the hallway took my breath away. My two women. My two angels. Why did Peng have to be so difficult?

When I first met Hope, I thought her mountains of hair were a sign of pretentiousness or insecurity. But I found out she worked in a specialized medical unit designed for kids with cancer, that she was a survivor of the disease herself, and that she used her hair as a beacon of light for children who were in a very dark place. But even Hope seemed to have difficulty getting through to Peng.

"I thought you said the new locks could not be defeated," Hope said.

"That's what the installer told me. Apparently the installer hasn't met Peng."

"Apparently not." Hope began to bounce Jin faster. Her voice was tight as she spoke. "What do you think he does when he leaves at this time of night? Do you think he's doing something . . . bad?"

I pulled on my pants, T-shirt, and socks. "With his ability to get around locks, maybe he's robbing a bank," I said. "At least we could recoup some of our adoption expenses."

"Matt." The tone in Hope's voice told me that now was not an appropriate time for me to act like me. "There are gangs on the streets. Drug dealers. Bad people. You don't think he's involved in something, do you?"

I thought before responding. "I've never seen any sign of drugs. And when I find him, he's not hanging out with gangbangers or junkies. He's not hanging out with anybody. He's always alone. He's always at a bus stop or Trax station. It's almost like he wants me to find him. But whether he's involved in something bad . . . well, your guess is as good as mine."

"Aren't you supposed to be good at reading people?" Hope was glaring at me now, and I wasn't too comfortable being on the receiving end of her wrath.

"I am very good at reading people," I said, pulling on my sneakers. "For example, I can see that you would really like to hit me right now."

Hope let out a large breath and stopped bouncing Jin. "I don't want to hit you. I'm just afraid. I'm afraid we are going to lose him. I'm afraid we *are* losing him. This is such a critical age. If he goes off the rails now, he may never come back."

"I'm not sure he's really ever been here," I said, pulling on my shirt. I put my hand on Hope's shoulder as I thought about Peng and the faraway look he often had in his eyes.

"Maybe we should be tougher on him," Hope said, bouncing Jin again and breaking contact with me. "Other parents ground their kids when they disobey. Maybe we are being too lenient."

"Maybe," I said. "But other parents don't have a kid that could break out of Fort Knox. Besides, he spends most of his time alone in his room anyway. Grounding him to his room might feel like a reward."

"We could take away his electronics."

I laughed. "He would probably just make more. I've never seen anyone who can look at a piece of machinery or electronics like he does and automatically know how it works. Maybe he's just another Einstein. Maybe he just needs the night air to incubate his genius."

"He's our son. We have to do something. We're his parents. We can't just let him dictate the terms. He needs structure. He needs discipline." She bit at her lower lip. She was looking at the wall, but her words were directed at me. "He needs a father," she said.

I stood, grabbed my jacket, and walked past her out the door. I should have just left without saying anything. I should have walked out the door and let the steam roll out of my ears. But I was never very good at keeping my mouth shut.

"I know what he needs," I said, disarming the house alarm and unlocking the several locks that were supposed to be undefeatable. "But I'm not sure I'm the one who can give it to him. I didn't grow up with the greatest of role models. My father was an addict who killed himself before I was born, so I'm flying a little blind here. Excuse me if I'm not very good at this." Before Hope could respond, I walked out the door and into the night.

* * *

It took me a little longer than usual to find him. Hope had trained me to pray before going out to look, and it really did seem to speed up the process. But I didn't really feel like praying this morning. I felt like running away myself.

The first time he'd gone missing, we'd panicked and called the police. They'd eventually found Peng at a bus stop a few miles from our home. This turned out to be a pattern. When Peng disappeared, which happened about once a month, he always seemed to end up near some form of public transportation: bus stop, bus station, Trax station, train station, and once the airport. He never left the Salt Lake Valley, and he wouldn't try to run when I found him. He would just sit there like he was waiting to be picked up from school.

This time he was on a bench at the Thirteenth South Trax station, the one next to the ballpark. The trains didn't start running until about five fifty, so I didn't think he was going anywhere. He had a hoodie pulled up over his head and was listening to his headphones.

I took a deep breath, walked over to him, and sat on the bench beside him. He knew I was there, but he didn't acknowledge me. The frustration in my gut as I'd stormed out the door flared up again. I reached up, pulled off his hood, and yanked an earbud out of one ear.

"Couldn't you do this when there is a ballgame going on?" I said, trying to gain control and drain the irritation from my voice.

He shrugged and looked at the ground. This was Peng's way of communicating.

"You know Hope can't sleep when you run out like this. She's home bouncing Jin up and down like a hot potato. She thinks that maybe you've joined a gang or become a drug addict."

I saw a glint of protest in Peng's eyes, but instead of denying it, he calmed himself and shrugged again.

I thought about what Hope had said about being stricter with him, about introducing consequences. I tried to imagine what a good father would do in this situation. I had no clue.

"If this continues, there are going to be consequences," I said. "No electronics for a month." The words sounded strange to me as I heard them come out of my mouth. They must have sounded strange to Peng too because he looked at me as if studying a puzzle.

He finally shrugged again and said, "Okay."

For some reason, his quick acquiescence didn't make me feel victorious. In fact, I felt like I'd taken a step back. "Look," I said. "I don't want to punish you. I'd rather just understand what's going on here. Why do you run off in the middle of the night? It makes Hope sick with worry, and it turns me into a father from a bad sitcom. We're trying to do the right thing here, but you're not making it easy. You need to talk to us. We're your . . . parents."

The last word didn't exactly roll off my tongue, and I could see that Peng could sense my awkwardness. He looked down at his shoes as if there was some hidden truth intertwined between the laces. I thought of Mr. Seng's final words at the orphanage and wondered if Peng thought of Hope and me as his guardians or as his guards. I thought about the locks I'd had installed on the doors with the express purpose of keeping Peng from leaving and wondered if they reminded him of the locks on the orphanage.

"You're a great kid most of the time. You're a good student. You don't cause problems in school or church. You even keep your room clean—which is kind of weird for a fifteen-year-old. If it wasn't for you running away in the middle of the night, I'd say you were darn near perfect. But this is a lot more serious than leaving the toilet seat up. There are dangerous people out at this time of the night. You could get seriously hurt. It's our duty to protect you, and we're doing the best job we can, but you've got to help us out a little bit."

Peng didn't answer and didn't raise his head. There were demons in his past. Demons I could probably help him with if he would talk about them. But he wasn't talking, and the truth was I wasn't sure I really wanted to know.

Mistress Wu and Mister Seng had been eager to get rid of Peng, but there was more to it than that. I remembered the look in their eyes when Peng had entered the room. *They were afraid of him.* After we left the orphanage, I made sure that some of my contacts went back to investigate their dubious dealings. It turned out they were involved in all sorts of illegal activities, and they were eventually shut down. *Why would a pair of hardened human traffickers be afraid of a young boy?* It was a question I'd been trying to avoid.

As I thought about it, I noticed Peng fumbling with something in his hands. It was something I recognized. Something of mine that he should not have had in his possession. "Peng," I said, slowing my breathing and forcing a calmness I didn't feel. "Where did you get my watch?"

He moved the shiny silver casing back and forth in his hands, studying it. "It looks like an old watch," he said. "Something from the 1940s. But it's not. There's a GPS inside."

"GPS watches aren't unusual," I said, worried about where this conversation was going. "And a lot of them are being made to look old style."

"I know," Peng said. "But this one's different. The gears and parts are all mechanical—like a real swiss watch. The GPS chip is hidden underneath the gears and camouflaged. I tried to find similar models on the Internet, but there's nothing like it out there. Other vintage watches look analog on the outside, but inside everything's digital. Not this one. I think if you hold down these two buttons, it might turn on a tracking beacon."

"Don't do that," I said quickly. The last thing I needed was Demetrius and Chico showing up with the cavalry. The hackles on the back of my neck stood up, and I suddenly felt like someone was watching me from the shadows. I looked around, but I couldn't see anybody. Probably just a case of déjà vu.

"Peng, that watch was locked in the safe in my den. Nobody knows the combination to that safe except me. Hope doesn't even know what it is."

"I'm good with locks," Peng said, still looking at the watch.

"Peng," I said, dread beginning to fill my stomach. "There was something else inside that safe that could be very dangerous."

"You mean the gun? I didn't touch it. I don't really like guns. I made sure the safe was locked so nobody would get into it."

I felt a long, slow breath of air escape my lungs. I didn't like having a gun in the house, but with my former occupation, I'd been convinced it might be a good idea. I was glad I'd ditched most of the other remnants of my prior life as a covert antiterrorist agent. It would be hard to explain a folder full of passports with my picture under several different names. "Peng," I asked. "How do you know what's inside my watch?"

"I looked," he said, handing it to me and finally meeting my eyes. "Don't worry. I put it back together." There was a question in his gaze that seemed to say, Why would an assistant college professor have a watch with a hidden GPS tracker? Why would he have a gun locked in a safe?

All of a sudden, I felt like I was back undercover—playing a role, hiding my identity, constantly in danger of being discovered, constantly in danger of losing my life. Once again I felt like someone was watching from the darkness. I subtly scanned the area around the Trax station again but still saw no signs of life.

I took the watch from Peng and put it into my pocket. "You shouldn't have taken it apart. It's a delicate piece of equipment. You could have broken it."

Peng looked back down at his shoes again, probably realizing I wasn't going to open up to him anymore than he was to me. "I didn't break it," he said. "I'm good with things. I know how to take them apart and put them back together."

I stared at him for several seconds. I was at a complete loss as to what to do. It felt like parts of my life were coming apart, but unlike Peng, I had no idea how to put them back together. Finally, I put my hand on his shoulder. He flinched a little, but I left it there. I had to try to be a father. It was what Hope expected me to do. "We need to get home. You've got a big day coming up, and Zack, Mimi, Shi-Shi, and Permelia are all coming to church with us. We're going to barbecue after in celebration of you and Shi-Shi. They're all very proud of both of you."

Peng looked confused for a moment, and then his head jerked up and his eyes went wide. This was a look I had never seen before from Peng—a look of pure terror.

I stood quickly and turned around, scanning the empty parking lot. I thought I saw a flicker of movement in the distance, beyond the lights in the shadows, but it was probably nothing. I looked back at Peng. A remnant of the terror still remained in his eyes, but he was not looking at the parking lot. He was looking at me, studying me like he had studied the watch, delving into my innermost secrets. Probably wondering why my hand had gone to the back of my belt as if I were reaching for a weapon. I took a deep breath and sat back down.

Peng's shoulders slumped like I had just placed a gold medal around his neck that weighed about fifty tons. I now understood the look in his eyes. It didn't have anything to do with the parking lot or somebody watching us. It had to do with the weight of responsibility. He was being called to be the teachers quorum president. I didn't think it was something he wanted to do.

I understood how he felt.

"What if I can't do it?" Peng asked.

I thought for a moment about life and church and family. About responsibilities being placed around my neck that I really didn't ask for. "I'm sure you'll figure it out," I finally said. "Tonight you were able to bypass an unbreakable security system, maneuver your way through several unpickable lock mechanisms, take apart a delicate piece of electronics, put it back together, and somehow arrive on the other end of town with no public transportation running. Being the leader of your teachers quorum should be a piece of cake."

Peng met my gaze, but I could tell what I'd said hadn't diminished his concerns. Not in the least.

"I'm good with things," he said again. "Not with people."

I shivered and looked around for movement one more time. Someone or something was watching us. I could feel it. Peng was good with things. I was good at sensing danger. I didn't know if it was a transient or a stray coyote. But there was something out there watching us.

"Let's go home," I said. "This place isn't safe."

Chapter 2
THE SHAM

"Report," Dempsey said as Buck stepped into the van and pulled off the black ski mask.

Buck shook out his curly hair and chuckled. "I tell you what, your man out there has some Spidey sense going on. I was a thousand yards away, looking at him through a night scope, and I swear he could feel me."

"Did he make you?"

Buck shook his head. "I told you. I was a thousand yards away. And even at fifty, there ain't no one out there who could make me. That's why you pay me the big bucks." Buck removed the scope from the gunstock and put it into a foam, padded case. He pulled himself into the front passenger seat and adjusted the mirror so he could see himself. Then he licked his fingers and tried to put his curls back into place. He was humming an old Hank Williams song.

Dempsey wondered for the fiftieth time if he had made the right decision in including Buck on this contract. The stakes on the job were enormous, and the young man was acting like he was getting ready for prom.

"Buck, I'm only going to tell you this once," Dempsey said. "Be careful with this one. Like you say, he's got some Spidey sense going on. You don't want to underestimate him. And we definitely don't need you going off on any tangents. There's a lot of money riding on this."

"When have I ever gone off on a tangent?" Buck seemed to be satisfied with what he saw in the mirror because he turned it back toward Dempsey and pulled a cowboy hat from under his seat, placing it lightly on his head.

"The real question is when haven't you gone off on tangents. I remember some significant collateral damage in Argentina, in Nicaragua, in Costa Rica, in Brazil. And those are just off the top of my head. Luckily nobody connected the dots."

"What makes you think those had anything to do with me?"

"It's evident by the tightness in your voice when you deny it."

Buck started to protest but then rubbed his hand against his throat and chuckled. "I guess you know me pretty well, Boss. Let's just say I've got a weakness for lovely Latina ladies."

"And you know me well too, Buck. So know this: I'm not going to stand for it this time. If I see even a hint of you heading down that path, I will remove you."

Buck's smile flickered but did not diminish. "What's the story with you and the spider man?"

"What do you mean?"

"Seems like you know this guy. Seems like there's something personal here."

"Nothing personal. Just a job. One that's going to make both of us wealthy men."

Buck grinned wider. "The tightness in your voice says different."

Buck was smarter than he sometimes let on. Dempsey was going to have to be careful around him.

"I just don't like working on home soil," Dempsey said. "This isn't a third-world country. If things go south, we won't be able to bribe our way out."

"No, it's more than that. You've crossed paths with this guy before. What happened? Did he defeat you at one of your own games? You look at him like you did at that Russian who used to beat you at chess—before you took him out."

Dempsey thought for a moment. He remembered a day a long time ago when Matthew Knight's fists had pounded into his face as he'd lain on the ground. He could still taste the blood. "You're right," Dempsey said finally. "We have crossed paths before. A long time ago, in grunt school. But he definitely didn't beat me at any of my games." *He just thinks he did.*

"It would have been a lot easier if you'd let me just take care of him and the kid tonight. We couldn't have asked for better conditions: middle of the night, no one around, crosshairs all lined up nice and pretty. Two quick taps on the trigger and our problem would have been solved."

"That's not the job," Dempsey said. "The client wants the packages delivered alive. If we drop them off in body bags, we don't get paid."

"Seems like unnecessary complications," the younger man said. "We both know that once the packages are delivered, the results will be the same."

"Maybe. But we follow the client's instructions on this. And we don't make any moves until the agreed-upon time. Is that clear?"

"Oh, it's clear," Buck said. "Clear as a warm Mississippi sky in the summer time. You want some gum?" He held out a pack toward Dempsey, who ignored it and started the van.

Buck shrugged, unwrapped the gum, and folded it into his mouth. "You're as tight as a garage door spring," he said. "I think you're still sore about that man beating you at something."

"I told you he didn't beat me."

"I'm not so sure about that. I've been watching him for about a week now. Comfortable house in a quiet cul-de-sac, steady job at a university, nice little family, and a drop-dead gorgeous wife. You may have gone to the same school, but I'd say he came out ahead."

"You'd be wrong," Dempsey said.

"Why's that?"

"Because it's a sham."

"It doesn't look like a sham to me. It looks like the American dream."

"Looks can be deceiving."

"I don't know about that. I think I could be happy walking a few hundred miles in his boots with that filly on my arm."

"Then you're a fool," Dempsey said. "Take it from me. I grew up in what was supposed to be a perfect family. We were featured on the cover of national magazines. We were the envy of those looking for the ideal life."

"That's what I can't understand. Why would you give all that up?"

Dempsey thought back to his childhood and immediately wished he hadn't. "Because it was a lie," he said. "It always is. Behind the façade, there is always darkness. My perfect mother tried to kill herself three times because she was so happy to be part of a perfect family. My perfect father spent more time with his perfect mistress than he did with his perfect kids. My perfect sister almost died from an eating disorder. The perfect family doesn't exist."

"That explains a lot about you," Buck said. "And heaven knows my own childhood was no picnic. But that doesn't mean it's that way for everybody."

"You really think that?"

"I think it's possible."

"Answer me this, then. If Matthew Knight has such a perfect family, why is he out in the middle of the night tracking down one of his kids at a train station?"

"He still gets to go back home to his pretty wife. It ain't all that bad."

"But all of that is about to change, isn't it?"

Buck grinned again. "I guess you're right about that, Boss. On second thought, maybe I wouldn't want to be in his shoes."

Chapter 3
CARPE LIMO

ONE LOOK IN THE MIRROR told me I'd tied my necktie too short. I pulled at the knot and muttered under my breath. I'd been regular at going to church since I met Hope, but some things still didn't feel natural.

The doorbell rang.

"Can you get that?" I called to Hope.

"Can't," she yelled back from the downstairs bathroom. "Jin's on the big-girl potty, and I think we are getting close."

"Peng?" I yelled down the hallway.

No answer. I threw my tie onto the bed and rushed down the stairs.

I opened the door to a bevy of voices and smiles.

"Where's my little peaches?" Mimi said as she hugged my neck. "I haven't seen her in days."

"First-floor bathroom," I said. "If you hurry, you might be in time for a break-through."

"Big-girl potty?" Mimi asked, pulling back to look at me.

I nodded.

"Then what am I doing wasting my time here with you?" She rushed past me without another word. Since Hope's parents lived in Montana, Zack and Mimi had become unofficial grandparents to Peng and little Jin. They were joining us for church today and a backyard barbecue afterward. We were celebrating Peng's getting a new calling and Shi-Shi's being accepted into a prestigious dance school.

"Hi, Uncle Matt," Shi-Shi said, stepping forward and giving me a hug. "Is Peng ready yet?"

"Your guess is as good as mine," I said. "Why don't you go knock on his door and see if you can shake him loose."

"I'm on it," she said and rushed up the stairs.

I watched her as she went. Shi-Shi had turned into an amazing young woman. I shuddered to think what might have happened to her had we left her in the orphanage. Even though the trafficking ring had been exposed and broken up, there was no telling what type of situation she might have found herself in. When we'd returned home with three orphans rather than one, we had immediately shared our concerns with Zack and Mimi about placing Shi-Shi in a good home. We'd wanted to take all three but had felt we should start our family venture with just the two siblings to make sure we could do the parenting thing okay. Our suggestion to Zack and Mimi that they might want to consider how Shi-Shi would fit in with their family was tentative. But they didn't hesitate. They filed their own adoption papers the next day.

I turned back to Zack. He was also watching Shi-Shi, and I don't think I'd ever seen his face beaming like it was now.

I reached for his big, dark hand and winced as he took me into his grip. Zack was getting older, but he was still one of the strongest men I'd ever known. When I'd first met him, he was my hand-to-hand combat instructor at Quantico. He'd weighed quite a bit more then, and his goal had been to use his weight and skill to crush me into the ground. My goal had been to gain enough skill to stop him. Later, I'd been assigned to work undercover in a Salt Lake singles ward in order to locate a potential terrorist. I'd been surprised when the bishop of the ward and my direct superior for the mission had just happened to be this giant black man. He was no longer trying to bash in my brains, at least not overtly, but he had threatened to cause me bodily harm if I brought harm or heartache to any one of his flock—especially a certain beautiful lady named Hope Winslow. He was probably the closest thing I would ever have to a father, and I loved him dearly.

"Come in, and have a seat," I said. "This could take a few minutes."

Zack watched Shi-Shi until she disappeared from sight. I motioned him to sit in my "papa bear chair," an insanely luxurious recliner that Hope had bought as a thank-you gift for me after we'd returned from China with the kids. Zack settled into it and sighed. I always felt like I was drowning in the chair, but it seemed built to fit Zack. Fatherhood also seemed to fit him a lot easier than it did me. He was still looking at the spot Shi-Shi had just vacated.

"Did Shi-Shi ever have any problems adjusting?" I asked. "It's been two years, but sometimes I think Peng still looks at us like we're aliens."

"Shi-Shi doesn't adjust; she conquers." He sighed and pulled the footstool up to rest his feet. "I don't think there is anything that girl couldn't do."

"Do you think we did the right thing?" I asked. "Letting them keep their Chinese names?"

"It hasn't slowed Shi-Shi down a bit," Zack said. "But girls seem to do well with unique names. If they don't have them, they just make them up anyway. I'm not sure it's the same with boys though. Is Peng still having issues?"

"You know Peng. He doesn't talk about it. I wish he would have considered changing his name. I know he gets teased. I even hear it in the halls at church. 'Did you get that name when your parents dropped a spoon on the floor, or were you just a royal *peng* in the neck?' Stuff like that."

"And how does Peng react?"

"He doesn't react, but I do. Sometimes I want to find a long spoon to shove down their insensitive little throats."

"Ah," Zack said with a knowing nod.

"What do you mean, 'Ah?'"

"I've got a friend who's a coach. He says there are two kinds of crazy. The kind that puts you in a psychiatric ward and the really crazy kind."

"The really crazy kind?"

"The kind where someone says something bad about your kid. That turns rational people into potentially violent psychopaths. Welcome to parenthood."

I knew what Zack was talking about. I'd probably go Rambo if anyone ever teased or threatened little Jin. But with Peng, it was different. Maybe it was because of his age when we got him, but I didn't really feel like his parent, even if I did want to punch the kids who teased him.

"How is it?" I said. "With you, Mimi, and Shi-Shi?"

Zack leaned back in his chair, and a broad grin stretched across his face. He sighed deeply.

"I owe you a great debt, son. A debt I know I will never be able to repay. When you brought Shi-Shi to us and suggested adoption, I didn't know what to think. Mimi and I were set in our ways and had pretty much prepared ourselves to be content as surrogate grandparents to the baby you and Hope were bringing home. We had given up on the idea of being parents long ago. But as soon as we met Shi-Shi, all of that changed. I can honestly say these past few years have been by far the best years of our lives. I can't imagine life without these kids in it." Zack had expressed this same sentiment several times before.

I watched Zack for a moment and felt a pang of jealousy.

He must have felt my gaze because his penetrating eyes turned to me, and he asked a typical Zack question. "What about you, Mr. Knight? How's parenthood treating you these days?"

I squirmed a bit in my chair. I should agree with Zack and say these were also the best years of my life, but I couldn't lie to him. After being my combat instructor, my boss, and my bishop, he would see right through me.

"Truthfully," I said, "it's been a struggle. Sometimes I long for the days when it was just Hope and me. Together. Alone. I mean, I can't imagine life without little Jin, but I also tend to worry a lot more than I used to. I think I found a gray hair the other day."

"What about Peng?" Once again Zack seemed to know how to get to the crux of the matter. I had been avoiding talking about Peng.

"I don't know," I said. "He's great with Jin, and when he visits Hope at her work with the cancer kids, you can tell he has a good heart. But he seems somehow disconnected. Maybe he's just a typical teenage boy, but that kid has more layers than an onion. I don't think he considers us his parents, and I certainly don't feel like his father. He barely speaks, he disappears at night to who knows where, and he causes Hope to lose a lot of sleep. You know, I've been able to work my way inside the heads of some of the most devious and secretive terrorists in the world. I've been able to understand them, even build relationships with them, but I tell you, Peng is still a mystery to me."

I heard a rustling behind me, and I hoped it wasn't Peng. It wasn't. It was worse. Hope had walked in, and she was glaring at me.

"How long have you been there?" I asked.

Zack stood, and Hope stepped over to him and gave him a hug.

"Long enough to hear Zack gushing about the best years of his life," she said, releasing Zack and turning to me. "Long enough to hear you comparing our son to a terrorist."

"That long," I said, really wanting to change the subject. "Any success on the potty-training front?"

Hope was about to say something else when a two-foot-tall missile launched herself into my arms.

"Daddy, Daddy," Jin said. "I get big-girl panties for church." She pronounced it "choach."

I held her up in the air above my head and twirled her around. "Did you go in the big-girl potty?"

Jin nodded vigorously.

Mimi followed her in and confirmed. "At first it was just a trickle, but then we got Niagara Falls. She's officially a big girl now."

Jin spotted Zack in the chair and almost jumped out of my grasp.

"Grampa, I'm a big girl." She ran to show him her panties. My guess was that she would be showing anyone who would listen to her today. I was glad we were still a few years away from when that would not be appropriate any longer. Thinking about that time, I felt a sense of loss for the innocence of a two-year-old. An innocence I wasn't sure Peng had ever had the chance to experience.

At that moment, Shi-Shi pulled Peng into the room by his tie. "Look what I found hanging from the handsome tree."

Mimi scolded her daughter, "Let go of that tie, girl. You're going to put a wrinkle in it." She grabbed Peng by the shoulders and swung him around so she could pull him into her arms. Peng wasn't really a hugger, but somehow Mimi could get away with it.

"Not only has he been hanging around the handsome tree, but apparently he's been visiting the smell-good tree too. What is that you've got on, boy?"

Peng looked at the floor. "Shi-Shi made me put it on."

"Well, she was right to do it. Now go give your gramps a hug before he falls asleep in that big ol' chair."

Zack stood, and Peng gave him the halfhearted hug of a teenager.

"You are getting tall, son. I swear you've inherited some of my genes."

"I don't think so, Pops," Shi-Shi said. "If he had your genes, he'd be a freakish giant by now."

"You watch your mouth, young lady. You're not too old for a spanking."

"But I am too fast. I don't think you could catch me, old man." Shi-Shi stood with her hands at her hips and her chin in the air as if in challenge.

Zack waved her off with a smile.

"Jin, come over here and get your dress on," Hope said. She was still eyeing me as if to say we would talk later. "We need to get moving, or we'll be late for church."

The doorbell rang again. I got up to answer because I wasn't sure that anyone else had even heard it. I opened the door to a horrifying sight: an elderly woman in a frilly white dress and a chauffeur's cap.

"I hope I'm not too late for the pickup, Captain," she said, saluting me.

"Permelia, why are you wearing a chauffeur's hat?" I asked, not knowing if I really wanted to know the answer.

"I'm your ride," she said, stepping aside and letting me see the white stretch limo sitting in front of our house. Permelia was also a member of the singles ward where I had once been assigned undercover. She had been Hope's roommate at the time and had been the first person who had asked me out on a date. She had also tried to kiss me. She may have been seventy, but I don't think she had really ever completely grown up. Everything she did was way over the top.

I stepped outside with her and pulled the door closed behind me. "Permelia, I really don't think this is a good idea. Peng already thinks we are making too much of this."

"Nonsense," she said. "You only live once, and you don't get any younger. My turkey neck can attest to that. This is one of the items on my bucket list, and the rope on my bucket is wearing thin. Lighten up, Matthew. Sometimes you just have to say carpe limo and take life by the horns."

As I tried to figure out how to get Permelia to remove the limo from our street, the door opened behind me, and I heard a loud squeal. Shi-Shi emerged, pulling Peng by his tie again and jumping up and down with excitement. "Aunt Permelia, is that your limo? Can we see inside?"

"You're not just going to see it, honey; you're going to ride in it," Permelia said. "We're all going to ride in it. I've got it rented for the rest of the day. Maybe later we can go cruising and see if we can pick up some hot guys, but right now we are going to celebrate your dancing and Peng's new calling by showing up to church in style. This is what I like to call making an entrance."

Peng looked at me with pleading eyes. I could only shrug. When Permelia got something in her head, it was impossible to stop her.

"Carpe limo," I said and stood back as everyone else flowed out of the door and into the fantasy world.

It was complete and utter chaos. We were a mixture of black and white, Asian and Caucasian, old and young, yet no one here seemed uncomfortable or out of place.

No one except me. I felt as out of place as Goldilocks trying unsuccessfully to get comfortable in the overwhelming vastness of the papa-bear chair.

Chapter 4
CELL BLOCK D

THROUGH SACRAMENT MEETING AND SUNDAY School, I was able to catch up a little bit on my sleep. With Zack and Mimi focused on the kids, it seemed I had been a bit forgotten. Hope elbowed me only once in Sunday School, and I think it was because I must have started snoring. Mostly she didn't talk to me. I wasn't sure if it was because she had sympathy for me for being called out in the middle of the night or if she was still mad at me.

Unfortunately I couldn't hide out during the third hour. I was assigned to the fourteen- and fifteen-year-old boys, and it was my turn to teach. I had planned to work on my lesson early this morning, but after having to chase down Peng, I'd forgotten all about it. Not that preparation would have done me much good anyway; the boys in the class didn't seem to pay attention no matter how much work I put in. For some reason, we referred to the fourteen- and fifteen-year-olds as teachers. I was pretty new in the faith, but I think the scriptural reason for this must have been because the word *devil* had already been taken.

I began my lesson, and as usual, the boys weren't listening to me. I didn't think it was because I was a bad instructor—my college students always gave me good marks—but today I was definitely overfatigued and underprepared. I felt like I might as well be talking to the walls—which would've been a lot less frustrating. They called our meeting place the Scout room, but I referred to it as Cell Block D.

In Cell Block D, we had four inmates. I was the assistant warden, Ron Kelton being the main adult in charge. Sometimes a member of the bishopric would also attend, but usually he didn't last very long before he found an excuse to meet with someone in the hallway. I wished I was in the hallway right now. The inmates were getting ready to revolt. I could feel it.

JR was the ring leader. Currently, he was leaning back on the rear legs of his chair and finding a position where he could achieve balance with no hands or feet touching the floor. He was compact and wiry, with visible cords of muscle running through his hairy forearms. He usually had a toothpick or straw in his mouth, and he was extremely creative in finding ways to interrupt our class. He seemed to have no respect for authority and, in that way, reminded me a little bit of myself. He was a royal pain, and I was more than a little bit ashamed that at times I wished Peng were more like him. Heck, I wished I were more like him. He seemed to be a natural leader, and heaven knows he had more control of the boys than I did.

JR coughed once. This was the signal for inmate number two—Eric Chase—to look at him. Once he had Eric's attention, JR coughed twice. I had come to learn that this was the signal to follow JR's example. Eric did so and began balancing his own chair on two legs.

Eric was tall and gangly, with a mop of curly blond hair that seemed to bounce no matter which way he moved. He was a follower and a laugher, and when he started laughing, he didn't seem to have the ability to stop. JR's major goal in life seemed to be to find ways to get Eric to do what he wanted him to do because then it would put Eric into a laughing fit.

I thought of JR and Eric as the two stooges. A third stooge would have made sense and would have added a symmetry to the mix, but the other two potential stooges didn't seem to fit the mold. Peng had his head down. He was probably listening, but I found it disconcerting to address the top of his bowed head, so I turned my full attention to the only other remaining boy—Joseph Johnson. His parents called him JJ, but JR wouldn't allow any other initial-bearing boys in the class, and Joseph seemed too formal for his short, pudgy body and perpetually dimpled apple cheeks, so we all just called him Joey.

Joey had his hand raised to dutifully answer one of my questions when I heard JR begin to cough again in short bursts.

Uh-oh, I thought and looked to Ron, our warden. I could see by the look in his eyes that he knew, like I did, what was probably coming next. But his expression seemed to say, "You're the teacher. You need to deal with it." I felt as helpless as I had the night before when Hope had said I needed to be Peng's father. I had no clue how to deal with this type of thing.

The third cough sounded. This was JR's signal for Eric to do something that would cause a disruption. It was only seconds after the signal had been given that Eric obediently did as he'd been instructed. He leaned back farther on his chair until he completely lost his balance and then flapped his arms as if to catch himself as he fell backward onto the floor in a clattering mess.

The sound reverberated off the walls, and I'm sure the class of girls next to us was in the process of sending someone to complain to the bishop.

Eric, lying in a heap on the ground, looked stunned at first and then said, "I think I just named a whole village in China." He turned to JR for approval, and when he got a smile and a nod, he laid his blond curls back on the ground and burst into laughter.

I looked at Peng to see if he'd been offended by the obvious slight to his name. However, the soon-to-be-president of this motley crew had barely raised his head. Joey was smiling, but he seemed unsure of whether he should laugh at Eric.

I felt heat filling my face, and I took a step toward Eric. I wasn't sure what I was going to say to him, but I was tired from the night before, and I'd pretty much had enough.

Luckily, Ron decided to take this moment to stand and step in. "Okay, guys, that's enough." His voice was quiet and composed, but Eric immediately stopped laughing and put his chair back into place. I had nowhere near the amount of respect from the boys that Ron did. Maybe it was because he'd been teaching boys this age a lot longer than I had; maybe it was because he really cared for the boys and they knew it; or maybe it was because he used to be in the special forces and could probably take any one of us out with his little finger.

He was in his early thirties, about my age. He was also close to my size and build, but when he stood up in the room, you would think he was ten feet tall. The boys called him Brother K, but it sounded like "Sir," when they said it. Sometimes they called me Brother N because of the sound of my last name, but usually it came out sounding like "You idiot."

"Eric, I don't want you to do anything like that ever again," Ron said. "I've seen a man break an arm from a fall at about that height. We were in the jungles of Nicaragua. He tripped on a root, reached down to break his fall, and drove the bones in his arms back up and through his elbow. One of the bones clipped an artery. A tourniquet finally stopped the bleeding, but the arm got infected. By the time we got him out, it was a green, stinking mess. The doc had to take the arm off at the bicep. I want you to think about that the next time you decide to lean back in your chair."

The boys followed Ron's story with their full attention. Even Peng looked up. Ron was always good about adding details to give the lesson a little more color, and for some reason, an arm with gangrene was particularly interesting. I was pretty sure Joey's mother would pass out if she ever heard what was being shared in class.

"What's my favorite scripture?" Ron said in his best drill-sergeant voice.

The stooges groaned. Joey raised his hand and recited, "John 15:13—Greater love hath no man than this, that a man lay down his life for his friends."

"Very good, Joey." He turned his attention to Eric. "Eric, does this mean that you need to die for the other boys in this class?"

"No," Eric mumbled reluctantly.

"What does it mean?"

Joey piped up again. "It means that we need to learn to live for each other. To be nice to each other and serve each other."

Ron's gaze was burrowing into Eric. He didn't say anything about Eric's jab at Peng's name, but I could see that Eric got the message all the same as he lowered his head in submission.

Ron looked around the room, making eye contact with each of the young men. "I want to tell you boys something. Brother Knight has given up precious moments of his life to prepare an excellent lesson, and I don't think you are being very appreciative of the gift he is giving you. Now, in the few minutes we have before our guests arrive, I would appreciate it if you would give him your full attention." Ron sat and looked back over at me.

I felt a little guilty at his words. I hadn't spent that much time preparing this lesson. In fact, the first time I'd even opened the book was this morning. And I didn't think that anything I could teach them from the manual would have near the impact of Ron's sharing some of his army experiences. He didn't ever actually say that he had been in Delta Force, but from some of the details of his stories, I was convinced this was the case. In truth, I was a little jealous of Ron. I had some good stories too. I just hadn't figured out a way to tell any of them. Maybe I should try.

I cleared my throat. "Thank you, Brother Kelton. Uh . . ." I glanced down at the manual, but I couldn't remember where I had left off. Maybe I needed to wing it. "Uh," I said again. "This reminds me of a time when I was in London, working undercover to stop a terrorist threat at Heathrow airport."

Every head, including Peng's, snapped up and looked at me with curiosity. *So that's how you get their attention.*

"I broke into the apartment of one of the suspected perpetrators and didn't realize until I was in his bedroom that he was on the floor behind the bed, prostrate on his prayer mat. I stood there in the middle of the room, not knowing what to do. I didn't bring a weapon with me because I was just there to gather intelligence, and he wasn't supposed to be there. He had an AK-47 lying next to him. If he noticed me, I was toast. I began to back away slowly, and somehow my foot found the creakiest floorboard in the entire city. Still, he did not look up but continued his prayers."

I definitely had their full attention now, though several of the looks I was getting were more than a bit quizzical. This was a true story, and the details got better from here, but it was probably time to retreat back into my cover and not let my pride or jealousy of Ron take me somewhere I really didn't want to go.

Joey raised his hand. "So what did you do?"

"I did the only thing I could do," I said. "I started to dance."

Eric looked at me like I'd gone mad.

"What?" I said, "I'm a really good dancer." I broke into what I thought would be some impressive urban dance moves.

There was a moment of silence, and then Eric blinked and began to snicker. That was all it took. The rest of the boys erupted in laughter.

Between guffaws, Eric said, "You had us going, Brother N. For a minute there, I thought you might have really been a spy."

"That's not the half of it," JR added. "Before you started moving, I thought you really might be a good dancer."

This brought even more laughs. From everyone except Ron and Peng, who both seemed to be studying me curiously.

It was at this moment that the bishop decided to stick his head into our room. I could tell from the look on his face that he was not pleased with what he saw.

I held up one finger, asking for him to give me a minute. "So the point of the story is," I said as the boys quieted down, "that reverence is not about being quiet. It's not about walking around with folded arms and a somber expression. Like the terrorist on the prayer mat, it's about being so focused on revering God that nothing is able to distract you, not even an excellent dancer like myself."

Eric's eyes lightened with understanding, and he began applauding. "Brother N," he said. "I think that's the best lesson you've ever given."

I looked over to the bishop as if to drive home the point. For some reason, he didn't look impressed. Maybe if he hadn't walked in during the laughing part. The bishop opened the door wider, and in filed the parents and guests. Both Hope and Zack gave me a scolding look. They must have heard the earlier commotion as well and, for some reason, thought I had something to do with it. Permelia had also joined them, but her eyes sparkled with approval. At least someone seemed to appreciate my methods.

The bishop said a few words and then proceeded to lay his hands on the heads of the boys, one at a time, to set them apart as the new presidency of the teachers quorum. Peng was the president, JR the first counselor, Eric the second counselor, and Joey the secretary. JR didn't look too happy about not being the president.

After class, as we were going out the door, the bishop stopped me. "Brother Knight. I'm wondering if you could visit with me for a few minutes in my office."

"About that lesson?" I said.

"It's not about the lesson. I'd like to meet with both you and Peng."

I looked over at Zack and our other guests. "I really need to get the grill fired up."

"It will only take a minute," he said.

I hadn't been active in the Church for much of my life, but I'd had a few meetings with bishops in their offices before. Most of them had been with Zack, but either way, I knew what these meetings meant.

I didn't know why or what for, but for some reason, I was in trouble.

Chapter 5
RESPONSIBILITY

As Peng and I entered the bishop's office, I looked around the room. Chairs lined the wall across from the dark cherry desk. The bishop shook our hands and motioned for us to be seated.

I decided I preferred the Catholic style of confessional, where you didn't have to look your religious leader in the eye when you spilled your guts.

But this was an unnecessary line of thought, right? I tried to convince myself one last time that we weren't here to confess. The bishop just wanted to meet with us. I glanced at Peng, and his expression told me he was thinking the same thing I was. Who was I kidding? One of us was definitely in trouble. I just hoped it was Peng and not me.

"Peng," the bishop began, looking intently at the boy beside me. This was a good sign. The focus was on Peng, not on me. "I wanted to speak with you about your new calling." I breathed a silent sigh of relief. Maybe neither of us was in trouble after all. Maybe this was just friendly instruction.

"The president of a quorum is a significant calling. It doesn't matter whether you are an adult or a young man. Being president means that you preside. And presiding means that you are responsible for each of the boys under your charge. When I laid my hands on your head, I gave you special keys associated with your calling. And with these keys, you will be able to know what is best for your quorum. But before you can be effective in exercising these keys, there is one thing you need to do first. Do you know what that is?"

Peng looked over to me as if asking for help, but I had no clue what answer the bishop was fishing for.

Peng returned his attention to the bishop and shook his head.

"You need to love the people under your stewardship," the bishop said. "Until you can do that, nothing else really matters."

Peng looked like he wanted to jump out of his chair and bolt from the room.

"Do you understand why this is important?"

"I understand," Peng said. "But I don't think it's possible."

I'd always heard that you should never lie to your bishop, but I thought that in this particular situation, Peng might have used a bit too much candor.

The bishop turned to me as if asking me to intervene. This was it. The moment of truth. The place where I stepped up and proved myself a wise and competent father. I realized I had no idea what to say, so I said the first thing that came into my head. "Don't look at me," I said. "I don't like them either—except for maybe Joey." As the words left my lips, I immediately wanted them back. But that was the problem with words: once escaped, there was no way they were going back into the cage.

I wasn't sure how I expected the bishop to respond. Maybe shake his head and frown gravely; maybe wag a finger at me and chastise my impertinent behavior; maybe throw me out of his office and tell me to learn to grow up. I surely didn't expect him to burst out laughing. But that was exactly what he did. He laughed so hard tears came to his eyes, and he had to remove his glasses and wipe his cheeks.

Peng's eyes met mine. He looked scared.

"Sorry about that," the bishop said, finally getting control of himself. "You'd think people would tell me the truth since I'm the bishop, but it's rare that people are as brutally honest as you have both been. That's not why I'm laughing though. I'm laughing because you both remind me a lot of myself. Those were almost my exact words when I was made bishop four years ago. The stake president told me I needed to learn to love the people in the ward, and I realized there were several I didn't even like.

"I had a particular neighbor at the time who constantly had her nose in my business. If my dog barked even once, she would call animal control. If I had mulch delivered and left on the street while I spread it, she would call the city to complain. I didn't like her. I didn't like her at all. And she wasn't the only person in the ward I felt that way about. I told the stake president that and asked him how I was supposed to be the bishop over people I didn't like. Do you know what he said to me?"

Peng and I both shook our heads.

"He said, 'The Lord isn't asking you to like them; He's asking you to love them. And you love those you serve. So stop whining, and start serving.' I took the stake president's advice, and even though my neighbor still drives me crazy at times, I can honestly say I love her. Not because she's any less annoying but because I've learned to see her potential. I've learned to see her as the Lord sees her. And I've been able to gain that perspective because I worried less about liking her and more about serving her.

"Peng, I'm not asking you to change your feelings for any of these boys. I'm just asking you to serve them. The Lord will take care of the feeling part. That's a promise. Do you think you can do that?"

"I guess I can try." Peng still sounded unsure, but apparently it was enough for the bishop.

"That's all I ask. Now why don't you go ahead and join your family. I know you have a lot of visitors waiting to congratulate you."

I breathed a sigh of relief. This meeting had been easier than I'd thought. We both got up to leave.

"Brother Knight, could you stay for just a few more minutes?"

I sighed and sat back down as Peng escaped out the door. I had been right all along. I was definitely the one in trouble. I decided to try a preemptive move. "I promise to try as well," I said. "To serve the boys."

"Good," the bishop replied, pondering me over his glasses. "Because the best place you can serve them is on the upcoming high-adventure trip."

"Uh, about that . . ."

"Brother Knight, you've been trying to find a way to get out of this trip since we announced it. Why is that?"

"It's just that I have a lot of demands at the university, and I'm not sure it's a good time for me to be away."

"You forget that I'm also a professor at the university, and the week of the trip is considered the ideal week for most faculty to take a vacation. I'm sensing it's something more than that."

"Because of your gift of discernment as a bishop?"

"No, because of the way you screw up your face every time the trip is brought up."

"Okay," I said. "You're right. I don't want to go. But it's not for selfish reasons. I just think it might be better for Peng if I sit this one out. Things with us are a little bit strained right now, and he's got such a good relationship with Ron that I thought the time away from the family might help him grow. When Ron talks with him, I see progress. When I step in, he seems to withdraw."

The bishop put his hand under his chin and seemed to consider my words. "You're right," he said. "Sometimes the right adult leader can help boys in ways parents can't. And Ron does have a way of getting through to teenage boys."

I sat up straighter in my chair. "So you agree. It would be better if I didn't go."

"Logically, that makes sense," he said. "But my powers of discernment as a bishop are telling me otherwise. I've considered letting you out of this trip for the exact reasons you mentioned. The problem is that every time I think about you not going, I get a strong feeling of unease. Call it my bishop powers if you want to, but something told me you definitely need to go with the boys into the mountains."

"Did your bishop powers tell you why?"

"Sorry, no. I just have a very strong feeling that it's important that you go. But I can make a pretty good guess. It's wrapped up in the nature and purpose of these high-adventure trips. I learned a long time ago that if we can get the boys in the mountains—away from cell phones and texting—if we can put them in a situation that tests them to their limits, miracles can happen. These trips aren't just for fun. They are a transformative experience. I've seen it again and again. Boys and leaders go off as a bunch of individuals who don't like each other and come back with a bond that can never be broken. It changes the very nature of the relationships. I'm not sure how, but it does."

"So shouldn't *you* be there to experience this change?" I said. "I mean, wouldn't it be great for the bishop to have that kind of relationship with these boys?"

The bishop stood. "You're not getting out of this, Matt. You can stop trying. And, yes, I would love to be there, but unfortunately I will be with the older boys at Lake Powell."

"Lake Powell? Sounds like a vacation, not a high adventure."

"I know. That's what worries me. Some of the youth leaders don't have the vision of providing a hard experience for the boys like Ron does. At least I know I can count on him to make it difficult."

The bishop had a gleam in his eye, and it kind of scared me. Then again, the whole trip scared me. I trusted the bishop and his feelings—I really did. What I didn't trust was his belief that this trip could transform my relationship with Peng. There was a gap there, one that I wasn't sure a walk in the woods could fix.

To be truthful, there was something else bothering me. I didn't have the spiritual sensitivities of the bishop, but every time I thought about this trip, I also felt something—a distinct sense of unease. It was a feeling I was familiar with. I'd felt it many times in my past life. It was a feeling that usually manifested when I was moving into serious danger—right before something bad was about to happen.

I wondered what the bishop would think if he knew I was considering carrying a gun with me in my backpack?

I decided he was probably better off not knowing.

Chapter 6
A CHANGE OF PLANS

DEMPSEY HEARD THE SHARP KNOCK and peered out through the hotel door peephole. When he saw Buck's distorted grin looking back at him, he relaxed his grip on the Glock 19 and let it settle back into its holster. He snapped open the locks and let Buck in.

"Hey, Boss." Buck's grin did not disappear as he pushed his way into the room.

"What's with the outfit?" Dempsey asked.

Buck looked down at himself in mock surprise. He was dressed in a light-tan, corduroy sport suit with a skinny brown tie. "You like it? I picked it up at a thrift store last night. Cost me twenty-five bucks for the whole get-up."

"Why would you need a suit? And why are you wearing it now?" Buck was supposed to be watching Matthew Knight's house, gathering intelligence.

"It's Sunday. You wouldn't want me goin' to church dressed like a heathen, now would you?"

Dempsey picked up a glass with ice in it and held it against his forehead. "Tell me you didn't show up at their church building this morning."

"I could tell you that, Boss, but I don't like to lie to you."

"Buck, if you've blown your cover, this whole job could be ruined."

Buck hopped up onto Dempsey's hotel bed, fluffed the pillows against the headboard, and leaned back, the toes of his cowboy boots pointing toward the ceiling.

"Take it easy," he said. "I was at their church building but not at the same time they were there. Did you know three different Mormon congregations meet in that same building, and each one of them stays for a full three hours? I can barely sit still for fifteen minutes. No sign of plural wives either. I guess you can cross Mormonism off my list of potential religions. Good thing that fifteen minutes was all I needed in this case."

"All you needed for what?"

"For me to confirm that our current plan of attack is not going to work. We need to scrap the blueprint and start over." Buck leaned back on the pillow and closed his eyes. "This is one fine pillow and comfortable bed. I think I'm going to join the church of Saint Mattress."

Dempsey walked over and shoved Buck's boots hard enough that his legs spun off the bed and he sat up. "No more games, Buck. Stop messing around and tell me what you found."

Buck met Dempsey's stare with a mischievous look. "Boss, did you actually just say 'No more games'? If there's one thing I've learned from you over the years, it's that life *is* a game. And *you* can't stand the thought of losing. It's a good thing you've got me here to keep you from screwing up."

Dempsey sighed. "Just tell me what you've got."

"You're going to thank me for this one." Buck reached into his pocket and unfolded a piece of paper. "I checked out the classroom where the target teaches the boys. Don't worry, I waited until after they were gone. I found this on one of the chairs."

He handed the paper over to Dempsey. On one side was a checklist of back-packing gear. The other side was an itinerary outlining a trip to the Uinta Mountains.

"So they're planning a campout. What's that got to do with our job?"

"Look at the dates," Buck said. "There's a detailed description of each night's camping site. There's also a list of adults and boys who are going on the trip."

Dempsey looked more carefully at the paper. Buck was right. This was important. Knight's name was on the list, as was that of his adopted son, Peng. There was one other adult listed and three additional boys. They were leaving on a Tuesday and planning to be back on a Friday. The dates coincided with the days Dempsey had been planning to make his move.

"Looks like grabbing the whole family that week isn't going to work," Buck said. "At least not all of them together at the same time. Half of them are going to be somewhere else. It's a good thing I decided to snoop around at the church and found that paper. I guess things haven't changed since I was a kid. I never seemed to manage to get notes home to my grandma."

"You never stopped being a kid either."

"I take that as a compliment." Buck stood, walked across the room, and looked at himself in the mirror. "So do we take them all early or bring in Carney and his crew for two separate grabs?"

Dempsey studied the sheet. "This might actually be better," he finally said. "That house is like a fortress, and they rarely emerge at the same time. I know Knight. He's not going down without a fight. If we can take him and the boy in the woods—away from prying eyes—so much the better. This itinerary tells us exactly where they will be each night. We can be waiting for them. I'm not sure what inspired you to go into that church to look around, but it paid off."

"Church always inspires me. And when you say *we* will be waiting for them in the woods, do you mean you and me, or are we talking Carney here? He and his crew seem to love dressing up in camo and playing soldiers in the woods. What's his pet boy's name? Jackson? He claims to have made it through Delta, and he doesn't frighten me nearly as bad as Jillian. She's a looker, but she scares the daylights out of me. I say we give them the mountain duty. They're the subcontractors; they should get the grunt work. Besides, I hate sleeping bags. They wrinkle my clothes." Buck looked down and brushed a speck of dust off his jacket. "And someone's got to be here to take the woman."

Dempsey considered Buck's words. He was right about Carney's crew being more equipped for mountain duty. But Carney's team in the woods would mean that he and Buck would be here. And Buck was just a little too eager when it came to Knight's wife.

"What're you thinking, Boss? You want me to call Carney?"

"I'm thinking that the thought of you being close to that woman makes me want to change my mind."

"C'mon, you'll be right there with me. You'll be supervising. How much trouble could I get into?"

Dempsey didn't answer. He stared at Buck, with his corduroy suit and pointed boots, and thought that man might be a lot more trouble than he was worth. "Call Carney," he said. "We need to be ready in a week."

Chapter 7
A SURPRISE

I heard the footsteps outside the door and was immediately awake.

I sat up and swung my legs over the side of the bed. The clock read 3:58—two minutes before the alarm was set to go off. Hope breathed peacefully beside me. I heard more sounds coming from the kitchen. Dishes clanking. A drawer opening. Cereal being shaken into a bowl.

I groaned inwardly. It was Tuesday. The day that I would leave my comfortable bed and beautiful wife and go into the mountains to sleep on rocks. Peng was in the kitchen getting ready for the trip. A typical fumbling teenage boy making his way through a tired breakfast. Funny how he never made any noise when he was escaping the house.

Hope stretched and yawned. "Is it that time already?"

I looked at the clock. "Go back to sleep," I said. "You have another thirty seconds."

She completed her stretch and then punched me in the arm. "Oops," she said. "Reflexes." And then her tone turned serious. "Be careful out there."

"Don't worry. I'll be fine."

"I wasn't talking about you," Hope said. "I meant be careful with the boys. If Joey comes back with so much as a scratch, I'll never hear the end of it from Mrs. Johnson."

I stepped out of the bed and onto the floor. "I appreciate your concern." I hit the alarm button just as it began to sound. I was going to try to dress in the dark, but instead, I turned on the bright overhead light.

Hope raised her hand to her eyes, then looked at me. "Stop it," she said when she saw my pout. "I worry about you too. But you're an adult. You can take care of yourself. I know how Mrs. Johnson feels. I don't want to see a scratch on Peng either. My motherly protective instincts kick in just thinking about you guys out there alone in the woods."

"Maybe Joey wouldn't be so soft if Mrs. Johnson let him take a scratch once in a while."

Hope looked at me with dagger eyes.

Jin began crying from the other room. The alarm clock and the voices must have woken her up.

"Maybe you should go pick up our daughter before I punch you again," Hope said.

I had just enough time to lift Jin out of her big-girl bed and calm her before I heard a soft knock at the door. With Jin in my arms, I went to greet our guest. Undoing the multitude of locks was not easy while holding a squirming toddler.

"I didn't miss breakfast, did I?" Permelia said, pushing past me into the house. She was carrying a sleeping bag under one arm and pulling a large wheeled suitcase with the other.

"I didn't think you were coming until later today."

"You boys are leaving in a few minutes, aren't you? Girl time starts as soon as the boys are gone. I'm not going to miss out on even one minute." Permelia dropped her bags on the floor and lifted Jin out of my arms. "We are going to have a grand old time with no boys around."

"No boys," Jin repeated drowsily. Funny how some phrases seemed to come easier to her than others.

"Why did you bring a sleeping bag? You know we have plenty of beds," I said.

She rolled her eyes. "You don't use beds at a slumber party. Any idiot knows that."

Hope and Peng came into the living room from different directions. Hope kissed Peng's forehead and said something to him, but I couldn't hear what it was over Jin's laughter. I motioned to Hope that I needed to brush my teeth and then I would be back.

"It's time for us to go," Peng said. "We need to be at Ron's house in five minutes."

"I'm sure he'd rather we be a little late than me kill everyone off with my morning breath. I'll be right back." We had already packed our gear in the trailer the night before. All we needed to bring this morning were the clothes on our backs and a small backpack with snacks for the car. "Besides, I'd kind of like a kiss from my wife before I go."

I quickly cleaned the night monsters from my mouth and returned with my pack in hand.

"That wasn't a very good brush job," Hope said. "I think you only deserve a peck on the cheek." She reached up to deliver on her threat, but at the last second, I turned my head, and our lips met.

"That's cheating," she mumbled through the kiss. But she didn't pull away. The kiss was a good one. In fact, it was great. But something didn't feel right.

Suddenly I had a bad feeling about leaving Hope. A really bad feeling. I pulled away and looked at her face.

"You look like the cat used your Cheerios as a litter box," Permelia said from the floor, where she was sitting cross-legged with Jin.

"What's wrong?" Hope asked.

I was asking myself the same question. But I couldn't find an acceptable answer. "Nothing, I guess. I just don't like leaving you here alone with a child."

"Don't be silly. Permelia will be with us all week."

"Permelia is the child I was referring to."

"Really," Hope said. "We'll be fine. You should be concentrating on the boys who are going with you into the wilderness. Remember what I said about no scratches."

I still had my arms around her waist, and I didn't want to let go. The feeling didn't make sense at all. It was as though if I left now, this might be the last time I ever held her.

She grabbed my arms and pushed me toward the door.

The moment of panic passed, but I still felt the lingering effects. "If anything happens, call Zack," I said, meeting her eyes in a way I knew she would understand. "Even if you think it's something small."

She nodded, affirming that she had gotten the message. We didn't talk much about my past and the potential for it to infringe upon our current lives, but we tried to prepare for contingencies.

"You boys have fun," she said as we moved out the door. "And don't forget to say a prayer before you start driving." She paused, and I saw a wrinkle knit her brow.

"You're feeling it too," I said. "Admit it. We should cancel this whole trip and stay home."

"No," Hope said, her face thoughtful as if she were listening to an inner voice. "You need to go on this trip. I'm sure of it. And you told me the bishop was convinced as well. I'm probably just having first-scout-trip mother anxiety. Just make sure that whatever you do, you bring those boys home unharmed— especially my son." These were Hope's last words as she pushed us out into the yard, fighting back tears.

The door closed, and Peng and I moved off into the dark. I held up my watch to check the time, but I couldn't see the hands. This watch had no illuminated dial. It had a vintage face and a secret tracker hidden inside.

* * *

Most of our drive was in the dark, but by the time we reached the Mirror Lake trailhead, the sun's rays were busily removing the dew off the leaves of the trembling aspens. Despite the sunlight, my darkness remained. I had a bad feeling I couldn't shake, and it wasn't because the boys were bouncing up and down in their seats and had decided to sing sitcom theme songs at the top of their lungs.

Something was wrong. I just didn't know what it was.

I was driving Ron's SUV. He said he had some last-minute preparations to take care of and was busy holding a flashlight in his mouth and scribbling on a map. So much for my plans to catch up on some sleep—although the singing probably would have killed that anyway.

"Can I drive?" JR asked. This was about his fiftieth request in the past two hours. I was tempted to let him take the wheel just so I could shut him up.

"Too late," I said. "We're here." I turned on my blinker to turn into the Mirror Lake trailhead, where we were scheduled to begin our journey.

"Keep going straight," Ron said.

I started to explain that this was our starting point, but when I looked at Ron, he shook his head and brought his finger to his lips. He darted his eyes back toward the boys, suggesting that he didn't want them to know about it.

Apparently he had a surprise for the boys. I didn't think this was wise since it would also be a surprise for everyone else, including the bishop, the boys' parents, and me. We had a very detailed and structured itinerary. People knew exactly where we were supposed to be at each leg of the trip.

I hoped he knew what he was doing.

* * *

"Carney, I think we've got a problem." Jackson spoke into the radio clipped to his shoulder as he balanced the binoculars with one hand, trying to get a good look at the target in the dim light of the morning. There were two men in the front seat of the SUV—the driver, who looked like your typical soccer dad, and the front-seat passenger. Even at this distance and in this light, even though this last-minute job hadn't included a picture of the target, and even though he could barely make out the figure through the windshield, there was something about the man that looked dangerous.

Jackson felt himself smiling. He liked dangerous.

"What do you mean a problem?" The voice on the other end sounded like chains being dragged through gravel.

"They signaled like they were turning into the trailhead but then just kept going. And they're not slowing down. I don't think they're going where we think they're going."

Jackson heard swearing on the other end of the radio.

"Did they see you?"

Jackson looked at his partner. Even at twenty paces, he wouldn't be able to see her if he didn't know she was there. "No way. Our position is secure."

"Then why didn't they stop? Could someone have tipped them off?"

"Who? We didn't even know we were going to be here until a few days ago. The guy in the passenger seat seemed to be looking at a map. Maybe they just decided to change their plans."

"Scout leaders don't go to the trouble of communicating every step of the journey and passing out flyers to the parents just to suddenly decide to change plans when they get to the trailhead."

"This one did," Jackson said. What had looked to be a routine job might actually turn out to be interesting.

"Can you catch them?"

"'Course we can." Jackson was already moving toward the car. "Don't worry. Jillian, Tiny, and I will be right behind them."

"Keep your distance. Don't let them see you."

"And what if they do? All they will see is a stunning woman and two extremely fit men out enjoying the mountains. We're just a group of ultrarunners doing some cardiovascular training at elevation. Our cover story is solid."

"The guy we're chasing is an expert on cover stories. Don't make contact until it's time to make a move. I don't want them to see us until it's too late. And, for heaven's sake, don't tell Jillian she's stunning. The team is small enough as it is without having to scrape you off the highway."

Jackson looked over at Jillian, who had moved from her position and was walking toward him. She looked annoyed. But, then, Jillian always looked annoyed. He was glad Carney had put her on the crew.

Now, *she* was *really* dangerous.

Chapter 8
PLANS AND LIFE

PENG CLOSED HIS EYES AND tried unsuccessfully to sleep. The raucous voices and jostling around him were annoying, but that wasn't what kept him awake. No matter how hard he tried, he could not erase the images that kept appearing in his mind.

He tried replacing them with happy thoughts: Shi-Shi pulling on his tie before church. Jin giggling as she tried to ride Permelia. Matt and Hope embracing before the trip. He told himself they were not his family—none except Jin. But he knew it was a lie. These people had taken him in as a son, without question. They had fed him, clothed him, and sent him to church and to school. They had worried about him. They had shown him what true, happy families were like. They *were* his family. Probably the best family he would ever have. But they didn't know who he was. They didn't know what he had done. His leaving them would cause them pain, and he was sorry about that, but leaving them would not be the worst thing he had ever done in his short life. Not by far.

The SUV pulled to a stop.

"Everyone out," Ron said. "Get into the trailer and get your gear. We've got some hiking to do."

Peng opened his eyes and pulled himself out of the vehicle. The cool air shocked him into alertness, and he was almost overcome by the vastness of the sky. It seemed to go on forever. He could easily lose himself in these mountains. He had a sudden urge to start running—right now. To run and never stop running. But no. It was not time yet. Well, that was also a lie. It was past time. Jin was safe. He'd kept his promise to his mother. Jin had Hope and Matt, Zack, Mimi, Permelia, and dozens of others who would take care of her. She didn't need Peng anymore. He was no longer responsible for her. He needed to leave before he messed things up. But he had also promised Hope he would come home safely and that he wouldn't let Matt do anything stupid. *One more promise to keep*, he told himself, and then he would go.

He dragged his pack out of the trailer and lined up with the other boys. Ron walked up and down the row, examining them as if they were soldiers. Peng felt himself straightening a little under Ron's gaze. When the man looked at him, he always felt he could be something better than he was. But Ron didn't know his history either. Nobody did. Ron was just another person Peng was going to miss.

Ron stopped in front of Peng, nodded, and waited. At first Peng was unsure what was wanted of him. Then he understood. He was the new quorum president. Ron was deferring to his position. Peng was silent. This was not right. Ron was the real leader here. Everybody knew it. It was dumb to pretend that one of the boys was in charge, especially Peng. Dumb and dangerous. Peng knew what could happen when he was made responsible.

"President, could you call on someone to give us a prayer? And then I need a few minutes, if that's okay."

Peng knew from experience that Ron would wait until he said something. "Joey?" Peng looked at the younger boy, but he wasn't sure what else to say. Luckily Joey seemed to understand, and he enthusiastically folded his arms.

After Joey blessed pretty much everyone and everything, Peng quickly nodded to Ron to indicate that he had control. It felt silly, but Ron wouldn't speak unless Peng authorized it.

"Boys, you've done well. You've planned well, you've prepared well, and I believe you are fully ready for this trip."

Despite himself, Peng felt a sense of pride as Ron commended them. He couldn't help it. Praise from Ron did not come easily. They *were* ready for this. All of them. Even JR and Eric, who didn't take anything seriously.

"I had a colonel once," Ron continued. "He used to say, 'There's plans, and then there's life.' What he meant was that even when you do the best you can do at planning and preparing, sometimes life throws you a curve ball. He taught us to prepare, but he also taught us something more important—he taught us to adjust when the situation changes. I want to give you boys the same gift my colonel gave me. I want you to learn that same lesson. I want you to go put your packs back into the trailer."

For what seemed like a long moment, the boys just stood there, looking at each other.

And then Eric blurted out, "Sweet. I knew it. We're going to the condo."

"Is that true?" JR asked Ron, his jaw dropping open.

"Yup," Ron said, a slight smile working its way across his lips.

Eric and JR nearly knocked each other over trying to get their packs back to the trailer. They did knock Joey over on their way back out, but they didn't seem to notice. Peng hoisted his comrade off the ground and helped him put his pack away as the others began dibbsing seats for the ride back to Park City.

But before they could get into the vehicle, Ron cleared his throat. "We *are* going to my condo," he said, "but not quite yet."

The boys stopped their excited shuffling for position and turned around.

"We have some miles to put in first," Ron said. Peng looked at Matt to see if he was in on Ron's change of plans, but Matt seemed as confused as everyone else.

"But you said we should put away our packs," Eric said.

"I said to put away *those* packs. They are not appropriate for what we're going to do. I have some others for you in the back of my SUV. Peng, if you and Joey could retrieve them, we can be on our way soon."

Peng nodded to Joey, who reached in through the back window and pulled out five smallish-looking rucksacks.

"But those are the crappy packs we made at your house," JR said.

"That's right. These are the packs we made at my house. But they aren't crappy. They're actually quite functional. And in these homemade packs are the sleeping quilts, rain ponchos, tarps, and pop-can stoves you made. These are what we will be using on the trail. Gentlemen, we are no longer on a backpacking trip. We are going fast packing."

Matt stepped over and picked up his rucksack, which appeared to be the sorriest of the lot. He looked inside and spoke quietly to Ron, but Peng could still hear him, even above JR's and Eric's whining. "I don't think there's enough food in there for a week."

Ron grinned. "There isn't. There's barely enough for two days, if you stretch it."

"I had Easy Cheese in my other pack," Eric moaned. "I can't survive in the woods without my Easy Cheese."

JR snickered. "Easy Cheese. That fits."

"What'd you mean?" Eric said.

"Your initials, *E. C.* They're also the initials of Easy Cheese. I think we found you a new nickname."

"But . . ."

"Okay, listen up," Ron said. As usual, his voice carried enough command in it that everyone immediately paid attention. Peng was curious, but he didn't much care what packs they used. He didn't care if they hiked fifty miles or went to the condo. All that mattered was that Ron was in control. As long as that was the case, Peng was confident things would turn out okay.

"If you remember, we spent a great deal of time on Wednesday nights working on orienteering. Well, I've mapped out an orienteering course." Ron held up a piece of paper. "These are your initial set of coordinates. They will lead you to your first campsite. Once you find this campsite, you will also find your second set of coordinates. These will lead you out of the mountains and to a vehicle that will transport you to my condo, where you can swim, play video games, and even eat a bathtub full of Easy Cheese if you want to. The course I've plotted uses trails but also some cross country. If you're resourceful and smart and use your orienteering skills, you could be out of the mountains by tomorrow night. If not . . . well, then you're going to need to learn how to use the fishing line and hooks to get your meals because you're going to run out of food."

"What about *your* pack?" JR said, pointing to a large Gregory Baltoro backpack that looked like it was stuffed to the gills.

"That's right," Ron said. "My pack looks a little different."

"I'd say it looks a lot different," Eric said, still grumbling.

"It *is* a lot nicer. And a lot *heavier*. This isn't a fast-packing pack. It's our backup plan. If something goes wrong, it has emergency supplies, including a satellite phone. Matt and I will be taking turns carrying it."

"But won't you slow us down?" Joey raised his hand before asking the question. "Trying to carry that heavy pack?"

"Good question, Joey. But, no, we won't slow you down because we won't be traveling with you. We will be following behind, and we will catch up to you at your camp. This is your experience. This is where you show what you're made of. We are only here for backup. Peng is your leader on this trip, and you are all responsible as a troop for finding your way and reaching your destination."

"This is a load of crap," Eric said. "The only reason I agreed to come on this trip was because I was looking forward to the Easy Cheese."

Ron smiled just slightly. "You're right. It is a load of crap. The only question is are you going to throw a tantrum or look for the pony?"

Eric stared blankly. "What's that supposed to mean?"

"Oh, I know." Joey was raising his hand again. "My mom likes to tell that story a lot. There's two birthday girls. The first one gets up in the morning, and her mom tells her that her present is in the front yard. She runs outside, excited, but all that's there is a pile of horse manure. So she runs into her room crying. The second girl starts the same way, but when she sees the pile of manure, she jumps in and starts digging. Her mom asks her what she's doing and she says, 'There must be a pony in here somewhere.' My mom always ends the story by saying that when life gives you . . . uh . . . crap, you should look for the pony." Joey's face turned bright red. "Sometimes she swears when she says that last part."

All of the boys turned to look at Joey.

"Your mom swears?" JR asked. "I don't believe it."

Joey's face turned even redder. "Maybe I shouldn't have told you that."

JR walked over and put his arm around Joey. "Joey, I think you've just changed my entire outlook on life. Picturing a swear word coming out of your mom's mouth, I may never be tempted to swear again. You've ruined me."

For some reason, whether it was the words or the arm around his shoulder, this made Joey beam.

Ron brought them back to the present. "President Knight, in your pack, you have a map, a compass, and the coordinates for your first RV point." It took Peng a moment to realize Ron was talking to him and not Matt. He didn't really like the title. But he pulled the items out of his pack and set them on the ground.

"Remember what you were taught. Locate your coordinates, orient the map, and then get going. Someone is coming to pick up my SUV. Our extraction point will be in a different location, and I will call someone when we get there. Coming back here is not an option. There will be no vehicle waiting. The bridges have officially been burned."

Joey bent down, looked at the coordinates, and began tracing his finger on the map.

JR moved in and bumped him out of the way. "Step aside, son. It's time for the real men to take over."

He looked where Joey had been pointing and announced. "Our destination is Ryder Lake. Easy Cheese, give me that pen in your pocket. The one you've been using to write all over yourself."

"Don't call me that," Eric said, but he handed over the pen anyway, then licked his thumb to wipe at the marks he had written on his arm. JR circled a small blue spot on the map. "That's our rendezvous point." He scanned the map some more and let the pen stop on a larger blue spot that designated another lake. "And here we are now. The Mirror Lake trailhead. So if we chart our course . . ." He took the compass and laid the edge from one circle to the other. "Then we can see the most direct route."

"That's not very far at all," Eric said, sounding excited.

"Only a few miles," JR confirmed. "But it looks like it's over the top of a ridge. And it's not on the main trail. So let's get an idea of what we're looking at." JR oriented the map to match the north of the compass and pointed. "We need to go that way." A pine-covered mountain stood in front of them, but it didn't look too high or too steep. "We could follow the trail that goes around that mountain, or we can take the most direct route and go over the top."

"That doesn't look too bad," Eric said. "I say we take the way that gets us to the condo the fastest."

"Agreed," JR said. "Easy Cheese, you are smarter than you look."

"But, guys . . ." Joey was frantically raising his hand.

"Quiet, Joey. There are men at work here. If you watch closely, you might learn something." JR folded up the map and put it in his pack.

"But . . ."

"You heard him," Eric said. "Watch and learn from the men."

Peng felt like he should say something. He knew why Joey was trying to speak up, but Peng didn't want to step in. He didn't want to be in control. He was perfectly content to let JR take the lead. JR might make mistakes, but at least they would be his mistakes. And Peng was convinced the consequences wouldn't be as bad as if he made the decisions.

He glanced back at Ron, expecting to see the disappointment in his eyes. Instead he saw a look of intense curiosity—as if Peng were doing something calculated and smart. Peng quickly broke the gaze. He turned his attention to Matt and saw an expression he was familiar with.

Bewilderment. As if he were observing an alien emerging from a spacecraft. Peng was sure Matt didn't know what to think of him, which was probably good. He was not an alien. Just a monster. A monster who had overstayed his welcome.

In that moment, he decided that after this trip, he would make his final escape and leave for good.

Chapter 9
STRANGERS ON THE TRAIL

I HEFTED OFF THE LARGE pack and dropped it on the ground. Ron had suggested that we hike to the top of a ridge to get a better view of the boys. Of course, he'd made this suggestion when it was my turn to carry the big pack.

Ron dug inside and pulled out a pair of binoculars that looked like they weighed fifteen pounds.

"Didn't you have a smaller version?"

"Couldn't find them," Ron said as he wedged his elbows into the ground and put the glasses up to his eyes.

I could see the small forms of the boys as they moved out of the pines and into a clearing. "Still headed the wrong direction?"

"Yup."

"Do you think they'll ever figure it out?"

"Oh, they've already got it figured out. At least Peng and Joey do. They've known from the start. The question is how long they'll let JR and Eric lead them off into oblivion." Ron continued to watch the boys. I could almost hear the gears grinding in his head.

"Are you sure our following behind like this meets the requirement for having two leaders present at all times?"

"I told you we will never let them out of our sight. They think they're alone, but they aren't. When do you think he'll make his move?"

"Who?" I had no idea what Ron was talking about.

"Peng. Our quorum president."

"You think he has a plan?"

"Don't you?"

I sighed and sat next to Ron. "I have no clue. To tell you the truth, most of what Peng does is a mystery to me."

"Huh," Ron grunted. But what I heard was, "Aren't you his father? Shouldn't you know this boy by now?"

"Who's that?" I pointed to a spot about a hundred yards to the left of the boys. Two figures had appeared, jogging through the clearing toward the boys. Ron turned his glasses on them.

"Huh," he said again.

"What?"

"See for yourself." Ron handed me the binoculars. "Maybe some ultrarunners training in the mountains?"

I focused the lenses on the two figures. A man and a woman. They carried medium-sized packs, wore trail-running shoes, and moved at a measured pace. Their movements reminded me of something. "Not ultrarunners," I said. "At least not like any I've seen before."

"And you've seen lots of ultrarunners?"

"As a matter of fact, I was a pacer for one once." Ron and I had spent a lot of time together, but I'd been careful not to share too much about my past—especially my past work.

"Huh," Ron said for the third time. I wasn't sure if he was commenting on my past or on the runners. I wasn't sure if he had handed me the binoculars because he wanted to see my reaction or to find out what I really thought. I told myself I needed to be careful not to reveal too much. Even to Ron. I didn't want to get into a discussion about how my experience with ultrarunners had occurred while I was acting as a pacer to my roommate, who was also a terrorist. I didn't want to bring up my former life at all.

Thinking of my past, I began to get a sick feeling in my gut. I'd finally figured out what the runners reminded me of. They reminded me of Ron. Their fluid, synchronized movement across the ground was typical of the few army rangers I had known. "I think we should get down there," I said.

"Not yet," Ron replied. "I want to see if the boys will follow instructions and refuse help from strangers."

I thought briefly about telling Ron everything, about telling him of the hidden danger my past might bring to those around me. But I choked it down. So what if the runners were military or ex-military? That didn't mean they were a danger. I wasn't worried about the military. I was worried about terrorists, those who might be ticked off that I had ruined their plans to reap vengeance on the West. These people were probably just enjoying the wilderness. Maybe a couple on leave from Afghanistan. Besides, it would take us at least twenty minutes to get to the boys. The encounter was going to happen whether we liked it or not.

"Keep an eye on them," Ron said as he dug into his pack. "Give me the play-by-play of what you see."

"What are you going to do?"

"I'm going to change my shirt. This T-shirt is too tight. I need something loose and with long sleeves. I don't want to get a sunburn."

* * *

Peng felt them before he saw them. He hadn't felt that sensation in a long time. Not since he had come to live with Matt and Hope. Not even when he ran alone in the darkness through the streets at night. Not since the orphanage.

He felt the bile rise in his throat and the lead sink into his legs. For a moment, he thought he had let JR and Eric's manic march go on too long, that he might be letting the group he was supposed to be leading march straight toward a cliff or a dangerous animal. Then he saw the man and woman jogging out of the pines toward them, and he knew where the threat was coming from.

The boys stopped in the clearing and gawked as the two figures came close. The man had his T-shirt pulled up over his shoulders, and his abs were defined in tight layers across his midsection. The woman looked beautiful from a distance, but as she drew closer, Peng sensed there was something wrong about her. Something hard.

"How's it going, boys?" The man pulled out a thirty-two-ounce bottle of yellow Gatorade and downed half of it while the sweat dripped off of him.

"Wow," Eric said. "Just like the commercials."

The woman didn't say anything. She looked like she was annoyed at the man for stopping.

"Are you training for the Olympics?" Eric asked, his voice filled with reverence.

The man laughed. "Naw, not Olympians. Just recreational runners enjoying God's beautiful creations." He winked at the woman, who scowled back at him.

"Where you boys headed?" The words were casual, but Peng sensed the man was forcing the lightness into his words. Like his pleasantness was just an act. Just like Mistress Wu at the orphanage.

"Ryder Lake . . . and then out of this place and into a condo," JR answered without hesitation. "A condo with a pool and loads and loads of junk food. Isn't that right, Easy Cheese?"

"Don't call me that," Eric snapped.

"Easy Cheese?" the man asked, a slight smile pulling at his lips.

Eric looked at the ground. "My name's Eric."

"That's too bad." The man seemed to consider Eric's words seriously. "I kind of liked the name Easy Cheese. It's got character. Smooth and cool. Kind of like real Easy Cheese, as a matter of fact. There's not many things in this world that I love more than Easy Cheese. But for a nickname, I think I would shorten it to just Easy. Now that is a seriously classy nickname."

Eric's head came up, and he beamed. He looked back at JR as if to say, "I am so much cooler than you."

"But if you're headed to Ryder Lake, I have some bad news for you."

"Wait." Peng heard the voice, an authoritative voice that got everyone's attention. It was a moment before he realized it was his own voice. He had stepped forward and was holding up his hand. "Remember the rules. We can't receive help from anyone else. We have to find the rendezvous point on our own."

"But we're lost," Eric whined. "We all know it. We're only following JR because he talks like he knows where he's going. If we were where he said we were, we would have already reached Ryder Lake." Eric stared at JR in defiance. He glanced quickly at the stranger to make sure he was watching.

"We aren't going the right direction, but we're not lost either," Peng said.

"If you knew we were headed in the wrong direction, why didn't you say something?" JR's tone was frustrated but reasonable.

"Because the *men* were in charge." Peng made sure he made eye contact with both JR and Eric. "And the men didn't want to listen to Joey." Peng turned his attention to the smaller boy. "Joey, why don't you tell everyone where we are and where we need to go to get to our camping spot."

Joey's face brightened. He stepped up to JR and held out his hand for the map and compass. "The mistake was an honest one. Our starting point was supposed to be at the Mirror Lake trailhead. My family goes there all the time for summer picnics, so I noticed when we passed it. But instead of stopping, we drove all the way to Christmas Meadows. So to get to Ryder Lake, we actually should have been following the trail mostly south and not cutting cross country. If we alter our course and go southwest, we should reach the trail pretty soon, and we can follow it right to the lake."

Peng didn't watch Joey as he spoke. Instead, he focused on the strangers—the man with the permanent smile and the woman with the scowl. The man nodded in appreciation. "It never ceases to amaze me how some of the most profound insights come from the quiet ones," he said. "What do you think, Jillian? You got to admit the little one is impressive."

Jillian turned her head to the side as if she was going to spit but then seemed to think better of it. Instead, she just continued to glare at her companion.

"She says she doesn't like kids," the man explained to the boys. "But I think she's just nervous 'cause I want a big family." The glare turned from disdain to poison.

The man was suggesting that these two were a couple, but something was off. They didn't seem anything like Hope and Matt—even when Hope and Matt were arguing with each other. He wanted to get away from these people as soon as possible. "We better go," he said. "We don't want to set up camp in the dark."

"I think that is a wise choice," the man said. "We best be moving too. Maybe our paths will cross again someday." The man pulled the pack onto his back. "Take it easy, Easy." He winked at Eric, and then in a matter of seconds, he and the woman were jogging away from them on the trail.

"I think I'm in love," Eric said.

"She *was* pretty hot," JR said as the woman glided away.

"Not her." Eric soured his face at the thought. "Did you see the abs on that guy? Did you notice how he talked? Did you see how he took your stupid nickname and turned it into something cool? I've just seen a vision of what I want to be when I grow up. That's it. I want to be that guy."

Peng continued to watch as the two moved out of sight. When they were gone, he said, "Let's go." He hoped to never see them ever again.

* * *

I put down the binoculars and studied Ron's expression. It was thoughtful—as usual. I had been giving him the commentary on what was happening with the boys and the strangers. I'd been a little surprised when Peng had stepped in and seemed to get the boys going on the right track.

"He's a good kid," Ron said. "You should have a little more faith in him."

"He doesn't make it easy sometimes."

"They never do." Ron had changed from his T-shirt into a long-sleeved, tan, UV shirt, supposedly so he wouldn't get a sunburn. It was loose fitting and looked like it would do a good job of keeping him cool. It also did a better job than the T-shirt of hiding the slight bulge behind his waist. When Ron said he was prepared for anything, he wasn't kidding. No wonder the pack was so heavy. I didn't bring up the fact that I noticed the weapon.

"So what do we do now?"

Ron watched the runners as they disappeared into the pine trees, moving in the opposite direction of the boys.

"I think it's time we hoof it to Ryder Lake. Now that the boys have the right scent, they'll be moving double time."

I looked at the large pack sitting on the ground.

"Do you mind?" Ron said. "It makes my back sweat."

By the look on his face, Ron knew I had noticed the gun. In fact, it felt like he had expected me to spot it, as if I had the type of background that I would notice such things. Sometimes I thought Ron might suspect just a little bit too much. Even so, after seeing the two strangers approaching the boys, I was glad Ron was here. And I was glad he'd brought a gun. I kicked myself for choosing reason over intuition and leaving my own weapon at home, and I prayed that I was wrong about my feelings of uneasiness.

Chapter 10
DANGER IN THE CUL-DE-SAC

ZACK WALKED INTO THE LIVING room and looked at his recliner. The newspaper sat on top of it, along with the remote control. Usually he spent some time every afternoon catching up on the news around the world and then taking a nap, but today he felt restless. He walked into the kitchen where Mimi was whisking up something in a bowl.

"What's that you're making?" He looked over her shoulder at a brownish batter.

"Oh, nothing much. Just zucchini bread, your favorite food in the whole world."

"That brown stuff is my favorite food? It doesn't look nearly as good before it's been cooked." He walked to the other side of the kitchen and stared out the window.

Mimi stopped whisking. "Okay," she said. "What's the matter? You've been pacing around all afternoon like a cat needing to go to the sandbox."

Zack continued staring out the window. "I'm not sure. Something just doesn't feel right. Where's Shi-Shi?"

"She's at dance class. I know that because she just texted me about thirty seconds ago. Are you having bad feelings about Shi-Shi?"

Zack moved away from the window. "I don't think so." He sat in a kitchen chair and rubbed at his chin. "Did Matt and Peng get off okay this morning?"

"Hope said they left before it was light. Permelia came over and apparently wore little Jin out. She's napping now, and then they were going to go out for a walk. Do you think the boys are okay? Is that what's bothering you?"

"I'm sure they're fine," he said and then stood, seeming to have come to some decision. "I'm going to go over and see how Hope and Permelia are doing with Jin."

"Wait a minute, and I'll come with you."

Zack thought about it. "No. You finish your bread. I'm just going to go check on them, and then I'll be back."

"Take your cell phone with you. You call me as soon as you get there. You've got me worried, Zackary Shepherd."

"I'm sure it's nothing. Just restless old bones and grandfatherly paranoia." But Zack knew it was something more. He'd had feelings like this in the past. Subtle promptings that he had learned not to ignore. There was something going on here—a sense of uneasiness about Shi-Shi, about Matt and Peng, but especially about Hope and Jin. He stopped in his room to get his cell phone. He also opened the safe and pulled out his holstered gun.

He didn't know what was going on—probably nothing. He was most likely just getting old. But in his line of work, in his years working for the FBI and other government agencies, Zack had learned to always prepare for the worst. Most of the time the worst did not happen. But if it did, he would be ready.

* * *

The Econoline van sat at the opening to the cul-de-sac, and Dempsey and Buck peered through the tinted windows at Matthew and Hope Knight's house.

"It looks quiet," Dempsey said.

"That's because it is quiet. I told you, Boss, the neighbors on either side were thrilled to win the free trip to Disneyland, and the houses farther down the street are far enough away that they won't see or hear anything."

"Let's go through it one more time."

Buck groaned. "You're killing me. We've been through it a dozen times already."

"And we're going to go through it again." If there was one thing Dempsey had learned from his time in clandestine operations, it was that rehearsals were critical. He'd also learned that no matter how thoroughly you prepared, there was always something that went wrong.

"I told you before. The kid likes to go outside in the afternoon. Sometimes the babe with all the hair likes to run, and sometimes she walks. She uses one of those running strollers for the kid. My guess is that they'll be walking today because the old lady is with them."

"And if they don't come out?"

"Then we wait until tomorrow. You said we didn't need to be at the rendez-vous point until Thursday. We've got plenty of time. It will be the smoothest snatch-and-grab we've ever been a part of. Carney and his crew pulled the hard duty. While they're up in the mountains trying to round up an ex-agent and a bunch of snot-nosed teenagers, we get the supermodel, an old lady, and a two-year-old. How hard could it be?"

Dempsey was about ready to lecture Buck about being too cocky when the door to the house opened and their targets began filing out. Dempsey opened the door and stepped out of the van. "Remember what I said. We don't want to make a scene."

Buck smiled and turned on the ignition. "Don't worry, by the time you get there, the princess will have fallen into my arms."

Dempsey was going to say something else about appropriate handling of the "princess," but Buck shut the door and began to drive away. Dempsey hurried, crossing through a neighbor's yard and behind a house. He wanted to be in position by the time Buck arrived at the curb, and Buck's speed was going to make that difficult. Dempsey hoofed it about a hundred yards and then stopped to peek through a hedge.

Just as Buck had said, the woman was adjusting a jogging stroller on the walkway. The old woman, dressed in spandex and bright-pink running shorts, stood behind her. The older woman had come out hand in hand with the toddler and was now adjusting the kid in the stroller. The old woman wasn't part of the plan, but since she was there, they would have to take her too. This shouldn't pose much of a problem—she looked like she was at least in her seventies—but Dempsey still didn't like it. He didn't like any changes to the plan.

He began jogging. He still had some ground to cover before he would be in position. If Buck slowed down, it wouldn't be a problem. But he knew Buck. Buck never slowed down.

Dempsey watched Buck pull up to the curb as the women made their way out to the sidewalk. Buck jumped out of the van, looking frantic. Dempsey couldn't make out what he was saying, but he knew the script. Buck would do some improvisation, but Dempsey was actually okay with that. Buck was good with improv. And he was very good at acting a part. He just wasn't very good at following orders.

As Dempsey got closer, he could hear what Buck was saying.

"My daughter." Buck was wringing his hands and looked to be almost physically ill. "She swallowed a tinker toy, and she isn't breathing. I don't think she's going to make it to the hospital. Is there a doctor in any of these houses?" He glanced up and down the street, a look of utter panic on his face.

As predicted, Hope immediately rushed forward. "Where is she? Take me to her. I'm a nurse."

Buck looked up to the heavens as if his prayers had been answered and then ushered her to the side door of the van. "She's in the backseat," he said, following Hope into the van.

Dempsey couldn't see them anymore, but as Hope neared the pile of blankets in the back, Buck would reach around to her face with a chlorophyll-doused rag and gently lower her into one of the seats. This was the part where Dempsey did not completely trust Buck. He didn't trust him anywhere around a beautiful woman, and Matthew Knight's wife was definitely beautiful.

"Hey," he heard the old woman yell as she rushed toward the van. Buck was just coming out, and the woman caught him with a front kick to the groin, causing him to double over. Then she hit and kicked him as he rolled around on the sidewalk, trying to protect himself.

"Uh-oh," Dempsey said under his breath as he rushed forward. The scene would have been amusing if the whole operation wasn't in danger. He wouldn't mind at all watching an elderly woman beat the tar out of Buck. But if somebody called the cops, it would all be over. He thought about rushing into the fray and pinning down her arms but decided against it. Instead he moved to the little girl, who was watching from the stroller.

"I think I would stop that if I were you."

The woman looked at him, noticing that he had control of the jogger and that he happened to be pointing his gun casually at the little girl.

"Don't you hurt her, you creepazoid. You can't even imagine what kind of pain I can cause."

"Oh, I think I can imagine." Dempsey nodded to Buck, who was pulling himself off the ground. "But we're done with the games now. Get into the van, or the little girl gets hurt."

"What have you done to Hope?"

"Nothing that won't wear off in a couple of hours. Now, please, move into the van. I don't particularly like hurting women and children."

Dempsey nearly jumped as a booming voice sounded behind him. "That's funny, Mr. Dempsey. Hurting innocent women seems to have become a pattern for you."

Dempsey knew the voice without having to turn around. And behind it was a six-foot-five black man who could grind a person to powder with his bare hands. Dempsey slowly placed his gun on the ground and turned to face the man who used to be his teacher. "Nice to see you again, Zack. You've lost some weight. Do they still call you the Hammer behind your back?"

"Usually they just call me Grandpa these days. And right now you are between an angry grandpa and his grandchild. Not a very good place to be."

Dempsey moved away from the stroller. Buck was on his knees, still trying to catch his breath.

"Nice to see you, Bishop," the old woman said. "I had it under control until the one with the crooked nose decided to pick on a little girl."

"These guys don't play fair. You did well, Permelia."

"You know these hoodlums?"

"I know this one." He gestured his gun toward Dempsey. "I'm ashamed to say he's a former student."

"Did you put that dent in his nose?"

"Naw. Not me. Matt did that."

"Huh. I didn't think the boy had it in him."

"Let's just say that some of my students were better at learning their lessons than others."

Dempsey smiled. "You're not talking about me, are you, Zack? Because I was actually a very attentive student. And you know the one lesson I learned from you that I will never forget?"

"What's that, Mr. Dempsey?"

"To never, ever rely on the first plan to succeed. To always, always, always have a plan B. Isn't that what you used to drum into us?"

Zack was about to respond when a shadow stepped out from behind a bush and hit him over the head with something hard and black. Zack went to his knees but did not go down. Dempsey marveled at how tough the man still was.

The shadow hit him again. This time Zack did go down. All the way down.

Permelia was about to scream when Buck reached around her with the chloroform rag and took her to the ground.

"Mean old biddy," he mumbled under his breath. "Reminds me of my grandma."

In the stroller, Jin began to cry.

"Buck, get the old lady into the van and then grab the kid. You"—Dempsey nodded to the man who had emerged from out of nowhere—"It's about time you showed up. Help me lift Zack."

The man from the shadows just grunted. Dempsey had worked with him many times before, and he had been expecting him, but he was still amazed at how his bearded colleague always seemed to appear out of nowhere.

Buck grimaced and rubbed at a bruise on his cheek. "Why don't we just take the old woman and the giant back in the house and put them on ice? They aren't part of the bounty, and neither of them looks to be a cooperative prisoner."

"We take them with us. The woman is old and harmless, and we have enough meds to keep the big one sedated. The last thing we need right now is someone finding a body."

"His wife's going to miss him. Someone's going to come looking," Buck said as he moved Permelia into the backseat, next to Hope. He stuck Jin between them and fastened her seat belt. She had stopped crying and was sucking hard on her hand.

Dempsey and the bearded man struggled to lift Zack into the middle seat.

"All the more reason not to leave any bodies," Dempsey said. But Buck was right. If Zack went missing, there was no telling what type of law enforcement would be on their tail. All they needed was a few days, but something would need to be done about Zack's wife. Dempsey handed Buck a handful of zip ties.

"Okay, let's sit him up." They struggled to get Zack's body into a sitting position in the van. "Is he secure?"

"His hands and feet are triple zipped. But I think he's going to be out for a few hours. Your mysterious friend did a number on his head. By the way, where is . . . ?" Buck looked around, but the bearded man was nowhere to be seen.

"He'll meet us at the holding site," Dempsey said. "He's not very sociable."

"But he's kind of handy to have around in a fight."

Dempsey fished around in Zack's pocket for his cell phone. "Okay, get me some ammonia. We're going to wake him up."

"Why would we want to do that? He's resting so beautifully. And the ghost is no longer here to help us put him back to sleep if we need to."

"You said it. His wife is going to be worried. We need him to call her."

"And what's he going to tell her? That he decided to suddenly take a week's vacation in Barbados?"

"He'll think of something good. He'll have to. Because I'm going to give him some real motivation."

Buck produced a small capsule of ammonia from a medical bag and crushed it under the big man's nose. Zack's eyes fluttered and blinked as he came back to consciousness. His legs and hands were tightly bound, and Buck had added extra protection by securing him to a post on the seat of the van. As Zack awoke and began to struggle, Dempsey thought he might pull the seat from its moorings and start beating Buck over the head with it. If anyone could do it, it would be Zack.

"I wouldn't do that," Dempsey said. "Your granddaughter is watching." Dempsey gestured to the toddler, who was staring intently at Zack. "I'm going to need you to call your wife."

"And why would I agree to do that?" Zack's eyes were deadly, and he reminded Dempsey of a caged bear.

"Because not only do we have the little girl, but I also have people following your daughter. Her name is Shi-Shi, isn't it? Such a great little dancer. But then again, she does take lessons every afternoon during the summer. Nice to have a studio so close that she can walk home afterward." Dempsey pulled a piece of paper from his pocket and held it out in front of Zack. "I believe this is the exact route that she takes. I wonder what would happen if someone pulled up and offered her a ride?"

The fire in Zack's eyes turned icy cold, and Dempsey was suddenly glad they had brought the pharmaceuticals. A lot was going to happen in the next week, but they needed to make sure Zack slept through it all.

"What do you want?" Zack had stopped struggling. His arms and voice were perfectly still.

"You are going to call your wife. You are going to tell her you were notified of a potential threat against Matt and his family. You are taking Hope and the little girl to a safe house, and you will be out of contact for about a week. You are sure there is nothing to worry about, but you want to take every precaution to make sure they are safe. You will contact her next week, but until then, tell her not to worry and not to talk to anyone else about this." Dempsey met Zack's stare with one of his own. "I think that should do it. Stick to the script, make it believable, and Shi-Shi will never know that friends of mine have been following her home."

"What are you up to, Dempsey? I thought you were strictly doing overseas jobs."

"I go where the money takes me. And you don't need to know what I'm up to. You just need to know that if you don't make that call, I will be forced to deal with your family."

Zack didn't say anything else, but he did give a slight nod. Dempsey dialed the number for Mimi in Zack's phone and punched the button to put it on speaker.

"I don't need to tell you what happens if you try anything funny."

"Hello." Mimi came on the line.

"Hello, Mimi."

"I was worried about you. Is Hope okay?"

"She's fine. But there's been a development. I got a call from Washington. There's been chatter about some terrorists digging into information about Matt and Hope."

"Oh dear. What kind of information?"

"They may have gotten ahold of their address."

"But that's not a secret. Why is that concerning?"

"It's concerning because they've been asking about it and apparently communicating it to other people. People that are in the profession of doing harm."

"Oh dear," Mimi said again. "You need to bring Hope and Jin over here right now."

"I considered that," Zack said. "But I think I have a better idea. I'm going to take Hope, Jin, and Permelia to a safe house . . . for about a week. I want to get them off the grid. Intel suggested that if something is going to happen, it will happen soon. I'll stay with them, but I won't be able to contact you for a while."

Zack looked directly at Dempsey. "I also want you and Shi-Shi to get out of town. I want you away from this as well."

"But where will we go? Another safe house?"

"No, not a safe house." Dempsey was ready to hang up the phone if Zack said as much as a wrong word. Telling his wife and daughter to get out of town was not in the script, but it also made Dempsey's job a little easier. He gestured to Zack with his thumb and little finger to make this short. Zack nodded, his eyes still defiant.

"You know that Disneyland trip we've been talking about? The one where we were going to stay at the Californian?"

"Yes, I know it," Mimi said. "The Disneyland trip to the Grand Californian."

"I want you to go with Shi-Shi. We've got the money saved up. It's in our savings account. Make the reservations as soon as I hang up the phone. Don't wait. These guys after Matt are the lowest of pond scum, and I don't want to worry about you and Shi-Shi. I will take care of Hope."

"What about Matt? He and Peng are out there in the woods."

"Matt can take care of himself," Zack said. "These guys aren't fit to even walk in his shadow." He was glaring at Dempsey again. Dempsey just shook his head. There were times when he missed Zack's not-so-subtle messages.

"Okay. I'll make the call, and Shi-Shi and I will leave as soon as she gets home from dance class."

"Don't wait for her to get home," Zack's voice seemed to soften. "I'd feel a lot better if you went and picked her up."

"Shall I call the hotel first?"

"Yes, do that first," Zack said. Dempsey was running his hand across his throat, telling Zack to end it. "Look. I've got to go. You keep Shi-Shi safe and have a good time at Disneyland. Don't worry about Hope and Jin. I will take care of them."

Dempsey hung up the phone. "You think sending them to Disneyland will protect them from us?"

"I think you got what you wanted—a plausible explanation of why I'm not coming home and a wife who isn't going to be contacting the FBI with questions about where I am."

"Also a wife and daughter who are far away so you can focus on putting a wrench in my plans without worrying about them." Dempsey sighed. "While I would seriously enjoy playing that game with you, there is too much money at stake." He nodded to Buck. "Unfortunately it's time for you to go back to sleep."

Before Zack could struggle, Buck pulled out a long syringe and jabbed it into the side of Zack's neck. In a matter of seconds, his eyes rolled to the back of his head and his chin fell to his chest.

"I don't know why we don't just kill him," Buck said as he extracted the needle. "A couple more shots of this and he won't be waking up."

"Because we don't have anywhere to stash the body," Dempsey said. "And dead bodies stink. Besides, when he wakes up and the job is all finished, I want Zackary Shepherd to know he's been beaten." Dempsey realized as he said the words that he meant them deeply.

Buck moved back into the driver's seat, took one more look around the cul-de-sac, and then slowly pulled away from the curb.

* * *

After hanging up, Mimi immediately went to the safe in the bedroom closet and began turning the dial. Her hands shook so badly she messed up several times and had to start over. When the door finally opened, she pulled a paper off the top shelf and quickly began to dial a number.

Zack had made her rehearse what to do in case of an emergency. There was code language involved. One of the codes had to do with calling on some of Zack's former colleagues for help. If the phrase involved *Disneyland* and the *Californian* or *Dolphins* and *Cancun*, she was to call Demetrius and Chico, two undercover agents Zack trusted above all others.

A man answered on the first ring. "What up, homey? You hit the butt dial again?"

"Excuse me," Mimi said. "Is this Demetrius?"

The voice changed from Harlem slang to Harvard educated. "Mrs. Shepherd? What's wrong?"

"I'm not sure," Mimi said. "Zack just called me. He went to check on Hope. He used a predetermined code that warns me of danger and directs me to call you."

"Hope? You mean Matt's wife, Hope? Where's Matt?"

"He's on a trip with the Scouts in the mountains."

"Dang, that man never goes to the mountains without getting into some kind of trouble. We'll be there tomorrow. Do you have any idea where Zack might be?"

"No, but he said not to worry about Hope and him. He seemed more concerned with making sure Shi-Shi was okay. He told us we should go to Disneyland, but I think he meant that we should just get out of town."

"Okay, you hang tight. I'll round up Chico, and we'll be there in the morning. Get your daughter and hole up someplace. If you think there's an emergency, call 911."

"I don't think that would be a good idea," Mimi said. "If Zack wanted me to call the police, there would have been a different code word. Shi-Shi and I will go to a hotel and stay there until you get here."

"Okay, Mrs. Shepherd. We'll be there as soon as we can."

Mimi hung up the phone and locked the safe. Her hands would not stop shaking. She didn't try to stop them. Zack was gone, and Shi-Shi was in danger. She reopened the safe and pulled out a gun.

For the first time in her life, Mimi thought she understood what it might feel like to be a mother grizzly protecting her cub.

Chapter 11
TAKEN

I SNAPPED AWAKE. I SLOWED my breathing and took stock of my surroundings without opening my eyes. I was on the ground in a sleeping bag on a backpacking trip with a group of boys. I listened to see if there was something out there that had caused my sudden alertness. I heard the chirp of crickets and the hum of other night insects. I smelled the remnants of the campfire from the night before. The boys had been tired, but they had also been glad they'd made it to the first camp. They hadn't been thrilled about the meager dinner of jerky and dehydrated mashed potatoes, but they had been excited that they'd found the instructions for the next rendezvous point. They'd been even more energized when they'd read, "Find the fastest, most direct, but safest route to the main highway and wait to be picked up." They'd searched their maps and actually consulted with each other on the best path out in the morning. JR had even deferred to Peng and Joey to make sure they hadn't made the same mistakes as before. Eric had fantasized about spending two full days at Ron's condo, playing in the pool and gorging himself on Easy Cheese and crackers.

The most direct way out looked to be over the top of a mountain. Following the main trail would take a lot longer but also looked much easier—and was probably a lot safer. The boys decided on a compromise between the two. They would follow a trail to where the contour lines on the map began to space out a bit and then hike over a pass and out to the main road. If the pass didn't look safe, they could always revert back to the trail. Either way, it looked like we would be at Ron's condo by tomorrow night.

I opened my eyes to slits. The light of dawn was just beginning to break through the trees. I'd slept restlessly the night before. For some reason, I kept worrying about Hope and Jin. I told myself that they were home in a warm, comfortable bed and they should be worrying about me, not the other way around. Still, something was bothering me.

I listened to the forest noises again. There was some scurrying in the underbrush, and a squirrel chattered in a faraway tree. Nothing that seemed out of place. Nothing that should have awoken me. Then I found it—the cause of my interrupted slumber. The alert was not coming from the outside but from within me. My stomach was turning over like a cold engine trying to start. Apparently the dehydrated potatoes and jerky didn't agree with me. Or maybe it was a touch of altitude sickness. Either way, I needed to get into the woods, and I needed to get there fast.

I groaned and got up. Ron was sleeping a few yards away in what looked to be a professionally built shelter made from a piece of tarp. This was a man who carried his condo with him wherever he went. It didn't matter the environment. Wherever he was, I was convinced Ron would be comfortable.

I rummaged inside the large pack, looking for toilet paper and a shovel to dig a cat hole, and came across something hard and plastic, but it wasn't the shovel.

"Need to make a call?" Ron asked. His voice sounded fully awake. I wondered how he knew my hands had just come across the satellite phone. I also wondered why, deep inside of Ron's pack, there was another holstered weapon. What did he expect to encounter out here in the woods? I wondered if he was really a paranoid maniac under his cool composure. I looked at him again. He was the picture of contentment. I decided I was probably the one being paranoid.

"I don't need to make a call," I said. "I need to answer one. Mother Nature is ringing, and she's being pretty insistent."

"The spade and paper are in the side pocket. The boys created a latrine area up behind those rocks a few hundred yards away."

"If it's all the same to you, I don't think I want any part of the boys' latrine area. I'm going to walk a ways and find my own private space." I located the spade and paper exactly where Ron had said it would be. "I may be a while. Don't leave without me."

"Don't get lost."

I walked as deep into the trees as I could until I began to think that I really would get lost. Now that I was relieved of carrying a pack, the sounds of the mountains took me back to a time several years ago when I had run over twenty-five miles through the dark in a place not too far from here. It had been my experience with my ultrarunner terrorist roommate. But somehow the memory was still a fond one. I realized I had not been in the mountains much since then. Maybe it was time for me to start running again.

On the way back, I took my time, enjoying the sunlight filtering through the aspens and the feel of damp pine needles under my feet. I heard voices up ahead and thought that maybe I would skirt around the camp and come in from the back side. Ron was right. Peng had shown leadership the day before.

I wanted to observe him this morning in his interactions with the group, and I wanted to do it without him seeing me.

As I crept up in a stand of pines behind the camp, some of the voices I heard were not familiar. A male voice was laughing, but nobody else seemed to be laughing with him. Needles began to rise up the back of my neck, and I wished I'd grabbed the weapon in Ron's backpack instead of the latrine spade. Where was Ron in all of this?

I answered the question when I made a small slit through the pine boughs to see the scene in front of me. The man and the woman we had seen through the binoculars yesterday were standing in the middle of the boys' campsite. They were both armed and pointing guns at the boys, who were my responsibility to protect. The tall, smiling man had a handgun sticking into Peng's back, and the woman was holding a pistol next to Joey's head. She looked like she really wanted to use it.

There were two other armed men in the camp. Both of them had guns leveled at Ron, who stood a few yards away with his hands in the air. Ron was wearing another loose shirt, this time a garishly colored Hawaiian one, which meant he probably still had his weapon tucked behind his waistband.

For some reason, I thought of how I would explain the situation to Hope in a "good news/bad news" fashion. First the bad news. You know those boys you told me to protect? Well, it looks like they've been kidnapped by well-trained militants with nasty-looking guns. Oh, and the good news? Well, the bad guys didn't know the Scoutmaster was probably an ex-Delta Force operative trained to deal with exactly this type of situation. I'd been invited to attend Delta training exercises on one or two occasions, and if Ron was given the slightest opening, the four kidnappers would be on the ground in a matter of seconds. I guess the other piece of good news was that I was still free—and I had my latrine spade.

Whatever optimism I had was dashed in the next few moments.

"Search him," the smiling man said.

The two other men carefully approached Ron. One of them, a huge man the size of a giant, covered him while the other man patted him down. He came away with the gun from the waistband, another small gun strapped to the ankle, and a wicked-looking knife that hung down Ron's back.

"Wow, Brother K. You . . ." Eric was staring at Ron's assortment of weapons. As Eric spoke, he seemed to catch himself and put his hands over his mouth as if to stop more words from coming out. He looked nervously at the smiling man.

"It's okay, Easy. You and me are compadres. You can speak whenever you like." He put his hand on Eric's shoulder. At first Eric beamed, but his smile halted as he looked around at the guns pointed at his Scout troop.

The man turned his attention back to Ron. "So tell me, Brother K, where's the other leader?"

"It's just me," Ron said. "The other leader went home. He was feeling ill."

The punch caught Ron square in the stomach. He stepped back but didn't go down. He was one tough dude. They had pulled his hands behind him and zip-tied them, but he still looked to be in control. At this moment, however, Delta Force or not, there wasn't much he could do. The laughing man smiled and hit Ron again. This time Ron went to his knees.

"Your dad thinks he's a tough guy." The man was looking at Peng when he said it.

As I asked myself why these men would assault a group of Scouts in the mountains, the answer came as clearly as the stars had shone last night in the darkened sky: they were here because of me. My past was finally catching up to me. More than that, it was catching up to the innocents around me. It seemed as if Eric's "Brother K" comment had made them think Ron was me. And Ron was more than willing to play along. But what would the boys do?

The smiling man picked up Ron's knife, unsheathed it, and placed it against Peng's cheek. "Our orders are to bring you and your son back alive. But alive doesn't mean undamaged. I could carve a nice memento in his face if you want to play it that way."

"We could waste the little fat one," the woman said, putting the barrel of her gun closer to Joey's forehead. "There's nothing in the job that says we need to bring out all the brats."

The man took the knife away from Peng's cheek and looked at the woman with admiration. "Jillian doesn't much like kids. And she's right. We don't need to bring out all these boys. Just you and your son. So why don't you tell me where the other leader went before your Scout troop starts to get a little smaller."

"He went to dig a latrine," Ron said, his eyes focused firmly on Jillian. "And if you so much as lay a finger on any one of these boys, none of you will make it out of these mountains alive." The words were calm, quiet, and utterly believable. I felt a chill run down my back, and I thought I saw the woman named Jillian ease up a bit on the trigger.

The tall man went back to Eric and put his hand on his shoulder again. "So. Easy. Why don't you tell me about your other leader?"

Eric's eyes widened as he looked back and forth between the man and Ron. He seemed torn but finally he started talking. Under pressure, Eric always started talking. I groaned inside. It wouldn't be long before he gave up all our secrets.

"He's just a teacher," Eric said. "Kind of nerdy. Not very good with Scout skills. He probably got lost going to the bathroom." Eric laughed nervously. He was going to say more, but the man interrupted.

"Thank you, Easy. That wasn't so hard, was it?"

Thank you, indeed. Nothing he'd said was critical. If I could make it back to the satellite phone to call Zack . . . I looked back at Eric and groaned inside once again. The man had taken his hand off Eric's shoulder and was turning away, but I could see by the look on Eric's face that he wasn't done babbling.

When Peng made the signal, I was surprised. I didn't even think he knew what it was. JR was always the one who initiated things. But the signal was clear, three distinct coughs. After years of practice in Sunday School, Eric should know that it was now his job to create a scene—something to distract the adults in charge from what they were trying to do. But I wasn't sure that Eric had recognized the signal in time. He'd already started talking again.

"But he's not really—" Eric blurted out before he could stop himself.

The smiling man was turned away from Eric, but his head snapped back. "He's not really what?"

At first I thought Eric would panic. But then I saw the look in his eye that I had seen a thousand times during class. He was good at distractions, and he knew it. It was maybe his greatest talent. He almost smiled.

"He's not really good in the woods," Eric finally said. "If we left right now, he probably won't even be able to find his way out." Eric's eyes steadied, and he looked directly up at the tall man. "By the way, did you say you had Easy Cheese?"

The man patted Eric on the shoulder again and said, "I've got some in my pack. And because you've been such a good sport, maybe you can share some with me later." He looked up, motioning to those with him. "Have the boys clean up their camp, and then let's get ready to move out."

Jillian was staring at Joey, a look of disgust on her face. "We're just making it harder with the extra baggage."

The man just shook his head and chuckled. "You're going to make a great mom someday, Jillian." Then his tone turned serious. "We're taking them all with us. The last thing we need is the body of a dead kid calling attention to us."

He turned his gaze back to Ron. "Look, Knight. This is nothing personal. We're doing a job here."

"And you do it so well," Ron said. "Did they teach you how to terrorize little boys in ranger school?"

The man shook his head and chuckled again. "Nice try. But ranger school isn't even the half of it. Look, we can do this the easy way or the hard way. The easy way is that we all walk out of here and I deliver you to the client, who wants you and your boy alive, and that's what they're going to get." He moved closer to Ron and looked down into his face. "But if you want to play the tough guy, if you want to mess with us and make our jobs more difficult, then I'm inclined to give Jillian what she wants. We could walk out of here a lot easier with fewer boys to attend to. I'm sure we could hide the bodies so they wouldn't be found for weeks. It makes no difference to me. But you should also know that you and the boy are only half the package. A second crew is on their way to pick up your wife and little girl. So if you all want to meet up as one big, happy family, I suggest the best way will be to cooperate."

My hand gripped the pine branch I was peering through, and I felt the rough bark and needles pierce into my palm. This wasn't just a kidnapping in the mountains. They weren't just taking Peng and me. They had Hope. They had Jin. Or they soon would if I didn't do something to stop it. I needed to get to the satellite phone in Ron's pack. I needed to warn them. I needed to act now. The situation here was dicey, but it didn't seem to be deadly at the moment. Hope and Jin needed my help.

Besides, the boys had Ron to take care of them.

I scanned the scene in front of me, but I didn't see Ron's pack. It must still have been at our campsite. Maybe he'd heard a commotion with the boys and had come to investigate. Or maybe he'd just come to check on them before they started the day's journey. Either way, apparently he hadn't brought his pack with him.

I heard the smiling man say, "Woolhead, Tiny, go find the other leader. Catch up to us when you have him."

"Why do we even need him?" one of the men said. "Like you say, he's not part of the package. Wouldn't it be better to just extract the man and his kid?"

"C'mon, Woolhead. You know the rules. We don't leave anyone behind."

"I thought that rule was only for us? In case one of us got into trouble?"

"It is, you idiot," Jillian said. "Jackson is messing with you. He just doesn't like to leave any loose ends." The woman's voice was monotone. Just listening to her made the skin on my neck prickle. A few minutes ago, she'd been holding a gun to Joey's head. I had no doubt she wouldn't have hesitated to pull the trigger.

"I thought we decided to use nicknames," the man who I now knew was called Jackson said. He was still smiling, but there was no humor in his voice.

"Should have thought of that before you outed me a few minutes ago," Jillian said. "But I don't think it's really going to matter." Her tone made it clear to me exactly what she meant. Whether Peng and I were delivered to the client or not, she did not expect any of us to survive the ordeal, and she didn't plan on leaving any witnesses.

"Maybe you're right," Jackson said, his tone softening a bit. "Sorry, I didn't realize I said your name."

"That's because you treat this like a game. But I agree with you on one thing: we need to find the other leader. Tiny, Woolhead, you go take care of him like Jackson said, then catch up with us. We're not waiting."

"Take care of him like Jackson said, or like you would?" one of the men asked.

"You know who the boss is," Jillian replied. But her tone was ambiguous. I began to back away from the tree. Not only was I about to have two thugs on my trail, but because they didn't know my real identity, they might decide they wouldn't want me along for the ride.

I needed to get to that phone before they did. And I needed to stay alive long enough to warn Hope.

Chapter 12
JILLIAN'S WAY

THE BACKPACK WAS LESS THAN 300 yards away, but I couldn't take a direct route without being seen. The mercenaries, however, weren't under the same restrictions. Because we had picked a campsite close enough to see the boys, they had direct sight and a direct trail to where Ron and I had laid out our bags.

I moved as quickly as I could back the same way I had come. As soon as I was confident they couldn't see or hear me behind a small hill, I began to sprint. If I could grab the bag and disappear before they got to the camp, I had a chance. If they got there before me, I would have to figure something else out. And if we arrived at the same time . . . well, that wouldn't be good.

I tried to quiet my breathing as I came out of the pines into the campsite. The pack was sitting on the ground where I had left it, along with my tarp and sleeping quilt. The place where Ron had slept was cleaned up and pristine— like no human had ever been there. Sometimes I wondered if Ron really was human.

I couldn't hear the mercenaries, but they had to be getting close. I didn't want to run or act hurried in case they saw me. If they thought I was ignorant, it might give me an advantage.

I slowed down and moved out of the trees. I took three steps toward the pack before I knew I was in trouble. I could sense them before I saw them. They were in the shadows of the trees to my left. Waiting for me. They had arrived first. It was time for me to do what I was trained to do. I gripped the latrine spade tightly in my hand and turned toward them.

"Oh, hey, guys," I said. "I didn't see you there. But then again, by the looks of your guns, you must be hunters, and you're probably used to being stealthy." I didn't mention how odd it was that hunters would be hunting with handguns. "You didn't by chance happen to see which way my Scout troop went, did you? I made a latrine run, and it appears they might have left me behind."

"Yeah, we seen 'em." The man who spoke had a crop of curly black hair that spread out under a knit cap. My guess was that he was the one they called Woolhead. The other man was the giant. He wasn't just tall but big all over too, and not in a soft sort of way. This would be Tiny, of course. Criminals were really funny people sometimes.

"We can take you to them if you want," Woolhead said.

"Hey, that's awfully nice. You know, I've heard that hunters are some of the most decent people in the world. You look all scary with your guns and stuff, but underneath that hard exterior and rather pungent scent, there truly lies a heart of gold. Would one of you mind holding this for a second?" I tossed the spade in their direction and bent down to dig inside the pack. Tiny caught it, blade end first. "I forgot to take my baby wipes with me and I thought it might be good to clean that thing before putting it away. I don't think wiping it on the grass really did much good at all."

Tiny dropped the spade on the ground. I began to dig inside the pack. I had them a little off guard for a minute, but it wouldn't take them long to recover. "Ah, here they are," I said as I dug in the pack, trying to get my hand around the butt of Ron's Glock. "I'll get that cleaned up in no time, and you boys are welcome to some of these wipes if you need to freshen up. I find they are almost as good as a shower when you're out in the wonders of nature."

"Jackson's way or Jillian's?" Tiny asked quietly.

"I always try to side with either the meanest one or the hottest one, and in this case, Jillian is both," Woolhead replied.

"Agreed. Do you want me to do the honors?"

"Nah, I got this."

When I saw the red dot appear on the backpack, I knew I was in trouble. I'd noticed that Woolhead's pistol had a laser sight under the barrel, and he was apparently lining it up on me. Then the dot disappeared. This could mean a couple of things: either Woolhead had decided not to shoot me, or the red dot was sitting squarely on my shoulders or the back of my head. I guessed it was the latter. Either way, the time for talking was over.

Woolhead had already started shooting when I dove to the side, brought the gun out of the pack, chambered a round and fired three times. They told us in training that if we practiced the actions enough, they would be forever stored in our muscle memory. Like riding a bicycle.

The movement itself was smooth, but my aim was high. I hadn't fired a gun in quite a while. I was aiming for Woolhead's center mass, the most likely spot for me not to miss. Instead, all three of my shots caught him in his forehead right under his ball cap. He sank to his knees and fell onto his face.

I leveled my gun on Tiny. "I would drop that if I were you."

Tiny stood there with a dumb look on his face. His gun was in his hand by his side. He hadn't even brought it up. My actions had completely surprised him. But then again, they had completely surprised me. He let the gun fall to the ground.

A voice came from the body of the dead man, and I jumped.

"Were those gunshots?" The voice was angry and filled with static. It took me a moment to realize that it was coming from the radio attached to Woolhead's shoulder. "I told you no killing. Your portion of the take just got cut in half."

I was thinking that Woolhead's portion was going to be a lot less than that when I realized my mistake. Tiny had been holding his gun in his hand, but he still had a bulge in his waistband. The voice on the radio had distracted me long enough for him to go for his second weapon. I snapped my focus back to him, but I was too late. He hadn't gone for his second gun. Instead, he'd taken the opportunity to turn and flee. I could hear him crashing through the trees as he ran away from me. I thought about firing at him but couldn't get myself to shoot at a man's back.

"Woolhead, you answer me. What's going on out there?" the voice from the radio continued to bark.

I heard Tiny answer between gasping breaths as he ran. "Woolhead is down," he said. "Dead. And that guy is no innocent nerd. He put three rounds in Woolhead's face before I could even blink. He was about to do the same to me. I don't know who this guy is, but he's no Scoutmaster. More like a paid assassin. What kind of job did you get us into?"

I wasn't an assassin and had never been one. But in my previous line of work as a covert antiterrorist agent, I had been trained well, from hand-to-hand combat to all kinds of weapons. Despite my training, the secret nature of my identity had always been my biggest advantage. But today, my cover had been completely blown. Whatever happened next, I would not be able to take them off guard.

I looked at the backpack and noticed that there were several bullet holes piercing the exterior—right where my back would have been had I not moved. I prayed that none of them had penetrated the satellite phone. I needed to warn Hope, and I needed to do it before it was too late. But there was something else I needed to do first.

I took a quick glance at Woolhead's body. The disembodied voice from his radio had gone silent. Everything had gone silent. Especially for Woolhead. He would never see or hear anything again.

In my entire career, I had never killed anyone. I didn't much like it now.

I went into the bushes and threw up.

Chapter 13
THE ASSASSIN

PENG HEARD THE SHOTS AND watched as Jackson began barking into his radio, chastising his men for using force. Chastising them for killing Matt. Peng looked around him. Everything seemed to be moving in slow motion. Joey put his face in his hands and began to cry. The woman called Jillian looked down at Joey, snorted, and then moved a few paces away as if she didn't want to be infected by his tears. Ron looked quizzical and calm.

Peng didn't know what to feel. He'd been planning on leaving Matt and Hope for a few years now. He'd been steeling his heart for the separation, trying not to become too attached. Maybe that was why he felt numb—he'd been successful at keeping himself aloof from his new family and he didn't carry the emotional baggage most sons would bear. Why else would he feel nothing when he'd just heard that his adopted father had been murdered?

And then he looked down at his hands.

They were shaking uncontrollably. Then a hole opened inside his chest that felt so large it could swallow all of the ocean in the entire world. He thought of Hope and Jin, how they would react when they heard the news. He felt their sadness so deeply that it might have been his own.

It was his own. Despite his plans to leave, despite his attempts at keeping emotionally separate, he felt like he had just lost a father. Not the stepfather he had known in China. Not his real father who had died when Peng was a baby. But a real father who had loved him and raised him and struggled with him. Peng realized that these past few years had been the happiest of his entire life. He felt the tears rising in his face and wondered where the well of water had been hiding all these years. He had pretended not to have a family, and now one of them was suddenly gone. Taken from him.

He looked to Ron again. Peng had experienced loss before. He had experienced grief. But he'd never known the right way to act, so he had always buried it deep inside. He needed an adult to show him the proper way.

But when he met Ron's eyes, Ron shook his head slightly as if to say, "Wait." He was listening intently to what Jackson was saying into the radio. At first Peng didn't understand. The words were fast and confusing, and Peng's brain seemed to have shut down. But gradually the picture became clear. Jackson was yelling and stomping around. Jillian looked more ticked off than usual.

Somebody had died, but . . . it wasn't Matt. It was the man they had called Woolhead. It sounded like Matt had shot him. But that didn't make any sense. Matt was a good person. Peng had watched his every move for two years now. He wasn't somebody who could kill another human being. But Ron didn't look confused. He didn't look disappointed in Matt either. He looked somehow . . . satisfied.

The wave of relief that flowed through Peng's body was almost overwhelming. But now he felt something else—something akin to regret. This made no sense either. Why should Peng be disappointed that Matt was alive and one of the bad guys was dead? The tears were still coming, and Peng wiped them away with his sleeve. He decided to stop trying to figure out his feelings and focus on the situation in front of him instead.

The voice on the other end of the radio had stopped talking. Jackson was still pacing back and forth and glaring at Jillian every few seconds as if the whole situation were her fault. Finally he stopped, fiddled with the channel on his radio, and said to Jillian, "Time to call the boss."

He tried to hand the radio to Jillian. She didn't take it. Instead she said, "You're the leader on this job. So lead."

Jackson reluctantly pulled the radio back and punched the button.

"Carney, you there?"

Static crackled for several seconds, and then the gravelly voice came on the other end. "I'm here. What's your status?"

"We have secured the primary target and his boy. We also have control of the other kids as well."

"That's good, then."

"No, it's not good. We're also a man down because you neglected to provide us sufficient intel on the other leader."

"What do you mean you're a man down?"

"The other Scout leader jacked a few rounds into Woolhead's brain and put enough fear into Tiny to make him run like a little girl. So what was it that you conveniently forgot to tell us about him?"

The static returned for several seconds, then the voice came back. "Is your position secure?"

"For now. Tiny's on his way back to join us. But we need to know what we're dealing with here. You've got to give me something on this guy."

"Sorry about that," the gravelly voice said. "You know this was a last-minute job. Dempsey gave us only the bare details. I didn't receive any intel on the other guy either. I thought he was just a Scout leader. What's his name?"

Jackson looked at Eric. "Easy, what's your other leader's name? Brother Walton or something?"

"It's Ronald Kelton," Ron said before Eric could answer. "And you've made a big mistake."

Jackson barked the name into the radio, and the voice came back saying, "Give me a few minutes, and let me run the name."

Jackson began pacing again as he waited for his boss to get back to him. Tiny came crashing into the camp and put his hands on his knees to catch his breath.

"He killed Woolhead," he said, panting.

Jillian scowled at him. "It was two against one, and you ran away?"

"He wasn't a normal guy. He talked all casual like he was an idiot, and then he put three rounds in Woolhead's head just like that. He would have killed me too if I hadn't run. That's not just some Scout leader."

Jillian turned away from Tiny in disgust. Peng didn't think she would ever run from anything, even if it meant dying. Tiny was huge, and it was hard to imagine him being scared either. But it was clear he was terrified. Of Matt.

The voice came back on the radio. "You were right. We missed on this one big-time."

"What do you mean?"

"Kelton used to be a ranger."

"I told you so," Tiny said to Jillian. But she still wouldn't look at him.

The voice continued. "But that's not the worst of it."

"What could be worse than that?" Jackson said.

"It's what happened after he was a ranger. Apparently he was assigned to a special ops unit and served for another five years before he retired."

"Which ops unit?"

"Doesn't say. There's no record. You of all people should know what that means."

Jackson stopped in his tracks and seemed to listen to the surroundings.

"What does it mean?" Tiny asked.

Jackson chewed on his cheek for a minute before answering. He was no longer smiling. "It means tier one," he said. "It means first special forces operational detachment." Jackson spat on the ground. "It means we've got Delta Force on our tail."

"We've dealt with special ops before," Tiny said, seeming to find his courage again now that he was back with the group. "We can handle it. There's three of us." He looked over at Jillian as he spoke.

Jackson stepped over and got into Tiny's face. "Do you know why Delta Force was formed?" he asked, but he didn't wait for Tiny to answer. "It was to deal with the threat of terrorism, to train a new breed of warrior to fight in a war without rules, to especially deal with terrorists who take hostages. It was to be able to step inside of a hijacked plane, differentiate the hijackers from the civilians, and take out the bad guys by putting a bullet in their head before they knew what was happening. Let me put it this way: Delta Force was trained to deal with exactly the situation we find ourselves in now. They were trained to deal with people like us. Three of us and one of him—we're just sitting ducks."

"How do you know so much about Delta Force?" Tiny asked.

Jillian answered. "Because he was there. He even made it through selection before they saw his true colors and kicked him out. Probably a good thing too. The way I heard it, if he hadn't been booted to the street, the Delta boys would have taken care of him on their own. They don't much like it when one of their brothers shoots one of their own."

"Shut up, Jillian." Jackson had a full-on grimace.

Peng looked over at Ron. All the boys were looking at Ron. They knew of his military experience, but Jackson's description of Delta Force's abilities in a hostage situation brought a whole new level of respect for their Scout leader.

Ron was looking at Jackson. His eyes had narrowed, and there was something in them that made Peng feel cold. He wouldn't want to be in Jackson's shoes if Ron ever freed himself from his restraints. Jackson was bigger, louder, and more muscled, but somehow Peng felt that Ron would have a significant advantage. Maybe that was just a foolish wish. Either way, Peng decided he needed to figure out a way to free Ron from the bindings on his hands.

"I don't like this," Tiny said. "If we try to hike out of here, this Delta assassin is going to choose his spots and pick us off one by one. Carney needs to send us some backup to take this guy out."

Jackson looked like he wanted to yell at Tiny, but he stopped himself. "Tiny, for once in your miserable life, you might be right."

Jackson touched the button on his shoulder radio. "Hey, Carney."

"Yeah."

"There's been a change of plans. We're going to hole up for a while to make ourselves less vulnerable. In the meantime, you need to send a backup team to take out the Delta."

There was a pause on the other end as Carney seemed to be considering. "I'll send a team," he said finally. "But it's going to take at least a day. You think you can survive for twenty-four hours?"

"I know a spot where we can wait. A box canyon that's only accessible through a small pass. Only one way in, and no trees to hide an approach. We'll make camp there and keep our eyes on the pass. He might figure out a way to get to us, but it will take him more than a day."

"Okay, I'll charter a wet team and get them there by tomorrow. We still have a few days before the package needs to be delivered, so it doesn't impact the job." The voice on the other end seemed to be talking with someone else and then came back. "There is another option, you know. You could use the leverage you have to get this guy to back off."

"What leverage?"

Jillian moved toward Jackson. "You know what he's talking about. We take out one of the kids and let him know that if he gets close, we pop the other ones. We could start with the little pudgy one." She looked directly at Joey. For some reason, his being there personally offended her.

"No," Jackson said into the radio. "Kidnapping is one thing, but killing kids is not good for the reputation. Mine or yours. That kind of thing tends to follow you. People don't hire kid killers, and I plan to have a long and profitable career."

"Guess you're right," the gravelly voice agreed. "Get to your spot. I'll contact the team. And try not to lose any more of my men. I guess I'm also going to need to send in a stump grinder to clean up Woolhead."

"Woolhead's not a stump," Jackson said quietly.

"He is now. If I were you, I'd get to the canyon as soon as possible. I'll take care of the Delta."

Peng felt the ocean in his chest open up again once more. Matt was alive, but the voice on the radio was sending men to kill him. Ron met his eyes. He looked calm; he looked confident; he looked like he was trying to tell Peng not to worry. The waters receded but not completely.

Peng knew what he needed to do. Ron had been in the Delta Force. He could save them. But not until he was free. Peng would help Ron escape. But for that, Peng would need the darkness.

Chapter 14
THE PUZZLE

I FELT I COULD HAVE spent a lot more time relieving my body of last night's dinner, but I didn't have time for a meltdown, not now, not while Hope was in danger. I needed to warn her, to hear her voice, to know she was safe.

I went back to Ron's backpack and dug quickly, throwing out punctured packages of dehydrated food and clothing until I found what I was looking for. The black housing was covered with Mountain House dehydrated lasagna powder, but the phone looked undamaged. I blew off the meaty tomato smell and examined the phone, pressing hard on the on button, praying for a signal. The lights began to flicker, and I slowly let out my breath, my prayer turning to one of thanks as I dialed our home phone number. No answer. It was early though. Probably no reason to worry. Hope was likely taking Jin out for a walk, maybe having some donuts with Permelia and making a sticky mess.

I hung up and dialed Hope's cell.

After four rings, the line connected. I didn't wait for Hope to say hello before I started talking.

"It's Matt," I said. "Listen to me. You need to call Zack right away and get out of town. There's a group of men coming for you and Jin. I don't know what they want, other than to take you. They've already made a grab for Peng and me. We are both fine for the time being. Call Zack now, and then get over to his house. When you get there, call me back."

There was a pause on the other end of the line. I was out of breath and probably sounded like a crazy person. It was a lot for Hope to take in all at once.

"Is that you, Knight?" a voice that sounded vaguely familiar said. "Unfortunately I don't think Zack is going to be able to help right now. He bumped his head, and he's napping. Maybe I can take a message."

I felt like a bag of wet cement had been dumped down my throat. "Dempsey?" I asked. "What have you done with Hope?"

"You're supposed to be tied up and heading for a box canyon," Dempsey said, ignoring my question. "Not making phone calls."

"I've never been good at doing what I was supposed to do. You know that. Now tell me what you've done with my wife."

"Huh," Dempsey said. "If you're on the phone, that means . . ."

"Dempsey."

"Oh, right. Your wife. She's napping now too. But don't worry, no bumps on the head for her. Just a little chloroform. She should be waking soon."

I wanted to scream, to find a rock and smash the voice coming through the phone. I was too late. Dempsey had Hope. He had Jin. He and his mercenaries had taken my whole family. And there was nothing I could do about it.

At least not yet. Not until I could find where they were.

"What're you doing?" I asked. "You're supposed to be off charging insane dictators boatloads of money to take care of their problems, not kidnapping innocent people."

"Are you innocent, Knight? The people paying me don't think so. And they happen to be offering me insane amounts of money to bring you to them."

"The only people who think I'm not innocent are terrorists. And what has any of this got to do with my family?"

Dempsey paused, then said, "I'm not sure. But my clients were insistent on that part."

I tried to force down the panic rising in my chest. I was too late to warn Hope, but I still needed to save her. Somebody from my past had paid a group of professionals to take my family hostage. But why was Dempsey involved?

"Listen, if this is about revenge, if it's about me getting you kicked out of school or breaking your nose—"

"You can stop right there," Dempsey said. "Getting kicked out of the agency was the best thing that ever happened to me. I've seen what kind of house you can afford, and that's with a wife who's paid pretty well as a nurse. I could buy your entire neighborhood. I could buy an island if I wanted to. And the nose gives me credibility in circles where meanness matters. My old face would never have done that. If you think about it, I should probably be paying you for what you did to me. Instead, it looks like you'll be paying me."

"I'll make sure I tell Becca," I said. "She'll be very proud of you."

Dempsey didn't say anything, but I could almost feel the coldness coming through the phone. Finally he spoke. "Someday, you're going to have to tell me how you survived so long undercover. I thought for sure your mouth would have gotten you killed by now."

I was starting to get under Dempsey's skin. I'd always been good at that. He'd come from an influential family, had gone to the best schools, had been a member of the highest social circles. He'd acted like he was above the rest of us, and in reality, he probably was. But I'd always been able to find ways to get him to lose his composure. "Becca really liked you, you know? You shouldn't have done that to her."

"Really?" he replied. "You think she'd enjoy playing a mercenary's wife?"

"If Becca had been your wife, you wouldn't be a hired gun. You'd be something better."

"That's where you're wrong, Knight. I am who I am. I always have been, and I always will be. I enjoy the game too much to give it up. You should thank me as much for hitting Becca as I thank you for giving me this crooked nose. I saved her from being with me."

He actually made a sick kind of sense. Becca had been one of my best friends when I was going through agency training. She'd ended up marrying Robbie, my other best friend, who was also in training, but there was a time when the three of us were just buddies. Through us, she met Dempsey, and he wasted no time asking her out. Both Robbie and I were jealous, but at the time, we were too caught up in our friendship to do anything about it. Dempsey and Becca went out a few times, and I could tell she was actually starting to like him.

Then Dempsey took Becca to one of his family's parties. His father was a senator and something of a socialite in Washington. Apparently Dempsey had a few too many drinks at the party, and things went south. Becca came home with a welt across her face, and I went after Dempsey. Luckily Robbie was out of town. I didn't find Dempsey that night, but he made the mistake of showing up for school the next day. I had him down and his face a bloody mess before Zack could pull me off of him. When I told Zack what Dempsey had done, I thought he might finish the job I'd started. Instead, he had Dempsey kicked out of school. Dempsey's family had pull, but Zack's pull was stronger. There was no way he would let an abuser remain with the agency.

Dempsey left in a rage and then disappeared for a while. A few years later his name began to pop up in Central American skirmishes, and it wasn't long before he gained a reputation as one of the most dangerous and effective mercenaries in the world. And now this man had my family.

"You don't have to do this, Dempsey. You already admitted that you have more money than you can possibly spend. We're talking about kidnapping a little girl. What would your mother and father think?"

Once again I thought I could feel a coldness through the phone. "My father was a womanizer who drove my mother to take the pills that eventually killed her. I don't think they've got any room to judge me."

I'd managed to get under Dempsey's skin again, but I was still no closer to finding out where he was keeping Hope and Jin.

"You should be worried more about your family than mine," he said. "The client demands delivery by the end of the week. I lose money if any one of you is not breathing. I don't like losing money, so I suggest you cooperate. For the time being, it looks like we're on the same side. You want your family alive, and so do I. So don't mess this up, Knight."

"Who's the client?"

Dempsey laughed. "You know I can't tell you that. I have a reputation to protect."

"You know they are going to kill us," I said. "Even though you may not play games of revenge, you know others do. Most of the people I have offended in my life are terrorists. They kill children all the time and justify it with their ideology. They're not smart enough to think through the morality of their actions. Are these really the people you want to work for? You may be a mercenary, but you're not a monster. You know what will happen when you deliver us to them—they're going to take my little girl and kill her in front of me. You talk about reputation? Is that what you want to be known for?"

"What happens after I deliver the package is none of my business." His words were ice, completely devoid of emotion. "I do my job, and then I get paid. I don't associate with my clients. I use them. I use them for their money. I don't really care what class of people they are. At the same time, once you are in their hands, I don't care if you find a way to escape. If these people are as dumb as you say they are, and if you're as smart as you pretend to be, you should have no problem wriggling out of their grasp as soon as I'm gone. So if you want to give your family any kind of a chance, I suggest you cooperate with me and my men."

"One of your men tried to shoot me in the back," I said.

"Yes, I heard. Although he's not technically one of mine. I had to farm out the mountain portion of this job. It's hard to find quality subcontractors these days. Not only did they almost lose me my money by killing you, but they also somehow got mixed up on identities. Apparently, they think they have you in custody, along with your son. They think the man who killed their associate is some sort of Delta assassin who is going to pick them off one by one like Rambo. It's quite comical. But you know what the really funny part is?"

"I'm sure you're going to tell me."

"They are so worried about the Delta assassin that they've called in an extermination team to take care of him. So think about this. You have about twenty-four hours before some very nasty men will be fast-rappelling out of helicopters, doing their best to find and shoot you. And all over a simple misunderstanding."

My stomach dropped. Once they knew who I was, once Dempsey told them I was still loose, they would call off the assassination team. This was good for me but not so good for Ron. It wouldn't take them long to figure out his real identity. The last person they would want around in a hostage situation would be a Delta operative. Maybe if I gave myself up, maybe if they had the real object of their mission within their grasp, just maybe they would let him go. But even as I thought about it, I knew what they would do. Once they knew who he was, Ron was a dead man.

"Don't worry about your friend," Dempsey said as if reading my thoughts. "If you give yourself up, I can guarantee his safety."

He was lying, and he probably knew I knew, but then again, he was always lying.

"But I think I'm going to make this interesting," Dempsey continued. "I think this little situation can actually be turned to my favor. I've decided not to tell anyone about your little subterfuge. Consider this a puzzle. A problem to solve. As I remember, you were adequate at solving puzzles in school."

I was more than adequate. I was great at it. There was nobody better than I was—nobody, that is, except Dempsey. He was the puzzle master. The more challenging the task, the more impossible the situation, the better Dempsey was at finding a solution.

"Here's the situation. I have your wife and daughter, and you have no way of knowing where they are being held. Even if you manage to capture one of my subcontractors and torture them to get them to talk, it won't matter. They don't know my location. They are waiting for instructions from me once they leave the mountains. Add to that the fact that they are holding your son, a group of innocent boys, and a Scout leader under an armed guard, and they are moving to a secure location where no one can approach within a hundred yards without being seen. If you try to get to them, you'll probably get yourself or at least one of the boys killed.

"But that's not all. Within twenty-four hours, an extermination team will be descending with the sole purpose of taking out a Delta operative. They happen to think that operative is you. Which means that in less than twenty-four hours, you will have trained assassins trying to kill you. So your puzzle is this: how do you turn yourself in to my men in the next twenty-four hours without having them shoot you or some of your boys? Seems like a challenge worthy of your wits."

I always hated these types of story problems in training. But if I had learned one thing from them, it was that there was always more than one solution. As my mind began to work its way through the maze, running down path after insidious path only to meet with dead ends, jumping over walls in the hopes of seeing the problem from a new angle, seeking for the actions that would help me save my family, I finally found myself at the edge of a cliff with the obvious solution staring at me from the abyss. I knew what I had to do, and it was the opposite of what Dempsey had said. I didn't need to find a way to *not* get shot. I needed to get them to kill me. If Dempsey didn't have me, there was no way he was getting paid.

Dempsey's voice sounded as if he was in my head, his words casual like an afterthought. "Oh, one more thing," he said. "If you come to the conclusion that the solution to your problem is to shoot the hostage or let the extermination team take you out of the equation to save your family, I would seriously reconsider. If you die, I will still deliver your family to my client. True, he will probably not pay full price, but my guess is that he will still give me something. And even a portion of this bounty is a lot of money."

I slumped to the ground. I would gladly give my life for my family, but even that was not going to save them. Suddenly I ached to be with Hope, to hold her in my arms, to push her mountain of hair from out of my face and feel the warmth of her cheek next to mine.

"I want to talk to my wife," I said. "I don't even know if she's still alive."

"I wouldn't lie to you."

"I want to talk to Hope."

Dempsey sighed. "Very well. I'll have one of my men wake her up. I'll call you in five minutes. Don't tie up the line trying to call the authorities. I have a lot of contacts. If you call someone from the agency or law enforcement, I will know about it. And if the line is tied up when I call back, you might just miss a chance to speak with your lovely wife. In the meantime, I suggest you come to grips with the fact that the best chance you have at saving your family will be to deliver yourself to my men. Like you say, the client may be rich, but they are probably not very smart. With them, you might even have a chance to escape; with me, your only chance is to cooperate."

Before I could say anything else, Dempsey hung up. His last words had sounded almost sincere, as if he really wouldn't mind if we escaped after he delivered us. But sincerity from Dempsey was as dependable as promises from a politician.

I pulled the map out of the pack and examined it. Dempsey had given me at least a little information. I could guess where the mercenaries were holed up with the boys—a box canyon on the end of a narrow pass. A place where it would be nearly impossible to get to them without being seen. There was only one place in the vicinity that fit the description, and it wasn't far. I thought for a moment about how I might approach the box canyon and give myself up before being shot. But the thought quickly left me.

I wasn't going to the box canyon, and I wasn't going to give myself up. I wasn't going to wait around for the extermination team to come after me either. Hope was in trouble. I didn't know where she was, and I didn't know how I was going to find her, but I was going to try. Ron was with the boys, and at least for now, the mercenaries thought he was me, and they thought the threat was coming from the outside. Ron would figure something out, and Dempsey's little game would backfire.

I was getting out of these mountains.

I put the map back in the pack and hoisted it onto my shoulders. When Dempsey called, I would make him think I was torn, that I was still trying to find a solution. But I was done sitting and thinking. There was only one path through this maze that made any sense to me, and that path led to Hope. The highway wasn't that far away. If I could get to the city, I would pick up her trail. Somehow I would find her.

I began to jog—away from Ron, away from the boys, away from Peng. I said a silent prayer asking God to forgive me for leaving them, asking Him to lead me to Hope.

Chapter 15
A MESSAGE OF HOPE

AFTER DEMPSEY HAD ENDED THE call with Knight, he had almost called Carney to tell him about the mix-up, but he had decided to wait. He pondered his decision now. This move could ruin the entire plan. If Knight got himself killed, it would mess everything up. Allowing the fiction to persist that Matt was an ex-Delta operator was playing a dangerous game.

Dempsey smiled to himself. He liked games, especially dangerous ones, especially when he had a worthy opponent like Matt. Especially when he knew that in the end he would win. Buck was coming toward him from across the wide, expansive room.

"You've got that look on your face, Boss," Buck said.

"What look is that?"

"The one where the cat has the mouse in its grasp but decides to bat it around for a while before he kills it."

Dempsey consciously made the muscles in his face relax. It might not be such a good thing for Buck to see him smiling. Buck liked games too, but his tended to lean toward the sadistic. If Buck had a mouse in his grasp, it would probably be missing a few limbs before he put it out of its misery. It was probably best to keep him focused on the job and not the game.

Buck's feet echoed loudly as they met with the cement floor. The space they were in was large and hollow, an abandoned airfield hangar that was now leased out to movie crews. Dempsey had the whole place rented out for the week—the hangar, the airfield, and the outbuildings—under the auspices that he was scouting potential sets for an upcoming film and the producer was an ex-film star who hated publicity and would pay well to keep prying eyes away from the set.

The women and child were locked in a small room at one end of the hangar, and Zack was sedated in a room at the opposite end.

Dempsey waited for Buck to get to him before he sent him back the other direction. Sometimes the man needed to know who was in charge.

"Go get the woman and the little girl and bring them to me."

"Okay," Buck said, but he didn't move right away, as if he knew Dempsey was trying to exert control and it wasn't working. "What about the old woman?"

"Leave her there." And then Dempsey quickly added, "Alive and unharmed."

"Don't you worry." Buck twisted a toothpick between his lips. "She reminds me of my granny."

"As I recall, you killed your granny."

Buck screwed up his face. "She forced me to eat mush," he said. "You should know better than to try to force a kid to eat mush." Buck started to walk away, then stopped and stared back at Dempsey. "I don't remember ever telling you about my granny."

"I had you checked out. I like to know who I'm working with."

Buck took the toothpick out of his mouth and waved it at Dempsey. "That's a smart thing to do, Boss. A really smart thing. I always do the same thing myself, and I have to say that you, sir, have a very interesting background. Senator's son and all that. Jilted by your country. Kicked out of the service. Somehow finding a way to build a reputation as a mercenary in foreign lands. By the way, who was that guy with the beard who showed up out of nowhere?"

Dempsey didn't like where this conversation was going. "I told you I always have a plan B."

"I'll bet you do. I'll bet you do." Buck stopped waving the toothpick and put it back in his mouth. "I'm the same way myself."

"Go get the woman, Buck. I need her to call her husband."

"Yes, sir." Buck saluted and clicked his heels. He walked away slowly as if making a statement. Dempsey was going to have to watch him. He'd hired Buck because he was known and didn't question the job, but if he kept digging, Dempsey might just have to put a bullet in his head.

* * *

Hope's ears were buzzing as she tried to open her eyes. For a moment, she thought maybe she had passed to the other side for the second time in her life, that she was waking up in another realm, ready to meet the angels. But that couldn't be. The first time she had died, her head hadn't hurt anything like this.

As the room came into focus, she saw the hospital bed she was lying on, but she wasn't in a hospital. She was in a room about twenty by twenty feet, with cold cement walls and three beds around the perimeter. Permelia was lying in one of the beds. Hope deduced that she was all right because she was smiling and snoring loudly.

The third bed was empty. For a moment, Hope felt a wave of panic, pain, grief, and anger that grabbed at her stomach so fiercely it frightened her. Then she saw Jin's stroller sitting a few feet away from the bed. Jin was playing with a dinosaur toy and smiling at her. Jin loved dinosaurs. She especially loved when Peng played dinosaurs with her. The knots in Hope's stomach loosened slightly.

She slid her legs over the side of the bed and stood. Flecks of light burst in her eyes for a few seconds and then cleared. She went to Jin and inspected her for marks.

Jin held out the dinosaur to her. "Play, Mommy."

"How are you, girl? You're not hurt, are you?"

Jin giggled and waved the dinosaur.

Hope shook her head to clear it. Why were the three of them in this room? She vaguely remembered the anxious face of a man in a van. He'd said his daughter was hurt. Was he some sort of predator? Neither she nor Jin seemed to be harmed. She looked over at Permelia. Her bed was now empty.

"Looks like we've got ourselves a situation."

Permelia's voice came from directly behind Hope, and she nearly jumped out of her shoes. "Permelia, don't do that. I thought you were asleep."

"Faking it," she said. "In case somebody came in. I thought I could get the drop on them. I wouldn't mind kicking that smug little hooligan a few more times."

"You kicked the man in the van?"

"You bet I did. Several times. I had him dead to rights on the ground and would have made short work of him if the guy with the broken nose hadn't come up with the gun and threatened Jin. And then the bishop showed up, and another guy whacked him over the head. That's when the young one got me with the chloroform, and now here we are."

"Wait a minute. Did you say Zack showed up?"

"Yeah, he got the drop on the ringleader, but then a guy appeared out of the bushes and cold-cocked him."

"Is he okay?"

"Don't know. The guy with the beard hit him pretty hard—twice. The bishop doesn't go down easy."

"Who are these guys?" Hope asked. "What do they want with us?"

"The bishop knew the one with the broken nose. Said he'd been one of his students. He also said Matt was the one who smashed in his face."

"If he was one of Zack's students, that would mean he's a government agent. Why would a government agent kidnap us?"

"Looks like Matt must have really ticked him off."

"Matt really ticks off about half the people he comes in contact with," Hope said. "But that doesn't make them kidnap his family."

Permelia walked around the room, lifting up the beds, poking at the walls and floors.

"What are you doing?" Hope asked.

"We're obviously prisoners of war. Time to implement the SED protocol?"

"The SED protocol?"

"Survive, escape, disrupt. I used to date a brigadier general from the Army National Guard. The relationship wasn't going anywhere, so I tried to get as much useful information out of him as I could, which included what to do if I was ever a prisoner. Your first obligation is to survive—no use throwing your life away needlessly. Second, you are obligated to escape if you can, and if you can't escape, you try to disrupt the enemy as much as possible so their focus is on you and not on the rest of the good guys who might be trying to get you out. SED. Survive, Escape, Disrupt."

"Let's focus on the survive step right now. We don't even know what's going on or why they are doing this." Hope looked around the room. "We don't even know where we are."

"Looks like an abandoned industrial or military installation of some kind, judging by the walls and the rust spots. I wish one of us had been awake during the drive; we could have estimated the amount of time it took for us to get wherever we are." She looked down at Jin, who held out a dinosaur and smiled. "I guess you wouldn't be able to tell us, would you, dear?"

"You said they used chloroform," Hope said. "The effects would last from several minutes to a few hours. My arm is also sore, so they may have given us an additional sedative to make us sleep. My watch says it's nine in the morning. And Jin has several empty granola bar and fruit snack wrappers in her stroller. I'm guessing it's Wednesday and we've been here all night. But who knows how long we were driving. We could be in California by now."

"What are the side effects of chloroform?" Permelia asked.

"Why? Are you feeling okay?" Permelia was in her seventies, and there was a reason they stopped using chloroform for an anesthetic.

"I feel fine. But our jailers don't need to know that. I need to find a way to get out of this room to figure out where they're holding us. If I can fake one of the common side effects, maybe they will take me out where I can see something."

"The main side effect is unexpected cardio arrhythmia and death. I'm not sure you should be faking that."

"What about nausea or diarrhea? Could those be side effects?"

"I suppose. Almost any medication can cause nausea."

"Then that's what I've got. I've always been good at faking nausea. Ever since I was a little girl trying to get out of going to school. I'm going to start pounding on the door and demand a bathroom, then maybe I can make a break for it and find out where we are."

As Permelia spoke, a noise sounded at the door—a lock being opened from the outside. Before the door swung open, Permelia rushed to her bed and sat on the edge, putting her head in her hands, moaning softly.

The door inched open a crack, and Hope could see a bright blue eyeball scanning the inside of the room from left to right like a vulture looking for stray bits of carnage abandoned on the asphalt.

The door opened slowly, and a smile appeared. Behind the smile was a round boyish face and, underneath the face, a body that seemed reluctant to follow. It was the man from the van.

"Sorry to bother you, ma'am," the boy said to Hope in an apologetic Southern drawl, but his eyes remained on Permelia. "The boss says I should bring you to him so you can make a call to your husband."

Permelia moaned more loudly.

"What's the matter with your grandma? Is she okay?"

Hope glanced toward Permelia, who had her arms wrapped around her body and was shivering violently. Permelia was overdoing it, but Hope played along. "I think she's reacting to the chloroform. You might want to get her to a bathroom if you don't want to clean up a mess."

The young man sighed. "All right," he said. "But after I take you to the boss. He says he needs you now. I guess you better bring the baby with you."

Hope didn't waste any time arguing. She wanted desperately to speak with Matt and to try to find out what was going on here. The young man held the door for her as she stepped out, but he didn't turn his back on Permelia as they left the room. He also didn't forget to lock the door on the way out.

They stepped out into a room large enough to fit a football field. The ceilings were so high Hope supposed she could fly a helicopter through the interior. It was open and largely empty. A few doors were etched along the perimeter, concealing rooms Hope guessed were like the one where she and Permelia had been sequestered. She saw a single table and some chairs near the other end of the building and the figure of a man in the distance.

She grabbed the handles of the stroller until her knuckles whitened. This place made her feel small—small and alone, as if she had been sucked off the face of the earth and been cast into the vast universe.

The sounds of their feet and the rubbing of the stroller wheels echoed as they inched their way closer to the man. When they reached him, he stood and held out a phone.

"Mrs. Knight, my name is Dempsey. I need you to call your husband. You can tell him you are okay and unharmed. You can tell him you are being held against your will by two armed men. You can even tell him you love him." The man's voice went from conversational to cold. "But if you try to give him any more information, if you try to give him hints about our location, if you try to convince him to go to the authorities, let's just say there will be consequences." As he said this last part, he glanced down at Jin.

Hope felt the anger start to rise in her chest again. She wanted to pounce across the table and scratch out the man's eyes, but instead, she took the phone from his hand and nodded.

"Just press the dial button. The number is already plugged in."

Hope did as he said and waited for Matt to pick up.

He answered on the first ring. "Dempsey?"

"Matt, it's me." She thought she heard him suck in his breath on the other end. "I'm okay. Jin's okay, and Permelia is okay too, just a little nauseated from the chloroform." Permelia would be angry with her if she blew her cover. "I think Zack is here too, but they knocked him out, and I haven't seen him."

"Where are you? Where are they holding you?"

Hope looked at Dempsey and spoke carefully. "I'm not sure, but they won't let me say anything about it. Only that we are being held against our will. There are two of them, Dempsey and another young man. The second one has been polite. Not so much with Mr. Dempsey." Hope glanced at Buck while she was speaking, and he beamed at her description. Dempsey glared at Buck. Maybe she could use that later.

"Matt, how are you? How is Peng?" The man with the broken nose narrowed his eyes. This was not part of the script. He held out his hand for the phone, but Hope didn't give it to him.

"Don't worry about us," Matt said. "Just know I will come get you."

The man was coming around the table. She didn't have much time. "Remember the last thing that I told you when you left the house this morning? When you held me in your arms? I don't want you ever to forget that." Dempsey pulled the phone from her hand as Matt responded.

"I love you too," came through the phone as Dempsey pulled it away from Hope's ear.

Dempsey spoke into the mobile. "Isn't that sweet. The celebrated covert agent has become domesticated. That's all for now. Stand by for a text with further instructions." He hung up the phone and then connected it to a laptop and began typing.

Hope breathed a sigh of relief and frustration. It appeared Dempsey hadn't picked up on the message she was trying to send Matt. The problem was, Matt didn't seem to pick up on the message either.

Sometimes men could be so dense.

Chapter 16
SPOILED BOOTS

As soon as Hope left with Jin and the young scoundrel, Permelia began testing the door, hoping the guy might have forgotten to lock it. There didn't seem to be any easy way out of the room; the walls were cement, and the door was thick metal. If only she had a blowtorch.

It wasn't long before the man returned with Hope, opening the door and gesturing her inside as if he were a doorman at a hotel.

"There you go, ma'am. Let me know if you need anything: any special food requests, toiletries, or toys for the baby. I apologize that there's no connected bathroom. Just holler when you need to use the facilities. I'll hear you."

The young man was obviously trying to impress Hope, trying to get on her good side. Just listening to him made Permelia want to throw up. Good. It was time to start acting. She held her stomach and started groaning loudly.

"I don't think I can wait much longer," she said. "I really need to get to a bathroom."

"Sorry about that." The man smiled and shrugged at Hope. "I almost forgot about her." He gestured toward Permelia. "This way, ma'am. The restrooms are across the building."

Permelia shuffled toward the door, still holding her stomach. She thought about kicking the man again as she went out, but he made sure to keep his body turned so he was out of range of her feet. He locked the door behind them, and the smile immediately left his face.

"Let's get a move on, old lady." He pushed her roughly out into the room. "I ought to break both of your ankles for what you did to me earlier."

"You ought to turn in your man card for what I did to you earlier," Permelia said, making sure to speak as if she were in pain. "You know Hope's going to see through your schoolboy act, right?"

The man grinned but not the innocent grin he'd used with Hope. This grin was malicious. Evil. "We'll see about that," he said. "I've found that most women like a nice schoolboy. And I've never met a filly I couldn't tame."

"Hope's not a filly," Permelia said, wishing she had a baseball bat. "And more than that, she's a married woman."

"I've never been one to let a piece of paper get in the way of a good time," Buck said. "Now git a move on. We haven't got all day." He pushed her again.

Permelia looked around as she stumbled across the room, trying to assess where they might be. If she was going to get them out of there, she needed to understand the lay of the land. The room was large, really large—almost stadium large—and mostly empty. She could see a table at the other end where the other man—the one who seemed to be the boss—sat on a chair, talking on a cell phone. There were no other people or furniture anywhere to be seen, just a large room big enough to hold a thousand people . . . or an airplane.

That was it. *This is an airplane hangar.* Permelia wondered if they were at the Salt Lake City airport. But the only way to find out would be to get outside. She could see the restrooms now, and they weren't far from the front door. If she could create a distraction, maybe she could make a break for it. She wouldn't get very far, but if she could get out of the building, she might be able to get a better idea of their position.

Permelia didn't think she could outrun the young man. But she had to try something. She wasn't about to take it easy on these yahoos. If they wanted a compliant prisoner, they had chosen the wrong senior citizen.

She staggered and fell forward. At first she didn't think he was going to catch her, but he finally reached out.

"Don't do that," he said. "I'm not going to carry you, and if you try to kick me again, I'll break your foot."

"Sorry," Permelia replied, grabbing onto his jacket to pull herself back to her feet. She quickly slipped her hand inside his pocket and was gratified to find what she was hoping for. "I'm just a little bit light-headed."

As she pushed away, she noticed a distinct scent coming from the man's collar. The smell made her stomach turn. "Are you wearing cologne?"

"Yeah, so what?"

"I thought this was a kidnapping. What kind of idiot wears perfume to a kidnapping?"

"It's not perfume. It's cologne. And I like to do things with style."

"I don't know if I'd call slapping on some Old Spice while you abuse innocent women and children doing things with style."

The man's face reddened. Permelia could tell she'd struck a nerve.

"This is not Old Spice," he said. "It's Clive Christian #1. It costs over $2,300 a bottle, and it's about as far away from Old Spice as you are from your reproductive years."

"That makes me sick," Permelia said.

"What? You don't believe in spending on the finer things in life?"

"No, I mean the smell. It really makes me sick." Permelia took a step back and then threw up on his boots.

Buck swore and jumped away. "Ahhh. You couldn't wait? We were almost to the bathroom." He pushed her toward the door that said Women and opened the adjacent door to the men's room. "Get in there, and don't move until I come get you out. I've got to get cleaned up."

Permelia turned on the sink in the bathroom and washed the taste out of her mouth. That wasn't exactly the distraction she'd had in mind, but it would have to do. The air was surprisingly fresh for a bathroom. The surfaces were shiny and clean, as if it had been serviced recently. There were eight stalls along the wall. *Why so many?* Permelia thought.

She left the water on and peeked out the restroom door. She could hear the guy cursing in the room next door, but she didn't see any sign of the man who had been sitting at the table. The door to the outside was less than thirty yards away. She ran for it.

As she flew out the door, the sun blinded her, and she held up her hands to shield her eyes. The air was dry and hot, and the wind blew dust into her face. She'd been right—this was an airport. Or at least there was a landing strip in front of her. The building she had been in was a large, mushroom-shaped hangar capable of opening its doors to allow a fairly large plane inside. This was not the Salt Lake City International Airport. There were no planes flying in or out, and the buildings that spanned the flight line seemed decrepit and deserted. Except for the wind, everything was eerily silent.

She was struck with the strong sense that she had been in this place before or at least seen it. From the outside, the hangar looked familiar. She raced through her memories, trying to put the pieces together, but she came up empty.

She looked around the corner of the building and saw an old, dusty motorcycle leaning against one of the walls. "Hallelujah," she said. "I've found the way out."

She moved toward the motorcycle and suddenly remembered where she had seen the building. It had been in the newspaper just a few years ago. She smiled. She knew where she was. Now she just needed to get this information to Matt so he could locate them, and then she needed to get to the police. She pulled out the cell phone she had lifted from the young man's jacket when she had fallen into him, pressed the icon to text, and put in Matt's number. She typed in "P here. R-way. Looking at Enola G," hit send, and then looked for the camera app so she could take a picture to accompany her words. She raised the phone in front of her, and then everything went black.

* * *

"Can't I just shoot her?" Buck asked.

"No."

"Why not? You clocked her pretty hard, and we don't really need her for anything."

"I wouldn't have had to clock her if you'd been doing your job. How hard can it be to keep an old lady in your sight for five minutes? And not only that, but she had your phone too." Dempsey was searching through the phone to see who the old woman might have contacted. A 911 call would be a major inconvenience, but they would be able to deal with it. There were no outgoing calls, only a single text message. Dempsey chuckled when he saw what she had sent.

"What's so funny?" Buck asked.

"That is one smart old bird," Dempsey said. "But you're lucky. She sent a text to Knight, but it's harmless. Not only is there no cell coverage where he is, but he will be giving himself up soon. And even if he did somehow get this message, I don't think he would figure it out."

He nodded to Permelia, who was lying on the pavement. A dark knot was starting to form on the side of her head.

"It looks like we're going to have to watch this one. There's more to her than meets the eye."

"Just let me kill her."

Dempsey turned and met Buck's eyes. "Let me say this one more time: if anything happens to the old woman, the little girl, or the wife, I will hold you responsible. Now carry her back to the room. We've been out in the open for too long."

* * *

Permelia was dreaming of aliens and spaceships when she began to regain consciousness. She was being carried over someone's shoulder. An alien? No, the shoulder was human, and whomever it was was speaking as they laid her down on the bed. But the voice wasn't talking to her.

"Sorry about this, ma'am. It was my fault. I let her out of my sight, and the boss cold-cocked her. I would've been more gentle had I been the one who found her, but the boss man, he doesn't know how to treat ladies."

Permelia felt someone take her hand. "Permelia, are you okay?"

A fuzzy alien with large tentacles coming out of its head looked down at her. But then her vision cleared, and she could see that it was just Hope, with all her hair. Permelia wondered if they had remembered to bring a brush.

"I'm fine," she said, using Hope's arm to help her sit up. "Just a little woozy. The hit on the head was bad, but I think the cologne was the worst of it." She looked past Hope to the man, who winked at her and put his hand on Hope's shoulder.

"Ma'am, if there is anything you need, you just let me know," he said.

Hope didn't turn around. She was busy examining Permelia's forehead. "Thank you, Buck," she said and patted his hand.

Buck smiled directly at Permelia, took his hand from Hope's shoulder, sniffed it deeply as if taking in her scent, and then turned to leave the room. "I'll see you ladies later."

Chapter 17
BRING THEM HOME

I LOOKED AT THE PHONE in my hands and felt the ache of the distance that separated me from Hope and Jin. I was breathing hard and sweating. In the minutes I'd been waiting, I had been running—running to find my way out of these mountains. I couldn't stand the thought of Hope and Jin being held hostage.

Hope had sounded confident, not scared at all. But that was Hope. She would not be intimidated by anyone. Even Dempsey. And she didn't sound like she was hurt or—

The phone beeped, and I pulled up a text. "Stay tuned for more messages," it said.

Dempsey was probably just tying up the line because he wanted me to wait, but I had waited long enough. I was going to need some help on this, and even though Zack was my obvious choice, there were others I could call, others who would not alert any government agencies and trigger Dempsey's contacts. I began to dial and then heard the beep of another incoming text. It was from the same number as before.

"So sorry about the virus," it said. "But you know I can't allow you to use this phone." The words flashed long enough for me to read them, and then the screen went blank. I pushed every button I could think of; I pulled the battery out and put it back in; I pounded the phone against a tree. To no avail. The phone was dead. Dempsey must have sent the worm when he sent the text.

I threw the satellite phone into the bushes and pulled out my cell phone. No bars.

I began running again. I needed to get out of these mountains to locate my family. I reached the edge of a clearing and stopped cold. It was as if a plate of invisible glass had been stretched across the finish line of a 100-meter dash and I had run directly into it. An unseen hand was holding me back, telling me to wait and listen. I suddenly realized what Hope's last words had been when she'd been holding me in her arms, the ones she had been so careful to urge me to remember in the phone call. She hadn't told me she loved me. What she'd said was *You bring back those boys unharmed—especially my son. I'm holding you responsible. You bring them home.*

Hope knew me well. She knew I would abandon everything and everyone to come for her. She knew it, and she was telling me not to. She wanted me to stay here and save the boys. But Hope didn't understand the situation. She didn't realize that the boys were in far better hands with Ron than they ever could be with me. She didn't realize that every second she was in danger took at least a year off my life. I could no more abandon Hope to Dempsey than I could try to survive without breathing. Without her, I couldn't live.

I began running again. I could see glimpses of the mountain pass before me. Once over the top, I would be at the road in a matter of a few hours. Somehow I would find where Dempsey was holding them—I would find him and hurt him, just as I had done the night he'd hit Becca. Dempsey claimed this was not about revenge, but I knew how badly he hated to lose. I'd always thought he'd be back again someday. But I'd never thought it would be like this.

I stopped to catch my breath, and the invisible hand pushed me again, urged me to stop and turn around. But my family was on the other side of that ridge, a family I had never expected to have, a family that meant everything to me. *Not all of your family*, a voice inside my head seemed to say. *Not Peng.*

I should have felt guilty for not including Peng in my thoughts of family; instead I felt angry. I thought back to the day at the orphanage, to Mistress Wu's insistence that we not bring the baby home without taking the brother. I should have seen the signs then. I should have paid more attention to the look in her eyes when Peng entered the room. She was afraid of the boy. She wanted him out of her orphanage; she wanted someone to take him away. In trying to make Hope happy, I'd let my guard down. I recognized now that bringing Peng home had been the beginning of a wedge between Hope and me, a growing rift in what had been a perfect union.

I slowed a bit. I was being unfair. Peng was just a kid. If there was something wrong with him, it was because he had been emotionally damaged as a young child. Even so, I couldn't help but think I had brought something unsafe into our home, like a pet rattlesnake in a box.

I began running again, and my thoughts came with me. My anger moved from Peng to God. Why couldn't we have been given someone more like Shi-Shi, an honor student who brightened every room she stepped into? Or even someone like Joey, far from perfect but lovable all the same, lovable and teach-able. I thought of all the boys in the Scout troop. If they survived this trip, they would probably all be going on missions in a few years—all starting families and bringing grandkids home for visits. I couldn't imagine what Peng would be doing. Maybe helping convicts escape from high-security prisons, maybe running an illegal drug ring back in China, maybe just disappearing into the mist. Of all the people we could have brought home, why did it have to be Peng?

Because I knew you would understand him. The words came into my head at the same time the invisible hand stopped me again. I had reached the top of the ridge, and I could see Mirror Lake and the highway next to it. I could see the reflection off the windshields of cars in the parking lot. I could see the path to Hope. Turning around made no sense now. Neither did the words that had come into my mind. If there was one thing I knew, it was that I did not understand Peng. Surely someone else, anyone else, could do a better job as his parent.

Bring them home. Hope's words were insistent in my mind.

Almost against my will, I found myself turning around. With tears streaming down my face, I began to make my way back in the direction I had come.

I remembered a conversation I'd had with Ron about how to tell the difference between a prompting from God and random thoughts that entered the brain. I tended to get a lot of random thoughts, and if I acted as if all of them were promptings, things would not turn out well. When I'd asked Hope the same question, she had just seemed exasperated. "You just know," she had said. But that was it. Hope just knew. She had the advantage of having once died and gone over to the other side. For her, the veil was thin. My veil seemed like a brick wall a hundred feet thick.

"You don't know," Ron had answered. "Not really. Sometimes not until years later. That's why it's an act of faith. You either act on promptings, or you don't, and then you learn from that when to pay attention in the future. You do your best to sort out the real from the random. If you are thinking about jumping off the roof because you think you might be able to fly, that's random. If you think you should go check on your neighbor because they've been sick, it's probably something else."

"That's not very helpful," I'd told him.

"Well, there's always the rule of threes."

"The rule of threes?"

"If the same thought hits you strong three times in a row, you can be pretty sure someone is sending you a message."

I'd had the strong impression to go back three times now. I was pretty sure I'd just encountered the rule of threes. And once I turned around, I'd somehow known it was the right thing to do.

In my mind, it still didn't make any sense. It seemed like I was playing the game Dempsey wanted me to play, making the moves he wanted me to make.

Should I do what he said and turn myself in? But then what would happen to Ron when they found out *he* was the Delta operative? Should I wait for the assassination team and try to fight them off? This made about as much sense as jumping off the roof and expecting to fly.

I didn't know what to do. I just knew I needed to head back toward the boys, back toward Peng. Difficult or not, he was my son. And I still had a day before the assassination team showed up.

Maybe I would think of something.

Chapter 18
SPIDER HOLLOW

As they marched toward a rocky cliff face, Peng studied the landscape ahead of him, noting every trail, every hill, every tree, and every stream of water—mapping out every possible opportunity for escape. He was good at identifying such opportunities. He always found a way out. It was what he did.

Peng had always imagined he would escape into a big city—maybe San Francisco or New York. Both of them had large populations of Asians, and Peng would be able to blend in and disappear. He'd never thought about escaping into the mountains before. Maybe the wilderness would be even better than the city. Ron had taught him enough to survive—he could build a shelter, purify water, and keep from getting wet in a rainstorm and contracting hypothermia. He could sneak into the packs of hikers at night and steal small quantities of food they'd probably never miss. Winters would be a problem. There wouldn't be any hikers; there wouldn't be any food. Maybe he could live in the mountains in the summer and move to the city in the winter. At least in the mountains there would be fewer people. Fewer opportunities for his actions to hurt someone.

A cold wind whipped at them as they hiked single file. The giant man was in front, keeping JR close to him, almost as a shield, and continually looking around as if a cougar might jump out and pounce at any time. The woman walked behind Joey, prodding him with the sharp end of a stick if he slowed down or began to cry. He'd been crying a lot.

Ron was next, walking in front of Peng, his arms pulled behind him and secured with zip ties. Peng could see that Ron was testing the nylon, pressing against it with his wrists, seeing if it would stretch. Like Peng, Ron was also trying to find a way to escape. Somehow this made Peng feel close to him, as if they shared a secret—almost as if they were friends. Peng quickly looked away from Ron. He had decided the path he would take a long time ago, and friends were not part of the equation. He couldn't falter now.

Suddenly, Tiny dropped to his knees, pulled JR close in front of him, and raised his gun. The others pushed Peng, Joey, and Ron to the ground as well.

"What did you see?" Jackson said.

"Just a flash. Something moved up there in the cliffs. You're leading us into a trap, Jackson. That Delta's probably up there, waiting to pop us like zits on a teenager's forehead."

"You're seeing things," Jillian said, spitting on the ground.

"It's just a goat," JR said, surprising Peng. Since their capture, the boys had gone silent with only the occasional sob coming from Joey. JR's voice shook a little, but he still sounded sure of himself. "A mountain goat next to that rock by the lone tree, moving up toward the top."

Jackson pulled out his binoculars and settled them over his nose. "The kid's right. It's a mountain goat. Looks like one of its horns is busted off. Must be a fighter." He pulled the binoculars from his eyes and squinted at the hill. "Dang, kid, you've got good eyes."

"I spotted it first," Tiny said.

"You've been seeing assassins behind every tree," Jillian said. "There's no telling what you saw."

A flash of white disappeared over the top of the ridge, and the goat disappeared.

"See where that goat went?" Jackson said. "That's where we're headed."

"Over that cliff face?" Tiny asked. "That's impossible."

"Exactly. So no one will be able to follow us in. But don't worry, we're taking another way."

They got up and started hiking again.

"How do you know about this place?" Jillian asked.

"I did my research."

"The box canyon wasn't on the original itinerary. It wasn't even close."

"It was within ten miles," Jackson said. "I made sure I was familiar with every option within that radius."

"Did you learn that in Delta school?"

"As a matter of fact, I did. You'd be surprised how much we talked about the importance of planning for contingencies."

Jillian said the next words softly, almost inaudibly, as if she were talking to Joey and no one else. "At least he learned something more than how to shoot a comrade."

Jackson's jaw clenched. "If you've got something to say, then say it."

"I thought Deltas were a tight brotherhood—no man left behind and all that. I'm still trying to figure out how you felt it was okay to pop one of your own in a training exercise."

Jackson chuckled. "Is that what's bothering you?"

"As a matter of fact, yes. Since I happen to be part of your current team, it bothers me that you would kill one of your own."

"Well, don't worry about it. I was just the scapegoat for somebody up the chain who messed up."

"So you weren't responsible?"

"Oh, I shot him, all right, if that's what you mean. But the two of us had been at each other's throats since selection. He was a sacrosanct son of a millionaire, who thought he was better than everyone else, especially me. Anyone with eyes could have seen there was trouble coming. And then they put us in the shooting house together with live ammo flying. He was behind me with a gun swinging in my direction. I reacted. What did they think was going to happen?"

"So they kicked you out to cover up their mistake?"

"Something like that."

"It was the other guy's fault? For starting to swing a gun your way?"

"That's the way I saw it."

"That's a convenient way to see the world, Jackson, blaming everyone else for your actions."

"Give it a rest, Jillian. You're starting to tick me off."

"And we know what happens to people who tick you off, right? They tend to have unfortunate accidents." Jillian paused, then said, "You should know something about me."

"What's that?" Jackson said.

"When I was fifteen, a man tripped me on the street. He said he was sorry, that it was an accident. He made like he was going to help me up, and instead he pinned me down and tried to take advantage of me." Jillian stopped for a second as if reliving the memory in her mind.

"What happened?" The question didn't come from Jackson; it came from Joey. Everyone looked at him in surprise. He had stopped crying and was turned around, looking at Jillian.

"I cut his lips off," she said and then used her stick to turn Joey back around to start hiking again. "I don't much care for accidents."

Tiny muttered something under his breath that sounded like a swear word. Jackson didn't say anything more for several minutes.

They reached a small hollow with a spring bubbling out of a rock, the trees around it forming a semicircle and the breeze that had been biting at them all day temporarily absent. This was the kind of place a travel agent would put in a brochure, a slice of paradise that disguised an angry world just outside of view.

"Time to stop," Jackson said.

"Is this the place?" Tiny asked hopefully.

"This is last water," Jackson said. "We'll stop for a few minutes and rest up before we hit the rocks. Fill up every container we have. We are going to need it where we're going."

"Why don't we just camp here?" Tiny asked.

"Because this is the perfect place for a Delta operative to sneak up in the night and cut your throat. Keep one of those boys in front of you at all times. Fill up quickly. We don't want this guy catching up to us before we get into Spider Hollow."

"Did you say Spider Hollow?" Tiny asked. Tiny complained a lot for such a big man.

"That's the name of the canyon," Jackson said.

"I figured. What I want to know is why they call it that."

"Not sure exactly. There's a legend that the Spider gang from Yuma, Arizona, decided to knock off a Park City bank in the 1860s. They killed a few bank employees in the process and got out of town with a posse hot on their trail. They made it this far and holed up in the box canyon. The legend says the law couldn't get to them for five days because the canyon was so well protected— anyone trying to get through the rocks could be easily picked off."

"So what happened to them?" This time it was Eric who asked. He had always had an obsession with cowboys.

"They ran out of water and decided to make a run for it. The posse gunned them down one by one as they tried to get out."

Eric seemed impressed.

"At least that's one version of the story," Jackson continued. "The other one says they were so freaked out by the giant spiders in the canyon that they couldn't take it anymore and fled in a crazed frenzy."

"You're making that up," Tiny said, but there was a question in his voice.

Jackson laughed. "Maybe, but modern-day hikers do talk of the spiders. Big ones that weave their webs between the rocks and make them dance when you approach, trying to warn you away. I don't think they're poisonous though."

"I'm not going in there," Tiny said. "I don't do spiders."

Jillian snorted in disgust. "When I took this job, I was told you were one of the toughest, meanest mercenaries out there. But you're just a pansy. Even Joey here's not shaking like you are."

"I collect spiders," Joey said.

"Put any man in front of me with fists or knives and I'll grind him into the dirt," Tiny said. "I just have a thing about spiders."

"Stay out here if you like," Jackson said. "But we're going in, and we're going now. Everyone load up."

Their water bottles filled, they all put on their packs and began walking again. Tiny grumbled, but he followed behind.

When they reached the rocks, they saw their first web. Jackson had not been exaggerating. The shining filaments began to dance in the sunlight, and numerous other webs stretched between the two cliffs that bordered the trail. The only way through the rocks was through the webs, which hosted fat, dark spiders with yellow-and-black legs.

Trying to avoid the spiders in front of him, Tiny stepped back into a web behind him and began jumping, screaming, and cursing. "We can't go in there."

Jillian rolled her eyes and stepped forward. She grabbed a spider with her bare hand and crushed it, a dark ooze leaking out between her fingers.

The boys looked at her in fear and awe, all except Joey, who said, "You didn't have to kill it. It wasn't hurting you."

Jillian wiped her hand on the back of Joey's shirt, took down the web with the stick she was carrying, then pushed Joey into the opening of the slot. "You can deal with the next one any way you like," she said.

Chapter 19
DISNEYLAND

I MADE MY WAY FROM the top of the ridge I was on back in the direction I had come. Dempsey had said the mercenaries were holing up in a box canyon, but I wasn't sure exactly where that would be. I was wondering if I would ever be able to find the boys again when I heard the screaming. I'd been running most of the way back, but I ran harder now. The scream was high pitched, and my first thought was that someone was hurting Joey. But as I got closer, the scream turned to cursing. I decided then that it couldn't be Joey. I reached the top of a rise just in time to see the group moving into a space between some large rocks. Joey went first, a woman with a stick behind him. Ron and Eric followed, with another man trailing them. Ron's wrists looked to be firmly secured. Peng and JR came last, with Tiny, whom I recognized from my previous encounter, behind them. Tiny was swinging his head from side to side and was continually swiping one arm behind him as if he were being attacked by invisible flies. He was the one doing the cursing, so I assumed the scream had also come from him. All of the boys looked unharmed. I breathed a sigh of relief. I hadn't let Hope down. Not yet.

I thought about calling out now, giving myself up, making the move Dempsey had said was inevitable in his game. But I didn't do it. I looked skyward, hoping for some answer from above for what I should do next. All I heard was Tiny's frequent cursing and the other man laughing at him. I'd listened to what I'd thought was a prompting and had come back to help the boys, but now I felt nothing—no inspiration, no revelation, no ideas.

I sat and pulled out the map. They were headed into a small box canyon. I didn't think I could follow them in without being seen, but at the same time, they couldn't leave without me seeing them. It looked like they were going to hole up for the night and wait for the reinforcements to arrive. I figured I had at least until morning. My best course of action was probably to wait to see if Ron would be able to make a move during the night.

I didn't like not doing anything, but there really wasn't anything for me to do. If morning came and nothing had happened, I would probably have to give myself up.

* * *

Peng watched the path carefully as they made their way through the rocks. In places, the trail was like some of the slot canyons they had hiked in as Scouts, boulders rising up on either side, making it impossible for more than one person to proceed at a time. Jackson hadn't said this, but if an outlaw gang had really hidden in this canyon, they would have had to leave their horses behind. There were a few spots where Peng could climb out of the labyrinth, but as he followed the routes upward, he saw only dead ends. He would find a way though. It was only a matter of time.

The trail was steep but not very long, and they made it to the end without any of the large spiders attacking them. They moved out of the rocks and into an open canyon, then hiked another couple hundred yards and approached a flat spot that had walls on three sides. As they approached, Peng heard the clattering of rocks up ahead, and the kidnappers all pulled their guns. A flash of white scrambled up the cliff face to their left.

Jackson laughed and lowered his gun. "No worries. It's just our goat friend with the broken horn. Looks like we took his favorite hiding spot. Okay, folks, drop your packs and set up camp. This is where we're spending the night."

"Here?" Tiny asked. "The ground is all rock, and there are spiders all around us. Not to mention how cold the wind is now. At night this place is going to feel like the North Pole."

Jackson studied the place with an air of satisfaction. "It's perfect," he said. "There's only one way in, and we can easily defend it. We'll only be here for one night. Tomorrow the wet team will arrive and take care of our problem on the outside. Tiny, since you don't seem to care for our camping spot, why don't you head a ways down the trail and take first watch. Find a place where you can see anyone who comes through that slot. If anything sticks its head in, you shoot it."

Tiny looked back the way they had come, then he looked at the spiderwebs all around them. He shivered once, then, grumbling, moved back down the trail to guard the entrance to the valley.

Peng watched the goat on the cliff face again. It had been outside the canyon and had found its way in, and it hadn't used the trail they'd used. Now, with their arrival, it looked like it was moving out of the canyon again. Peng tried to memorize the path it was taking and thought he could see a faint line of a trail weaving back and forth across the cliff face. Jackson was wrong. There was more than one way in and out of this canyon. The goat had found it, and so could Peng. Once it was dark, he would leave.

He wondered what would happen when they found him gone in the morning. Would they harm the other boys? Peng decided Ron would protect them. Besides, the kidnappers said they only wanted Peng and Matt. Maybe they would let the others go. He looked over at Jillian and knew that was a wishful thought. He wasn't sure why people like this would be after Matt, but Matt must have some secrets. Peng was okay with that. He had secrets of his own.

"You boys drag some of those big logs over here," Jackson said. "And pick up some of that deadwood. If we're going to sleep in this hole tonight, at least we can build a fire."

The boys did as instructed. When the fire was going, the boys found a place on the log and sat around it.

Jackson pulled something out of his pack and tossed it to Eric. Eric caught the can in his hand and looked at it—Easy Cheese. Jackson fumbled around in his pack and pulled out a packet of crackers. "There's nothing like Ritz and Easy Cheese to make a man feel better." He walked over to Eric and held out a cracker. "Why don't you load me up?"

Eric pushed the nozzle and sprayed the cheese onto Jackson's cracker.

Jackson popped the whole thing in his mouth and closed his eyes. "Now that's a good cracker." He gave the rest of the package to Eric. "Help yourself."

Eric looked at Ron for permission, and Ron nodded. Eric grinned and began his feast.

"See?" Jackson said. "This doesn't have to be that bad. Think of us as your protectors. Our job is to get you out of here safe and sound. You help us, and we'll help you. Now, why don't you all break out your stoves and get something hot to eat. This canyon is a little chilly."

Ron still had his hands tied behind his back, but he nodded to Peng to pull the stoves out of the packs. Peng gave one to JR and was going to hand one to Joey, but Joey was sitting on the log, his head in his hands, tears dripping onto the ground.

Jillian moved over to Joey, sat next to him, and poked him in the side. "Snap out of it, doughboy. I'm not going to listen to you sniveling all night."

Joey looked up at her. "Why are you so mean all the time?"

"This isn't mean. This is doing you a favor. It's time for you to grow up and get tough."

"I don't want to grow up," Joey said. "I want to enjoy being a kid."

"What's there to enjoy? You're crying in the dirt like a little girl," Jillian said. "Weren't you ever a little girl?"

This question seemed to take Jillian off guard, and she paused before answering. "Yeah, I was a little girl once," she finally said. "Let me tell you about it. When I was five years old, I saw a commercial on television for Disneyland. I got it in my head that it was the best place on earth. I begged my mom to take me. I begged her until I was blue in the face. We lived in Southern California, so it wasn't a far drive, but she said we didn't have the money. We probably didn't. She was a single mom with a blue-collar job, and the place we lived in was a dump. But she had just hooked up with a new boyfriend, and he had a nice car. I thought maybe he could buy us some tickets. She said he didn't like kids, and anytime he came over, they made me go to my room.

"Then one day my mom came home with two long pieces of cardstock in her hand. They had mouse ears on them, and I think I almost wet my pants with excitement. 'Dan bought us tickets,' she said. 'Go get your jacket.' Dan drove us to the park in his new car. My mom sat right next to him, almost on his lap, and I sat in the backseat.

"'I'll be waiting out here,' he said to my mom as we got out. 'Don't take too long.'

"When we got inside, I couldn't even speak I was so thrilled. Everything was so clean, and everyone looked so happy. I begged my mom to take me to Small World first thing, and she didn't argue with me at all. She just took me right there. She let me get into the boat first, and then as she was about to step in, she pulled her foot out and said, 'Mommy has to go to the bathroom, honey. Why don't you do this one on your own? I'll wait for you at the end.'

"Now, understand, my dream in life, my whole goal as a five-year-old was to ride that Small World ride and revel in the experience. But the girl who got in next to me was sitting in my mom's spot and was a pimply, sweaty teenager with a head cold, who snorted the contents of her nose up into her brains about every fifteen seconds. That's what I remember about my first Small World ride: not the singing, not the smiling robotic children, not the journey through different countries and cultures—just a snotty teenager and worrying about whether my mother would be there when the ride ended." Jillian paused, her eyes looking into the distance as if remembering every detail of the experience. "Well, she wasn't. Nobody was waiting for me when the ride ended.

"So I got back in the line and rode around again, thinking that maybe my mom had gotten sick, maybe she was just taking a little longer than she thought she would. I rode that ride all day long until the park closed. And every time, I thought for sure my mother would be waiting for me at the end. I remember it like it was yesterday, as vivid as a high-definition picture. But you know what? I don't remember the ride itself. I barely even remember the song. I didn't enjoy it, not any of it. Even the times without the snotty teenager. Because I was worried about some stupid adult waiting for me at the end so they could take care of me." Jillian glared harder at Joey as if she were trying to penetrate his skin with her eyes. "So, yeah, Mr. Doughboy, I was a kid once. But in the foster homes that followed, I grew out of it real fast."

Jillian stopped talking and looked around her as if waking from a dream. Everyone in the camp had been listening. Everyone had heard her story. No one was willing to meet her eyes.

No one except Joey, who had stopped crying and was staring Jillian in the face. "Jillian?" he said.

"Yeah."

"This trip was supposed to be my Disneyland."

Jillian blinked and looked away.

Joey stood and moved to a spot on the other side of the fire.

"It's amazing the kinds of things you learn on camping trips," Jackson said, shaking his head.

Jillian gave him a look that stopped him from saying anything else.

"Well, that was pathetic," Ron said.

"Get over it," Jillian shot back. "The kid needs to be introduced to reality sometime."

"I wasn't talking about the kid," Ron said. "I was talking about you, letting your mother control your life like that."

Jillian pulled out her gun and pointed it at Ron's face. "You want me to paint these rocks with what's left of your face?"

Ron didn't even blink. "She was a bad mother," he said. "She should have been there waiting for you. It wasn't your fault she abandoned you. You were a kid. You needed her to be there. But living your life trying to prove that you don't need anyone else means she's still in control. She's still the one pulling your strings. You need to learn to let her go and truly become your own person."

Jillian's hand began to tighten on the trigger. Jackson stepped in and gently pushed the gun away. "I think it's time we concentrate on the task at hand and remember that if we don't bring him and the kid in alive, we don't get paid. Now, why don't we work on getting some hot food into us. It'll be dark in a few hours, and we still need to set up the tents. I think all of us would be a bit better off if we evened out our blood sugar some."

Jillian scowled, lowered her gun, and stomped to the other side of camp. The boys got up slowly and dug inside their meager packs for some food.

Peng just watched. He watched Jillian as she circled the camp like a cat; he watched Joey as he pulled out his pack of dehydrated food; he watched JR and Eric trying to ignite their backpacking stove but having difficulty in the swirling wind; he watched Ron as he seemed to be studying every rock and every burning tree limb inside the camp as if assessing what weapon to use and the right time to use it. Ron would probably wait until it got dark to make his move, after some of the kidnappers were asleep. But Peng didn't intend on sticking around long enough to find out.

Jackson was looking at Ron, staring at him as if he were trying to work out a puzzle.

"You know this would go a lot faster if you untied my hands and let me help them," Ron said.

Jackson started to shake his head and then seemed to change his mind. "All right," he said, walking over to Ron and grabbing his arms. "But if you make one wrong move, Jillian over there is going to put a bullet in one of your boys. By the look of her pacing, she's itching to kill something. So I suggest you let me see your hands at all times."

Jackson cut the zip ties with his knife while holding his gun to Ron's head. He then backed away as Ron turned around, holding up his palms in front of him. Jackson seemed to study Ron's hands with great interest, and then Ron moved to help JR and Eric set up a windscreen so they could get their stove lit.

Jackson bit his lip. "Hey, Easy," he said to Eric. "I'm wondering if you could do something for me."

"Sure," Eric said, standing up. He seemed a little less wary of Jackson since they'd shared the cheese and crackers.

"Tell me about your other leader again. The one who's still out there somewhere."

"Sure," Eric said, the wariness returning to his voice.

"What was his name again?"

Eric glanced quickly at Ron. "It's Kelton. Ron Kelton."

"There's something puzzling me," Jackson said. "When we picked you up, you called this man over here Brother K." He motioned to Ron. "But your other leader also has a last name that starts with a K. So what do you call him?"

"Well," Eric said, beginning to stumble over his words. "We just, uh, call him Ron. Because having two Brother Ks would just be confusing."

"Ahh," Jackson said. "Makes sense. You wouldn't want to confuse the two. But is calling a leader by their first name allowed in your church? Wouldn't that be disrespectful?"

"He asked us to," JR said, stepping in and picking up on the tag-team routine he and Eric had performed so many times. "He doesn't like being called Brother anything. He's more like one of the guys than a leader."

Jackson chuckled and shook his head. "I'll bet he is. I'll bet he is. It must be quite a thing to have an ex-Delta as one of your Scout leaders. Thanks for helping me make sense of this puzzle. I have to admit it was bothering me."

He turned his gaze to Ron again, who was standing over the burning stove. Once again, Jackson seemed to be studying Ron's hands. "Brother K," he said, chuckling to himself. Then he lifted his pistol and shot Ron twice, once in the right hand and once in the lower leg.

The pot of water Ron had been holding went flying, and Ron went down on one knee, holding his hand.

Peng was stunned. So was everyone else, including Jillian, who stopped her pacing and moved quickly into camp, her gun up and pointing at Ron.

Jackson continued talking as if nothing had happened. "It seems to me that Ron Kelton would be the more likely one to be referred to as Brother K. Knight doesn't even have a hard *K* sound to it. I think you boys have been trying to pull the wool over our eyes. All along we've had the wrong Brother K. We've been holding Ron Kelton, while Matthew Knight—the one we're supposed to be taking back to the client—has been running free and making us feel like we had a Delta on our trail. But the Delta man has been right here in our midst, just waiting for the right time to strike."

"How could you know that?" Jillian said, not lowering her gun.

"That's easy. In the Delta OTC, we spent eight hours a day in a place we called the shooting house. We endlessly practiced breaching a room and shooting cutouts of terrorists, making sure we didn't hit the hostage. We practiced so much that the flesh between our index finger and thumb became blistered and then calloused. We used to joke that no Delta man could really go undercover—you'd be able to pick them out by looking at the palm of their shooting hand." Jackson spat on the ground. "I should have seen it from the first. Our man over there has a Delta palm. Our real target, Matthew Knight, is still out there. Probably long gone by now."

"Why'd you shoot him?" Jillian asked.

Ron continued to hold his hand to him while at the same trying to stop the bleeding in his calf.

"I hit his shooting hand to take away his major advantage. I hit his leg so he won't be able to follow us when we get out of here. We're taking the boys and leaving, and I don't want a Delta with us, wounded or not."

"So you're telling me Matthew Knight killed Woolhead, not a Delta?" Tiny said.

"That's exactly what I'm saying," Jackson said.

"And you're going to leave the Delta alive?"

Before Jackson could answer, Jillian tightened her finger on the trigger and shot Ron three times in the chest. The impact knocked him backward, and he rolled over once, his face in the dirt.

"Why'd you do that?" Jackson said.

"Tiny's right. You don't leave a Delta alive," Jillian answered. "Wounded or not."

Peng felt all the air go out of him. This could not be happening. Ron was their leader, their rescuer, the one who was going to get JR, Eric, and Joey out of here safely. He ran to Ron and knelt beside him.

Ron was still breathing, and his lips were moving. Peng leaned down to hear what he was saying.

His words came out distinctly but only loud enough that Peng could hear. "It's up to you now. Keep them safe."

"No," Peng said, shaking his head violently.

Ron's breathing was becoming more labored. "Peng?"

"Yes?"

"Whatever happens, don't let them shoot me in the face. I don't want a closed coffin."

And then he let out a long breath, and his chest stopped moving.

"No," Peng said again. "You can't die." But Ron didn't move, and he didn't respond.

Jillian was coming closer, her gun in front of her, pointed at Ron's head. "Let's finish this and get out of here."

Peng placed himself in front of Ron. "No."

"You might as well move out of the way, kid," Jackson said. "Besides, he's already dead. She triple-tapped him in the heart, and I bet you could cover the strike pattern with a playing card. That Jillian is one good shot."

"No," Peng said again. "You will not shoot him anymore. If you do, you'll have to shoot me, and then you'll have nothing. No money. No payout."

Jillian turned her gun to Peng and seemed ready to come away empty-handed if it meant killing someone else. Then Joey stepped in next to Peng. "You'll have to shoot me too. Ron was right. You are as bad as your mother." Joey's whole body was shaking, but he didn't back down.

Jillian moved her gun back and forth between the two of them, trying to decide which one to shoot first.

"Do you think you missed his heart?" Jackson asked.

"I never miss."

"Then let's stop playing and get out of this hole. He's either dead or close to it. If he hasn't bled out by nightfall, the hypothermia will do the rest." He looked at Tiny. "Or we can move back through those spiders in the dark."

Tiny lowered his gun and began packing his stuff. "I agree with Jackson. We need to get out of here."

Jillian lowered her gun and studied Joey for a minute before turning away. She turned her attention to JR and Eric, who were standing with their eyes wide and mouths open, obviously terrorized by the events.

"Don't just stand there; get packed up." She glanced once again at Ron and then back at Joey. "I'm tired of this place."

Within minutes, they had killed the fire, packed up their things, and started on their way out of Spider Hollow. Peng looked back at Ron's body, looked up at the goat trail he had planned on using that night, and looked at the dejected figures of the boys Ron had left him in charge of.

His biggest fear had come to fruition. He was now responsible.

Chapter 20
THE SHIRT AND THE SHOOTING HOUSE

I'D BEEN SORTING THROUGH RON'S pack, looking to see what other useful items—and food—I might find that would help me through a restless night when I'd heard the gunfire.

Two shots, a pause, then three more in rapid succession.

I hadn't heard anything since then. Had the mercenaries decided to dispense of the excess baggage? What if they'd discovered Ron wasn't who he'd said he was? Five shots, five hostages. Or what if Ron had made a move on the kidnappers? What if he'd tried something and failed?

Dark images flashed in my head: explaining to the parents of the boys that their sons had been killed because of me, explaining to Hope how I was not able to follow through on my promise to protect Peng and the boys, explaining why I had not given myself up and been there for the boys like Dempsey had suggested.

I wanted to rush into the canyon to get the answers, but that would be a mistake. I needed to wait, let the scene play out, find out what really happened before taking any action. I just hoped I wouldn't have to wait all night and that my worst fears would not be realized.

It wasn't long before I heard voices. First came the big man, Tiny, roaring as he came out of the rocky passage and into the open. The rest followed a few minutes later. First Jocy and Eric, followed by the woman, and then Peng and JR, followed by the leader. I breathed a sigh of relief. All of the boys were there, and although they hung their heads, they didn't look injured.

And then I realized who was missing. Ron wasn't with them. Ron, whom they'd sent a special team in to handle because he was so dangerous; Ron, who was a great leader to the boys and a great friend to me; Ron, who was not with the group. They wouldn't leave him alone, and he wouldn't have escaped without the boys. That could only mean one thing: Ron's true identity had been discovered, and he was now dead.

I waited for the group to move past me, then followed them for a time. They traveled only about a thousand yards before coming to a flat, protected area near a stream. They stopped, took off their packs, and began to set up camp. It looked like they planned on staying the night. I moved as fast as I could back to the opening in the rock. The entrance to the canyon was narrow, and I quickly realized why they had chosen it as a place to hole up. One glance also told me why Tiny had been yelling—the bouncing webs and the huge spiders looked menacing among the rocks. Other insects kind of freaked me out, but for some reason, spiders didn't bother me. Besides, I wasn't concerned about the spiders. I was concerned about Ron.

As I burst through the passage into the open, I could see the remains of their earlier campsite. Near one of the edges of the site lay a body, the large Hawaiian shirt whipping in the wind. As I got closer, I could see that one of the pant legs was soaked, and blood had also seeped out from under the dirt near the torso where Ron's arm was pinned beneath his body. I felt the awful despair rising in my throat, and then I looked at the scene again and thought about the whipping shirt. I thought about Ron's need to change clothing as we watched the mercenaries through the binoculars. I thought about the way he'd looked even more buff in the baggy shirts than he had in his T-shirt. "Are you going to lie there in the dirt or let me patch up your wounds?" I said.

Ron groaned and turned over. He was holding his hand and wincing as he blinked the dust from his eyes. "Good," he said. "You brought my pack. There's a compression sleeve in there that I need for my leg. I think I blacked out from the loss of blood." He winced again. "And I can tell you with absolute certainty that wounds to the hand hurt worse than in any other part of the body."

I pulled off the pack and dug out the sleeve Ron was looking for, along with as many other first-aid supplies I could find. I helped him clean the wound on his hand and bind it up. The bullet had torn the webbing between his thumb and finger, but it didn't look like it had penetrated the bone.

"Let's go to the leg next," he said.

"What about your chest?" I pointed to the three bullet holes peppering his shirt on the left side, directly under the breast.

"Hurts like crazy," he said as he used a knife I'd given him to cut away his lower pant leg. "I think I might have broken some ribs."

"I don't see a vest."

"It's not supposed to be visible," Ron mumbled as he held the knife in his mouth and pulled the compression sleeve over his leg. "It fits the contour of the body, and it's flesh colored. But when I tried it with a T-shirt, I looked like Batman. With a baggy shirt, however, it's almost undetectable." Ron gestured to the Hawaiian shirt he was wearing. "A friend of mine in law enforcement asked me to test it for him to see if it could feasibly be worn during long periods of high physical exertion. It was developed for undercover officers."

"Maybe they should have toned down the pecs and the six pack a bit," I said. "How did you know to put it on yesterday?"

"I just had a feeling." He grunted as I helped him wrap his leg wound and pull the sleeve up tight around it. "I've learned not to ignore those types of things."

With the bleeding stopped and all visible wounds dressed and wrapped, Ron grabbed my shoulder and tried to stand. He turned pale and made his way gingerly back down to the ground. "I was afraid of that," he said.

"What?"

"My leg's broken. I'm going to need to splint it, and even with a splint, I'm not going to be much help to you catching those guys."

"Who says I want to catch them? Maybe we should just worry about getting you out of here and calling in the authorities."

"If that was your plan, you would already be out of here. But you stuck around."

"I just had a feeling," I said.

Ron grunted again and then began shaking uncontrollably.

"You mind if we restart the fire? My body's starting to figure out that it's been shot."

"Sure thing," I said, stirring the coals and adding some small bits of kindling to encourage the flames. "You should get something hot in you."

"Just start the fire and leave me some grub. You don't want to lose their trail."

"I don't think they are going anywhere tonight," I said. "When I left them, they were setting up camp in a nice meadow with a rolling stream and protection against the wind." I pulled out a compressed down coat and helped Ron pull it on, then added some additional layers to my own skin. The wind felt like it was blowing off a glacier. "Besides, they're sending in a wet team tomorrow morning because they got me mixed up with you."

"The wet team's been called off," Ron said as he settled himself in a wedge between two logs close to the fire. "I heard them on the radio. They think you abandoned the mountains and headed for the city. Apparently they're holding something you want."

"They've got Hope," I said. "And Jin and Permelia and I think Zack. They want me to turn myself in and come quietly."

"But instead you are taking out the mercenaries one at a time like Rambo."

"Uh . . . that was an accident."

"Which part? Shooting a man in the forehead or following us around like a sniper?"

"Both," I said. "I was planning to get the drop on them, and then they decided to try to shoot me in the back. Remember, they thought I was you. I was aiming for his chest and missed. And as far as following you and the boys, I was halfway to the highway when Hope reminded me I had promised to bring the boys home safe and sound."

"You talked to her?"

"Yeah, for a few seconds before they sent a virus and fried your sat phone. Sorry."

"You know who's taken her?"

"A guy called Dempsey. A professional mercenary. He says he's working for a client who wants me and my family delivered intact."

"John Dempsey, the senator's son? The international criminal with the broken nose and the nasty reputation?"

"That's the one."

"I thought he only worked abroad."

"Apparently he made an exception in this case." I stirred the coals until the flames began to take. "I'm the one who broke his nose."

Ron chuckled. "You've got all sorts of surprises in your past."

"Me?" I said. "You're the Delta Force phantom who had these guys almost wetting their pants. I'm just a college professor who apparently ticked somebody off bad enough to take it out on my family."

Ron looked directly at me. "I know exactly who you are. You were part of an elite group of undercover agents specifically trained to infiltrate and expose terrorists working in the United States."

"And how would you know that?"

"You don't remember me, do you?" Ron said. He was either grimacing or smiling; I couldn't tell.

I thought through my past. I was pretty sure the first time I'd met Ron was when we had purchased our house and he'd brought over some chocolate chip cookies to welcome us to the neighborhood. My mind started to wander to those cookies. They were really good.

I think Ron noticed me starting to lose my train of thought. "The shooting house," he said. "We brought a group of you guys in for hostage training."

"What's a shooting house?" I wasn't sure why I continued to play dumb, but maintaining a cover was second nature to me.

Rather than calling me on it, Ron said, "We spent months in the shooting house, eight hours a day, practicing killing terrorists and saving hostages. When it came time to graduate, they upped the ante. Rather than using fake targets, we got to take turns playing the hostage and the rescuer. Live people and live rounds. It was the most intense experience any of us had ever gone through, but it prepared us like nothing else for the feeling of a real operation. Mess up and either you or one of your brothers would be dead."

"Sounds like fun," I said. "What does this have to do with me?"

"One day we got a call saying they were going to bus in a bunch of trainees from a new antiterrorist program. At first we thought the trainees were going to be given firearms training, but that wasn't the point of the exercise. These trainees were most likely to find themselves as hostages, not rescuers. They very likely could be part of a Delta Force rescue operation and needed to know how to act so as not to get themselves or other hostages killed. So they were brought in and given some instruction, and they got to play the hostage role in the shooting house while Delta rescued them."

"Doesn't sound difficult. Stand still, don't move. You guys had the hard job."

"There are no easy roles in the shooting house," Ron said. "When the lead starts flying, sometimes the hardest thing in the world to do is stand still. But to their credit, most of the trainees—both men and women—stood their ground admirably and didn't panic, although none of them came out as cocky as they'd gone in. None, that is, except one guy."

Ron seemed to study me for a moment before moving on. "This guy came into camp, and everything he said seemed to be a joke, like a day at the shooting house was a continuing education class at a community college. Our guys were chomping at the bit to get him into the house and watch his expression change. We made sure the rounds placed next to this guy were extremely close and extremely hot. After the smoke cleared, he stood, walked over to me, pale and a little shaky, and placed a small paper bag in my hands.

"'What's this?' I asked him.

"'It was my body armor,' he said. 'I wanted you to have it.'"

"I opened the bag, and inside was a wrapped-up diaper. The guy stopped his shaking act, punched me in the shoulder, and thanked me for not shooting him. Then he walked out, slow and confident, whistling to himself like he was just coming out of a movie. So, yeah, I remember you pretty well. I never did open that diaper to find out what was inside."

"Probably wise," I said, deciding it was time to stop pretending. "I was a bit of a smart aleck back then. I think it was a Baby Ruth. But the truth is I don't remember you because I was scared out of my mind and just happy to be alive. The whistling thing was a complete act."

"I knew that, but it was a dang good one. Most Delta guys don't come out of the shooting house looking that cool. With that kind of poise, you must have been good undercover. Are you still playing in that world?"

I laughed. "I gave up the undercover life the day I proposed to Hope. But apparently something from my past is catching up to me."

"Do you know who's behind this?"

"Not a clue." I stirred the fire a bit and added more wood. Ron's shivering was lessening, which was a good sign. "Tell me something," I said. "Which was harder: being on the shooting end or the receiving end in the shooting house?"

"That's easy," he said. "Being responsible for someone else's life is a hundred times harder than worrying about your own. I used to have nightmares about what would happen if I messed up and plugged someone by mistake."

"Did anyone ever mess up?"

"Just once that I know of. An operator killed one of his comrades in a plane-breach scenario."

"What happened to the shooter?"

"He got kicked out of the unit and became a mercenary. He's got a reputation for putting on a smile right before he shoots you. His name is Jackson, and he's holding our boys at gunpoint right now."

"What are we going to do?" I asked.

"Make a plan," Ron said, adjusting his homemade down comforter up around his chin. "A really good plan."

And then he passed out.

Chapter 21
PENG'S CONFESSION

WHILE RON SLEPT, I SAT by the fire trying to keep the chill wind from finding the seams in my clothes, trying not to think about the spiders that seemed to inhabit every corner of this little valley, trying to figure out what to do next.

My first thought was that with the wet team out of the picture and both Ron and me free, we could tag team the mercenaries, drawing them away from the boys and picking them off one at a time. But Ron looked awfully pale, and it was clear he had lost a lot of blood. Ex-Delta Force or not, he wasn't in shape for a battle.

He'd said we needed to come up with a good plan, but for all I knew he could be out for days and I would be no closer to freeing the boys or finding Hope.

I wondered briefly if I should be watching the entrance to the canyon rather than sitting by the fire. But there was no reason for anyone to come back here. They thought Ron was dead, and they thought I had fled the mountains.

The wind blew harder. I could understand why nobody would want to stay in this spot.

I should be trying to get some sleep while I had the chance. I told myself that tomorrow Ron would awaken, and together we could come up with a plan to rescue the boys and then go after Hope.

Just when I had settled into a semisoft, semiwarm position in between the rocks, I heard a noise. At first I thought it was a small animal or a really large spider moving through the bushes, circling our camp. I reached for a gun and remembered I had stuck both Ron's and Woolhead's weapons back inside the pack, which was leaning against a rock several feet away. I tried to move quietly as I raised myself up and began to inch my way toward the pack.

A face suddenly appeared in the firelight, and I almost screamed like a girl.

"It's just me," Peng said as he moved fully into the light of the fire.

I let out a breath but kept moving toward the pack. I pulled out one of the guns and scanned the dark landscape behind where Peng had appeared.

"I'm alone," Peng said.

"But how did you . . . ?" I stopped before finishing the sentence. Peng was good at escaping into the dark.

"Where are the other boys?" I asked quickly. I was almost afraid to hear the answer.

"Sleeping."

I breathed out a sigh of relief.

"How is Ron?" Peng looked at him as if trying to work out a puzzle.

"He's sleeping too. He's lost some blood, but he's okay."

"I saw him die." Peng's voice was expressionless. Watching a beloved leader murdered in front of his eyes must have been a traumatic experience, one that would burn a deep and lasting scar, yet Peng's face revealed nothing about what was going on beneath the surface.

"He was wearing a vest," I said. "The bullets to his chest hurt him but didn't penetrate the skin. His hand is damaged, and his leg is broken, but with medical help, he'll be fine."

"They have Hope and Jin," Peng said. His voice was steady and didn't crack.

"I know," I said. That was all I could say without choking up myself. I tried not to think of my wife and daughter in captivity.

"What are you going to do?" Peng's words were almost a challenge, like it was my fault my family had been taken. I started to get defensive, and then I breathed myself down. After all, it was my fault—or at least my responsibility. In my earlier career, I'd made it a point to be a thorn in the side of numerous bad guys, and one of them was returning for a little payback. What *was* I going to do? It was a fair question. "I'm going to wait for Ron to wake up," I said. "I'm going to try to tap his Delta-Force brain to come up with a plan. First, to free the boys and get them safe, and second, to locate Hope and Jin and go get them."

Peng nodded as if satisfied. He sat on a log a few feet from me and stared into the fire.

But my words weren't satisfying to me. They sounded hollow as they bounced off the walls in the canyon and then quivered along the shimmering spiderwebs before dying in the night. I really didn't have a plan. Even if Ron and I were able to free the boys, I still had no idea where they were holding Hope. Maybe they would take me in exchange for the boys. They wanted my whole family, but maybe they would let Peng escape with Ron if they had me as their prize catch. It would be a checkmate.

Peng and I both stared into the fire for a while, neither of us looking at the other, each of us lost in his own dark thoughts.

"Why do you run?" I asked after a while. "At home, in the middle of the night, with all of the doors locked? Why do you escape into the darkness?"

"I like to run," Peng said. I knew from past conversations that this was as much of an explanation as I was likely to get, so I didn't do what I usually did: I didn't press him for more. I just let his words sit and crackle in the burning embers of the fire. I almost jumped in surprise when he continued speaking. "I like the wind in my face. I like the sound of my feet on the empty streets. I like the feeling of freedom."

Not only were these the most words I had probably ever heard Peng speak at one time, but I think it was the first time I'd ever heard Peng express his true, authentic feelings about anything—other than not liking the other boys. Maybe the bishop had been right; maybe there really was magic in a campfire. "So when you run, you are actually running? Like you're training for a race?" I thought back about his patterns—each escape taking him farther and farther away from the house. This last time, he had been more than twenty-five miles away from home, and he'd been gone less than three hours. That would easily qualify him for the Boston Marathon if he was old enough to enter.

"Not for a race," Peng said. "I just like to run at night."

Maybe Peng and I did have something in common. "I used to run at night too," I said. "I've got a place I could take you sometime. A friend of mine showed it to me once. It reminds me a little bit of this place—except without the biting wind and giant spiders. If you start on the trail after midnight, by sunrise you can look out over a lake and watch the moose as they feed in the shallows. I think you'd like it." Peng reminded me a lot of the imposter Joseph Hadadi, which wasn't necessarily a bad thing.

Peng didn't say anything, and I could feel the door that had begun to open between us starting to close. I took a guess at what he was thinking. "You're not planning on being around for any future runs, are you?" I asked. "It isn't a coincidence that you always end up at a bus or a train station. You're planning on leaving us." I should have drawn this conclusion a long time ago, and maybe I had. But I was either too afraid to admit it or too ashamed that I had fantasized what our family would be like without him in it.

"I can't stay," he said. This time his voice did crack. "It's not safe."

"I'm sorry about that. As you've probably realized by now, there are things about my past that I haven't told you. I've managed to tick off a lot of bad people."

"No," Peng said, this time his voice showing real anguish. "It's not safe because I'm not safe. I make bad things happen to people."

I probably should have tried to comfort him, tell him that was ridiculous, but instead, I thought about the day we had picked him up from the orphanage, the fear in the staff's eyes, and their determination to pass him on to us. I thought about all of the nights I'd tried to tell myself I'd been imagining things, that I hadn't brought something dangerous into our home. I thought it was time we both stopped running and faced the truth. "What happened in the orphanage?" I asked. "Why were the people there so afraid of you?"

Maybe it was our position, both facing the fire and not each other; maybe it was the influence of the mountains and the crispness of the air; maybe it was the nature of our situation and the fact that we might not make it out of this alive; or maybe it was the hand of God and a delayed response to Hope's fervent prayers. Whatever the reason, this boy who normally barely said two words most of the time opened up and spilled his guts like a pumpkin. "My real father died when I was a baby," Peng said. "My mother tried to make it on her own, but she fell behind obligations on our farm and lost it to the bank. A man stepped forward—a farmer whose wife had also died—and said he would take care of us. My mother married him and soon found that what he was really looking for was someone to take care of him. My mother and I would do all the chores on the farm while he sat back and drank his rice wine. When he was drunk, he got angry and would beat my mother. When I tried to step in to help her, he would get even angrier and beat her more. But I couldn't just stand back. He encouraged my mother to get pregnant. He said it was because he loved children and wanted one of their own, but we both knew it was because he wanted more workers for his farm.

"When my mother did become pregnant, he was excited. For a short time, he stopped beating her. He even stopped beating me. Then Jin was born—a baby girl and not the boy he'd wanted. He was furious. He beat us both so bad I thought he was going to kill us. He *was* going to kill Jin. He wanted to put her in a bag and take her to the river. But my mother begged him to let her sell Jin to an orphanage—to at least bring in a little bit of money in exchange for her nine months of carrying the child. My mother was just appeasing him; she loved Jin more than anything else in the world, but the next day she asked me to go with her to the village.

"At the orphanage, they wanted Jin badly. I could see it in their eyes. My mother made them promise that Jin would be given to an American family, one that could take care of her. Mistress Wu said not to worry. They had many foreigners wanting girl babies. It was not like our country, where baby girls were seen as a burden.

"We turned to go, and Mistress Wu said there was also a good market for strong young men. She was looking at me when she said it. My mother started to shake her head and then stopped as if she'd had an idea. She pulled me aside and whispered to me. She said that I should stay with Jin—stay until she was sold to a nice American family but that once I knew Jin was safe, I should escape and come back to her. She said Jin was my sister, my blood. That she was my responsibility."

Peng stood and poked a stick into the fire. The large moon behind him looked like it was resting on his shoulders.

"I knew my stepfather would beat my mother for taking me away from the farm. She was still feeble from delivering Jin. She would be expected to do double the work, and when she couldn't, she would pay for it. But she had made me promise I would not leave Jin until she was safe with a good family. At the same time, I made her promise she would walk by as often as she could so I could see her. I entered the orphanage, watched over my sister, and began to plan my escape. I was already good at escaping. I had been breaking out of the farmhouse for a long time to run at night. To taste the air of freedom.

"My mother kept her promise. I saw her walk by the orphanage a few times a week. I knew it wasn't easy for her. The farm was over ten miles away. Making the walk would take her away from my stepfather and his demands. I knew he wouldn't like this. I knew he would beat my mother even harder. I should have gone back to her. I shouldn't have let her face him alone. My mother began to look different as the days went on. She walked with a limp and moved more slowly. Then I didn't see her anymore. There was only one reason for her not to keep her promise. I heard from someone in the village that she had died in a farm accident. I knew what had really happened, and I knew I was the cause. If I had not been so selfish . . . If I had not made her promise to come see me . . ." Peng's voice trailed off as he continued to stare into the fire.

I let his story sit for a while. Then the words that had been whispered to my mind came back to me. Peng had come into my life *because I would understand him.* At the time, I couldn't comprehend what the words meant. But I now knew two things Peng and I had in common: we both liked to run at night, and we both felt responsible for our mothers' deaths. I was overcome with a wave of guilt. I was Peng's adopted father. I should have known these things about him before now. But I'd been afraid to find out.

Peng poked a stick repeatedly into the fire, and I knew there was more to his story. "Why were they afraid of you?" I asked. "The people at the orphanage?"

Peng let out a deep breath. "A few weeks after my mother died, they brought Shi-Shi into the orphanage. Her parents had been killed in an accident, but there were whispers that this often happened with girls who were young and pretty. The rumors were that they were sold to sea merchants who came to the orphanage twice a year. Shi-Shi thought that this was just talk to scare the children into obedience, but one of the guards looked at her with hunger in his eyes. His name was Fong, and I heard him tell another guard the sailors were going to have to settle for seconds with Shi-Shi. The other guard derided him, saying he was all talk, saying he was a big bag of wind. But Fong told him to watch the girl. To look into her eyes the next day and see if her innocence was still there.

"I had to do something. The orphanage's electrical wires were exposed, and I passed word to the older girls that no one should touch their door that night, and then I went to work on the wires. I was curious about them. We didn't have electricity on the farm, so I studied the wires and I learned their secrets. I learned to make a shock when the wires were crossed in a certain way.

"When Fong tried to enter the room that night, the current in the doorknob went through his body. He was thrown across the room and hit his head against the wall. I just wanted to stop him from getting to Shi-Shi. I didn't mean to kill him. But when I found out he was dead, I didn't feel bad. I felt happy. Maybe happier than I have ever felt in my life. I found myself wishing that all of the adults in the orphanage were dead. I started thinking of ways I could use the power in the wires against them. I didn't do it, but I wanted to.

"I learned then that I was not a good person. I have darkness in my heart. That's why I need to escape. I need to take my darkness far away from Jin, far away from Shi-Shi, far away from you and Hope. Bad things happen because of me."

We were both silent for a long time. I now knew why the people at the orphanage had been afraid of Peng, but it wasn't because he was a monster.

"Did anyone try to harm the older girls after Fong was killed?"

"No."

"So you stopped them."

"Yes, I stopped them. But I also killed someone. And I enjoyed it." Peng threw the stick into the fire.

"It's called survivor euphoria," I said. "When you or someone close to you survives a near miss with severe bodily harm, your body sends waves of chemical relief into your brain. It's a natural reaction to surviving a life-threatening situation. Let me ask you something; since Fong's death, have you ever hurt anyone else?"

"No, but I told you, I fantasized about hurting the guards at the orphanage. I might have done it too, but you and Hope came and took me away."

"Have you ever hurt anyone since you came to live with us?"

"No."

"Do you continue to think about hurting people day in and day out?"

Peng thought for a minute and then said, "I think about hurting the guys who are holding us hostage."

I barked a short laugh. "I do too. Because they are trying to harm people we love. I killed one of them, and even though it made me sick, my first reaction was relief. It wasn't because I was a murderer; it was because he was trying to take my life and I stopped him. I don't think you are a bad person, Peng. At least no worse than me. Right now I'm planning a way to get my family and those boys to safety, and part of that plan may include hurting some more of the bad guys. I wouldn't hurt them if they would leave me and my family alone, and I regret killing that man. I might even have nightmares about it for the rest of my life. But I *am* going to save my family, and the fact that I'm worried about hurting the bad guys at all says something about the kind of person I am. I don't think the bad guys are worried too much about who they hurt. The fact that you worried about your feelings after killing Fong tells me a lot about you."

"You're not afraid to have me in your home?"

"No, I'm just an idiot for not finding a way to talk to you about this sooner. I thought you might be doing drugs or something."

"Why would I do drugs?"

Peng's expression was so serious that it made me laugh. I stood up and put my arm around him. "You wouldn't," I said. "I should have known that. But because I was afraid of the truth, I didn't ask the right questions." I'd put my arm around Peng before, but it had always felt stiff, unnatural. Now it just felt right.

"What are we going to do?" Peng said. "How are we going to save the other boys and find Hope?"

"I might have an idea," Ron said from under his quilt. "It's time to start planning."

Chapter 22
SETTING THE TABLE

DEMPSEY WATCHED BUCK UNLOAD A folding table and chairs from a truck outside the building and carry them inside, where he set them up. Dempsey stood and started walking across the large, empty floor. By the time he reached Buck, the younger man was draping a white tablecloth over the fiberglass table.

"What are you doing?"

"I think that's pretty obvious. I'm setting the table." He pulled out a package of Chinet paper plates and red Solo cups. "I brought the good china."

"Why are you setting a table?" Dempsey tried to keep his voice level.

"Our guests need a place to eat. It would be a bit uncivilized to make them eat in their room, don't you think?"

"They aren't our guests," Dempsey said, feeling the blood rising in his face and knowing that this was exactly the reaction Buck was looking for. "And we are not supposed to be civilized."

"I beg to differ," Buck said. "They are our guests until we deliver them to the client. There's no use treating them badly just because we took them against their will and used a little chloroform. I figure if we treat them kindly, they are much less likely to try to escape or call for help. It increases our chances of a payoff. Isn't that what you want, Boss? A big payoff?"

"The more you drive in and out of that gate, the more you increase the chance that someone starts to ask questions."

"You should tell that to your elusive bearded friend. The guard at the shack wasn't at all interested in what I was bringing in or out. He was pumping me about all of the camera equipment and explosives the guy with the beard was hauling in. I would think a guy like that would be a little more discreet. Why do we need cameras and explosives anyway?"

"Because we are supposed to be a film crew." The voice came from behind them, and both Dempsey and Buck jumped and reached for their guns. They relaxed when they saw the man with the beard emerging from the shadows.

"Sometimes the best way to hide is not to be seen at all." He continued to walk until he was fully in the light. "And sometimes it's to hide in plain sight. We rented this place as if we were working on an action movie. We demanded complete privacy, and we paid them a bunch of money. It would be a bit suspicious for a movie crew not to have cameras, and the explosives will reinforce the fact that if they hear any loud noises, they can chalk it up to an action scene."

The man's name was Morgan. Dempsey had worked with him many times before, but never on a job with Buck. Morgan talked to Dempsey when he spoke. He didn't pay any attention to Buck, and Dempsey could see it got under Buck's skin.

Morgan moved across the room toward the door. "I'll start setting up the cameras," he said over his shoulder. "You go ahead and have your picnic." Then he walked out the door.

"That is one strange dude," Buck said under his breath. "Why didn't you tell me you were letting someone else in on our end of the job?"

"You know what you need to know," Dempsey said. "And know this: don't get any ideas about the woman. If we don't deliver her, we don't get paid, and if we don't get paid, I have no use for you."

"You worry too much, Boss. Hey, could you help me haul in that cooler?"

Chapter 23
SACRIFICE

DEMPSEY WATCHED AS BUCK COMPLETED setting the table and brought the women out of the room to eat dinner. Buck helped Mrs. Knight situate her child in a high chair he'd bought somewhere, and then he helped Mrs. Knight into her seat. The younger woman nodded and graciously thanked Buck, but the older one pulled the chair away and seated herself. At least someone didn't seem to be falling for Buck's antics. He was a lot of things, but a conscientious host was not one of them. He was a psychopath—a useful psychopath at times but a psychopath all the same. It was the reason Dempsey had hired him. Many people would have qualms about kidnapping a woman and young child on US soil. To Buck, it was just another job. He would be just as unbothered if he were instructed to drown a baby puppy. He didn't have a conscience, and this made him a very valuable employee.

"You gonna come eat with us, Boss?" Buck yelled from across the room. "We've got a place set for ya."

Dempsey thought about just getting up and leaving, going for a walk around the perimeter, maybe finding the ghost to see how the preparations were coming, but as much as he really didn't want to engage the prisoners in conversation, he was even more afraid of leaving them alone with Buck. If there was going to be a tea party, he should probably at least be there for damage control. He rose and made his way across the large room toward the table. Knight's wife started in as soon as he sat down.

"Mr. Dempsey, you don't look happy to join us."

"I'm not really much on fraternizing with the guests," Dempsey said. "I don't see how it serves any real purpose."

"So you would rather we eat on the floor of that small room you have us locked in?" The woman didn't seem intimidated in the least. Anyone observing the conversation might think she was the one with the upper hand. Dempsey had to give Matt credit; he knew how to surround himself with strong women.

First Becca, and now this Hope. As he thought of Becca, a sudden wave of emptiness hit him. He quickly pushed it down. He rarely thought of her anymore, and now was not the time to reminisce.

"I'd rather get this job over quickly and efficiently," he said. "I'm not a big fan of drama and useless questions. So why don't you just eat and go back to your room."

"Why are you doing this?"

Dempsey sighed. "And so the useless questions begin. I told you before, but you don't seem to want to hear. I'm doing this for the money—lots of it. I'm being paid to do a job. I could speculate as to why the client wants you and your family delivered at a certain place and time, but I really don't care. I just want to get paid."

"I wasn't asking about this job," Hope said. "I was asking why you are in this line of work at all. Young Buck I can possibly understand. He's been telling us about the horrors of his childhood. But you grew up in a respectable family. Why would a man like you choose a profession like this?"

Dempsey wondered what tales Buck had been telling about his childhood. It truly had been horrible, but most of the horrors had been enacted on the people and animals that had had the misfortune of crossing Buck's path. He looked over at Buck, who was smiling broadly at him.

"I'd like to know the answer to that question as well," Buck said.

Dempsey looked Hope directly in the eyes. "I do this type of work because I enjoy it. I enjoy the money. I enjoy the danger. I enjoy the notoriety it brings me. But most of all, I enjoy the game, the opportunity to play in an arena with real life-and-death stakes, where one wrong move can bring disaster, the opportunity to test myself against the best and win. That's why I'm in this line of work. I get to play the game at the highest level and consistently prove I am the best at what I do."

Hope's eyes seemed to bore right into him, past his eyes, through his brain, and deep into his heart. She would know it if he lied to her. But he was not lying. At least not about the game. Above all else, he had always enjoyed the game.

"It sounds very lonely," Hope said finally.

"Now how could I be lonely with colleagues like Buck around?" Dempsey meant for his tone to be light, but his words seemed to echo hollowly across the big room.

"Do you have a family?" She said it gently, but for some reason, to Dempsey, it felt like a slap in the face. His mother and father were now long dead. They had been the outward persona of a perfect couple and had hid the cold war that had been the reality. His memories of family were not fond ones. He wasn't sure why anyone would want one. And then, for some reason, he thought of Becca again and wished he hadn't.

"There are certain sacrifices in my line of work," Dempsey said. "Family is one of them."

The woman continued to study him and then looked at her child and the old woman next to her. "Mr. Dempsey," she said finally. "I don't think you under-stand the meaning of sacrificing for family."

"Maybe I don't really care to," he said. And then to Permelia, "Please take that spoon out of your sleeve and put it back on the table." He was glad to have something to distract him from the direction of the current conversation. "Grinding a spoon into a shiv takes a lot longer than you might think, and it really isn't going to do you any good."

Permelia let the spoon fall out of her jacket pocket onto the table with a clang. She sniffed with disgust.

"What's the matter?" Buck asked Permelia. "You don't like Thai food? I assure you it is some of the best in the county." He emphasized his point by taking a big bite.

"I don't think Wendover, Nevada, is known as a Thai food mecca," Permelia said. "And the current company makes just about anything hard to swallow. Especially when it could be our last meal."

Buck looked at Dempsey as if to say he wasn't the one who had revealed their location. Dempsey studied Permelia with a fresh sense of appreciation. Despite her age and size, she had put Buck on the ground, found a way to escape to the outside, nearly gotten away, and figured out their location. She would definitely need to be searched before being put back in the room. Who knew what else she had managed to appropriate in her sleeves.

"Permelia, it really would be easier on all of us if you would save your escape plans until after we deliver you to the client. And you might as well eat while you can; that bit about this being your last meal is a little overly dramatic," Dempsey said.

"Is it?" Permelia asked. "I know how this works. If you're going to let the hostages go, you don't let them see your faces, you don't let them know your real names, and you definitely don't sit down with them and have dinner. You might as well have spelled it out in block letters. We're toast, and you know it."

"In most instances, you would be right," Dempsey said. "But not in this case. First of all, I don't do much work in this country, and I don't plan on sticking around after this job, so alerting the authorities to my identity is irrelevant. I'm already on several most-wanted lists. Second, in my line of work, I deal strictly with referrals, and referrals come from reputation. If I kept a mask on during each job, how would anybody know it was me? And Buck likes to see his name in the paper. So you don't have to worry about us feeding you dinner and then putting a bullet in your head. Our job is to deliver you alive, and that's what we will do. Otherwise, we don't get paid."

"And what about after you deliver us?" Hope said. "The only people I can think of who would hire you to kidnap Matt and his family are terrorists. Do you think they will also give us the courtesy of keeping us alive?"

"That's not my problem," Dempsey said. "But I'll tell you this: your husband has a knack for working himself out of some seemingly impossible situations, and I'm really curious to see if he can get himself out of this one."

Dempsey began eating his food. With a full mouth, he said, "Permelia, could you please remove that fork from your sock?"

Chapter 24
POKING THE GIANT

"THE FIRST THING WE NEED to do," Ron said, "is anticipate their response when they find that Peng is gone."

"I think we still have awhile," Peng said. "They said they would rotate the watch every two hours. They weren't really guarding us; they were patrolling the camp perimeter. Tiny had the first watch. The other two were sleeping when I left. I don't think they'll notice I'm gone until they change shifts."

"Maybe they'll think you ran for the highway," I said.

"No. They'll know I came here. Eric saw me leaving, and he knows I was coming to see if Ron was really dead. Eric can't keep a secret."

"No, he can't," Ron said. "Although I have to admit he did better than I thought he would earlier today. So that means as soon as they find out you're gone, someone will be coming here looking for you. Since you are the only one of the boys they really care about, they will probably send two people and leave one to watch the others. And I don't think Tiny will be coming back into this spider hole, so that means we should expect Jackson and Jillian pretty soon."

"Can't we just pick them off when they come through the rocks?" I asked.

"I think they'll probably be too careful to let that happen. They think I'm dead, but they can't be completely sure. Although I'd love to get them in here alone with me. What time did the first watch start?"

Peng looked down at my wrist. "It's been longer than I thought," he said, surprised at how much time we had spent talking. "It's almost time for the second watch."

"Too bad," Ron said. "I was hoping to get you two out of here before they started coming through the pass. I wish there was more than one way out of here."

Peng straightened and looked up at the rocks behind us. "There is. Up there."

I looked to where Peng pointed, but all I saw was a sheer cliff face.

"The goat?" Ron asked.

Peng nodded. "I watched the path he took. It's not as bad as it seems. The goat didn't even stumble."

"Do you think you could find your way out of here?"

"I know I could," Peng said. "I was planning on using that path to escape earlier."

Ron didn't question him, which made me wonder how much of our conversation he had heard.

"Okay," Ron said. "You and Peng sneak out the back way, find the boys, and free them. I'll wait for Jackson and Jillian to arrive, and we'll have a little fun."

"But your leg . . ." I said.

"My leg will be fine for what I need to do. Leave me with my pack. There's a knife in there that I can use to make a splint and arrange some surprises. Just make sure you get the drop on Tiny. The guy might be afraid of spiders, but he has a nasty reputation: he's big, he's strong, and he likes to play with his food before he kills it."

I thought about the plan, and I didn't like it. I didn't like the thought of Peng leading me up the wall of a cliff; I didn't like leaving a wounded Ron to deal with two armed opponents; I didn't like that I would be putting them both in more danger. There were too many things that could go wrong.

"Why don't you just let me walk out of here and give myself up?" I said. "I'm the one they really want. I'll tell them I won't go with them unless they let the rest of you walk out of here."

"Nice in theory," Ron said, considering my words. "But it wouldn't go down that way. They aren't going to want to leave any loose ends. They might agree to your terms, but they would still come after Peng, at the very least. And I don't think they would let the other boys go either."

Ron must have seen my shoulders sag. "Look," he added. "We'll find a way to locate Hope and Jin. But we have to deal with first things first. We need to get those boys away from the kidnappers. I'll take care of Jackson and Jillian; you take care of Tiny and get the boys out of here. We can rendezvous at the road. Now, you really need to get moving, otherwise our options are going to disappear quickly."

He was right, and I knew this was what Hope would want me to do. But I still didn't like it. We got Ron to the point where he could hobble around, and then he took his knife and gun and headed for the entrance to the canyon. He seemed confident, but I wondered about his chances. I wondered if we would ever see him again.

I didn't have a chance to wonder for too long because Peng and I were soon looking for a goat trail on the cliff face in the dark because we couldn't use our headlamps for fear of providing an easy target. I determined not to look down as

I focused on the placement of Peng's feet in front of me. Not once did he falter; not once did he slip. Not once did he act like he did not know the way perfectly. Although the canyon side of the cliff on the way up was steeper, the side outside the canyon going down was even more disconcerting. Peng suddenly stopped, and I almost ran into him, taking both of us down off the ledge. At first I thought we might have hit a dead end, but I looked up and saw that he was listening. There were voices down below—a man's voice and a woman's. Although we could not hear what they were saying, it was clear they were moving in the direction of the entrance to the box canyon. Peng and I had made our escape just in time.

I hoped Ron had enough time to prepare a proper welcome for them and wasn't just passed out on the ground somewhere.

* * *

"Stop," Jackson said as Jillian began to walk into the narrow slot leading into Spider Hollow.

Jillian stopped. She didn't like taking orders from Jackson, but ignoring his directives on a mission could have serious consequences. She didn't hide her irritation. "What now? Are you afraid of the spiders too?"

Jackson pressed up behind her, and at first she thought he might be using this opportunity in the dark to make unwanted overtures. But as he got close, he bent down near her feet, studying the ground in front of her.

"Well, that answers one question."

"What?" she said, still not moving.

"You didn't kill the Delta after all."

"What makes you say that?"

He pointed at the dirt. At first Jillian didn't see anything. Then she noticed a fine wire about a foot high running parallel to the ground. One more step and she would have tripped it.

"How do you know it's him?" she asked, taking a careful step backward.

"The design." Jackson followed the wire across and upward with his eyes. "Although he must be hurt pretty bad. It's a little sloppy. See that stick up there where the wire connects?" Jackson nodded in the direction of a large boulder. "Even if you had tripped it, I don't think the rocks would have hit you square. They probably would have filled in behind us."

"Maybe it's just a warning."

"Delta Force doesn't do warnings. If they want to take out an enemy, they take them out."

Jillian looked ahead of them and into the darkness. She wasn't too thrilled about becoming a sitting duck as they popped out the end of the crevasse. "What now?" she asked.

She could see Jackson's perfectly straight and probably professionally whitened teeth gleaming in the moonlight.

"We need to be a bit more careful. We aren't stalking a boy anymore. We're going after some real prey."

"You picked that canyon for us to hole up in because no one could get into it without you seeing them. Sounds to me like we might be the prey."

"His advantage isn't as great as it seems," Jackson said. "I watched for problems with our defense when we set up camp in there. There's a small fissure right before the trail empties out into the flats. If someone was expecting to be ambushed, they might be able to use that fissure to pull up and out of the slot and enter the canyon without being seen."

"And when did you realize this flaw in your perfect campsite?"

"About the same time we found out that it didn't matter anymore," Jackson said, stepping carefully over the trip wire. "C'mon, I'll show you what I mean."

"I don't think so," Jillian said.

"You aren't going to go all Tiny on me, are you?" Jackson asked. "You gonna start whining like a little girl?"

"The day I start whining like a little girl is the day I give you permission to put me out of my misery. You go in your way. I'm going to go in from the back side."

"There is no back side."

"Tell that to the goat," Jillian said, and then she moved off into the darkness.

* * *

Peng and I continued our journey away from the voices, toward the camp of a giant who enjoyed hurting people. Before long, we could see the glow from the dying fire. I tapped Peng's shoulder and whispered in his ear.

"I'll distract Tiny," I said. "You get the boys out of camp and out of these mountains. There should be plenty of people camping near the road. Find one of them and have them help you get to a city. Don't waste any time. I'm not sure how long I will be able to keep him occupied."

Peng shook his head to protest leaving me alone with Tiny, and for some reason, this made my chest swell.

"You heard what the bishop told you," I said. "Those boys are your responsibility."

Peng shook his head more vigorously. "I can't. Bad things will happen."

I saw the look of panic in his eyes and realized that underneath his stoicism, he was just a kid.

I took a deep breath. "How do you think Jin and Shi-Shi have adjusted with their move to the United States?"

Peng thought for a minute and then said, "They are doing great. Shi-Shi is amazing at just about everything, and Jin is happy."

"How do you think Shi-Shi would be doing if that guard had gotten into her room?"

"I don't want to think about it," Peng said.

"I don't either. But if that guard hadn't died, everything might be different."

Peng just looked at me.

"I'm saying that maybe that guard dying was the best thing that could have happened. Without that, they wouldn't have wanted to get rid of you when they placed Jin, and who knows what would have happened with Shi-Shi."

"I would have escaped with her into the countryside."

"And do you think her life would be better then?"

Peng shook his head.

"So maybe this one isn't all on you. Maybe God had a hand in the guard's death. Maybe you taking on the responsibility to protect those girls was not such a bad thing after all."

I saw the folds in Peng's forehead push against each other as if working their way through a maze. What I was asking of Peng was not fair. What had been asked of him his whole life wasn't fair. He'd never had a chance to be a kid. He'd always had to be in charge. But right now we didn't have a choice. "Look, you just led me out of a box canyon that was supposed to be impossible to escape. You can easily get those boys out of these mountains and to safety." I could see that he was almost convinced, but he was still struggling with something, and I thought I knew what it was. It was the same thing I was struggling with. "Once they're safe, we can focus on Mom and Jin." That might have been the first time I had referred to Hope as Peng's mom. It was probably the first time I had actually *thought* of their relationship in this way.

"Okay," he said. "I will get them out."

"Move quietly around to the other side of the camp. When you hear my signal, get the boys and get out of these mountains as fast as you can. At the top of that pass, you will be able to see the road. Find an adult and get those boys to safety."

"What's the signal?"

"I'm not sure yet. But you will know it when you hear it."

Peng looked at me as if he wanted to say something, but then he held out his hand for me to shake. I guessed he wasn't quite ready for a hug. As I took his hand, he put his other one on top of my wrist, shook it once hard, and said, "Thank you." And then he was gone into the darkness.

I gave Peng a few minutes and then began to work my way toward the firelight. I avoided snapping any branches as I walked, but I didn't avoid the rustle of bushes against my legs. I wanted to sneak up on the camp, but I also needed Tiny to hear me. I hoped he was at least a decent lookout.

As I got closer to camp, I wondered if he had flown the coop. I could see the three boys huddled together on a log, warming themselves by the fire, but there was no sign of the big man. There was also no sign of Peng. I hoped he had not inadvertently stumbled into the mercenary.

Then a voice behind me said, "Why don't you take that gun out of your waistband and slowly toss it over to me."

So far my plan was working perfectly. I turned around, slowly pulled the gun from my belt, and held it with my thumb and forefinger before tossing it toward him. I put my hands behind my head and looked up. Tiny seemed bigger than I remembered. A lot bigger.

"Where's the boy?" he asked.

"Which one?"

"The Chinese kid. The one who took off."

I twisted my head toward the camp. "What do you mean, he took off? What kind of professional killer are you if you can't even keep a kid under your custody? There's going to be hell to pay when my wife finds out you let him out of your sight. He's probably lost and hurt somewhere. Maybe a bear ate him. I hear there's lots of bears in these mountains."

Tiny squinted his eyes like a bear in these woods was a new thought to him, and then he seemed to remember he was pointing a gun at me. "Shut up," he said. "I'm sure the kid's fine. He went to look for the Delta. Jackson and Jillian are going to get him."

"The Delta? You mean Ron? Ron's dead. I found his body. Somebody shot him in the chest. I couldn't even bury him. That awful canyon was too rocky. I just had to leave him there, lying on the cold stone with all those spiders around." I shivered. "Why would Peng go back into that canyon? I wanted to get out of there as soon as I could."

Tiny shivered too. It was clear he didn't even like thinking about the spiders. But he did seem relieved when I said Ron was dead. I needed to keep him a little off balance. I needed him to relax. Most of all, I needed him closer.

I heard JR's voice calling from the camp. "Who's out there?"

Tiny looked past me and yelled, "Shut up, and sit down. If you move, I start breaking fingers."

I looked over my shoulder and then back at Tiny. "That fire looks nice," I said. "I don't know about you, but I'm freezing. I hate camping. And those spiders." I shuddered again. "I keep feeling like they're all over me." I swatted at my hair to emphasize the point.

Tiny shifted his gun from his right hand to his left and brushed at his hair too. "Okay," he said. "Start moving. But no funny stuff. You killed a friend of mine, and money or no money, if you try anything, I'll put a bullet in you."

"You've got my gun. What am I going to do? And for the record, I didn't mean to kill your friend. I just reacted. I didn't think I would really hit him."

My mention of my gun seemed to remind Tiny that it was sitting at his feet. He crouched and picked it up. With my gun now in his right hand, he put his own gun behind his belt. "Get moving," he said, still standing at least ten feet from me. I needed him closer. A lot could be done when facing an armed opponent but not when there was too much space between you. The space made all the difference.

I followed Tiny's instructions and started walking. Then I looked for a convenient tree branch to trip over. I hoped Tiny wouldn't interpret my falling down as an offensive move. As I fell, I began flailing my arms and yelling, "I think there's one of them on me. Get him off."

I heard Tiny sigh heavily and move toward me. I took a peek toward the boys. I didn't see any sign of Peng yet, but he had to be right next to them. The other three were watching me, taking in my act of flailing and ineptness. It must have been convincing because they looked a bit embarrassed. I was no Ron Kelton, that was for sure.

I nodded to the darkness behind the boys and coughed loudly. With Tiny's attention on me, it was time for Peng to make his move. I watched as one by one the boys disappeared from the fire into the woods behind them. I gave them a few seconds to get away and then began to stand. I needed to make sure the boys were out of the field of fire before I tried to disarm Tiny. Fighting over a loaded weapon was dangerous for everyone around.

As I stood, I felt Tiny's gun barrel dig into the small of my back, and I breathed a sigh of relief. The most dangerous part of disarming an opponent behind me was not knowing the location of the weapon. Tiny ground the gun harder into my spine, telling me exactly what I needed to know. It was time to make my move.

I thought back to the countless hours of close-quarters-combat instruction I'd received in my training. We'd spent a great deal of time on how to escape an armed opponent. It was a skill undercover agents often had to use. I remembered the rules: locate the barrel of the gun, move into the opponent, push the weapon up and away, and then remove the threat by taking out the central nervous system of the attacker. Lots of rules, but they all boiled down to a few movements: twist, push, attack.

I spun back toward Tiny, my right hand finding the wrist of his gun hand and my left forearm going up into the side of his neck. The blow should have taken him to the ground, but he seemed barely dazed. His wrist felt like a tree trunk in my hand. I felt him try to pull away and begin to sit. If he did, I was a dead man. It seemed Tiny had received some of the same instruction I had. The rule of thwarting someone who was trying to disarm you was to pull your weapon away from them and sit down. The inertia of sitting while pulling away would line the barrel up on their torso. From there, all you needed to do was pull the trigger. No aiming necessary, no fancy moves. Just sit and shoot.

I pushed tighter up against him and followed him down, continually pushing his gun hand away, feeling the recoil as it fired again and again, hoping against hope that none of the shots would find their way to where the boys were. Finally I heard a click and knew the magazine was empty.

I quickly rolled off Tiny and backed away out of his reach. There was a crazy look in his eyes, and he pointed the weapon at me and fired off several empty rounds.

"I surrender," I said, holding up my hands. "I give up." This had been my plan all along. It was the only plan that really made sense. If I was ever to see Hope and Jin again, I would need to be taken to them. And this meant I had to go as a prisoner. Peng could get the boys to safety, but I needed to stay with the mercenaries.

I was just hoping Tiny's head cleared a bit before he figured out where his spare ammunition was.

Tiny shook his head and rubbed at his neck. "It's been a long time since anyone has taken me to the ground," he said. But his eyes seemed to be losing their crazed look. He almost seemed thoughtful.

"I surrender," I said again. "Your job is to capture me—to take me in alive. You've done it. It's over. All you need to do now is deliver me to the client. Mission accomplished."

Tiny looked over to the campfire and swore. The boys were gone.

"They don't matter," I said. "They are minor players in this game. I'm the one you want, and now you've got me."

"They want both you and your son."

"Peng ran off, remember? Jillian and Jackson are after him. You've got the big prize. You'll be the hero. The other boys are nothing."

He rubbed his neck again, and a smile began to form on his face. I breathed a sigh of relief.

"You're right," he said, beginning to move closer. "I will deliver you to the client, and I will take the credit." He seemed to be looking me up and down. "How much do you weigh?"

A cold shiver began to creep up my back. "Why do you want to know that?"

"No reason. Just calculating how hard it's going to be to haul you out of here on my back."

"I'm perfectly capable of walking."

"You are now," he said, his smile getting broader. "But you decided to engage me in combat. And you killed a friend of mine. You don't think I can let that go, do you?" He continued to move toward me in small steps.

"The client won't like it," I said.

"The contract said to bring you in alive. It didn't specify in what kind of shape. There's a lot I can do to you and still keep you breathing." He looked down at the gun in his hand and threw it off to the side. Then he began laughing.

All I could think of were Ron's words of warning: *he likes to play with his food before he kills it.*

Chapter 25
A LITTLE HELP FROM MY FRIENDS

I SAW THE GLEAM IN Tiny's eyes and wondered how I was going to get myself out of this one. I decided I had only one chance.

"Wait. Is that Ron?" I said, looking behind him.

As Tiny's head whipped around, I gathered my strength and started sprinting the other direction. I didn't like abandoning my plan to surrender myself, but I wouldn't be much good to Hope and Jin if I was missing some essential limbs. I figured Tiny's bulk might hinder him in the trees. If I could get even a small lead, I was confident I could lose him. The first hundred yards would be the key. If he caught me in that stretch, I would be like a mouse in the grasp of a mountain lion.

I prayed that he would trip and fall.

He didn't.

As I entered a clearing, I heard his footsteps, and I swore I could feel his breath on my back. It smelled like stale Easy Cheese. His legs must have been as strong as the rest of him because he seemed to cover the distance about three times as fast as I did. There was no way I was going to escape. So I did the next best thing. I dropped to my knees and threw my fist into his approaching groin. His momentum took him through the air and over the top of me. I got up and ran again. Between the placement of the blow and his speed coming toward me, he'd be on the ground for several minutes.

But within seconds, he was standing in front of me, smiling his sadistic smile, stretching to crack the bones in his neck, waiting to inflict some serious pain. "The smaller guys always go there," he said. "That's why I started wearing protection on every job."

I had no choice now. I took a deep breath and tried to remember my training. *Self defense will get you killed,* Zack's voice boomed inside my head. *The only thing that will keep you alive is eliminating the threat.* I began to locate the targets on Tiny's body that would disable his central nervous system and make it impossible for him to hurt me: eyes, temple, neck, throat, bladder, knees . . . I ruled out the groin. If I could strike one or multiple of these targets, any man, no matter how large, would go down. The problem with Tiny was that he was not only large, but he was also so layered with muscle that it was almost as if he were wearing body armor. I'd felt it when I'd hit him in the side of the neck earlier. I'd felt it when I'd pushed against his wrist to keep him from shooting me. Anything short of a crippling blow would just incite him into a murderous rage.

I took another breath as he circled and tried to think back to more of Zack's training. *The advantage of facing a big man is that you can use his own momentum against him.* I told myself this was no different than facing Zack. He was about Tiny's size—bigger in those days—and Zack had been wearing full body armor when we'd faced him. But then again, Zack had been trying to teach us, not cripple us.

Tiny got tired of circling and stepped in with a roundhouse punch. He probably expected me to move backward, away from the punch, or put up my hands to try to block it. That would have been the reflexive thing to do, but my reflexes had been trained differently. I moved into him and slightly to the side. My left arm came up, not to block his fist but to guide it past me as I stepped in even more and used the leverage of his swing to put my right arm against his head and let his momentum pull us both down in a circular motion toward the ground. I hoped his head would land on a rock. Instead, we landed on grass softened by a trickling spring. When his head hit, it sounded like he had landed on a damp, squishy pillow. I rose to continue my attack, but he pulled up his knees and threw me through the air and past him.

My back hit a tree, and the air went out of me. For a moment, I panicked. I couldn't feel my legs, and I couldn't catch my breath. Tiny bellowed into the night like a wounded bear, and I feared I had awakened a hidden beast. At least I wouldn't be able to feel anything as he ripped my legs from my body.

But then I felt the tingling return to my limbs, and my struggling lungs finally found the air they sought. I was still seeing stars as I heard Tiny approaching. I thought about playing dead but, for some reason, remembered Ron's instructions about dealing with a bear encounter: if the bear is just surprised, playing dead might work to let it know you are not a threat, but if the bear is predatory, you'd better just fight for your life. I thought that Tiny could safely be classified in the second category. I didn't think he was used to being taken down in a fight—especially by a smaller man. I might not have hurt him, but I had deeply wounded his pride.

I lay there and tried to control my rapidly beating pulse, realizing that surprise might be the only weapon I had left. I could feel his body towering over me, and I heard his heavy breathing.

"You're going to pay for that," he growled through his breaths. "Nobody takes me down like that. Nobody." He stopped speaking for a second, and it sounded like he was pounding the palm of his hand against the side of his head. "And you got water in my ear," he said finally. "I hate water in my ears."

For a big, strong guy, Tiny seemed to have a lot of little things that bothered him. The problem was I now seemed to be on the top of that list.

I felt his large hands reaching toward me like crab claws, threatening to crush me in their grip.

I kicked out, and my foot caught the inside of his knee. I felt his kneecap move from the front of his leg over to the side, and he roared in pain. I tried to follow with another kick to the bladder, but I was in an awkward position, and I couldn't get much leverage. Instead, I caught him in the stomach. For most people, that might have also been a desirable target, but Tiny had abs like corrugated iron, and I thought the impact might have broken something in my foot, not in him.

But I didn't have time to test it because Tiny's rage overcame his pain, and his hands finally found their way to my body. He lifted me as if I were a rag doll and shook me as he roared. I tried to put my thumbs in his eyes, but he flipped me around, pulled his forearm into my throat, and locked it in place with his other hand. I was officially done. Once again the air was driven from my body, and I was sure this time that I would not get it back.

There were moves I had been taught to escape such a hold, but for some reason, my brain couldn't remember what any of them were. I watched as the light began to fade. I heard a loud crack and thought that maybe the bones in my neck had broken, but then Tiny said, "Ouch," and loosened his grip just enough that I caught a quick breath.

"Ouch," Tiny said again. "Hey, stop that."

Out of the corner of my eye, I saw movement. Someone was attacking Tiny, hitting him on the head with large sticks. At first I thought maybe Ron had dispatched Jackson and Jillian quicker than expected, but then my heart sank. The four boys that I'd thought were long gone, the same four boys Hope had made me promise to keep safe, were now moving around like dwarves attacking a cyclops. Not only had I failed to win the fight, but it had all been for nothing.

Their efforts were valiant and extremely courageous as one by one they darted in and whacked Tiny's head, but aside from a slight lessening of Tiny's grip around my throat, the blows weren't having much impact. Mere mosquitoes buzzing around a dragon's head. Enough to annoy but not to inflict any real damage.

"You boys just wait," Tiny said between curses. "I'm going to tear you limb from limb."

But the boys didn't stop. Eric stepped in for a swing, and Tiny caught the stick in his free hand. With one motion, he threw the stick, and Eric went flying with it. Eric got up quickly from the ground, but this seemed to make the other boys more cautious.

"Oh, I'm gonna have fun watching you boys cry," Tiny said as he once again increased the pressure on my throat. I felt myself blacking out.

"Let him go," Joey said, stepping in front of the big man. Tiny was on one knee, the other one grinding into my back. Joey looked him directly in the eye.

Tiny laughed. "What are you going to do, little man?"

Joey didn't say anything; he just held up one hand in front of Tiny's face and arced the other arm behind his head in what looked to be some sort of martial arts pose.

I felt Tiny's chest heave up and down as he began to laugh. "Is that supposed to be some sort of Power Ranger move or something?"

Joey nodded. "I call it the spider," he said, and then he opened his outstretched hand, revealing one of the large arachnids from Spider Hollow. He pushed it toward Tiny's face. The man began to yell, and as he opened his mouth the spider jumped inside, perhaps searching for a place of refuge. Tiny began flailing, but he didn't release his hold on my neck. He did, however, ease up enough for me to catch a few precious breaths, and suddenly I remembered clearly what I had been taught about escaping the grip of a choke hold.

In training they referred to it as joint manipulation. In practicality, it meant finding and breaking the little finger. I found Tiny's little finger, and I broke it. He screamed, but it was muffled by the gagging noises he was making trying to expel the spider from its new hole. As I took control of his hand, I spun around and used his weight against him, pulling his arm behind his back and dislocating his shoulder with a nasty pop. That was also joint manipulation. A normal person would have been out of commission at this point, but this was Tiny, and his strength was anything but normal.

I followed up with a fist to his windpipe and then a hard forearm to the temple. Despite all of this, he rose to his full height, holding at his throat and slapping at his open mouth. I hit him in the throat again with little impact. But with the third blow, his eyes rolled to the top of his head. He tottered for a minute and then crashed to the ground like a mighty redwood bouncing hard before settling into stillness. The spider crawled out of his mouth and scampered quickly into the underbrush. Joey breathed a sigh of relief.

I was also breathing, deep and clear, but still trying to recover fully. Peng, Eric, and JR tentatively made their way up to where Joey and I were standing. We all looked at the fallen giant, and for some reason, it felt like we were looking out upon the Grand Canyon, awestruck at the spectacle.

"That was one big dude," JR said.

Eric turned to me, his mouth still open in awe. "You took him out, Brother Knight. I can't believe it."

"I had some help from my friends," I said, suddenly realizing I didn't just like these boys; I loved them. I held out my arms, and we shared a group hug that somehow didn't seem the least bit awkward. "I wouldn't have made it without you guys. Thank you."

I released the boys and looked at Peng. "I thought the plan was to take these guys out of here."

Peng shrugged. "Joey wouldn't let us leave without you."

"And you can't say no to Joey," JR added. "He's a tough kid."

"That he is," I said as I ruffled my hands through Joey's hair. "You all are. I think you are some of the bravest people I've ever known."

"Hey, Brother Knight," Eric said. "You should be a cage fighter. That was awesome. Where'd you learn those MMA moves?"

I thought about it and almost laughed. "You wouldn't believe me."

"C'mon," JR said. "You have to tell us."

"My old bishop taught me," I said, silently grateful to Zack for his training. "It's amazing what you can learn from a good bishop."

Chapter 26
A TEA PARTY

HOPE FELT THE HAND OVER her mouth and opened her eyes to darkness. The room was completely black. She could hear Permelia snoring and Jin babbling the way she sometimes did in her sleep. Then the stale smell of cologne assaulted her senses and made her want to gag. She was getting ready to bite the hand and begin screaming when a small penlight came on. She could see Buck in front of her, his eyes bright with excitement, and his finger over his lips. He took his hand away from her mouth.

"It's time," he whispered.

"Time for what?"

"Time for escape." Buck turned around and began heading for the door.

Hope sat up and began to reach for Jin.

Buck turned around and shook his head. "Just you."

"I'm not leaving my baby," Hope hissed.

"We're coming back," Buck whispered. "I'm just showing you the way." He shrugged. "Or don't come. It's up to you."

The light went out. Hope heard the door open, and she hurried to follow. Had she made some inroads with Buck? Was he really going to help them escape? Something bothered her as she moved behind him in the darkness. But maybe it was just the way he seemed to be one with the night.

Before she knew it, they were across the empty expanse of floor and outside in the night air. She breathed in deeply and looked up at the stars, saying a silent prayer to protect Jin and Permelia while she was out of the room.

Buck kept the light off as they moved past several outbuildings. He darted his head from side to side. Several times he stopped suddenly, listening to the sounds of the night. He seemed worried about getting caught. Hope took this as a good sign.

In the glow of the night, she could see that Permelia was correct—they were at some kind of abandoned airfield. There was a line of mostly dilapidated buildings set back from the runway, as well as a few larger hangars like the one they had just left. The wind blew furiously, pushing tumbleweeds across the ground and drowning out all noise. They were headed toward what looked to be an old house—an old haunted house. It was a two-story wood structure that seemed to want to collapse in on itself. The wind rushing through it made a howling noise, and one of the shutters on an upper floor slammed rhythmically against a window, just like a scene from an old horror movie. Hope shivered. Ghosts didn't scare her, but there was something about this situation that made the hair on the back of her neck stand up and take notice.

They moved around to the back of the house, and Buck led them down a set of steps to a basement entrance. He opened the door, and they stepped in. Hope stopped, stunned at what lay in front of her. The inside of the creepy old house looked nothing like the outside. No rotting wood, no spiderwebs hanging eerily from the ceiling, no darkness at all. Just warm, glowing light coming from hundreds of small lit candles. In the middle of the room was a high four-poster bed with the comforter pulled down like she would find in an expensive boutique hotel. On the side of the room was a small table with two chairs and a flower arrangement in the middle. Two plates were topped with round aluminum covers, and Hope could smell the aroma of the food wafting out of the small holes in the centers. There was a bottle of wine in a canister of ice and a crystal goblet next to each plate. The linens were snow white, and the silverware was expensive.

She looked back and forth from the table to the bed, confused. How was any of this going to help them escape? And then, to her horror, she understood.

She spun around on Buck. He had moved from directly behind her to the small table and was pouring the wine into a glass.

"What is this?" she said, her voice sounding stronger than she felt. How had she allowed herself to be led out of the room, away from Jin and Permelia? How had she allowed herself to even be in this situation?

"I told you," Buck said, swirling the wine in the glass and sniffing it. "This is a stressful situation. I'm here to offer you some escape."

"You lied to me."

"Excuse me, ma'am, but technically I did not. I offered to help you escape, and that's what I'm doing. I never said I would let you run away. So why don't you just sit down, enjoy a fine meal with some good company, and then let's just see how the night progresses."

Hope looked at the bed and felt sick. "Nothing is going to progress any-where."

Buck followed her gaze. "Oh, don't worry about that. That's just for ambiance. Let's just focus on having a nice bite to eat and some good conversation."

Hope reached for the door behind her and found it was somehow locked from the outside. She felt her heart beating in her throat. She realized it had been a long time since she'd felt real fear. Oh, she had feared for her children, for Peng and where he disappeared to at night, for Jin when her fever was high, but since she had passed over to the other side that night years ago and felt the light and the overwhelming love and the reality of what death was like, she had no longer ever feared for herself. But she was afraid now—not for what lay on the other side but for what could happen to her in this world. She knew one thing for sure: she would much rather taste death again than be in this room with this man.

"You might as well just take me back," she said. "There's no way this evening is going to play out like you want it to. I'll die before I let you touch me."

Buck smiled and shrugged, buttering a small roll and popping it into his mouth. "I thought you might say that," he said, not bothering to swallow his food before he spoke. "And that's the one thing I learned from Dempsey: always, always, always have a plan B."

"Dempsey isn't going to like this," Hope said, barely able to catch her breath. "He said he would kill you if you touched me."

Buck shook his head, still grinning. "He's said things like that before. He hasn't killed me yet. You sure you won't reconsider? These rolls are divine."

Buck reached behind him and pulled a gun with a large rectangular barrel out of his belt. Something seemed off about it, but Hope still began to silently pray again, for Jin and Matt and Peng, begging the Lord to watch over them when she was gone. She braced herself. She wasn't ready to leave her family behind, but even so, she was not going to indulge Buck.

"You might as well shoot," she said. "I'm not going to play your games."

Buck nodded as if resigned and raised the gun. She waited but heard only a loud pop and then a whirring as silver filaments of light reached toward her and buried themselves in her chest. She now realized what was wrong with the gun. Buck was not going to kill her—he was going to tase her.

He chuckled as he saw her understanding. "There's no need for you to die. We'll just have a nice dinner, maybe a little snuggle, and you'll be back in your room before you know it."

Hope looked down at the prongs that had lodged in her chest and felt a wave of panic rising. Then everything turned white. She had to be falling, but she couldn't see, hear, or feel anything. There was just whiteness and a static-like buzzing, like someone had found an empty channel on the television and forced it inside her head.

It felt like a long time before sound began to return, like someone talking from another room—talking and humming. She recognized that voice, a chillingly cheerful voice that seemed out of place like raucous laughter at a funeral. She tried to place a name to it and finally landed on Buck. He was saying something to her about relaxing and having a good time.

He was carrying her, and although his voice sounded far away, his face must have been right next to her ear. Why wouldn't her eyes work? She tried to blink, but nothing happened. Were they open or closed? She couldn't tell.

She tried to move her arms, to kick, to make something in her body respond to her slowly awakening brain. Nothing worked. She had never felt so utterly powerless in all of her life.

She felt something hard press up against her back. She was relieved that it didn't feel like the soft pillow on the bed. She tried blinking again, and this time it worked. She still couldn't move her limbs, but the whiteness in her vision began to fade, and suddenly she could see again. She looked down at her body. Silver prongs like fish hooks were still stuck inside her blouse. She took her eyes from her chest and looked in front of her.

Buck had set her in a chair beside the table like a little girl would place a doll at a tea party. Hope expected that she would be stiff as a board, but her body looked limp and loose. Periodic spasms ran through her, and she could see that her hands were shaking. It was as if she were looking at somebody else's hands.

Buck was talking. She realized he had never stopped talking. He was carrying on a conversation as if he were out with his best girl on a date. She couldn't feel much, but she was sure she could feel a coldness running up her spine. This man was insane. How had she ever thought to appeal to his inner sense of decency?

She tried hard to concentrate on his words. If she could keep him talking until her body woke up, maybe she could do something. She almost laughed at her predicament, but her throat wouldn't let her. She was barely even able to breathe, though, so what was she going to do to keep him talking? His words seemed like a litter of small puppies, each one trying to go off in its own direction as she attempted to shoo them back to the center. She squeezed her eyes shut, and finally Buck's words started to form into sentences that made some sense.

"I always knew I was special," he said. "Even as a small boy. I was different from the other kids. They would get upset when others were angry at them. Not me. If the teacher was displeased with me, I just thought it was funny.

"Sharp things have always fascinated me. The doctor told my momma— this was before she ran off and left me with Granny—that most kids and most people had a natural aversion to sharp things and sticking them in others. Not me. I wanted to see what would happen. That got me in big trouble when I stuck a freshly sharpened pencil in the neighbor boy. I'll never forget his look of surprise. The doctor said that less than one percent of the population would be able to do what I had done. The thing is I never felt bad because I never felt I'd done anything wrong. I'm kind of missing the guilt gene. I guess you could say I'm one of a kind.

"Say, you don't mind if I have another roll, do you? I know I've been taking more than my share, but I don't think you're quite ready to chew yet."

Hope watched him put another roll inside his mouth and could smell the garlic on his breath. She really wanted to throw up, but her body wouldn't cooperate. Maybe if she could ruin his dinner party, he would leave her alone. It had worked for Permelia. But Hope couldn't even manage to make herself sick. She tried to scream with frustration, but all that emerged was a small squeak.

Buck stopped chewing and smiled. "You're getting your voice back," he said. "That usually comes first. I'm going to have to eat more slowly. I really am looking forward to some good conversation."

Hope tried desperately to get her throat to work. A few more squeaks came out of her mouth, and then she forced herself to relax and actually managed a hoarse whisper. "Why?" she asked.

Buck's eyes lit up. "That was good," he said. "Usually it takes a lot longer. You should be proud of yourself."

"Why?" The word was still a whisper, but this time it at least sounded more like a word.

"Why should you be proud? Because not only are you probably the prettiest woman I've ever had dinner with, but you may also be the strongest. Usually there are a lot of tears. Tears and begging. That can be interesting at first, but it gets tiresome after a while. You didn't do any of that. Even when you thought I was going to shoot you. You should be real proud of yourself. I don't think you are like any other woman I've ever met."

"Why?" Hope asked a third time. This time her voice was no longer a whisper, but her tongue felt like it kept getting in the way, like when she answered the dentist's questions in the chair.

Buck sighed and smiled. "You know I'm just messin' with you, right? I knew what you meant when you asked it the first time. You want to know why I would do something like this. But if you'd been listening—and I know that might have been difficult in your current state—but if you'd been listening, you would know that I already explained it. I'm not like other people. I'm curious about things most people won't let themselves think about. And one of the things that fascinates me the most is beautiful women and how they react to me. Some of them say I'm evil. That seems to be easier for them than to acknowledge the truth. I'm just curious—curious about a lot of things. But if you want to think of me as evil, that works too."

Hope looked into his eyes. What Buck was doing to her was terrible, but the fear had left her. For a moment, she saw him as a little boy, as a baby growing up in an abusive home, hiding himself behind some dark psychology to protect himself against the pain. She tested her tongue and found that she could move it a little. Her words were slow and thick, but she managed to almost produce another word. "Please."

Buck shook his head. "I guess it was inevitable. Now comes the begging and the pitiful pleas. I was hoping for better from you."

"Not begging," Hope said. "Not for me." She tried with great effort to make her words understandable. "For you. For your sake. Don't do this. You don't have to be like this. You can be better."

Buck's smile came back. "Look around you. I created an imaginary tea party so I could pretend we were dating. When you refused to eat with me, I hit you with a taser. Haven't you been listening to anything I've been saying? I hurt people, and I don't feel bad about it. I find it amusing. If you're not pleading for yourself, you should be. As for me, I'm beyond fixing."

Hope felt her tongue loosening. The words were coming easier now. "Please," she said again, tears filling her eyes. "You don't understand. No matter what you do to me, I will be okay. I've felt the light before. I've felt its power. There's nothing you can do to me physically or emotionally that won't heal. But you're headed down a path that leads to misery. Please don't do this. You can change. It's not too late."

Buck stopped smiling and jumped out of his chair. "Don't give me that garbage," he said, pointing an accusing finger at Hope. "Granny used to tell me the same thing. She used to say I could be good if I wanted to. The last time she said it was the last time she spoke. Maybe you're right. Maybe I'm not evil. But if that's the case, there's no such thing as evil. It's like one of Dempsey's little games—good and evil are just the rules people make up to help them feel better about playing. And then it's game over. Do not pass go, do not collect $200. That's it. There's not even anyone around to know who the winner was and who the loser was. At least the way I play makes it interesting."

"You're wrong."

"And how would you know that? I have just as much right as anyone else to say what the game is."

"I know because I've been there," Hope said, her tongue finally allowing her to speak powerfully without slurring. "I had cancer. I died. I've seen what's on the other side, and it's full of light and love and goodness for those who try to do their best. Your game theory is just a fantasy you've made up to cope with life, and it's not going to end well for you. It's not game over when we die. It's just the beginning."

Buck reacted as if she had slapped him, and he reached again for his taser. "I think the effects are wearing off," he said. "You need another jolt."

"It won't change the truth," Hope said. "I'm right, and you know it. You think you're brave by hurting people and not feeling anything. But you're a coward. You're afraid to face the truth, not because you don't believe it but because you don't want to feel the hurt. So you tell yourself there's nothing. You say you're special, but you're just like all the rest of us, trying to get through the pain of life and crying out for help in the darkness. It wasn't your fault. You were just a broken little boy in a messed-up home. But you don't have to stay broken. You have a choice."

Buck leveled the taser at her. "Stop talking." His relaxed smile and manner were gone. "I can't listen to this anymore."

"Then shoot me," Hope said. "It's your choice. But do it like a man. Admit that you're angry at me because I won't play your game. Don't blame it on a fake childhood derangement you've decided to use as an excuse."

Buck raised the gun, but then his hand seemed to relax a bit. "And what if I decided not to zap you again? If I just take you back to your room? What will you think about me then? You've seen what I was going to do to you. You've heard what I've done to others. One act of kindness won't change any of that."

"It would be a start," Hope said. "Despite the situation we're in, you are someone I thought could be decent—someone I really wanted to like."

Something changed in Buck's eyes, and he began to lower the taser gun.

The door burst open, and Dempsey walked in, a pistol leveled in his hand. His eyes swept the room and then landed on Buck. His voice sounded almost regretful. "I warned you about this, Buck. You just can't help yourself."

The shot rang out before Hope even had a chance to scream. Just before Buck crumpled to the floor, he looked in Hope's direction. A look of realization filled his eyes. A look of realization and utter terror.

Hope felt her chest begin to rise and fall with sobs. She'd been so close. She'd been getting through to him. Now it was too late.

"Are you . . . uh . . . hurt?" Dempsey asked.

Hope's sobbing was now uncontrollable. Her hands spasmed as some of the feeling came back into her body. She shook her head no, but she didn't mean it. Yes, she was hurt. She hurt as much as she'd ever hurt in her life. The tears poured out of her like a river of blood. Dempsey picked her up and headed out of the room. She looked at Buck as they left, his body lying on the floor, his dead eyes staring out into nothingness.

She had been so close.

She had been too late.

* * *

Dempsey carried Hope back to her room. She was lighter than he'd imagined she would be. He realized how small she really was and how much her strength of personality made her seem larger. The old woman came at him as soon as he opened the door. When she saw Hope crying in his arms, she backed off but was poised to pounce.

"What did you do to her?" she asked.

"Easy," Dempsey said. "I saved her. She'll be all right. Buck used a taser."

"Where is that little psychopath?" Permelia said. "Just let me get my hands on him."

"He's dead. I shot him."

Dempsey laid Hope on her bed, and Permelia went to her. Hope was still sobbing uncontrollably, and her whole body was trembling. Permelia bent over her and stroked her head.

"Did he hurt her?"

"I don't think so. I think I got there in time."

Hope whispered something to Permelia that Dempsey couldn't hear and then began crying again.

"She's probably in shock," Dempsey said. "She's been through a traumatic experience."

Permelia looked at Dempsey like his mom used to. "You know for someone who thinks he's smart, you can be pretty dense sometimes."

"What do you mean?"

"She's not crying because of what Buck did to her; she's crying for what you did to Buck."

"But he tased her," Dempsey said. "He had a bed set up. Who knows what else he was planning. Buck was a predator, and this world's probably a better place without him. Why would she be crying for him?"

"Because there was a chance," Permelia said. "Or at least Hope thought there was a chance. I can't say I agree with her, but Hope's not just her name; it's who she is. Right now, she's crying because you took away that boy's opportunity to change his life."

Dempsey was a little taken aback. The woman was crying over Buck? The man who had stolen her away in the middle of the night and used electricity to paralyze her body?

"That's not the worst of it," Permelia said. "She's probably praying for your soul right now too. Now get out of here. You aren't worthy to be in her presence."

Dempsey turned around and left, still shaking his head.

Chapter 27
ATTRACTION

RON WAITED. EARLIER, HE HAD heard the faint sound of voices approaching the entrance to the canyon. He hadn't heard the crashing of rocks or the cursing of surprise. They had discovered his trap. It was to be expected. Even though Jackson hadn't officially graduated from Delta school, he had been through the training. If he was smart enough to avoid the trip wire, he surely wouldn't be stupid enough to come into the canyon through the main entrance.

Ron had steadied himself under his homemade crutch and hobbled off to a secondary location. He hadn't hurried. After discovering the trip wire, they would be moving more slowly. And slowing them down was his prime purpose in this fight. He had lost a lot of blood. The odds of him engaging two trained killers and coming out on top were not very good. But that didn't really matter. As long as Matt had enough time to get the boys to safety, his mission would be accomplished. He'd already died once today—already seen the highlights of his life pass before his eyes. He'd always known he'd get the chance to sacrifice his life someday. He'd known it since he was a kid. He just didn't think it would be this soon.

He imagined the route they would take in their approach. It wasn't hard to do. He just needed to try to think like Jackson. That was easy. Jackson would think like a Delta. He would think like Ron. Jackson would take the same route he would take in a similar situation—the fissure that cut off a few meters before the entrance to the canyon. That was the easy part. The hard part was to know what Jackson would do after he emerged from the fissure. Unlike the main entrance, there was no good vantage point where Ron could see them when they came out. There was good cover for at least thirty yards. The best Ron could do was pin them down until his ammo ran out, which wouldn't be very long. There were two of them, and they could take turns providing cover fire as the other one moved to flank him. His Glock 23 held thirteen rounds. He figured this would give him about five minutes once the shooting began, maybe ten or fifteen if they were really cautious and he was really lucky. He had no illusions as to what would happen after that. Even with the crutch, he couldn't move fast, and his shooting hand had already been rendered useless.

He still might be able to take one of them out in the encounter, and he wanted it to be Jackson. Despite Jillian's shooting him, he didn't harbor any ill will toward her. She was a product of her environment. Jackson, on the other hand, had managed to receive all the advantages of Delta operator training and was still screwed up.

Ron winced as he wedged himself into position. He thought he heard a rattling of rocks near where the fissure would be. Soon it would be time.

* * *

It was easier than Jillian thought to find the back trail into the canyon. What looked precarious from below was actually not too bad, except in a couple of places. The trail was easy to find and easy to follow, and from the markings on the ground, she got the feeling it had been traveled recently by more than just a mountain goat.

She wondered if this had all been a ruse and whether she and Jackson might find nothing but an empty canyon when they got inside. But the one thing she didn't see was blood. If the Delta had come out this way, he probably would have left a trail.

She thought about turning around, finding Jackson, and telling him the prey had most likely left the area, but every step she took into the canyon made the hair on the back of her neck stand up. There was danger in front of her, she was sure of it. So she pressed forward, turning what should be fear into excitement, proving to herself that she was not a whiny little girl.

And then she rounded a corner and saw the body. It was wedged into the hole of a rock, and all she could see was the tip of a gun and a few fingers on one hand. The hand wasn't moving. Maybe the Delta had set his trap and then crawled into a hole to die. But then the hand moved. Just slightly, but it moved.

Jillian wasn't sure what she had expected to feel at seeing the Delta alive. Maybe the furious anger she had felt earlier when he had said the things he'd said about her mother, maybe satisfaction at getting the opportunity to kill him again, maybe anything other than what she was feeling right now, which was a sense of relief that he wasn't dead. Why would she feel relieved? The thought of killing someone had never bothered her before. At least not for many years. She shook her head to clear it. The encounter with the little chubby kid had rattled her. And what was the Delta doing down there in those rocks anyway?

Then she realized: the Delta knew exactly what Jackson was up to. He wasn't watching the front entrance; he was positioned to catch someone shimmying up a hidden fissure and coming into the canyon from a more protected location. He was positioned perfectly to intercept Jackson when he emerged.

She felt the rush of exhilaration again and wondered what was happening to her. She was just curious, she told herself. It would be interesting to watch a battle between two men who had been trained in the unit. Of course, one of them was wounded pretty badly. He must have been wearing body armor under his shirt to have survived the shots to his chest, but the wounds in his hand and leg were no illusion. Jackson should have the upper hand in this contest. She suppressed the urge to laugh.

Her smile turned into a grimace when she realized how exposed her current position was, moving across the trail along the face of the cliff. If the Delta poked his head out and looked in her direction, he would surely see her. She needed to get to better cover before the shooting began. She also needed to make sure she didn't dislodge any rocks and accidentally expose herself. She started to move to a more secure spot.

Jackson's head popped up from the fissure, and he immediately nodded in her direction, letting her know he had seen her. She was too visible in the waning moonlight if he had spotted her that quickly.

A few large boulders blocked the Delta's view of Jackson, but as soon as Jackson moved a few yards farther, he would become an easy target. For a moment, Jillian nearly allowed things to play out, not letting Jackson know he was heading for an ambush. She wondered if the Delta would give any warning or just take Jackson out. He was a religious man, after all, and a Scout leader, but he had also been trained to kill. Would he have the guts to take the shot?

She sighed, put two fingers to her eyes, and then pointed to the Delta's position, letting Jackson know he was being watched. Observing a death match between two highly trained gladiators would have to wait. They had a mission to complete, and the Delta was in the way.

"Hey, Kelton," Jackson yelled into the darkness. "You might as well give it up. You're wounded pretty badly, and we've got you surrounded."

What was Jackson doing?

"You don't believe me? Take a peek behind you on the cliff. Jillian's got a bead on you."

Jillian swore and began to move faster. Jackson had just given up her position. He was using her as a distraction to improve his own situation. Before she could take two steps, the Delta emerged from his hole, leveled his pistol with his left hand, and pulled the trigger. No hesitation, no yelling for her to drop her gun, no special treatment because she was a woman. The bullet barely clipped her shoulder, nothing more than a crease, but the impact still spun her around, and she lost her footing on the narrow ledge.

He had shot her. Despite the wound, despite her frantic efforts to stop her slide down the talus slope, despite the fact that she soon might be face-planted on a rock, all she could think about was the Delta.

He had shot her.

She couldn't help but smile. There had been no hesitation. *He had shot her.* She didn't think she had been this attracted to anyone in her entire life.

Chapter 28
GOING BACK

THE BOYS AND I HAD reached the top of the pass and could see the highway below when we heard the first gunshot. All of us turned and looked back in the direction we had come, back toward Spider Hollow, where a wounded Ron was facing two heavily armed mercenaries. I glanced at the boys to see the expressions on their faces and found that they were all staring at me.

"We can't just leave him," Joey said. The countenances of the other boys said they agreed with him. I started to go through all the reasons in my head why going back was a bad idea. Ron was a trained combat operative. He wasn't expecting any of us to be around. Adding a person to the equation might not only be dangerous, but it might also interfere with his plans. Yes, he was wounded and operating on one arm and leg. Yes, he had passed out for over an hour from loss of blood earlier that evening. Yes, it was two against one. And yes, I felt I had received clear instructions from Hope and maybe someone higher that my first priority was to make sure these boys were safe . . . Going back was definitely a bad idea.

Light seemed to be creeping up the backs of the mountains. It would be dawn soon. I looked down at my watch, but it wasn't on my wrist. I must have lost it in the fight with Tiny. It was a small thing, but I felt a sudden pang of loss. That watch had helped me get out of some tough situations, and it probably could have been useful in the very near future. Turning on the GPS would have allowed someone to locate my position. But no one would be looking for my signal unless I alerted them.

I turned around and looked toward the road. I could see a light down below, a camper or maybe a motor home beginning to come to life. No more than an hour's hike and the boys would be safe. I swore I smelled pancakes cooking.

I tried to listen to my heart, but I kept hearing Joey's voice in my head. *We can't just leave him.* "Okay," I said. "Peng, you get the boys down to that camp-site. Tell the people there that you've been separated from your leaders and have been lost in the woods all night. Ask them to take you to Park City, where your parents have a time-share. Have them drop you off at Ron's condo, and wait for us there." I pulled a key out of my pocket. "Here's the extra key." Then I pulled out my wallet and handed Peng a fifty-dollar bill. "Order some pizza. I'll call you as soon as I get out of the mountains and have cell coverage."

"Where will you be?" Peng asked.

"Joey's right. We can't leave Ron. I'm going back to help him." I didn't want to leave the boys, but we had taken care of our giant. The lights below represented the promise of safety and civilization. Ron was still out there, wounded and with two killers to face. Right now he needed me more than the boys did. But still . . .

Peng must have seen my hesitation. "Don't worry," he said. "I'll make sure they're safe. They're my responsibility."

I nodded and began running back down the mountain.

Chapter 29
GRAMS AND PAPA

THE SMELL OF PANCAKES AND frying bacon intensified as they got closer to the camp. Peng's stomach growled. He hadn't realized he was that hungry until now, but he could almost hear the eggs cracking onto a hot skillet and smell the maple syrup warming in a pan.

"I can't take it anymore," Eric said. "I'm going in." He moved to take the lead on the trail.

Peng stopped him with his hand. "We need to wait. We at least need to get a look at them first. We don't know who's down there."

"He's right," JR said. "If I've learned one thing on this trip, it's that we need to listen to Peng. He's our leader."

Peng looked at JR to see if he was being sarcastic, but his expression was serious, and the other two boys nodded in agreement—although Eric's nod was a bit reluctant. Peng felt a sudden wave of emotion that nearly squeezed the air out of his chest. He felt genuine affection for these boys, and he would do anything to protect them. He also felt a sense of power, as if invisible hands were lifting him, helping him to stand straighter and think more clearly. And he understood that the affection and the power were inseparably connected, although he didn't know exactly how.

"Let's move to that hill above the camp," he said. "We'll be able to see who's down there." They followed him without saying a word.

The light of dawn had replaced the darkness in the sky above the hills, but in the hollow, where the motor home was parked, shadows were still in full force. There were two large picnic tables in the campsite, a fire burning in the fire pit, and two camp stoves with empty skillets on them. The food they smelled had been transferred to plates and now sat on the table, covered by tin warmers like in a hotel. Inside the motor home, the light was on, but the door was on the other side, and there was no sign of people.

Then the door opened and slammed shut, and in the firelight, a shadow of a huge misshapen creature holding what looked to be a battle-ax reared.

The other boys gave a simultaneous gasp when they saw it. The great shadow lumbered its way around the front of the motor home and then shrank into the figure of an old, gray-haired woman holding a spatula.

"That's my grandma!" Eric said a little too loudly.

The old woman cocked her head as if listening.

JR put his hand over Eric's mouth and pulled him down behind the bushes. "That's your grandma down there? Like some sort of divine, bizarre coincidence?" He took his hand off of Eric's mouth to let him answer.

"Not my literal grandma, idiot," Eric said, lowering his voice to match JR's. "But she might as well be. She looks just like her. And my grandma makes the best blueberry pancakes in the world. So why are we whispering? Why aren't we down there throwing ourselves at her feet and worshipping her bacon and eggs? What's she going to do? Spatula us to death?"

JR looked up at Peng and raised his eyebrows. Peng shrugged, and with his silent permission, they made their way down to throw themselves at the mercy of the woman who reminded Eric of his grandma.

Peng was afraid they might startle the woman, coming up on her in the semidarkness, but she barely blinked when she saw them, as if she had been expecting a group of scraggly boys to show up for breakfast before it was light. "You boys are out early," she said. "Getting a head start on the trail?"

"Actually, we've been lost all night," Joey said. He seemed to be the one most determined to keep to the agreed story. And it didn't hurt that he looked like he needed to be mothered. "We got separated from our leaders and have been trying to find our way back to our camp." His voice cracked when he said it. Eric stared at him in admiration and added his meek nod to the act.

"You must be freezing," the woman said.

"Not really," Eric replied. "We've been hiking pretty hard all night. But we are a little bit hungry."

"Of course you are. And you are in luck. Some of our kids were supposed to meet us this morning, but I don't think they're going to make it. I've just made enough food to feed an army, and I was wondering what I was going to do with it all. You boys go get a plate and then get around that fire. I'll go find Papa and get you some blankets. We'll get you warm and fed, and then we'll help you find your leaders. They must be awfully worried."

"Thank you, ma'am," Eric said, already moving toward the plates. "Those pancakes smell really good."

"I think you'll like them. They're my specialty. And call me Grams—everybody does. Eat as much as you like. I can always cook up more if need be."

"Thank you, Grams," Eric said. "You are one of the most awesome people on the planet." Eric dug into the food, and the other boys were quick to follow.

"I'll be right back," the old woman said, moving around to the door of the motor home.

Peng needed to use the restroom, and after looking around, he spotted a small wooden building about fifty yards up the road. He told the other boys where he was going, but he wasn't sure they heard him. Their complete and total focus was on what they were putting on their plates.

The woman reminded him of someone. She was old like Permelia, but Permelia was thin and wiry; this woman was large and doughy. He was on his way back to the camp before he figured it out. It was her eyes. They reminded him of someone from his past. They were dark and hard. No matter how kind her words or how light her tone, the hardness never left. Her eyes reminded him of Mistress Wu. Peng picked up his pace.

He breathed a sigh of relief when he hit the camp. The boys were sitting around the fire, eating, joking, and having a good time. He walked past the tables with the food and picked up a large knife by the bacon and slipped it under his shirt.

Finally the woman came out holding a stack of blankets. For an instant, with the door open, Peng could hear a man's voice. He recognized it immediately as the voice from Jackson's radio—the gravelly voice that sounded like the rattle in someone's chest when they were dying. It was Jackson's boss.

For a moment, Peng was paralyzed. He had led the boys directly into harm's way. This was the man calling the shots. This was the man telling Jackson and Jillian what to do. They were all practically prisoners again. Despite the smell of the food, Peng felt sick.

Then realization hit: if this was the boss, maybe he knew where to find Hope and Jin.

Suddenly Peng knew what he had to do. He stepped out from behind the tree and quietly let himself into the motor home, removing the knife as he did so. The light inside the vehicle was bright, and although sunlight was also gradually displacing the darkness outside, Peng still needed to pause for a moment to let his eyes adjust.

The man had his back to Peng, and he was talking into his radio. "Yes, all the boys are here, even the son." The man was wearing headphones, and there was silence for a moment as he listened to someone talking on the other end.

"I told you I haven't heard from Jackson in almost an hour, and I don't know the status of the main target." More silence.

"Well, you could have told us the other Scoutmaster was former Delta Force. We might have approached the situation a bit differently . . . Uh-huh . . . Yes . . . I understand. But if you want the kid, I'm still expecting full payment. Uh-huh. Uh-huh. Well, have you ever thought that he will just come to you? Once we bring the kid in, you'll have his whole family. Just send him a text with instructions. As soon as he gets out of these mountains, he'll see it and know what to do. I'd say we've more than held up our end of the bargain."

Once again there was an extended silence.

"You can hardball if you want, Dempsey. But that just means we leave a bunch of unexplained bodies at a campsite and have the authorities asking all sorts of questions. Or we can bring these boys to you and you can pay us the price we agreed on. It's really your call.

"Uh-huh. Well, I can't just leave the other boys to go around talking, and you don't seem to want me to leave any more bodies, so my only choice is to bring them with us. We'll tell them we're taking them to their folks. Maybe Grams can give them some of her special hot chocolate and knock them out.

"Uh-huh. Okay, sounds easy enough to find. We'll see you in a few hours, but Grams is going to be disappointed. She hasn't killed anyone in a long time, and she hates playing grandma to kids."

The man finished his conversation and pulled the headset off. He looked up and paused when he saw the windshield. "I wish you hadn't heard that, boy." The man got up and turned around.

Peng held out the knife in front of him.

"Now, what are you going to do with that?" the man said. "Put it down before you hurt yourself. I'm a trained knife fighter. You're no match for me, son."

Peng believed the man, but he didn't put down the knife. Instead he held it up to his own throat and pressed hard enough to draw blood.

"Son, I'm not sure which school you go to, but I think you might have missed some of the finer points of taking a hostage."

"You will do what I say," Peng said, surprised that his voice was not shaking. "You will call the woman inside, turn on the vehicle, and we will drive away. Once we are far enough down the road, I will give you the knife. You can turn me over to the man on the radio and collect your money."

"And if I call your bluff?"

"Then you will have no Chinese boy to deliver. You will have failed in your mission, and you will not get paid."

"I don't think you've got the guts to do it," the man said.

"Then you don't know me." He saw the man weighing his conviction and met his eyes without wavering.

"One problem," the man said. "If you kill yourself, what's to stop me from doing whatever I want to those other boys?"

"Nothing." Peng tried to keep his voice firm. "But more importantly, you wouldn't get paid. Those boys are of no worth to you. Your contract says you must deliver me. Killing a bunch of Scouts will just put you on the FBI's most-wanted list."

"Already on it," the man said, but Peng could see that his words were getting through. "All right," he said finally. "I wasn't looking forward to riding with a bunch of brats anyway. I'll get Grams in here, and we'll leave your friends to their breakfast. Don't do anything stupid." He opened the door. "Grams," the man yelled. "Could you come in here for a minute?"

Peng began to inch his way slowly toward the back of the motor home. He wanted to keep his distance from the man with the voice of death and the smiling woman with the evil eyes.

The woman appeared in the doorway and said, "Oh my, what have we here?" Her voice still held the singsong friendliness of a helpful matron, but her eyes seemed to turn even darker.

"This boy says he will off himself if we don't take him and leave the other boys. Says he will mess up our payday."

"Oh my," the woman said again. "We can't have that, can we?"

"Pull in the awnings. We're leaving."

"But I was just starting to get to know those boys. It would be rude to leave them without saying anything."

"Just do it."

The woman huffed but did as instructed.

Peng continued to move toward the back.

The man sat in the driver's seat and started the engine. "The only door is up front if you're thinking about sneaking out the back way."

Peng looked around him. The side windows would pop out, and there was a hatch in the top if he needed it, but he wasn't thinking about escape. He just wanted to get one last look at the boys before he left. One last look at his friends.

He made it to the back window just as the motor home pulled away. JR, Eric, and Joey all looked on in shock as distance began to separate them. He still held the knife to his throat, but with his other hand, he motioned for the boys to stay put. "Wait here," he mouthed to them. "Wait for Matt." Then, as he thought about it, he pointed down to the watch around his wrist and mouthed, "Tell Matt." He continued to emphatically point at the watch and mouth the words as the motor home pulled away.

Looking at their faces, Peng felt a sense of loss. He turned away and caught the woman inching toward him, her foot in the air as if she'd been stopped in a game of Mother May I.

"Sit down," he said to her. "You have what you want. Now take me to my mother." Thinking of Hope as his mother didn't feel strange anymore. It felt right.

These awful people would take him to her and to Jin. He would find them, and then he would figure out a way to help them escape.

He sat at the back of the motor home and smiled at the old woman.

She did not smile back.

Chapter 30
GUNFIGHT AT SPIDER HOLLOW

RON CONSCIOUSLY SLOWED HIS HEART rate and tried to assess the situation. His brain wasn't working as efficiently as it normally did, and this made his circumstances even more dangerous. When he'd seen the figure behind him on the cliff face, he'd acted out of reflex. Find the threat, and take it out. When he saw her fall, he felt a tinge of regret. He didn't like having to shoot a woman, but she'd put herself in this situation. And the way she fell made him think his shot had not been a direct hit. She had turned just as he'd shot. If she hadn't died on the way down, he might have to contend with her again. But first things first.

He turned his attention back to Jackson, who had used Jillian as a way to find better cover. He'd darted into the next outcropping of rocks, and Ron considered taking a shot. Maybe if he'd still had the use of his shooting hand, but a snap shot at a moving target with his off hand while balancing on one leg would probably just be a waste of ammunition. And he might need every round he had left.

He had to move. Jackson's current position gave him enough cover to get behind Ron, and he was moving fast. There was no way Ron could match his speed, so he would have to rely on his brains and his training. But Jackson had received the same training. Ron pulled his homemade crutch underneath him and hobbled as quickly as he could toward a small stand of trees. It was the darkest spot in his line of vision and would afford him some cover—at least until daylight came. The full moon, which had highlighted Jillian against the cliff, had moved behind a cloud. Darkness and cover seemed like his best options.

His situation wasn't good. The lay of the land, his opponent's experience, and the condition of his body all worked against him. All evidence suggested that he would not make it out of this canyon alive. He looked at his watch. How long had it been since Matt and Peng had left? His mind was cloudy, and he somehow couldn't make the calculations in his head. He stopped trying and kept moving. He hoped he could give them enough time to recover the boys, get out to the road, and get to safety. That was all he could ask for. That was enough.

He made it to the dark stand of trees and breathed in deeply through his nose. His whole right side throbbed. He needed to find cover so he could drop the crutch, steady his arm, and get off a good shot when Jackson came out of the rocks.

He quickly found the right spot—a fallen log on top of a small rise. A place to rest his arm and steady his aim. Much of the wood was rotten, and though it was still solid enough to use for his arm, it wouldn't give him any protection from return fire. He looked around for a better spot, and then he stopped. There was movement in the rocks.

Jackson was already at the far edge of the outcropping. One short dash through the open and he would be in the rocks, which would conceal him until he could get behind Ron and have his choice of spots from which to pick him off. Ron needed to stop him here, now. But as soon as he fired, he would expose his position, and any return fire would cut right through the log.

He felt his hand shaking. *I'd give my right arm to have my shooting hand back*, he thought, and then he almost started laughing out loud. He forced himself to breathe, to concentrate, to focus on the mission.

Jackson darted across the opening, and Ron fired three times in rapid succession, hoping one of the shots would hit the mark. Jackson jerked unnaturally. He'd been hit but unfortunately not enough to slow him down. He disappeared into the rocks, and Ron waited for the return fire to begin. Instead he heard cursing. Maybe Ron had hit his shooting arm. At least they would be almost even now. Two one-armed shooters trying to kill each other. But Jackson still had both his legs and kept the advantage.

Just the thought of moving again made Ron cringe. The sky was lightening, the fresh air filled his lungs, and although his body hurt in multiple places, he was quite comfortable in this spot. He'd always dreamed of going out like this—pinned down on a lone hillside, sacrificing himself for his friends. He'd pictured it in his head a thousand times. It was why he had never married. Even after leaving the force, Ron had been sure this was the way he was going to go out. This canyon filled with spiders wasn't the best spot in the world, but he figured it was good enough. He wanted so badly just to close his eyes . . .

Move. Ron snapped his eyes open, looking around to see who had spoken to him. No one was there. Jackson had gone silent, which meant he'd probably finished tending his wound and was ready to fight again.

Move. He heard it again, except he didn't really hear it. It was more of a feeling than a voice.

He sighed. "I guess this isn't the place," he said quietly, and then he grabbed his crutch and began to hobble away as quickly as he could.

No sooner was he free from his nest than the bullets came. The spot where he had been lying was being peppered with shots, and the log disintegrated in a cloud of wood dust. He took one more longing look behind him as he lurched over a rise to a point of temporary safety.

The crutch jarred his entire body with every step. But he moved, not sure exactly where he was going but finding himself heading back toward the entrance to the canyon. Maybe he could get out in time to set off the trip wire and trap Jackson inside. Except he wouldn't be trapped. There was a back way out.

He wondered whether Jillian was dead or just wounded. He hoped she wasn't lying somewhere injured with no one to come to her aid. And then he wondered why he would hope for any such thing. Was it because she was a woman? Was it because he had heard her story of her childhood and it had almost broken his heart? Or was it just because his brain was still cloudy and jumping from one strange thought to another?

The opening to the canyon appeared in front of him, and he pushed himself to get there before it was too late. The last hundred yards would be completely unprotected, and he would be an easy target if he didn't make it unseen.

He was almost there and nearly ready to breathe a sigh of relief when he heard the unmistakable click of a bullet being chambered.

"I think that's far enough," Jackson said. He must have sprinted to catch up, but he didn't even sound winded.

Ron looked behind him. He'd been right. Jackson's right hand was wrapped in a bloody bandage. He was holding the gun with his left hand, but his aim looked steady. Even so, if Ron dove for the opening, he might have a chance. Jackson was at least thirty yards away, not certain range for a handgun, especially shooting with the wrong hand.

"I wouldn't even think about it if I were you." This time the voice was different, more feminine yet harder. Jillian stepped out from the canyon opening, her gun leveled at his head. She was scraped and tattered, but she was alive. "Why don't you take that gun out of your belt and set it on that rock over there." Jillian spoke low and soft, almost gently now.

Ron did as she said.

"You shot me," Jillian said, her eyes accusing him.

"You shot me first. Three times in the chest. I think you might have cracked some of my ribs."

"Your bullet pushed me off a mountain." Jillian turned, showing her scraped and bleeding back.

"But you didn't die."

"Neither did you."

"I guess that makes us about even, then," Ron said.

To his surprise, Jillian lowered her gun and smiled. "I guess it does."

"Boy, am I glad to see you," Jackson called out as he made his way toward them.

Jillian's smile turned to a grimace. She raised her gun again, but this time she pointed it toward Jackson. "Why don't you stop right there," she said.

"What are you doing?" Jackson said, continuing to walk toward them.

"I said stop." Jillian's voice was icy, and this time Jackson did as she said. "You gave up my position on the hill."

"He had me pinned," Jackson said. "It was nothing personal, just good tactics. Besides, it all worked out in the end."

Jackson said it nonchalantly, but Jillian was watching his gun. "Why don't you put your weapon on that rock next to you," she said.

Jackson's eyes flashed humor, but there was a dangerous note in his voice. "Now, why would I do a thing like that?"

"Because if you don't, I'll put two rounds in your forehead. You know I'll do it, so don't waste any more time."

Jackson's humor disappeared as he placed his gun gently on the rock. "What are you doing, babe? You know we have a mission to complete."

Jillian barely moved as she adjusted the barrel of the gun and fired.

Jackson dropped, holding his ankle and swearing. "You shot me," he screamed.

Jillian looked at Ron, smiled slightly, and then turned back to Jackson.

"You called me babe," she said. "I warned you never to do that. Besides, it's even now, and I didn't even hit the bone."

"What do you mean, it's even?" Jackson yelled. "You've gone completely crazy."

"Two Deltas trying to kill each other, both with wounds in their shooting hand and a leg. Both with their weapons several feet away from them. One young and cocky, one older and experienced. I couldn't draw up a better scenario if I tried, and I don't think I'll have this opportunity again. I wonder who's going to come out on top."

"You're setting up a duel?" Jackson's voice was incredulous.

"That's right, cowboy. On the count of three, go for your weapons."

Ron could see by the look in Jillian's eyes that she was not joking. Jackson was making a lot of noise, but his leg wound looked to be not much more than a scratch. Despite what Jillian said, the odds were not even. He'd lost a lot more blood than Jackson. And Jackson was not going to wait for the count of three.

"One." Jillian's voice rang out clear in the morning air as Jackson lunged for his weapon. There was no way Ron would be able to beat him to the gun, so he didn't even try. Instead, he reached behind his back and grabbed his knife. The throw with his left hand felt awkward, but the knife flew straight and true. Jackson looked up at the impact, his eyes wide with surprise, and then he fell forward on his face. Dead.

Ron waited for the bullet to come from Jillian.

"Huh," she said. "That was unexpected."

When the shot still didn't come, Ron turned to look at Jillian. She was sitting on her haunches in the morning sun, her eyes on Jackson's body. "Do you think he would have made it?" she said finally.

"What do you mean?"

"If Jackson hadn't been kicked out, do you think he would have made it in Delta Force?"

Ron didn't hesitate. "No."

"Why not? He was skilled. And he was clever. If you hadn't had that hidden knife, he would have had you dead to rights."

"Delta's not just about having the right skills. Jackson was more skilled than a lot of guys I knew in the unit, but being part of Delta is more about the heart. A real operative never would have given you up like he did. A real operative would have drawn the fire and given you a clear shot at my back. That not only would have been the smart move, but it would have been the right move. If you're not willing to die for your comrades, you never become a real Delta. Jackson never had a chance. He didn't care for anyone except himself."

Jillian picked a piece of long grass out of the dirt and began to chew on it. "You never expected to make it out of this canyon, did you? You thought you were going to die."

"I thought it was a distinct possibility."

"Then why'd you try?"

"Because it gave Matt and the boys the best chance to get away. Because it's what I was trained to do in Delta."

"Why'd you leave, then?" Jillian said. "If Delta was so great, why did you abandon it?"

Ron shrugged. "I guess I didn't trust the people calling the shots anymore. I didn't trust that they had the best interest of the unit or even the people we were assigned to protect. It started to feel more like a game than a cause, and we were just pawns on a chessboard. I'd still give my life for any one of those guys, but I couldn't stand around watching them get played."

Jillian nodded as if the answer satisfied her. "You married?" she asked.

Ron was caught off guard by the question. "No."

"Why not? I thought you Mormons were big on marriage."

Ron didn't know exactly how to answer. All of his reasons tumbled through his mind, and then suddenly he heard a voice, like his own voice, faintly in the back of his head. *Giving your life doesn't mean dying for someone. It means living for them. We all give our lives for something. We just need to decide what that is.*

"You still with me, Delta? I asked you a question."

Ron shook his head to clear it and chuckled to himself.

"What's so funny?"

"I think you just helped me figure something out. I thought I had good reasons for not being married, but they don't seem legitimate anymore."

"Is that a proposal?"

Was Jillian hitting on him? "I don't think that would work out very well," he said. "Considering the circumstances."

"Yeah, probably not." She had a glint in her eye. "You gonna dive for your gun now?"

He'd thought about it. Catch her while she was talking. Catch her while her defenses were down. It might be the best chance he would have at getting out of this thing. Instead, he shook his head. "I don't think so."

"Why not?"

"I guess I just don't feel like shooting you again."

"I'd probably shoot you first anyway."

"You probably would."

Jillian rose and spat the piece of grass she'd been chewing on the ground. It appeared that their conversation was over. She raised her gun and pointed it directly at his head. "I want you to do something for me," she said.

"Let me guess. You want me to stay dead this time?"

"Good answer, but the wrong one." A smile played across her lips, then disappeared, and she looked at him intently. "I want you to tell Joey something for me. I want you to tell him not to let the idiot adults in his life ruin it for him. They're not worth it. Tell him to sit back and enjoy the ride no matter what. I wish I would have."

"You're not going to shoot me?"

"I don't feel like shooting you again either." Jillian lowered her gun and stuck it into the back of her belt.

"What about the job?"

"What job? I'm a free agent. I choose the jobs I take, and I'm choosing to opt out on this one. I don't let others control my actions." She smiled at him again. "I think you helped me figure something out too. See you later, Delta. Don't forget to give Joey my message." Jillian turned away from him and began jogging toward the back pass, where she'd come in.

Ron staggered backward and rested against a rock. He watched her as she glided away through the morning mist like she was moving in and out of one of his dreams. It sounded like she was humming as she ran, a tune that was both familiar and out of place. His cloudy and overstressed brain struggled to identify the song, and then he had it.

"It's a Small World."

Chapter 31
ALIVE

As I GOT CLOSER TO the canyon, I slowed from a run to a walk. There had been several shots fired, and I had told myself that was a good sign—each shot had meant Ron had survived the last. But in the past thirty or so minutes, with the sun rising above the peaks, there had been only silence.

I reached the slotted opening and pulled the gun out of my belt. I was thinking more and more that this was a bad idea. Although I'd been trained in using firearms, I was nowhere near Ron's level, and I didn't have any knowledge of the current situation. If anything was still happening, I'd probably just get in Ron's way or get myself shot. My best bet was to stay quiet, stay out of sight, and find out if Ron was still alive or not.

I moved toward the slot, trying to make as little sound as possible. The spiders were awakening, their webs dancing in the morning sunlight and causing shadows of movement along the rocks that made me jump at every turn. I had nearly fired at imaginary foes a dozen times when I finally tripped. I looked down at what looked like fishing wire, probably set by Ron to catch the mercenaries off guard. I started to move backward, but I was too late. The smaller rocks above me were beginning to rattle down the side of the wall.

I turned, expecting to see a boulder before it caught me in the face, but instead, I saw Ron holding his crutch above him as he slid down the wall face.

"It's a good thing I disabled that," he said. "I almost forgot about it."

I breathed a sigh of relief, lowering my gun and placing it back in my belt. "I guess this means you won?"

Ron grimaced as he pulled his crutch back under his arm. "You could say that."

"Jackson?"

"Dead."

"The woman?"

Ron smiled. There was something in his eyes that almost looked like admiration. "Gone," he said. "She decided she's out of the game."

"Your doing?"

Ron shook his head. "I think it was Joey. That boy has a way of growing on you." As he said Joey's name, Ron stiffened. "Matt, where are the boys?"

"They should be to the highway by now. Peng is leading them out."

"Why aren't you with them?"

"They wouldn't leave unless I came back to check on you."

Ron studied my face more carefully. "You look like you've been in a fight with a grizzly bear."

"Worse," I said.

"You took on Tiny?"

I nodded. "That is one strong man."

"Yet you're still alive."

"Thanks to the boys."

He shook his head. "You never cease to surprise me. Did you run all the way back here?"

"Pretty much."

He raised his eyebrows. "You don't look too winded."

"I used to run a lot in the mountains," I said. "I kind of enjoy it."

"In that case, I think you should turn around and get back to the boys as soon as possible. Even though the team on the ground is out of commission, we don't know where the mother ship is. I don't like those boys being out there alone."

"Hopefully they've already flagged down a camper and gotten some help."

"Let's just hope they picked the right camper."

I hadn't thought about that. I'd figured with Tiny, Jackson, and the woman out of the way, the boys were home free. A bad feeling started to creep up the back of my neck. "What about you?" I asked.

"I'll hobble along behind as fast as I can, but I would just slow you down."

I nodded, pulled out my water bottle, and took a long drink. And then I turned around and once again began to run.

Chapter 32
GONE

I RAN AS FAST AS I could to get back to the boys. I had a nagging feeling that something was wrong, and I hoped it was just my imagination. I passed Tiny on the way, still securely attached to the tree where we had zip-tied him. I thought about making some bear noises to give him a scare, but my heart wasn't in it. I needed to get to those boys.

I topped the last rise before the highway and immediately saw them, blankets over their shoulders, sitting around a fire. They looked tired, they looked deflated, but they were alive. I breathed a sigh of relief and continued to jog in but more slowly now. Running back and forth through the mountains and fighting a crazed giant was starting to take its toll on me. I smelled the food from the campsite and realized I badly needed something to eat. I was ready to get some food, take a nap, and wait for Ron to help me figure out what to do next to find Hope. I'd been so focused on the boys and Ron that I'd let my concentration slip on my wife and daughter. The emptiness of my separation from them hit me suddenly, like falling into a dark, empty cave.

When I came into camp, I didn't see the relief I'd expected on the boys' faces. They were anguished. "What's wrong?" I asked.

"They took him," JR said.

I looked around. The only one missing from the group was Peng. My heart began to beat faster. I wondered if Jillian had returned to finish the job. "Who took him?"

"I'm sorry," Eric said. "She looked like my grandma."

I was confused. Eric wasn't making any sense.

JR must have seen it on my face. "There was a motor home parked here," he explained. "An old lady made us pancakes and bacon and gave us blankets. There was a man too, but we didn't see him. We were just eating, and the next thing we knew, they were driving off in the motor home with Peng. We saw him in the back window. It looked like he had a knife to his neck. He told us to wait here for you."

"I didn't know she was a serial killer," Eric whined. "Honest, she really looked like my grandma."

"Peng was holding the knife," Joey chimed in. "The old lady was way behind him."

"Why would Peng hold a knife to his own neck?" JR said. "It doesn't make any sense."

"None of it makes any sense," Joey said. "Peng kept pointing the knife at his watch and saying, 'Tell Matt.' But he didn't say what to tell you."

I blinked my eyes and shook my head. It was all coming at me too fast, with bizarre images, like in a bad dream. "Peng doesn't even have a watch," I said.

"Sure he does," Eric said. "We could see it in the window as clear as day."

I looked around the camp, hoping there was some clue that would help me piece this together. They'd left the camp stoves behind, and they were still burning. I walked over and turned them off. There were still plates piled high with pancakes, bacon, and eggs. I grabbed an empty plate, filled it with food, and started chewing. Eating often helped me think, and although I was no longer hungry, I needed the calories.

It made no sense. A motor home with an elderly couple, a kidnapping where the victim was holding the weapon, and food enough to feed a crowd.

And then it dawned on me.

"This was the base camp," I said. "They were expecting Jackson to bring back the prisoners this morning. That's why there's so much food." I pushed in a few more bites of a pancake, which seemed to be helping my brain. "Peng must have figured it out and convinced them to take him and leave you here."

"He gave himself up for us?" Joey asked.

"That's the way it looks." I was appreciating my adopted son's qualities more and more. But I wished he would have waited for me to get here before doing anything.

"Is Ron okay?" JR asked.

"He's fine," I said. "I came ahead because he's moving slower with his leg. But he should get here soon."

"Did he kill them?" Joey asked. His voice was tentative, like he didn't really want to know the answer.

"Jackson is dead, but apparently the woman decided to abandon ship. I didn't get the full story."

Joey screwed up his face like he wasn't sure how he felt about that answer.

I put down my plate and began pacing back and forth across the camp, trying to think of what to do next. They had Hope, they had Jin, and now they had Peng. And I had no idea where they were or what to do next. It looked as if Dempsey held all the cards again. I was sure he would contact me as soon as I had cell coverage . . . and he would be able to lead me like a lamb to the slaughter.

I wasn't any closer to finding a way out of my predicament when Ron staggered into camp. The boys nearly knocked him over when they saw him, and I filled him in on what had happened.

"You're right," he said after I explained it to him. "They've got the upper hand. I could call some ex-companions to go in with you, but that will take time, and I don't think they're going to give you a lot of time. So I guess it's just you and me."

"Not you," I said. He was struggling to even sit upright. "You need a doctor."

Ron looked like he wanted to argue, but he didn't. "I know a guy in Park City," he said. "I'll have him patch me up at my condo. It sounds like these guys have connections to local law enforcement, and it's probably better to keep any word of Scout kidnappings and gunfights on the down-low for a while. There should be some cars passing by here soon. We can flag one down."

As if on cue, lights appeared on the highway, coming toward us. The driver stopped, but he was in a Mazda Miata convertible, and there wasn't enough room for all of us.

"Me and the boys will catch the next vehicle," Ron said. "You need to go find Hope. I'm sure there will be an SUV or a van coming along soon."

I opened my mouth to argue, but he pointed up the road at an old VW microbus chugging its way down the highway.

"Okay," I said, getting into the Miata. "Call me when you get a chance." I looked at Ron, looked at the boys, and felt a sudden wave of affection for all of them.

"Good luck, Brother Knight," Joey said.

The others boys nodded in assent.

I turned around and watched them as we sped off.

Chapter 33
THE ROAD BACK

MATT WAS GONE IN THE Miata before the VW bus reached Ron and the boys. In fact, the bus never did quite reach them. About 100 yards up the road, it weaved into a gravel pull off and stopped. Ron got the boys moving, and they jogged up the highway toward it. Ron limped along behind.

The windows were tinted, and Ron could barely make out the figure inside once he got up to it. He moved to the driver's side, and the window slowly began to roll down. A thin man with long stringy hair and half-closed, bloodshot eyes looked out at him.

"Hey, man," he said, his voice distant, like he was talking from another dimension. "What's up?"

"We have an emergency. Can you to take us into Park City?"

"Yeah, no problem, man. The van's yours. But I don't think I can drive right now. I tried that already. It didn't work out too well. I need to get in the back and sleep for a while. Just leave the keys in the ignition when you're done." The man began to get up and crawl across the seats toward the back of the van. A mixture of alcohol fumes and marijuana smoke escaped the open window as the man shifted position.

"You sure it's okay?" Ron asked. The man looked back over his shoulder and shrugged before he tipped over in the seat, unconscious.

Ron poked his head inside the window and looked down at the floorboard. The van was an automatic. Ron had only one good foot, but that was all he would need. He pulled his head out of the van, and the sudden movement sent bright streaks racing from his pupils back to his brain, leaving darkness in his wake. The last thing he registered was his body falling to the ground.

"You okay, Brother K?" JR was helping him up to a sitting position.

Ron felt a strange urge to join the van's owner on one of the backseats in a two-day sleep-a-thon. It wasn't a good idea for him to drive, but he really had no choice. Then his eyes cleared, and he took another look at JR. The boy seemed to have matured five years in the last few days. "JR," Ron said. "It's your lucky day."

"Whadda you mean?" JR asked, his eyes brightening. "Are you going to let me drive?"

"No," Ron said. "But you *are* going to be my copilot."

"Copilot?"

"Yes. That means you need to keep me awake on the way to Park City. If I start to drift, poke me. If I pass out, put your foot on the brake until the van stops. I'll be going slow, so it won't be hard."

JR's face went pale. "But I've never driven on the road before."

"You aren't driving. You're copiloting."

JR bit his lip.

"Would you rather Eric do it? We could ask Joey, but I don't think he would be able to see over the dashboard or reach the brake."

Eric started to look excited.

"I'll do it," JR said quickly with a sidelong look at Eric.

"We just have to get to Park City. It's a straight shot, and the road doesn't wind too much. Let's all get in the van. Roll down the windows to air it out, and try not to disturb our sleeping host. As promised, we're headed to my condo."

The boys piled in, and Eric said, "Easy Cheese, here I come."

Ron smiled. It was almost as if they were back to where they had started before they'd set out on this trip, back to a time of innocent adolescence. But who was he kidding? The road back never felt the same as the one that brought him. Even if he traveled the same route, even if he was looking at the same trees, even if he was talking to the same people, the road back was always different. Always quietly satisfying. And a little bit sad.

* * *

Tim looked too large for his Miata, and he wasn't a great conversationalist, but that was just fine with me. I needed to think, and making small talk while we traveled would just be a distraction.

Tim had the top of the convertible off and the radio turned up and was humming along to the tunes. He seemed to be enjoying himself—maybe a little too much. For a moment, I had an awful thought: what if Tim was another one of Dempsey's mercenaries? What if I was playing right into their hands? What if the reason Tim was so happy was because he was getting an extra bonus for bringing me in?

But as I studied Tim further, I had a hard time believing it. He just didn't fit the part. His humming and happy façade were a little too convincing. Also convincing was the red patch that lined half his forehead. He was obviously no stranger to driving around in his convertible. And he didn't seem to be aware of me at all. Not that I looked like much of a menace, but if Tim was one of the mercenaries, he would have been told to be careful. He was no villain. He was just . . . oblivious. And though he seemed to be plugged into nature, I didn't feel like he had much connection to the human race.

For some reason, this thought almost disturbed me as much as thinking he was a cold-blooded killer. I turned around and looked behind me. The road was empty. Ron and the boys were back there somewhere, hopefully finding transportation to get Ron to a hospital. Leaving them behind made perfect sense—at least in my head. But my heart felt a sense of loss, like I had disconnected from the mother ship and was floating alone out in space. I turned my attention forward, and my sense of loss deepened. I had no idea where Hope, Jin, and now Peng were being held. I was sitting here with a guy named Tim who was lost in his tunes. I was stuck in the in-between.

Tim continued humming, and I continued thinking. We might have gone on like that for a long time, but both of our phones began to make angry buzzing noises at the same time and nearly scared us to death.

Tim sighed. "Looks like cell phone coverage is back on. Whaddya say we throw the darn things out? That would really help us disconnect."

I reached inside my pocket, pulled out my phone, and scrambled with shaking fingers to open my messages.

Tim just shook his head in disgust.

I had two texts. One was from an unknown number and said only a few words. "P here. R-way. Looking at Enola G." The text was from yesterday. It was clearly from Permelia. She always started her texts with "P here," even though her caller ID would identify her on my phone. I'd told her this several times, but it didn't make any difference. I was glad of that now, but I had no clue as to what the rest of her message meant or whose phone she had been using. What was R-way, and who was Enola G?

I stashed the questions in my head and looked at the next text. It was from the same number. The message was also short and succinct, but this time the meaning was clear. "If you want to see your family alive, call this #."

Apparently Permelia had gotten hold of the phone for a few moments and tried to give me some information before it was taken away. At least I knew how to find my family. All I needed to do was call the number and get instructions on where to turn myself in. But I was at the point where I didn't want to give Dempsey an advantage. If I could just figure out where they were without running through a bunch of check points, maybe I could tip the scales. But Permelia's message didn't make sense to me.

What was R-way? Could it be a railway somewhere, maybe a train station? A roadway? And "looking at Enola G"? Was Enola a person? A place? I almost started dialing my phone when I realized Dempsey had been planning this operation for some time and could have compromised my phone. Would he be privy to any call I made?

"Hey, Tim," I said. "What cell phone provider do you have?"

Tim looked annoyed but stopped singing long enough to answer. "Verizon. Why?"

"I'm getting no bars, and I need to make a call. Any chance I can borrow your phone for a minute?"

"Knock yourself out. It's in the glove box." And then under his breath he mumbled, "Can't even disconnect for five minutes."

I was about ready to connect my foot to Tim's body, but I restrained myself. I grabbed his phone, texted nasty messages to everyone on his contact list, and dialed a number. Okay, I didn't send any nasty messages, but I really wanted to.

Tim jammed earbuds into his ears with disgust. Perfect. He probably wouldn't know what to think, but I really didn't want him listening to my conversation.

The phone on the other end rang but didn't pick up. When it stopped ringing, it went silent. No answering machine message, nothing. Strange. I hung up and wondered what to do next. That phone was supposed to be active 24/7. I only had to wait a few seconds before Tim's phone began to ring. I didn't recognize the number, but I picked up anyway. "They're calling me back," I mouthed to Tim.

He rolled his eyes.

"Hello," I said, wondering if I was going to get Tim's mother on the line.

"It's about time you called, homey," the voice on the other end said.

"Demetrius?" I asked. "How'd you know it was me?"

"I've been expecting you, and my tracer says the call is coming from the Uinta Mountains. Who else would be calling me on my secure line that only about five people in the world know about?"

"Why have you been expecting my call, and why didn't you answer the first time?"

"Zack was with Hope when somebody took them, but he passed a code to Mimi. She called Chico and me, and we moved Mimi and Shi-Shi off the grid."

"That answers my first question. But why didn't you answer the first time? And why did you call back on a different phone?" Something about this whole situation was starting to bother me.

"Because I can't be sure it's secure. As soon as we made Mimi disappear, we had all sorts of people on our tail, setting off alarms all over the place. I'm not sure what you've gotten yourself into, but it goes high and deep."

"How high?"

"High enough that to keep Mimi safe, we couldn't go to our own people. High enough that we'll probably get fired if we ever decide to officially check in. Either that, or we might meet with a mysterious accident. Who did you tick off this time?"

"A guy named John Dempsey kidnapped Hope, Permelia, and Jin. Zack apparently caught them in the act, and they took him as well."

"The international-gun-for-hire Dempsey? I didn't think he worked on US soil."

"Apparently he made an exception. He says he has a client who will pay him handsomely for delivering me and my entire family intact."

"So you did tick someone off."

"Probably."

"Do you know who?"

"Not yet. But they've got lots of money if they hired Dempsey."

"Huh," Demetrius said.

"What?"

"It just doesn't make any sense. Every time I tried to raise the subject of Zack's disappearance through back channels, I was told to stop before I ended up on the wrong end of an investigation. They seemed a lot more interested in knowing where Chico and I were vacationing than in going after the people who took Zack. And they were even more interested in finding out about you."

"Me?"

"Mainly about your current location. I was told it would be very good for my career if I were to report any contact with you. And damaging if I didn't."

"Dempsey said he would know if I tried to involve the authorities. It sounds like he has someone on the inside."

"That would be one heck of a mole. The guys I've been talking to aren't interns. And it's not just coming from one place. Something strange is going on."

"You can say that again," I said, a dull pain starting to form in my temple. None of this made any sense at all. "Are you being watched?"

"We would be if Chico didn't have some extended family nobody knows about. We're in the clear as far as I can tell."

"Good. Do you still remember my tracking coordinates on my watch?"

"You think I could forget?"

"Can you pull them up?"

"Sure, give me a second. Don't you know where you are?"

I did know where I was, but I'd finally figured out what Peng was trying to say through the back window of the motor home. He'd taken my watch. He knew what it was for. He knew exactly what he was doing. "Peng has my watch," I said. "I think he's on his way to where Hope and Zack are being held."

Demetrius whistled. "How'd you get him to do that?"

"I didn't. He did it on his own. He might have a future in the business."

"Wasn't he giving you some problems earlier?"

"I thought he was. I was wrong. He's an amazing kid."

Demtrius paused, then said, "Okay, I've got him. Looks like he's moving out across the west desert, headed toward the state line. Next stop, Wendover. You think they're headed to California?"

"No, it's got to be closer. They're going to want me to meet them, so they can't be too far." I thought for a minute about the text from Permelia. "Can you do a Google search for me? Type in *Enola*, *railway*, and *Wendover*. Let me know what kind of hits you get."

"That didn't take long," Demetrius said after a few seconds. "Except you probably meant runway instead of railway. A page popped right up: Wendover airfield, historical home of the Enola Gay hangar. Wasn't that the plane that carried the nuclear bomb? Says the airfield is no longer operational, but they have a museum, do some air shows, and film movies there."

"I'm pretty sure that's where they're being held. How far off the grid are you? Somewhere in Central or South America?"

"No way, man. We're just down the road in Midway."

"I thought you said you were with Chico's long-lost relatives."

"We are. Who would have known his relatives are Swiss? That's why no one is going to find us."

"Look, I'm going to rent a car in Park City. I'll pick up another burner phone there as well. Do you think you can find a stoplight in Heber that isn't being monitored with cameras where you can jump in my car?"

"Have you been to Heber lately? I'm not sure any of the stoplights have cameras."

"In the meantime, see if you can do some research. I want to know what else is going on and who Dempsey's client is."

"You got it, Home Skillet. I'll see you soon."

"Did you just call me Home Skillet?"

"Don't worry about it, man. Chico's Swiss relatives don't get me either."

I finished my call with Demetrius, confirmed that Tim could indeed drop me at a rental car agency in Park City, and then picked up my own cell phone again. It was time to make contact with the enemy.

"Okay," I texted. "You win. I'm coming in. Where can I find my family?"

It was less than thirty seconds before I heard my phone tweeting in reply.

"Hey, I thought you said you didn't have any bars," Tim said, his earbuds now removed.

"Just got them back."

I read the words on the return text. No surprise. "Get to Salt Lake City. When you are near the airport, call me for more instructions. Be ready to fly."

Dempsey was cryptic, as usual, and he was trying to make me believe I would be taking a plane somewhere. Knowing him, he would play out the game for as long as he could. He liked to be in control.

But I knew where he was hiding.

Chapter 34
THE PRINCE AND THE TERRORIST

TIM DROPPED ME OFF AT the Hertz 24/7 car rental building in Park City. I tried to say thank you, but as soon as I was out of the car, he was gone, singing and muttering to himself. I wondered if and when he would notice that I had stolen his phone. My plan had been to stop at a convenience store to buy a prepaid unit, but I was kind of in a hurry, and Tim was kind of a jerk. Besides, he'd said a number of times that he wanted to disconnect from the outside world. I'd left a granola bar and twenty bucks where the phone had been sitting in the glove box. I guessed he would think it was a fair trade. And I planned on returning the phone to him when I was through with it—if I was still alive.

I asked for a compact car with good gas mileage, but for some reason, the rental car employee kept trying to upgrade me to an SUV. After saying "No, thank you" several times, I finally discovered that the reason he wanted to upgrade me was because SUVs were the only cars they had left. I drove away in a dark-red Chevy Tahoe with leather seats. It was shiny and new and would be easy to spot, but I wasn't trying to hide my identity. I'd used a credit card and flashed my driver's license liberally while renting the car. If Dempsey's people or the Feds had their feelers out for me, I wouldn't be hard to find.

Despite what Demetrius had said about traffic cameras in Heber, I decided it would be better not to meet with him in person. He and Chico were some of my only advantages in this game, and I wasn't going to give them up.

I connected Tim's phone to the Bluetooth in the Tahoe, dialed Demetrius, and began driving.

"If it isn't my pasty-white friend Tim," Demetrius said when he answered.

"I think I want to talk to Chico."

"Chico doesn't talk much."

"That's why I want to talk to him."

"Ahh, that hurts, man. You almost to Heber? I can be there in ten minutes. I bet I can jump in the backseat of your car without you even knowing it."

"Demetrius?"

"Yeah."

"How many people that look and talk like you have you seen in Midway and Heber?"

"I think I might have caught a glimpse of one the other day."

"I've got people watching me. My guess is they've got access to rental car computers. I just used my credit card to rent a car, and I'm driving a shiny red SUV. I don't think it's a good idea for you to jump into my car at a stoplight."

"Hey, man, you're ruining my fun."

"Let's just do this over the phone. I don't think anyone's listening in on Tim—he's not the most engaging conversationalist—and I'm assuming this last number you gave me is untraceable."

"Tim must be a nice guy to lend you his phone like that."

"He's a sweetheart. Have you got anything for me?"

"Oh yeah, you won't believe what I've got. Ever hear the name Prince Abdullah bin Sayami?"

"It sounds vaguely familiar. But after a while, all those bin's and ibn's start to sound the same."

"Racist."

"No. I'm just really bad at Arab names. I'm assuming, however, that since you used *prince* in front of the name, we are speaking of someone from the Saud family?" In Saudi Arabia, they took their royalty seriously, and only a select group of people would have the title of prince.

"Now you're getting it. A distant cousin to the current rulers, but one who seems to have his fingers on the pulse of the people and his pockets in the hands of the terrorists. Some say that if it came to a popular vote, he would be the clear winner out of all the Sauds."

"I didn't realize they were a democracy."

"They're not. But we tend to forget that the current stretch of stability is an anomaly where the Saudi state is concerned. Some experts seem to think the country is ripe for a revolution, and Saudi succession may be one of the pivotal questions not only for the Middle East but for the whole world too. We get the wrong guy at the top over there and everything changes. Not that it's great right now. But at least our relations with Saudi Arabia are fairly stable when compared to the rest of the Middle East."

"And this bin Salami guy figures into the mix." I was picturing a large salami wearing a keffiyeh headdress to help me to remember his name.

"It's Sayami, with a *Y*. And yes, he could figure in big-time. He's got lots of friends with lots of money, and not all of them live in the Middle East. Some think his frequent visits to the United States are more than just spending sprees in Vegas. He's been meeting with some pretty powerful people."

"So what does this guy have to do with me and my family?"

"That's the real question, isn't it? Lucky for you, I think I might have found the answer. Do you remember the Yehudi brothers?"

"Yeah," I said. "I remember them." I couldn't help but swallow hard when I heard the name. I'd infiltrated the Yehudis in Miami. My cover had been blown, and they were getting ready to take my head off when my friend Robbie arrived with the cavalry. One of the brothers was killed trying to resist. The other was executed a few months later.

"Well, it seems the two you sent to Allah aren't the only ones in the family. They have a fanatical mother and a little brother who was barely fifteen when his older siblings went to meet their God. The mother put the younger brother under the keeping of one of her distant cousins and closest friends."

"Let me guess, Prince Sayami."

"You got it."

"So you think Sayami's doing a favor for a family friend, exacting revenge on the western dog responsible for killing his brothers?"

"That's the way I read it."

"And this same Sayami has influential friends on our side of the pond?"

"Let's just say our government has a history of building relationships with those who might end up becoming leaders of powerful and influential countries. If there is even a slight possibility that he could become the Saudi successor—even if it is through revolution—you can be sure our guys are talking to him."

It made sense that the attack on my family was instigated by the Yehudis—I had put a serious dent in that family's terrorist reputation. It appeared they were using the diplomatic privileges of their friend the prince to get to me.

"What about Dempsey?" I asked.

"That's the weird part."

"What do you mean?"

"You'd think the CIA wouldn't want a known assassin like Dempsey anywhere near an asset like the prince. You'd think they'd be happy to pay for information about a confirmed Dempsey sighting on US soil. But when I started to raise the issue with an old colleague, he told me point blank that the CIA already knew Dempsey was here and that if I knew what was good for me, I would stay out of it."

"Did you tell them Dempsey had kidnapped an innocent woman and child?"

"I tried, but the conversation never got that far. It appears that the name Dempsey is on the do-not-talk-about list. He told me that if I brought up Dempsey again he would be obligated to report me."

"Why would the CIA be protecting Dempsey?"

"Maybe they want to get to him first."

"I don't know . . ." Something wasn't right about this, but I needed more time to think—time I didn't have. "Looks like no additional help is on the way. It's just us."

"You really going to just turn yourself in to them?" Demetrius asked. "If Yehudi gets off that plane and sees you, the first thing he's going to do is put a bullet between your eyes."

"They have my family," I said. "I have no choice. Besides, you're going to be there to make sure nothing happens to me."

"You don't make it easy on Chico and me."

"No, but at least I keep it exciting. You said you wanted action. I'm giving you some."

"I'd forgotten what action looked like when you were involved."

"Dempsey told me to get to Salt Lake and wait near the airport for further instructions," I said. "My guess is they will tell me to come to the airfield in Wendover either in the middle of the night or tomorrow morning. You think you can set up a perimeter without being spotted?"

"Don't worry, man. We got this."

Demetrius was confident, but as I hung up the phone, I was hit with a wave of anxiety. The Yehudi brothers were not only terrorists, but they were also fanatics, and their mother was reputed to be the craziest of them all. If there was a little brother who had been raised as an instrument of revenge, I had no illusions for the safety of my family. What Demetrius had said was true. If Yehudi stepped off a plane and saw my family and me, the first thing he would do would be to start shooting.

Chapter 35
THE DELIVERY

DEMPSEY WATCHED AS THE MOTOR home rolled up in front of the hangar. Carney had phoned ahead so Dempsey was expecting him, but it was still a bit disconcerting to see a man with Carney's reputation arrive looking like a grandpa on a road trip.

The motor home pulled to a stop, and Carney's wife emerged. Dempsey had never met her, but she also had a reputation in the business for cruelty, cunning, and ruthlessness. To Dempsey, she just looked old. Old and tired. For some reason, he caught himself wondering who would win in a fight between her and Permelia.

The boy came out next, followed by Carney. The teen looked alert. His eyes darted around the airfield, taking in everything. And then they landed on Dempsey. There was a fierceness in those eyes. Despite his being adopted, it appeared that some traits ran in the family.

"How'd you finally catch him?" Dempsey asked.

Carney huffed and cleared his throat. "I think you got it backward. The kid hijacked us and demanded we bring him to you. I don't know what you got us into this time, Dempsey, but my crew is dismantled, some of my best men are dead, and I think Mother and I are ready to retire. So if you don't mind, we'll just take our money and be on our way."

Dempsey pulled the handle up on a Samsonite bag and wheeled it across to Carney. He stopped a few feet short of giving it to him. "You didn't deliver the main target."

"We did what we could, and you held back information we needed. Besides, you owe me for collateral damage. I'm going to have to build a whole new team."

"I thought you were ready to retire?"

"Maybe. If that's the case, we are going to need every penny we can get. Are you going to pay us or not?"

Dempsey rolled the bag the rest of the way over to Carney. "At least you won't have to split it as many ways."

Carney huffed again and shook his head. His wife wheeled the bag to the motor home and went inside.

"What about the father?" Carney asked.

"We've been in contact. I've got him in a holding pattern until just before the client gets here. I really don't want him around for very long."

"Don't blame you. From what the kid says, he did a number on Tiny. And I didn't think I would ever say that about anyone. He's got to be tougher than he looks."

"He's tough enough," Dempsey said. "Who do you think put this dent in my face?"

"So he's the one. I would've thought you'd learned your lesson the first time."

"This one's a big payoff. You know how it goes."

"The older I get, the more I think that sometimes the payoff isn't worth it. Don't call me again, Dempsey," Carney said. "We're done." He didn't look back as he climbed into the driver's seat and drove away.

The boy stepped forward. "Take me to my mother," he said. His voice was quiet, almost polite but also insistent. Dempsey studied him. He should have been in shock after having been kidnapped by mercenaries in the mountains, but you wouldn't know it. He was a little dirty, and he looked like he hadn't slept, but there was a calm about him that shouldn't have been there. Dempsey would need to be careful around this one too.

The Ghost appeared from behind him, and Dempsey forced himself not to jump.

"You need any help?" the man said.

"I think I'll be okay. It's just one boy, and he wants to go where I'm taking him. Did you get the cameras set? The client will be arriving tomorrow."

"Working on it," the bearded man said.

"What's the matter?" Dempsey sensed something tentative in the man's voice.

"Nothing." The man sighed. "Sometimes I just really hate this job."

"Me too. But you know the stakes."

"Yes," he said. "Yes, I do." And then he was gone as suddenly as he had appeared.

Dempsey led the boy to the room where Hope, Permelia, and the child were being held. He wondered if Hope was still crying from the night before. And then he wondered why he would be concerned about that. In his line of work, he often caused tears, and he usually never gave it a second thought.

He unlocked the door and opened it. Hope was sitting on the bed on the other side of the room, and Permelia was sitting next to her, her arm draped over her shoulder. Dempsey couldn't see Hope's face because of all the hair, but he was sure her cheeks were stained with wetness. She'd probably been crying all night. Dempsey felt a flush of indignation. It was stupid to shed tears over Buck. Dempsey had saved her from who knows what terrors he might have inflicted on her. She should be grateful to him. Instead, she acted like he had killed a member of her family, not some psychopath who had meant to cause her harm.

Dempsey put his irritation in check. What was he thinking? He had taken her family and yanked them out of a peaceful existence. Of course she wouldn't be grateful to him. And why would he even want that?

"Mom?" the boy said as he saw her.

Hope's head snapped up. The lines in her forehead disappeared, and a wide smile brightened her face.

"Peng." She stood, and he ran into her arms.

They hugged for a long time, and then she held him by the shoulders and pushed him to arm's length so she could study him.

"Did they hurt you?" she asked, examining every bruise and scratch she could see. She spared Dempsey a single menacing glare and then returned her attention to the boy.

"I'm fine."

A loud squeal came from the stroller where the toddler was sleeping. It was so loud that Dempsey wanted to put his hands over his ears.

"You better pick her up," Hope said to the boy. "You know she won't stop until she sees her brother."

Peng went to the stroller and lifted the toddler. She kicked and squealed and giggled as he did. He held her up in the air, twirled her around, and then enveloped her in his arms. The boy smiled and laughed. This was the first time Dempsey had seen him smile. It seemed as if everyone was smiling except Dempsey. He felt a sudden sense of loss, like a hole had opened inside his stomach and something important had fallen out.

"You called me Mom," Hope said. "When you came in the door. You've never done that before."

Peng stopped swinging the girl and met Hope's eyes. "I figured some things out," he said. "In the mountains. Matt helped me."

"How is he? How are the boys?"

Peng grinned widely. "They're great," he said. "Ron got shot, and we thought he was dead, but it turned out it was just his hand and his leg. He stayed to fight Jackson and Jillian in the canyon with all the spiders.. Matt found us with the giant, but then he fought him and told us to run, but he was in trouble, so we all came back and helped him fight . . ."

"Stop right there," Hope said. "What do you mean you helped Matt fight a giant?"

"They called him Tiny," Peng said. "But he was huge, and I think he liked hurting people. Matt was beating him, but then Tiny grabbed him around the throat. Eric, JR, and I started hitting him with sticks, and then Joey put a spider in his mouth—Tiny was afraid of spiders—and Matt got away and knocked him out. Then we tied him to a tree."

Hope sat down hard on the bed. "I think you're going to have to slow down. That's a lot to take in. You said Ron got shot? And Matt was attacked by a giant?"

"It was actually Matt who attacked the giant. He's tougher than he looks."

"Yes, I know. But he's not very responsible sometimes. He let you boys get involved in the fight?"

"No, he told us to run away. Joining the fight was our idea."

"I think I like these Scout trips," Permelia said. "Sounds like they put some hair on your chest."

"I'm not sure I agree with that," Hope said. "I think I need to have a talk with my husband."

"He'll be coming soon," Peng said. "He'll get us out of here."

As if on cue, they all turned and looked at Dempsey. For a moment, they'd forgotten him. Now they were all glaring at him like they wanted to punch him in the face.

Had to be something that ran in the family.

Chapter 36
ANOTHER PROMISE

A<small>FTER</small> D<small>EMPSEY</small> <small>LEFT</small>, H<small>OPE</small> <small>SAT</small> Peng on the bed and made him give all the details of the time in the mountains. Jin interrupted every few minutes, demanding that Peng play with her, until finally she fell asleep on his lap. The room reminded Peng of the orphanage in many ways—the gray walls, the sterile furniture, the lock on the doors. But something was different. Peng struggled to figure out what it was, and then he had it: the difference was in the smell. There was no smell of fear. Despite their being held captive, despite the locks on the door and the threat of being sold to terrorists, there was no fear here. Hope seemed more interested in the small details of how Peng got along with the boys on the camping trip than in what was to come. Her eyes lit with emotion whenever he spoke of Matt. He felt sorrow that his birth mother hadn't had anywhere near that relationship with his stepfather but also comfort, like a warm blanket, that he and Jin were with the family they had now. The room didn't feel like the orphanage after all; it felt like family.

He wasn't used to talking so much, but the words spilled out of him. Hope was a good person, and Peng was determined to get her out of this situation safely. He could have Hope, Permelia, and Jin out of this room within a few minutes, by the looks of the locks; however, getting out the door would only be the beginning. What lay outside the door was what worried him.

After a while, Hope seemed to be running out of questions. Jin's breathing became deeper, and her body felt heavier than it had moments earlier. Peng looked Hope in the eyes. "I can get us out of here," he said. "Tonight, when it's dark."

"I hate to tell you this," Permelia said. "But those are good locks on that door. I've been trying to pick them since we got in here."

"I'm good with locks," Peng said. "I can get us out."

"No." Hope stared at Peng with a sudden intensity in her eyes. "We are not going to try to escape without Matt. I forbid it." Her voice was loud. Almost shouting.

Peng was taken aback. Hope had never talked to him like that, not even when she'd scolded him for sneaking out of the house at night. "But it will be easier for Matt to take care of the bad guys if he doesn't have to worry about us." Peng had complete confidence that Matt could and would take care of the bad guys.

Hope's eyes softened, and she put her hand on Peng's arm. "You may be right," she said. "But I don't think I can handle another night like the last one. I tried to escape. A man was killed. I can't go through that again. He . . ." She shivered as if a cold wave had passed through her. "Please, let's just wait for Matt."

"A man?" Peng asked.

"More like a psychopath than a man," Permelia said. "But there's no use arguing with her. The scar's a bit too fresh. I've seen this look from your mother before, and she's not going to be moved."

"No, I won't," Hope said. "I just want one night of peace, reunited with my son, not having to worry that anyone is going to get killed. When Matt arrives, we can start talking about getting out of this place."

Peng looked back longingly toward the door. The locks would be so easy to defeat. Hope followed his eyes and seemed to be reading his thoughts. "Promise me, Peng. Promise me you won't try to escape. That you won't leave us. That you will stay here and wait for Matt."

Peng thought carefully before he spoke. A plan was beginning to form in his head. He would not try to sneak his family out in the middle of the night. Hope was right. Trying to move that many people without being seen would be dangerous. But he needed to help Matt, and to help Matt, he needed more information—information he couldn't get if he was stuck in this room. Hope was asking him to promise not to escape. But sneaking out for a few hours after it got dark to look around would not really be escaping. And he was never going to leave this family. Never again. It seemed like he had just found them. He would stay here and wait for Matt, but *here* was bigger than just this room. Matt needed him. His family needed him. If he waited until they were asleep, Hope wouldn't even realize he had gone. "I promise," he said finally.

Chapter 37
THE SLEEP-N-SAVE MOTEL

WHEN I GOT TO SALT LAKE, I texted Dempsey as instructed. His return message did not tell me to board a flight. No surprise. Instead, he sent me to a hotel near the airport. Except it really couldn't be called a *hotel*. Not even a *motel* really—unless you put the word *roach* in front of it. And it wasn't exactly *near* the airport—more like an area where the noise from approaching planes would put a serious dent in property values. More like an area where nobody would want to live, visit, or do business unless there were no other choices.

The name of the place was the Sleep-N-Save Motel. It sat off an industrial road near an airport park-and-ride facility. The twenty-four rooms sat on either side of a gravel access road that led to a trailer park in the back. The rooms on one side of the road were dirt colored. The other side was painted vomit green. The front-desk attendant's ears perked up when he heard my name—and it wasn't just a figure of speech. He had overly large ears, and they actually moved up and down with excitement when I came in. Dempsey must have offered a bonus if I made it to the place.

The room itself smelled like mildew and had black mold growing up the sides of the shower walls. Which was too bad because I really could have used a shower.

The phone in the room rang. The kid with the ears must have let Dempsey know the target had arrived. I let it ring about eight times and then finally picked up.

"I trust you are enjoying your room," Dempsey said.

"Yeah. I'll be sure to repay you someday."

"Oh, no need for that. The pleasure is all mine."

"You know, there are other hotels near the airport. Some that people might actually want to sleep in?"

"I wanted you someplace inconspicuous."

"Inconspicuous? Half the meth deals in the county probably go down here. I'd bet I'm under surveillance right now by at least four federal agencies, including the Department of Health."

"Oh, I wouldn't worry about that. The meth heads won't go near the Sleep-N-Save, and neither will the FBI, the DEA, or the FDA. They're afraid they might catch something. There's a rumor that there's a virus in the furniture that causes your ears to swell. I'm surprised the place is able to stay in business."

I thought of the kid at the front desk, and my ears began to itch. I resisted the urge to scratch them.

"What about the NSA?" I said. "This seems like their kind of place." I didn't really care about the NSA, but I did want to feel Dempsey out to see if he suspected my contacting Demetrius and Chico. It was a long shot that anyone—even the NSA—would have time to pick up Tim's cell phone chatter and feed it into something that made sense, but I didn't know how deep Dempsey's connections with the government went.

"Oh, I wouldn't worry about the NSA," Dempsey said.

"Why's that?"

"Let's just say they may have visited the Sleep-N-Save at one time and have no intention of returning."

"So this room is bugged?"

"You might say that," Dempsey said. And then he started laughing. Laughing hard. Really hard. He was barely able to compose himself for several seconds. It wasn't like Dempsey, and I wondered what game he was playing, but the laughter sounded genuine.

"What's so funny?" I asked.

"Trust me," Dempsey said as he tried to catch his breath. "You'll find out. And that part I said earlier about me not wanting to get revenge for you breaking my nose? Well, that was a half-truth. Kidnapping your family wasn't about revenge. The Sleep-N-Save Motel, however . . ." He let his voice trail off, and then he turned serious again. "Just know this—you'll receive a call with further instructions on where to find your family. The call will come on your room phone, not your cell. It might come sometime tonight; it might come tomorrow morning. It might come in a few days. Do not, under any circumstances, leave your hotel room. Do not try to contact anyone else. If you do, we will know, and bad things will happen. My client wants you and your family delivered alive, but there's someone here who's not technically a family member—an elderly woman with sharp elbows and a sharper tongue. She would make a fine object lesson if you decide to step outside the lines. Do you understand what I'm saying, Knight?"

"I hear you," I said. But I wasn't anxious for Permelia. I was relieved. It didn't appear that Dempsey knew that I had contacted Demetrius and Chico. And if I had to stay for a day or two holed up in a run-down motel, I could handle that. I could always order pizza and a Dr. Pepper, which sounded pretty good right now. However, I couldn't risk making any more calls to Demetrius. I wasn't sure what Dempsey was hinting at with the room being bugged, but I couldn't take any chances.

It wasn't long after I hung up the phone that I found out why Dempsey had been laughing, and it had nothing to do with audio surveillance. The room had bugs, all right, but they were of a different kind. As soon as the light started to dim outside, the scratching noises in the walls began.

At first it was so slight I had to stop and wonder if I'd really heard something. Then it became louder, as if an army of vermin were multiplying between the thin layers of sheetrock that pretended to be real walls.

Brief glimpses of antennae feeling their way between the darkest cracks, testing to see if it was safe to venture out, followed the noise. I moved the bed away from the wall and into the middle of the room. And forgot about ordering pizza. There was no way I was going to bring even a morsel of food into this room.

I started to open the door to flee to my car and then remembered Dempsey's words and his demonic laughter. I needed to stay in the room to wait for his call. If I wasn't in here when he called, he was going to hurt Permelia.

I stood there for a long moment, one foot in the room, one outside, looking at the shiny red Tahoe and the cleanliness and safety it represented, then looking back into the room, where the darkness was slowly edging out the light and night creatures were waiting to be unleashed.

For some reason, an image of Tiny, his eyes wide and terrified while Joey held the spider in front of his face, flashed into my mind. Then came an image of me as a little boy, traveling from one low-rent apartment to another with my mother and needing her to hold my hand each night to help me get to sleep.

"The bugs won't hurt you," she said. "They're just looking for table scraps. As long as you wash your hands and face before bed, you'll be fine."

Although I'd believed my mother about many things, I hadn't believed her about that. I'd known what the bugs had been after—they'd been after me. I'd overheard their dark whispers and understood their devious plans. If she'd left me alone, they would have come. If I stayed in this room now, they just as surely would come. I needed to get away, and I needed to get away now.

I was inside my rented Tahoe before I realized what I was doing. The kid with the twitching ears was watching me from the office. He looked like he was eager to run and pick up the phone to let Dempsey know I hadn't been able to follow instructions.

I tried to let the oxygen fill my lungs and abdomen, to push out the horror that had taken over my body. I could hear Dempsey's laugh and wondered how he'd known about my bug phobia. I hadn't told anyone except my mother about it. And then I realized I had told one other person—the agency psychologist who had poked and prodded and hypnotized me until nothing was hidden from her. She must have placed a note in my file, and somehow Dempsey had gotten access. He knew exactly what he was doing when he put me in this motel. He was doing what he always did—he was playing games, trying to mess with my head, trying to get the upper hand so that when I arrived at the playing field tomorrow, he would have the full advantage. He'd said it was about revenge, but I didn't believe it. For Dempsey, it was always, always about winning.

The thought made me furious. I couldn't let Dempsey win. I pictured his face in front of me, my fists smashing into his jaw until he no longer had the ability to smile. But I still didn't get out of the car.

I looked at my hands. My knuckles were white, gripping hard around the steering wheel. Every corner of my brain seemed to be filling up with visions of roaches, and the thoughts were paralyzing me. I had to think of something else.

I tried to focus on the future, on tomorrow, on Wendover airfield and my reunion with my family. The roaches disappeared, but they were replaced by even worse thoughts: What if I failed? What if I couldn't rescue them? What if Yehudi started shooting before I had a chance to act? What if I had to watch Hope, Jin, and Peng get gunned down in front of me?

My hands gripped even tighter around the wheel.

Let go. The thought that came into my head was clear and strong, but I didn't let go. Instead, I gripped the wheel tighter.

Let go. The thought came again, this time even stronger. It made no sense to me. If I let go and went back into that room, I was convinced I would either be consumed by insects or be plunged into a raving madness.

Let go. The thought came a third time. *It will be all right.*

I pushed back against the voice in my head with all the strength and anger I could muster. "You don't understand," I said aloud. "If I go back in there, I will die."

Maybe, my mind spoke back. *But it will still be all right.*

As I began to respond that that wasn't particularly comforting, I remembered Hope lying next to me in bed, telling me about her struggle with cancer. At first they'd thought the hysterectomy had removed all of the mutated cells. The doctors were ready to pronounce her cancer free. Then, in one of her follow-up CT scans, they'd noticed a shadow on her spleen. Even though the lymph nodes they'd removed had been clear, somehow the minuscule cancer cells had managed to migrate. They needed to do another surgery. They also prescribed a round of chemotherapy.

"There were only two things in the world that terrified me," Hope told me. "One was chemotherapy—I can't stand being nauseated. The other was stupid but very real—I was terrified of losing my hair. I prayed and fasted. I fasted and prayed. I asked God to let me die. I asked for a miracle, and eventually I received peace."

"You didn't have to do the chemo?" I asked.

"Oh, I did the chemo. It was even worse than I'd imagined. And I lost every bit of my hair."

"That doesn't sound very peaceful," I said.

"It wasn't. The peace came from somewhere else. It came after the pleading, when I told God that even though I didn't want to go through any of this, I would submit to His will. I would go through it if that was what He wanted from me. I can still remember the feeling. After I submitted to Him, the peace wrapped around me like a blanket and didn't go away. It didn't make any sense at all, considering my circumstances, but still, it was as real as the nausea and baldness. It was more real because it was eternal."

Let go. The thought came to me a fourth time.

"You want me to go back in there and get eaten by bugs?" I said to the car roof.

I didn't receive an answer, but I knew what I had to do.

I sighed and let go of the steering wheel. I got out of the Tahoe, pulled my sleeping gear from the back, nodded at the kid in the office as if this had been my plan all along, and headed back to my room. I thought my legs might buckle before I reached the door, but they held strong. And even though I was still seriously creeped out when I entered the room, I was somehow able to function.

I turned on every light that worked. I turned on the water in the bathroom sink and the static on the clock radio to drown out as much of the scratching sounds as I could. I still didn't like being here, but for some reason, this ordeal seemed a little smaller than it had before. I laid my mummy bag on top of the bed, sprayed it liberally with mosquito repellant, and then crawled inside, pulling the drawstring tight over my head, leaving only my nose exposed so I could breathe. I lay back and prepared to spend an uncomfortable, sleepless night filled with worries and night terrors.

But somehow, within a very few minutes, I fell into a deep and dreamless sleep.

Chapter 38
ESCAPE

PENG AWOKE ABRUPTLY IN THE darkness. He looked at Matt's watch. It was nearly three in the morning. The breathing in the room was soft and deep. He was sure everyone was asleep. He rose silently from his bed, made quick work of the locks, and was outside in a matter of minutes.

The openness of the space beyond the door nearly overwhelmed him. He had never seen a room so large and empty. When they'd brought him here, he'd been anticipating seeing Hope and Jin and had taken special notice of the locks, so he hadn't fully grasped the enormity of his surroundings. It reminded him of the sky at night when he sneaked out of the house.

He pushed himself against the wall and tried to fade back into the shadows. There was a table with a lamp at the far end and a couple of chairs with no one in them. There was another table with several chairs directly in front of him, where they had eaten earlier in the evening. Other than that, the room was devoid of furniture.

He moved toward the table with the lamp, careful to keep his steps soft. He had the feeling that any noise might echo throughout the entire chamber. Permelia had said they were at an abandoned airstrip and this was a hangar where airplanes had been kept and serviced in the past. Peng would have liked to examine the airplanes to see how they worked, but there were no airplanes here now. Only the one lamp. The air smelled like dust that had been recently swept out of an old garage.

As he neared the lamp, he noticed two doors at this end of the building. One looked to be the door to an interior room, similar to the one in which Hope, Jin, and Permelia were sleeping. The other led to the outside and had a small window in it. Peng could see shadows moving through the glass and thought he heard faint voices. He crept up next to the door and moved to where he could see out the window into the darkness. Two men stood talking about thirty yards away— Dempsey, and a man with a beard, whom Peng had seen earlier. Peng had the feeling that if he blinked, the man might disappear.

Peng was careful to move slowly. A sudden darkening of the window might draw the attention of the two men, but he nearly jumped out of his shoes when he heard a sound behind him. He waited for someone to grab him and throw him to the ground as they spoke threats into his ear with stinking breath. But this was not the orphanage, and there was no one behind him. He heard the sound again, a low groan coming from behind the door by the table. The door had a lock like the ones on his room, but it also had a padlock on the outside.

Permelia had said they were holding Uncle Zack here somewhere. This must be the place. He took a quick peek out the door and saw that the men were moving away from the building as they talked, then he placed his attention on the other door. Getting through the padlock would have been a problem from the inside of the room, but it only took him a few minutes to release it from the six-inch piece of plate metal that spanned the door. The lock on the door itself was even easier. He'd stolen some bobby pins from the sink in the motor home, which made perfect picking tools.

He stepped inside the room and saw Zack lying on a hospital bed, an IV cart next to him and a tube running into his hand. There were straps across his arms, legs, and chest securing him to the bed, but that wasn't the reason he hadn't escaped. His eyes were rolling around in his head like he was trying very hard to focus but couldn't.

Peng studied the setup. He didn't know a lot about medicine, but he'd had his appendix removed, and he remembered that his pain medication had been fed through the transparent plastic bags on top of the IV cart. There was an empty bag on the table, but the one that hung on Zack's cart looked mostly full. They must have changed it recently, which meant they might not come back and check it for a while. Maybe not until tomorrow morning. He could remove the IV from Zack's hand or cut the tube running from the bag, but if anyone came in, it would be obvious that it had been tampered with.

Peng looked for options. There was a roll of adhesive tape sitting on the cart next to Zack's head. Peng carefully removed the tube connected to a shorter section plugged into the back of Zack's hand. The liquid drug pulsed out of the end of the tube in slow, steady drips, like grains of sand counting out the seconds in an hourglass. An additional piece of tubing on the table had a blue connector like the one stuck in Zack. He plugged the IV into this one and taped it next to the one running into Zack's veins. He angled the drip so it would go down along Zack's side and into the mattress. It would soak everything, but the men might not notice it unless they looked carefully.

Peng unbuckled the straps holding Zack down and then rebuckled them loosely. They still looked like they were in place, but if Zack woke up, he could easily escape them.

Peng took one last look at the room, making sure it appeared the way it had when he'd come in, and then he opened the door a crack and scanned for danger before stepping outside. The large room was still empty. He could leave Zack's door unlocked, but the padlock was a problem. He went back inside and pulled off a few inches of the adhesive tape. He came back out and stuffed it down into the padlock hole. When he moved the bar of the lock back into the hole, it held but didn't lock. If Zack pushed hard on the door from the inside, it would swing open.

Peng moved back to the outside door and found the two men still talking, now nearly fifty yards away, their backs to him. They were near the corner of a fence that would take them outside his vision.

Peng took a deep breath and slipped outside the door to see if he could determine what they were talking about. He waited, crouching in the dark for a few moments, and listened for the footsteps that would tell him he had alerted the men to his presence. There were no footsteps. Only the faint voices of the men, who started to move away from him again.

Peng found the shadows and made his way toward them. If he could hear what they were saying, he might be able to find out something useful for Matt. The men rounded the corner of a small outbuilding, and their voices no longer moved away from him. Peng crept up to the corner of the building to a place where he could hear without being seen.

"So tell me what's going on." The voice was Dempsey's. "It's clear something is bothering you. You've been antsy all day. Normally you're so cool that most people wonder if you're human."

The other man didn't say anything for several moments, and Peng wondered if he had arrived just in time for the conversation to end. Then the man sighed and spoke. "It's this job," he said. "I don't like it."

"I haven't liked most of the jobs we've done together. It doesn't seem to have bothered you before," Dempsey said.

"This one's different. The woman, the old lady . . . the girl. We have no way of knowing how things will go down tomorrow. Yehudi's a certified psycho. I wouldn't be surprised if he starts shooting as soon as he steps off the plane."

"I don't think that's going to happen. Yehudi's mother is crazier than he is, and word is she's ordered him to bring them back to the homeland so she can observe the bloodletting in person. He's going to want to keep them alive."

"And you're going to let them go?"

"We've got our orders. Our job is to capture the video. That's it. Once that's done, you can take out Yehudi. I doubt the prince will have any need for hostages after that. We get the evidence, the prince flies away angry, and we're done with this job."

"Provided Yehudi doesn't take you out first."

"That's why you're going to be holed up in your nest with a sniper rifle. I'm counting on you to keep me alive. And I'm counting on them not spotting you. Just focus on doing your job."

"What about the women and the kid?"

"What about them? Once we get what we need, they are no longer relevant. They can safely go back to where they came from."

"And what if it's a choice between their safety and completing the job?"

"What do you think?"

"The job always comes first. No matter what."

"No matter what," Dempsey confirmed.

There was a moment of silence, then finally Dempsey asked, "How are the cameras coming?"

"They're placed and well camouflaged."

"I want you to turn them on now."

"Are we expecting an early arrival?"

"I'm expecting the plane to arrive at noon tomorrow as planned, but you know me."

"Always have a plan B?"

"You got it."

"Okay, then. I'll go turn on the cameras. And, Dempsey . . ."

"Yeah."

"Watch your back tomorrow."

"I won't need to," Dempsey said. "You'll be watching it for me."

The talking seemed to be over. Both men began to move.

Peng barely had time to scamper out of sight as Dempsey made his way back toward the main building. It would be impossible for him to return to the room without being seen. But then again, Peng had never really meant to return. He promised Hope he wouldn't leave, and he would keep that promise, but he could probably be of more help to Matt on the outside rather than locked up in that small room. Still, he was ashamed at the disappointment Hope would feel when she awoke and found him gone.

When Dempsey was far enough away, Peng sneaked back around the building and moved in the direction the bearded man had gone. At first he thought he'd lost him, and then he spotted an elusive dark shape moving toward a small grouping of buildings that sat near the edge of the runway. One appeared to be an old radio tower, a place where a flight controller could watch a plane come in and give directions.

The bearded man looked around before climbing the tower stairs. At the top, he moved back and forth in front of the windows, and it looked like he was speaking to someone on a phone.

After about five minutes, he came down the stairs again and melted into the shadows. Peng tried to follow him, but he was just gone. Peng stood in the shadows for a very long time. He wasn't sure what to do. He tried to process what he'd heard. Apparently there was a plane arriving tomorrow at noon with a prince on board, as well as a man named Yehudi, who wanted to either kill Peng's family on the spot or take them with him and kill them in front of his mother. There was also something about cameras that Peng didn't fully understand. These men had a job to do that involved recording video, and once the job was done, it sounded like they might allow Peng's family to go free—if they were still alive. It was all very confusing. He tried to think about it like it was a machine, gears connecting with other gears, all working together for some end purpose. But without knowing what the purpose was, the machinery didn't make any sense.

After a while, he decided he needed to see more of the individual pieces. Maybe if he could see all of the parts laid out, he might be able to put the whole picture together.

He moved quickly and silently to the tower the bearded man had been in. There was dust everywhere, and Peng had to fight back a sneeze. There were cameras in the tower too, but not the type he was expecting.

There were three of them, all mounted on tripods, with camouflage webbing covering them.

Peng lifted the webbing and nearly gasped. The brand name Arri stood out in bold letters along the side. These were not just cameras; these were Hollywood movie cameras. Each of them probably cost about $65,000. Technology was Peng's hobby, and cameras were a specialty. He could tell the difference between the models and could even list which ones had shot the different Oscar-nominated films. These particular cameras were some of the best out there—the ones the biggest studios used. But why would these men need Hollywood cameras?

There was a small monitor along the wall that wasn't turned on. Neither were the cameras, which confused Peng since he had heard Dempsey's instructions to the bearded man. The cameras were all plugged into an eight-plug outlet surge protector, but the button on the surge protector was turned off. Peng hesitated for only a moment. He flipped the switch and watched the cameras and monitors come to life. All three of them were focused on an area in front of the hangar, where Peng assumed an airplane would arrive tomorrow. He followed the wires from the cameras and noticed two black cylindrical objects that looked like guns pointed toward the same area as the cameras. He knew immediately what they were—shotgun microphones. This meant they wanted sound as well as video. Just like Hollywood. They would likely have additional microphones somewhere close to the subjects if they wanted the audio to be cinema quality.

One last bit of camouflage webbing hung off to the side. There was a tripod there too, but it was empty. And it wasn't built for a camera. This was where the bearded man would be watching the action through his scope. It was the sniper's nest. Peng looked around for the rifle and saw a long, dark case lying on the floor. Why had the man not placed the rifle on the tripod? Maybe that was something he would do later. Peng moved to the sniper's nest and settled in to see what the sniper would see.

He tried to envision what would happen tomorrow when the plane arrived. It would taxi to the point where the cameras were aimed. Peng didn't know what size the plane would be, but he guessed it would be a small private jet. The door would open, and the stairs would extend to the ground before the people exited—the prince and Yehudi. Maybe others. Probably men with guns. Dempsey would come out to meet them, and the cameras would be recording them and their conversations the whole time. The bearded man would be up here in the sniper's nest, and when Dempsey got what he wanted, the man would shoot Yehudi and allow the prince to leave in the airplane. Maybe Dempsey would then allow Peng's family to leave as well. It was all like some big movie production, scripted down to the last detail.

Peng went to turn off the switch on the surge protector and then stopped himself. He still felt like something wasn't right. Dempsey had asked the bearded man to start the cameras recording. The bearded man had come up here, but he hadn't turned the cameras on. Peng looked back at the empty sniper's nest and wondered again why the man hadn't set everything up now. Maybe he was disobeying for a reason. Maybe he knew more about cameras and guns than Dempsey. Maybe he knew they would function better if he set them up closer to the time when he knew they would be used.

Or maybe he was operating off a different script. One where Yehudi was not hindered from taking his victims and that didn't have a happy ending. The man's responses to Dempsey had made Peng suspicious, and all of this was getting complicated. He looked at the wires again. To someone else, they might look like a mass of confusion. To Peng, they all made perfect sense. He wished he could read the paths of people the way he could read the wires.

The wires didn't connect logically. Wires that were supposed to attach didn't. Wires that should be doing one thing were doing something else. Cameras that were supposed to be recording had been turned off.

Peng looked at the cameras one more time, and it was as if he were seeing them with new eyes. He found the record buttons and turned them on. If the bearded man came back, he would know someone had been here, but Peng wasn't too worried. He was pretty sure the bearded man wasn't coming back.

Then he noticed the bag of explosives in the corner.

Chapter 39
REUNION

I WOKE UP AFTER WHAT seemed like only a few minutes of sleep. Everything was dark, and I felt like I was suffocating. I pulled my nose out of the hole in the mummy bag and put my eye where my nostrils had been.

"Ow," I said as sunlight hit me squarely in the pupil. It was morning. I had slept through the entire night without waking once. I pulled myself out of my bag and looked around. The water was still running, the static remained on the radio, and my sleeping bag smelled like mosquito repellant. But the sound of the bugs in the walls was gone. In fact, the bugs were gone altogether. I hadn't been consumed in the night. And I'd gotten perhaps the best night's rest I'd had in years. And there was something else. During the night, my brain had been able to put together some of the pieces that had been bothering me. I knew a lot more about my situation now than I had when I'd fallen asleep.

I began whistling to myself. I crammed my stinky sleeping bag into the stuff sack, stomped happily on a last errant roach, opened the door to let some air in, and sat on the bed, waiting for Dempsey's call. The entire situation suddenly made sense—the kidnapping, the government's connection with Dempsey, even Dempsey's actions with Becca years ago. I should have seen it before. It had been staring me in the face all along.

I now knew what Dempsey's game was. And knowing gave me an advantage.

* * *

Dempsey woke up feeling fatigued. Not only had he not slept much, but there was something else. Usually at this point in the game he was wired with excitement. This time he felt different. Mainly, he just felt weary. Maybe he was getting too old for this line of work. Maybe he should follow Carney's example and think about retirement.

He thought about calling Knight directly to hear the stress in his voice after what Dempsey was sure had been a long and restless night in the motel. Usually he would have enjoyed this, but for some reason, this morning he just didn't feel like it. Instead, he texted Knight the directions to the airfield and told him to get here as soon as possible.

He spent a long time going through the final pieces of the mission in his mind. After a while, he realized he was hungry and should probably get some food while he could.

He looked through the cooler for something to eat for breakfast and wrinkled his nose in disgust. There were two gallons of milk sitting in cold water that had once been ice. Also in the water were two large, soggy, open boxes of Cinnamon Toast Crunch—Buck's favorite cereal. He had put the boxes in the cooler instead of where they belonged. Sometimes Buck had no more sense than a twelve-year-old kid.

Dempsey started to call out and then caught himself. He was never going to have to chastise Buck again—never going to have to deal with his foolishness. For some reason, the thought caused a wave of sadness to wash over him. He threw the soggy cereal in a garbage bag and then hauled the bag, the thoughts of Buck, and his own melancholy emotions out to the trash bin. He couldn't afford to be distracted by sentimentality. Today was proving day. This was where all the threads came together and where the game would be either won or lost. This was what he lived for.

His cell phone buzzed.

"Mr. Dempsey, sir?" It was the elderly security guard at the front gate.

"Yes, Elwin, what is it? Do we have a guest?" Dempsey looked at his watch. It was about time for Knight to be here.

"I guess you could say that. The man says he is here from the office of the health inspector. Says there's been a report of rather large rats that need exterminating."

Dempsey frowned for a moment and then smiled. "Is he driving a red SUV?"

"Yes, he is. How did you know?"

"Send him in. Tell him the king rat is waiting for him."

"Yes, sir." Elwin sounded a bit confused.

Dempsey choked down a granola bar and then went to make final preparations.

* * *

The Enola Gay hangar looked exactly like it had on Tim's smartphone. I tried not to think about the hundreds of thousands of deaths associated with the plane that had once been parked here and the atomic bomb it had dropped. I didn't want to think about death today. There was only one thing I wanted, and that was to keep my family alive.

Dempsey was waiting for me outside the hangar. It had been years since I'd seen him last, but I would have known his profile anywhere. He'd bulked up some, but other than that, he was the same old Dempsey, standing confidently like he was privy to a secret nobody else had access to. I felt like taking my rented SUV and running him over before he had a chance to speak. That would be something he probably wouldn't expect. It would almost be worth it to see the surprise on his face.

I pulled in fast and close enough that he had to back up or risk me going over his toes. I opened the door quickly, wanting him to back off even more, wanting him to be at least a little off balance. But he sidestepped like a boxer who knew where the next punch was coming from and smiled knowingly.

"Well, if it isn't Matthew Knight. It's been a long time."

"Not nearly long enough. Where's my family?"

"They're safe inside. We've got a lot to talk about."

"I didn't come to talk to you, Dempsey. No conversation until I see them."

"As you wish." Dempsey motioned me toward a gap in the large sliding doors of the hangar. I stepped in, and he followed me. I didn't see any of his minions in the immediate area and wondered if I should make my move now, but his catlike gait and hint of a smile told me he was expecting me to try something. I wouldn't give him the satisfaction. Besides, I wasn't even sure he was telling me the truth about my family being safe. The closer I got to them, the more I ached to see them.

He led me across a cavernous space to a door on one end of the hangar. I thought I could hear talking inside, and then I recognized Hope's voice. My heart leaped into my throat, and I felt like a teenager picking up his crush for prom. Dempsey opened the door, and the most beautiful face I've ever seen was looking out at me. Granted the face looked extremely ticked off and quite a bit worried, but it was still the most beautiful face I'd ever seen.

Hope rushed into my arms and nearly knocked me over, her hair almost suffocating me. "You're here," she said through sobs. "You're finally here."

"I am definitely here," I mumbled through a mouthful of hair.

Hope pulled away from me, and Jin squealed "Daddy" from her stroller and held out her arms. I moved to her without fully letting go of Hope and pulled her up to my chest. She hugged me hard, and I wanted to squeeze her even harder. I nodded to Permelia, who was also in the room and was mouthing something to me. It looked like she was saying, "When are you going to take him out?"

Hope held my face in her hands and examined me. I'd forgotten that Tiny had tried to use me as his punching bag. My bruised cheek and forehead must have been a sight to behold.

"Peng told us you picked a fight with a giant. I thought I told you to be careful."

"Did he also tell you I won?"

"He told us you got the Scouts involved."

"I didn't involve them," I said. "I just . . . Where is Peng?" I looked around the room and didn't see him.

Hope let go of my face and stepped back. "He left us, Matt. He was here, he told us everything—he talked more than I've ever heard him talk before—but then he broke out and ran away. He promised he wouldn't leave, but then he disappeared . . . like he always does."

"He did what?" Dempsey's voice boomed from behind me.

"He escaped," Hope said, glaring at Dempsey. "He wanted to take us all with him, but I told him I wasn't going to watch you murder anyone else."

I was confused and a little angry. Just when I thought Peng had changed, he was back to his old tricks, sneaking out. Then I caught myself. For the first time, I felt I understood Peng, and I understood why he had done what he'd done. I pulled Hope close to me and said, "I'm sorry." Then I whispered in her ear so only she could hear. "He didn't leave us. I'm sure of it. He's still here somewhere. He'll try to help."

I turned to Dempsey before Hope could respond. I needed to turn this conversation in a different direction. I definitely didn't need Dempsey sending out a search party after Peng.

"You know, Dempsey, last night as I slept with the roaches, I think I finally figured you out. What would the criminal community think if they knew one of their favorite mercenaries was actually working for the CIA?"

Dempsey smiled slightly. "I doubt there's too many mercenaries out there who haven't done at least some work for the company. I'm not unique in that regard."

"I'm not talking about a contract job, and you know it. I'm talking about a full-time, permanent position with health benefits and a pension. Tell me this, was hitting Becca your initiation? A test to see if you would follow orders no matter how despicable they were? You know she really liked you. I think she was about ready to tell Robbie and me that the three musketeers were going to need to disband. And then you hauled off and smacked her like she was an insignificant pawn on one of your chessboards. I'm sure your bosses were very proud."

A dark cloud moved across Dempsey's eyes, and his mask of composure faltered for a fraction of a second. I'd tried to get under his skin many times, but this was the first time I'd really succeeded.

"This isn't helping your family," he said in a calm, composed voice.

"Neither are you," I said. "Not one bit. But know this, whatever your game is—government-sponsored or not—I'm holding you responsible. And this time you're going to lose more than the use of one of your nostrils."

Dempsey was about to say something else when a bearded man appeared out of nowhere.

"The plane's about to land, Boss. They'll be taxiing up in a matter of minutes," the man said.

"Have you seen any sign of the boy?" Dempsey said. "Apparently he escaped sometime last night. He probably could have made it to the Wendover police station by now."

The bearded man looked surprised. "I'm sure if he'd contacted the police, we would have heard about it on the scanners. There's been nothing. The airwaves have been quiet as death."

The color returned to Dempsey's face. "Okay. We can't worry about the boy now. Get into position. Tell Elwin to send a couple of his people to put the ramp in place."

The bearded man looked hesitant, as if he was ready to say something, and then he nodded and disappeared as quickly as he had come.

"Let's go outside," Dempsey said. "There's someone you need to meet."

We stepped out through a small slit in the hangar doors, and I handed Jin back to Hope, who put her in the stroller and opened her mouth to say something just as a large jet proceeded to touch down on the runway and taxi to a stop directly in front of us. When Demetrius had said the prince was coming in a private plane, I'd been expecting something a little smaller, maybe a Gulfstream 550. This was a full passenger jet, an Airbus 380, by its markings, and now I understood why Elwin needed to send his men to roll the ramp up to the plane. It was either that or have the passengers slide down the safety chutes.

The two men moved quickly and efficiently to put the ramp in place and then jumped in a Jeep and drove off. I didn't think they were part of Dempsey's crew. They didn't look sinister enough. They were probably Elwin's nephews. So far, it appeared that Dempsey had only one man with him, which should have been comforting, except I knew Yehudi was on that plane.

The door opened with a hiss as the engines powered down, and the smell of jet fuel drifted through the dry air. There appeared several hard-looking men in robes and keffiyeh head scarves, swinging submachine guns in arcs like they were clearing a room. Dempsey smiled and held up his hand in greeting. The men ignored him as two more people emerged on the ramp before the door hissed shut once again.

These men also wore keffiyeh, but while one of them had robes that looked clean, pressed, and expensive, the other looked like he'd been living in a sheep pen for about a month. I recognized the second one immediately, even though I'd never seen him before. The Yehudi nose was hooked and prominent, and the wild, murderous eyes reminded me of his brothers. He was also carrying a submachine gun and had a long, wicked-looking knife in his belt.

Luckily, Prince Sayami looked like he wanted to do some talking before beginning the mutilations. I was hoping he wanted to talk for a long time, and I really hoped Demetrius and Chico had been able to get into position. Now would be a good time for them to show up and save the day. I looked around the airfield but saw no sign of them. I scanned the surroundings, looking for places of safety if one of the men with submachine guns started shooting.

We stood about fifteen yards in front of the sliding metal doors of the hangar, which were mostly closed, leaving only the small gap we had just walked out of. The doors were made of thick metal, and getting back inside and behind them would be our best protection against a spray of bullets. The only problem was making it to the doors before the bullets made it to us.

Directly to our right was a wheelchair ramp leading up to the doors. The ramp was protected by a short cement wall along the outside edge. This was closer to us than the door and would also offer protection from bullets but only temporarily. The wall ended well before the outside corner of the hangar building, and if we moved behind it, we would be pinned down.

To our left were my rented SUV and a van I assumed belonged to Dempsey. Both vehicles would offer some cover and potentially a means of escape, but right now they were too far away to do us any good. A few hundred yards beyond the vehicles was a tall control tower, its windows reflecting like mirrors on the desert sands.

We had to get back inside the building, but in order to do so, we needed a pretty big distraction. And I was hoping it was going to get here soon.

"Mr. Dempsey," the prince said, holding out his arms in a magnanimous gesture as he stepped down the ramp to the tarmac. "It is good to finally meet you."

"You as well, Your Highness." Dempsey nodded slightly. "As you can see, I've brought you what you requested. I trust that you have brought the agreed-upon payment."

"Of course, Mr. Dempsey. Of course. But you jump to business so soon. I find that Americans have very little patience. In my country, this would be seen as rudeness."

"I mean no disrespect, Your Highness. It's been a long and trying week, and I'm feeling a little bit exposed out here."

"Yes. I understand you lost some men in this venture."

Dempsey's eyes narrowed. "Where did you hear that?"

"Let's just say I have my sources."

While the prince talked, Yehudi stood behind him, looking at each member of my family with daggers in his eyes. I thought about winking at him, but I was pretty sure he'd start shooting—prince or no prince. As he looked at each of us, his eye began to twitch, his scowl deepened, and his breaths came harder. He leaned toward the prince and whispered in his ear. I thought it might be, "That man over there. He is very good-looking, no?" But I was probably mistaken.

The prince listened with interest and raised his eyebrows. "It seems you have not fulfilled your part of the bargain after all, Mr. Dempsey. You were instructed to bring me the whole family, and it appears you are short one person."

"The boy escaped, but we've replaced him with a close family friend." Dempsey nodded toward Permelia, who actually winked at Yehudi.

"I'll reduce the fee by one quarter. The boy is adopted, after all. I'm sure Mr. Yehudi will find satisfaction enough as he tortures the wife and young daughter. The absence of the boy is inconsequential."

Yehudi whispered something again to the prince; he seemed to be working himself into a frenzy.

"My friend says you have not fulfilled your contract. He says we should kill you now and keep all the money."

To Dempsey's credit, he didn't flinch. "With all due respect, Your Highness, your friend wants to kill everybody he sees. We had a deal. You paid me to do a job that no other mercenary would take. At great danger to my own life, I returned to American soil, committed a number of federal crimes—including kidnapping an innocent woman and child—and am about to turn over one of America's greatest antiterrorist agents to a prince of Saudi Arabia. I may be missing one of the minor pieces, but I think I deserve to get paid."

The prince smiled widely. "Of course you are right." He motioned to one of his men, who in turn waved to one of the windows on the plane. A door opened near the wing of the plane, and a black duffle bag dropped onto the tarmac. One of the bodyguards ran to the bag and brought it to Dempsey. Dempsey knelt and unzipped the bag. Stacks of crisp bills were bundled inside.

"You could count it," the prince said. "But I think that would take a very long time."

Dempsey looked to be satisfied with what he saw. He measured off about a quarter of the bag and began removing stacks of money.

"Oh, no need for that, Mr. Dempsey. You can keep it all. As you say, kidnapping innocents on American soil is very hard work. It is a heinous crime. One that a prince of Saudi Arabia would not want to be associated with. But here I am, paying off a renowned mercenary for such a terrible act. And what is more, the kidnapping will be only the beginning. My friend here, Mr. Yehudi, made a promise to his mother that he would find the man who caused the death of his brothers and bring him and his family back to the Yehudi village to march them through the streets, where they would be tormented and spat upon. And then he would make the man watch as he flayed the skin from his loved ones while they were still yet alive and screaming. These would be great crimes indeed, don't you agree, Mr. Dempsey? It is a good thing we are out here in the middle of nowhere, away from the knowledge of anyone."

I noticed a change in Dempsey's demeanor. He glanced quickly behind him at the flight tower. Something was wrong. I could see it in Dempsey's eyes.

And then someone moved near one of the outbuildings behind the plane, working their way closer. At first I thought it might be Demetrius or Chico, but the figure was too small, too slight. An adolescent. An Asian. Peng. All it would take was a small turn of the head for one of the terrorist guards to spot him and take him out.

Hope pushed into my side and hissed with urgency, "What is he doing?" She had obviously seen him too.

"I don't know," I whispered back. The prince was still talking, and Dempsey still looked disconcerted. No one except Yehudi seemed to be paying any attention to the rest of us, and he was mainly just scowling at us.

"Do something." Hope's grip on my hand was forceful. "Stop him." The message was clear. I was the father. It was up to me to protect my family. Peng was putting himself in harm's way, and I needed to save him.

I could see where Peng was headed now, inching his way between small bits of cover, working carefully toward the landing gear at the bottom of the plane. I didn't know what had happened to Demetrius and Chico, but things seemed to be going south quickly with Dempsey and the prince, and I didn't think it would be long before Yehudi's murderous expression would manifest into tangible actions.

"Matt," Hope hissed again, squeezing my hand even tighter.

"We need to trust him," I whispered back. "He knows what he's doing."

"I don't like that answer," she said. Her grip did not lessen.

I didn't like it either, but I didn't see that there was much we could do. "They'll see him."

"We need to distract them," I said, looking around for options.

Permelia stepped closer. She had also apparently noticed Peng's movements. "I got this one, Captain," she said. I wasn't sure why she was calling me captain, but there was no one else around who she could be talking to.

"Don't," I told her. "It's too risky."

She snorted. "At my age, getting out of bed in the morning is risky—and don't even talk to me about going to the bathroom. There's a little Indian motorcycle around the corner. I saw it when I busted out the first time. It reminds me of the one Anthony Hopkins drove on the Salt Flats. I'm going to get to the motorcycle and drive the other direction like a bat out of Hades. That should give Peng time to do whatever he's doing."

Both Hope and I started to protest, but before any words came out, Permelia was making her break toward the side of the building.

Yehudi, the only one who seemed to be paying any attention to us, began pointing and shouting. "The old one," he said. "She's getting away."

The prince just shrugged. "She was not part of the bargain. Where is she going to go?"

I heard the sound of a small engine trying to catch. After several sputters, the spitting noises turned into a whine, and Permelia appeared, hunched over a small dirt bike heading down the runway in the opposite direction from Peng. The good news was that all eyes turned toward her. The bad news was that this particular Indian dirt bike seemed to have the acceleration of a push lawnmower.

Despite the frantic, mosquito-like buzzing of the engine, Permelia didn't seem to be getting any farther away. A few of the guards pushed at each other and laughed. The prince was also smiling. I stole a glance in Peng's direction as he scampered up the large tires of the landing gear and disappeared into the plane's underbelly. Despite her pitiful progress, Permelia's distraction had worked.

Yehudi stepped forward, his face flushed with rage, and waved toward the guards. "They are letting her get away."

"I don't think she will get very far," the prince said, chuckling. "By the time she reaches the authorities, we will be crossing the ocean. It would be a waste of ammunition."

"Then let me do it," Yehudi demanded. "She is their friend. Let me make them feel pain."

"Shooting a defenseless old woman," the prince said with mock gravity. "But that would be cold-blooded murder."

"My prince."

The prince frowned at Yehudi and then shrugged. "All right," he said. "You have my permission."

Yehudi smiled and pulled the assault rifle up to his shoulder. Hope was squeezing my hand, and I heard her begin to cry.

I looked around for something to use as a weapon. Dempsey wasn't close enough for me to grab his gun, and Yehudi wasn't close enough for me to throw anything at him. So I was left to use the only weapon I had—my tongue. "Your brothers used to call you the flea. Did you know that?" Yehudi swung his weapon toward me. "I don't think it was a term of endearment. They used to say the best thing about coming to America was that they no longer had to put up with the constant nagging from the hag and the constant pestering from the flea. From the pictures, I'm pretty sure the hag they were talking about was your mother."

"You lie!" he screamed, but I could tell I had scored a point. And I wasn't lying. His brothers really had said that. Permelia's buzzing was fainter now, and I hoped she was moving out of firing range, but Yehudi's rage was building, and I was afraid he was going to start shooting at me instead.

"I promised my mother you would not die until we reach my village," Yehudi yelled, the spittle flying from his lips. "But I will not listen to any more of your lies. I will have your tongue, and I will have it now." He lowered his gun to the ground and pulled out his knife.

"Easy, Yehudi," the prince said, holding him back. "You can cut out his tongue later. But right now it looks like we have other guests."

I was thinking it was about time that Demetrius and Chico showed up, but when I turned, I didn't see what I had hoped to see.

It was Demetrius, all right, but he was being herded toward us by the man with the beard. I wasn't the only one who seemed genuinely surprised. Dempsey also seemed to be caught off guard. The prince, however, looked like he was getting exactly what he'd expected.

"Did Knight bring any more soldiers with him?" the prince asked the man with the beard.

"One other. A big Hispanic. He wasn't going to come easily, so I had to lay him out. He won't be conscious for several hours."

Demetrius looked at me and shrugged. So much for the cavalry.

The bearded man also looked apologetic, but he was focused on Dempsey. "Sorry, Demps. Just following orders."

Dempsey nodded to the tower behind the bearded man's shoulder. "So there are no cameras? I thought the prince was being a little too theatrical with his remarks."

"I was instructed to turn them off." The man spoke like each word pained him.

Dempsey rubbed his nose and studied the situation around him and then turned back to the bearded man. "Why not just tell me? Why keep me in the dark on this? Did they think I would do anything different than follow orders? Have I ever not done exactly as they said?"

"It's a new regime, Demps. They don't know you like I do. Their assessment was that you would work best if you thought you were the one pulling the strings. They call you the Game Master."

"It was a good plan," the prince interjected. "Get a potential successor to the Saudi crown on tape implicating himself in kidnapping and murder. Show the tape to the royal family, and eliminate one of the more radical factions. But that plan was no longer feasible once I convinced your government that I was actually one of their better options for succession and that doing me and my friends a favor might be in the best long-term interests of your country."

"Only one problem with that," Dempsey said. "Your friends are criminals and terrorists."

"Yes, they are, Mr. Dempsey. As are many of yours. It is an occupational hazard. Let's just say there are certain members of your government who feel more comfortable dealing with someone who has influence with the criminal element. Isn't that why they put you in the position you are in?"

"I don't know how you talked them into this," Dempsey said. "They've got to be out of their minds."

"But I'm a good actor, Mr. Dempsey. Admit it, I had you fooled earlier. I took two semesters of drama when I was at Princeton. It was my favorite class. You, of all people, should appreciate this. It's not who we are that matters, it's who people think we are. But alas, I'm getting weary of this conversation. I think it's time for me to retire to my plane and take a nap on my ridiculously expensive bed."

He nodded to his guards. "Bring the prisoners, but only after I am in my quarters. I don't want to hear their screams. Let Mr. Yehudi do with them as he wants. I don't think his mother will argue their condition as long as they are alive." The prince turned and began walking up the ramp toward the door of his plane.

I looked at Dempsey in desperation.

"Wait," Dempsey said. "You can't tell me they agreed to let you take the prisoners."

The prince turned and smiled. His voice was quieter now, less flamboyant, less like he was playing a part in a movie. "That is exactly what they agreed to, Mr. Dempsey. And that is exactly what is going to happen. They did say that you were to be spared, but only if you stayed out of the way and didn't cause any trouble. You like to play chess, no? This is what they call checkmate. Your only move at this point is to step back and stay out of the way. You may keep the money if you like. I have more of it than I know what to do with."

Dempsey looked to the bearded man. "You realize what this means," he said. "My cover's been blown. A target's just been placed on my back. Did they ask you to make it official from the sniper's nest?"

The bearded man shook his head. "I don't think they've thought that far ahead. But I'd be careful from here on out. Take the money, Demps. Disappear."

The prince had turned and was on his way up the ramp, and Yehudi's grin was widening.

"Dempsey," I growled. "Where's your plan B?"

But when I looked into his eyes, I saw only defeat.

Chapter 40
BOOM

TIME SEEMED TO MOVE IN slow motion. The prince made his way up the ramp, step by step. His guards closed in around us, careful to keep their guns trained on both Dempsey and me. I looked for any move I could make, but there was none. Yehudi continued to glare at me and my family, fire in his eyes and no doubt about his intentions once we were in his control. Demetrius was poised and ready to move, but the bearded man kept him at gunpoint, a look of resignation on his face.

As the prince neared the door, I heard a slight buzzing sound in the distance. He must have heard it too because he stopped momentarily and cocked his head. The sound got louder, and slowly a figure appeared—a small figure on an Indian dirt bike. A heroic figure who should have been going the other way.

The prince shook his head. "Your friends are valiant, Mr. Knight, but not very wise." He turned to Yehudi. "When the old hag gets within range, shoot her."

Yehudi happily nodded.

I wanted to jump one of the guards, but they were ready, waiting for me to make a move. There was nothing I could do.

The prince tapped three times on the plane door and waited.

I expected to hear the hydraulic hiss of the electronic door opening. Instead there was a deafening boom as the door exploded outward, coming completely off its hinges and carrying the prince with it, over the top of Yehudi's head, away from the plane, and down onto the tarmac. The prince landed on his back with a thud, the heavy door on top of him. He didn't move.

For the space of a few heartbeats, everyone stood and stared in stunned silence. And then everything seemed to erupt at once.

I grabbed Jin from the stroller, pulled Hope with me, and rolled over the top of the cement wall in front of the wheelchair ramp. I heard the bullets tearing away great chunks of concrete as Sayami's guards opened fire on us.

"Keep your head down," I said to Hope as I transferred Jin from my arms to hers. Jin turned her face into Hope's chest and clung to her tightly.

Dempsey was also moving. He grabbed the bag of cash, dove inside the hangar doors, and came up holding a gun in his hand. We needed to get inside those doors if we were going to have any chance.

"Cover us," I yelled at him.

He hesitated for a moment, then shook his head. All we needed were a few seconds to get across the walkway and through the doors, but we weren't going to make it without some cover fire.

"We're on the same side," I said. "You're CIA."

"Not anymore," Dempsey said. "I think I just received my burn notice."

"Mr. Dempsey." It was Hope's turn to yell at him. "Please, I have a little girl. We need your help. I know you've got some good in you. I've seen it."

By the look in his eyes, I thought Hope's words might have gotten through. But then a shower of bullets peppered the door next to him, and Dempsey disappeared into the dark abyss of the hangar.

I turned my attention to where Demetrius had been. The man with the beard seemed conflicted about keeping his gun on Demetrius or turning it toward the prince's guards. He seemed to make up his mind when one of the guards opened fire on him. Both the bearded man and Demetrius leaped behind the van on the other side of the hangar opening.

The bearded man raised his gun above his head and shouted, "Stop shooting. Stop shooting. I'm on your side." This prompted an immediate barrage of bullets from one of the guards who seemed to be enraged. It also prompted Demetrius to punch the bearded man in the face and take the gun away from him. The man crumpled to the ground like a wet blanket.

I took a quick peek over the wall. Four of the six guards were pulling the plane door off the prince, who was groaning and holding his ribs. The other two guards were raining focused volleys on the wall and the van. I peered around the side of the wall and immediately got cement chips in my eye. Demetrius was in a similar predicament, even though he had a weapon. He tried to return fire but was quickly forced down by a barrage of bullets.

I wondered where Yehudi had gone, and then I heard the cackling of his maniacal voice. It was coming from above the guards, and it sounded like he was shouting out instructions in Arabic.

My language skills were rusty, but I picked up enough to know the gist of what he was saying, and I felt a cold dread creep up my spine.

"Focus your fire on the dark one," he said in his own language. "Keep him pinned down." And then in English. "Let the infidel and the woman raise their heads. I want them to watch while I take the life of their son."

Hope stood before I did, but only by a fraction of a second. We were completely exposed to the guards, but they had done as Yehudi had instructed and had Demetrius completely pinned down.

At the top of the ramp, where the plane door had been blown off, Yehudi stood with an arm around Peng, his long knife held against my son's throat.

"Take me instead," Hope shouted. "Take me and not my son."

"There will be plenty of time for you," Yehudi screamed. "Plenty of time for your husband to witness that as well. The prince was right. I will be patient. I will take most of you back alive. But I will also give you a taste of what is to come. Look on your son, Matthew Knight. Know what happens when you cross the Yehudi family."

I glanced wildly around, looking for any way to stop the events from transpiring. Hope was pleading with Yehudi, sobs wracking her body. Demetrius was hopelessly pinned down by the gunfire from the guards. The prince was slowly regaining consciousness but was not aware enough to take control of the situation. Chico was lying unconscious somewhere in the desert, Dempsey had fled, and Permelia was approaching on the dirt bike at a pace that might get her here by next Tuesday. Peng didn't look scared. He looked proud. Yehudi stood behind him, the sacrificial knife in his hand. I needed to do something. I needed to save Peng. I was his father. He was my responsibility. Hope was counting on me.

But there was nothing I could do. The situation was beyond my control. All I could do was watch—watch, pray, and trust that God was in control.

I'd never been to the other side, but when Hope talked about her near-death experience, her face glowed with light. "Death is no tragedy," she often said. "It's like going home."

What if it was Peng's time to return home? What if it was God's will that he should leave us? Could I accept that?

Let go. It will be all right. The thoughts from the night before returned.

I took Hope's hand and tried to comfort her. I ignored Yehudi and met Peng's eyes. I looked at the exploded door and the prince lying on the ground and nodded to Peng as if to say, "Good work." I hoped he got my meaning. I was proud of him. He had done well.

I thought I saw the tug of a smile on his lips, and he turned his eyes from Hope to Jin and then back to me. "Take care of them," he said with his eyes.

I knew exactly what he meant. We didn't need words. We were family. I nodded to him that I understood.

Yehudi laughed again and held the knife in the air in dramatic emphasis.

"Close your eyes," I told Hope, pulling her head into my chest. "You don't want to see this."

She did as I said. I should have done the same, but I couldn't look away. I kept my eyes locked on Peng's. In his final moments, in the moments before he passed into a realm where beings of light would embrace him with warmth, I didn't want him to be alone.

The knife descended onto its target, and Peng dropped to the ramp.

My heart dropped with him. I had known grief before. I had seen my mother murdered in front of my eyes. I had lost my best friend, Robbie. I had awoken with night terrors, dreaming that Hope's cancer had come back and that she had been called home. But none of this had prepared me for a grief like this. A grief that could only come by the death of a child. The death of *my* child.

I looked from Peng to Yehudi. Something had changed in his expression. His eyes went from triumphant to confused. He looked down at the blood on his hands and dropped the knife. He reached up toward his forehead, where I now noticed that two small holes had appeared. And then he toppled off the ramp. Peng was moving now, scrambling back inside the plane. I struggled to piece together what had happened. Peng's throat had not been cut. Someone had shot Yehudi before the knife had found its mark.

I pulled Hope back down behind the wall and tried to identify where the shots had come from. There was somebody in the control tower with a sniper's rifle. At first I thought it was Chico, awakened from his slumber, but as I looked closer, I recognized the familiar figure. From this distance, I couldn't see the broken nose, but I knew where it sat on his face. Dempsey had returned. He'd saved Peng's life, and he was starting to pick off the prince's guards one by one.

Two of them were down, but the other four concentrated their fire on Dempsey. Dempsey took out one more of the guards before the barrage of fire hit him and he fell backward off the tower.

Demetrius rose and opened fire on the remaining three guards. One of them went down, but the other two trained their weapons on him and forced him back behind the van. Dempsey's sacrifice had been valiant, but it had not quite been enough. The closest fallen guard lay at least twenty yards from me, next to the prince, who sat on the ground looking bewildered. If I could just get to his weapon . . . but they would cut me down before I made it three steps.

Peng peeked his head out from the doorway of the plane. He had Yehudi's gun in his hand. I shook my head at him. As soon as he started firing he would be an easy target for the two remaining professionals. I waved at Peng to get back. For once in his life, Peng heeded me. He nodded and stayed concealed. The two guards began a flanking maneuver. It wouldn't be long before

Demetrius was exposed. I looked around frantically. There was no weapon in sight, except a metal piece of rebar that would be of no use at this distance. Unless . . .

I picked up the rebar, held it like a rifle, and nodded to Demetrius to be ready.

He signaled back by holding out his arms as if to say, "Are you crazy?"

I popped up from my position and yelled, "Drop the guns, or the prince dies." I hoped the rebar looked enough like a rifle at this distance to at least make them hesitate.

They did, but not for long. Both rifles swung in my direction. Hope was pulling at my leg to get down, but there was no time.

Demetrius took the opportunity to take out the guard in his line of vision, but he didn't have a shot at the other one.

The prince seemed to have recovered his senses and was getting to his feet. "Kill him," he shouted. For some reason, he was pointing at me. "This infidel has ruined everything."

The guard raised his gun obediently, but as he did, Peng stepped out into the open. He didn't fire on the guard, although he could have. Instead, he trained Yehudi's gun on the prince. "Don't," he said.

I waved at Peng to go back inside, but it was too late. The guard still had the black barrel of his assault rifle pointed at me, but I could see he was gauging the time it would take for Peng to react.

"You might shoot me," Peng said. "But not before I kill the prince." Peng's voice was confident. He didn't sound like a kid anymore. He didn't sound like he was bluffing either.

The guard didn't seem as convinced as I was. He was hesitating. I could tell that any second he would make his move. Peng would probably be able to kill the prince before the guard shot him, if he even knew how to operate an assault rifle, but either way, the guard was going to take him out.

The guard smirked, and Peng tightened his grip on the rifle and kept it steady on the prince. Demetrius was working his way around the wall for a clear shot, but he wouldn't make it in time. The stage had been set. The pieces were in place. And I didn't like the way this scene was going to end. The guard's eyes no longer showed any sign of hesitation. He was going to act.

The only sound on the airfield was the buzzing of Permelia's motorcycle, still too far away to make any difference.

The prince had turned and was looking back and forth between his guard and Peng. The guard began to move.

"Stop," the prince yelled. "Stop, you fool."

The guard stopped his movement.

"How dare you risk my life with your bravado."

"But, my prince, they have killed your royal guard."

"I can replace my royal guard, you idiot. I can buy a thousand royal guards. I cannot replace my life."

"But they will take you captive. They will shame your family."

The prince smiled. "Drop the gun, Ahmed. There is nothing they can do to us. We are diplomats on foreign soil. We have immunity."

The guard lowered his gun. Demetrius came out from behind the wall. "On the ground," he ordered. The guard went to his knees and put his hands behind his head.

"I don't think you know how diplomatic immunity works." Demetrius kicked the guard's rifle safely away from him and turned his gun on the prince. "You've committed terrorist acts on American soil." He nodded in Dempsey's direction. "You've murdered a member of an American security agency. Diplomatic immunity doesn't apply here. Put your face on the ground."

I walked out, picked up one of the dead guard's guns, and joined Demetrius.

The prince just smiled. "I believe it is you who does not understand diplomacy, my friend, or the politics of power. You see, I have an agreement with a member of your government. Someone who outranks you by many levels. Someone who wants me in power. Someone who was willing to give me Mr. Knight and his family in order to secure my loyalties. Do you think the killing of Mr. Dempsey is going to change any of that? Officially he is an outlaw mercenary. I might even get a reward. Put your guns down, gentlemen. I am no longer a threat to you. With Yehudi dead, I don't need his loyalties. Mr. Knight, you and your family are free to go."

"I don't think so." I kept the gun pointed at the prince's head and looked over at Demetrius. By the look on his face, I could tell he was having the same doubts about our government handling this that I was. If what the prince said was true, the CIA might not like us messing with someone they viewed as an asset.

A deep and booming voice sounded behind us. "Your agreement with the government ends here, Prince Sayami."

Zack appeared in the hangar door. He had his forearm tightly around the neck of the bearded man, who I realized had disappeared at some point during the firefight. The man was squirming, but I knew there was no escaping that grip.

"Little Gerald Morgan. Always sneaking out of my classes at Quantico and trying to slither away now. I think he will make a great witness of today's events when they are presented to a grand jury."

Gerald's face was beginning to turn purple.

The prince was nonplussed. Even in his burned and tattered robes, even with two guns trained on his head and the remains of his royal guard lying dead around him, he still looked like he believed he was in charge.

"It will be my word against his," the prince said. "And your word against the deputy director of your CIA. You can't win here. None of this ever happened. If anything, the evidence will suggest that I was the one attacked." He nodded to Demetrius and me. "Your country has special offshore prisons for men like these— suspected terrorists and enemies of the state. Do you think this will ever come to a trial? Who do you think is going to win here? All of the evidence will support my position. You can either let me go, or I guarantee you will all go away to a very dark place for a very long time."

"What about the video?" Demetrius said. "Dempsey said this was being taped."

The man in Zack's grasp was shaking his head. Zack released his throat long enough for him to speak. "The video doesn't exist," he said. "I unplugged the cameras." He rolled his eyes up toward Zack as Zack began to retighten his grip. "It was orders," he said desperately. "Orders from above. They told me to turn the cameras off." Zack looked like he wanted to keep squeezing, but he eased up.

"Not true." Peng stepped forward. He'd made his way down from the top of the ramp and was holding Jin and embracing Hope.

"That man did unplug the cameras, but I plugged them back in."

"Impossible," the bearded man said. "Those aren't your everyday Walmart cameras, kid. They're sophisticated equipment. It took me years to learn how to use them."

Peng just shrugged. "I'm good with cameras."

The bearded man started to protest again, and Zack squeezed a little harder. "Gerald. Don't argue with my favorite grandson."

Gerald passed out.

All eyes moved toward the observation tower. The windows were pockmarked with bullet holes where the shots had been fired at Dempsey. If there were cameras, there was no guarantee they were still in working order.

"I guess we better go take a look," I said and started walking in that direction.

About that time, the buzzing noise heightened, and Permelia pulled around the corner on the motorcycle. She looked around at the bodies on the ground and the rest of the bad guys in custody and snorted. "I missed out on all the fun," she said. "These bikes look a lot faster in the movies."

Chapter 41
PLAN C

THE CONTROL TOWER WAS TALLER than it looked at a distance, probably about sixty feet high, the metal support structure alternating colors between ghostly white and blood orange. Peng led the way, the rest of us marching single file behind him. A wind picked up, and it moaned and wailed as it whipped the grit off the desert floor and threw it into our eyes. Maybe I would suggest to Hope that we get a summer home here.

"Peng, go see if there is any camera footage left in that tower."

Peng scurried off without a word while the rest of us looked for Dempsey.

We found him lying on the ground behind the out buildings.

Hope rushed over and pulled his limp head up into her lap. "No." Tears poured freely from her eyes. "Please, no."

That was one of the things I loved about Hope. This man had kidnapped her, threatened her, and almost gotten her family killed, yet she was still openly worried about his well-being.

Dempsey coughed and opened his eyes. I nearly jumped in surprise. There was no way he should have survived such a fall, whether he had been shot several times in the chest or not. I looked closer at what appeared to be a square metal storage structure and saw it ripple in the breeze. It wasn't metal at all but was only painted to appear like metal. It was an inflatable blow-up rescue mat that firemen placed under a jumper. Probably something Dempsey had gotten from a movie set. It appeared he had landed there and then rolled off onto the pavement, where he now lay. Still, he had been shot by real bullets, and ragged holes peppered the front of his shirt. But I had seen this movie before.

"Thanks," I said to him as his eyes began to clear. "For saving my son."

"I didn't do it for you." His voice was hoarse, and each breath seemed to pain him. He looked up at Hope and then back at me. "How is it that you got so lucky with the women in your life?"

He was right about that. I was the luckiest man in the world.

"Becca really liked you," I said. "You didn't have to hit her. You didn't have to choose to work for the CIA. Nobody messed that one up except you."

Dempsey nodded, and then he began coughing. He held one arm around his chest and another to his mouth. When he spoke again, there was blood on his teeth. He smiled at me. "I would appreciate if you told Becca I finally did something right. Tell her I did it for her."

He began coughing again, and he winced in pain with each spasm. Hope was getting blood all over her clothes, but she didn't seem to notice. Her only concern was to comfort Dempsey. She was too good for me. She was definitely too good for Dempsey.

"Tell her yourself," I said. "We're through playing your games."

"Matt." Hope looked up at me in exasperation. "He's dying."

"Maybe," I said. "But only if I decide to strangle him."

"Matt . . ." Hope's voice was getting more insistent.

I bent down and dipped my fingers into the pool of blood. It was thick and sticky. I touched my fingers to my lips and tasted. I'd heard of the sweet taste of blood, but this was a little too sweet. "Karo syrup?" I held out my fingers to Dempsey. "Really?"

"Matt, what are you doing?" Hope asked. "He was shot. We all saw it."

"He also seems to be extremely well defined under his shirt," I said, standing up. "The Dempsey I knew never had pecs. It just so happens that a friend of mine has been testing some new body armor recently. It's at the prototype level and is only available to a few people. But I'm sure with your connections, it wasn't difficult."

"Matt, he's not faking the pain. I can feel his ragged breathing. He really is hurt."

"I don't doubt that. The impact of the bullets probably broke a couple of his ribs. But that's not real blood, and he's definitely not dying."

Hope looked down at Dempsey, and he gave a slight shrug. "It was worth a try."

She dropped his head from her lap onto the pavement.

It bounced.

Hard.

"Ow. Was that necessary? I saved your son's life a few minutes ago."

"That's the only reason I'm not strangling you right now," Hope said.

I smiled. There was another reason I loved this woman.

Peng returned from his trip to the tower. He was carrying a canvas sack.

"Were the cameras damaged?" Zack asked as if he was briefing one of his agents, not a fifteen-year-old boy.

"Yes." Peng was matter-of-fact. "None of them are functional now."

"You see?" Prince Sayami stepped forward, his nose tipping in the air. "This situation is beyond you. But if you let me go now, I might decide to forget that you have ruined my plane and killed most of my guards."

I ignored the prince and kept my focus on Peng. "What's in the bag?"

"The hard drives," Peng said. "One of them was destroyed, but the other four are intact."

"And the video is on those drives?"

"Yes." Peng looked at me as if I should know. "I tested them on the monitor. You have video from four angles, and the sound is pretty decent too." He patted the bag. "We have the whole thing in here."

"It won't matter." The prince continued to push his way toward us. "As soon as you leave this place, those drives will be seized. You can't win. You don't know who you're dealing with."

"No," I said. "You don't know who you're dealing with. Prince Sayami, meet Zack, the hammer."

I nodded to Zack. He stepped forward and brought a huge fist down on the prince's head. The prince crumpled silently to the ground.

Permelia pushed at the prince's body with her foot. "I want you to show me how to do that," she said to Zack. "It might come in handy someday."

"What would it take to send that video to a few of my friends?" Zack asked.

"We need a laptop and a wireless connection," Peng said without hesitation. "The file is too large to send, but we can create a Dropbox folder and send the link. It would probably take about fifteen minutes." Peng nodded at Dempsey, who was now sitting up and rubbing his ribs. "He's got a computer inside the building. We can tether into a cell phone for the Wi-Fi."

Zack glared at Dempsey. "Mr. Dempsey, you are going to take us to your laptop. Now."

Dempsey winced and reached again for his ribs, but his hand came away holding something that looked like a can, and he said something that sounded like, "Plan C."

"Get down," I said, pulling Hope behind me and reaching for the stroller to cover Jin's ears.

The flash-bang grenade did exactly what it was supposed to do. I was temporarily deaf and blind. Dempsey must have followed up with a smoke grenade because when my senses began to return, I still couldn't see more than a few feet.

People were staggering around, attempting to get their bearings. The one remaining guard was trying to crawl away, but Zack's foot had come down on his back. When the coughing finally subsided, I began counting heads. Everyone was present, accounted for, and in reasonably decent shape, except for Dempsey—he and the canvas bag Peng had been holding.

"We need to find him," I shouted to Zack.

He nodded, a grim look on his face as he scanned the surroundings. Everything was flat, dusty, and empty. Dempsey was nowhere to be seen.

Jin was crying. Hope picked her up and held her close. Peng looked down at his side, where the bag had been, blinking his eyes as if he were surprised it still wasn't there.

"This is bad," I yelled. I was only a few feet from Zack, but I wasn't sure he could hear me.

Zack nodded in affirmation. "You don't need to yell." He must have prepped his ears for the bang better than I had. I'd been focused on protecting Jin.

I held my hands against my ears and made yawning motions, trying to bring back my hearing. There was an annoying buzz in the back of my head that reminded me of Permelia's motorcycle, but I was slowly starting to hear things again.

Dempsey had disappeared into the dusty barrenness like a hero at the end of a Western movie—and he had taken our evidence with him. We still had Morgan and the prince. We still had the eyewitness testimonies of three current or former antiterrorist agents. We still had Hope and Permelia, two innocents who'd been kidnapped and nearly killed. It should have been enough to secure justice. But I knew the people we were dealing with. People like Dempsey, who liked to play games. We really needed those drives.

"Let's fan out," I said. "Demetrius, you take left, Zack take the center, and I'll take the right. Any sign of Dempsey, make your voice heard."

"What about me?" Peng was still looking down at his side.

I wanted to tell him it was okay. That he had done enough. That his actions these last few days—from stealing my watch and showing me the position of the bad guys to rigging the plane door to explode and prevent Yehudi from leading us all into an unimaginable terror—were more than anyone could ever ask of a young man like him. But I could see from his face that my words would not be enough. Peng didn't want comfort; he wanted to help.

"You check the buildings in the back."

"What about—"

"You go with Peng." I cut Permelia off before she could finish. The longer we talked, the easier it would be for Dempsey to escape.

Zack and Demetrius had already started fanning out. I tried to think like Dempsey, and it made my brain hurt. Playing games with him was like going against a Sicilian when death was on the line. But I thought that maybe if I were Dempsey, I would have gone back toward the plane. The desert might be safer, but it would also take a lot longer before he could connect with his people. And the desert would be dirty and dusty. Dempsey had always liked his creature comforts. Using my skills of deduction, I headed toward the plane.

None of us had gone very far before I heard a yelp that reminded me of a dog that had been accidentally stepped on. It was coming from the desert across the runway, somewhere in the direction Demetrius was heading. So much for my skills of deduction.

"Hey." It was Dempsey's voice, and he seemed to be in distress. "Hey. Ow. That was my nose. What did you do to it?"

"Fixed it for you." The other voice was also familiar.

"I don't think Dempsey understands that the *C* in plan C stands for *Chico*," Demetrius said, a grin beginning to spread across his face as two figures appeared and began to move closer. "Hey, Chico, it's about time you woke up. They don't pay us for sleeping on the job."

"Where's the one who cold-cocked me?" Chico was holding Dempsey by the back of his neck, his fingers almost meeting on the front side of Dempsey's throat. Anytime Dempsey tried to speak or struggle, Chico would just tighten his grip.

"He's sleepin' for now," Demetrius said. "You can pay him back later. Maybe fix *his* nose too."

As Dempsey got closer, I could see that Chico had indeed fixed Dempsey's nose, putting it back in the middle of his face where it had been so many years before. But in doing so, he must have broken some cartilage because Dempsey was bleeding heavily from both nostrils.

"Get the bag." I nodded to Peng.

"What'll we do with him now?" Permelia was licking her lips. "I've always wanted to try waterboarding. Do you think it would work with a bloody nose?"

Peng retrieved the bag, and Chico dropped Dempsey in the dirt in front of me. I looked down at him and thought about all the grief this man's actions had caused my family and me these last few days. I thought about Peng and the other Scouts being terrorized by armed mercenaries in the mountains; I thought about Hope, Jin, and Permelia being taken from our home and held hostage as pawns in a game of politics and power; I thought about Yehudi's knife and how close we had all come to being put into the hands of a raving maniac.

Hope was examining Dempsey as well, her eyebrows knit in thought.

"Don't look at me like that," he said. "I am the man I am, not the one you'd like me to be."

"And yet you saved my son."

"I went back for the hard drives. My agency has blown my cover, and I'm going to need all the leverage I can get. End of story."

"You thought the cameras were turned off," Hope said. "There was no reason for you to go back for the hard drives."

"I had to be sure."

"Then why didn't you just take the drives and run when you had the chance? None of us would have seen you. You could have been miles from here by now. And Yehudi would have killed my son. You may not be willing to admit it, Mr. Dempsey, but there is good in you somewhere. You know what else I think? I think you hit Becca because you cared about her. You knew the life you were going to be leading with the CIA, and you didn't want her to have to endure it. You needed a way that she would let go of you forever. You did it for her."

Dempsey acted as if he'd been slapped. Hope had been able to see truth behind Dempsey's mask that I'd never gotten close to discerning. He turned to me as if asking for help.

"Don't fight it," I said. "She has that effect on everyone."

Zack stepped up next to me. "What do you want to do with him? It's your call."

Hope was still staring at Dempsey with a curious mixture of anger, disappointment, and . . . something I'd seen many times before when she'd looked at me. Something that always made me want to stand a little taller.

"Let him go," I said.

Everyone, including Hope, turned to stare at me in stunned silence.

"We don't need Dempsey." I directed my comments to Zack. "With the video, the bearded man, and your relationship with the president, I think we have more than enough to make our case."

"You have a relationship with the president?" Permelia asked. "Why didn't you ever tell me about that?"

"He was a student of mine," Zack replied. "I choked him once until he passed out."

"I've been wanting to do that for years," Permelia said. "Can you teach me?"

Zack ignored Permelia's request. His eyes met mine. "I'm afraid he'll be back to his old games in no time."

"Let him," I said. "Someday he'll realize he's playing a game he can't win."

"I always win," Dempsey said.

"Not in this case. You made an errant move early on, and you never really had a chance to recover."

"You're right, but I'll make sure the new deputy director doesn't underestimate me in the future. I should have anticipated the little weasel throwing me under the bus."

"I'm not talking about the deputy director," I said. "You made the wrong move long before that. You had a chance at a real life with Becca, one with real friends and real family. One where you wouldn't have to worry constantly about people stabbing you in the back. You should have moved right, and instead you moved left. After that, you had no chance of winning. The game was already decided."

Dempsey shrugged. "If that's true, I guess my only choice is to play it out until the end."

"No," Hope said. "You could admit defeat and start playing a different game. One where you aren't forced to shoot your friends in the head."

For a moment, I thought he might listen. Dempsey had a faraway look in his eyes that suggested he longed for something more. Then he came back into focus and deliberately looked away from Hope toward me.

"How about a vehicle?" he said.

"Don't push it," I replied. "You get to walk your way out of this one. I think some long hours of self-reflection might do you some good. The desert is that way."

Dempsey shrugged, stood, and began to walk away.

"Wait," Demetrius said. "What about that bag of money?"

"I'm sure he's stashed it somewhere only he can find," I said. "Let him take it. He's going to need it."

"Wait." This time it was Chico who spoke. "If he's got a phone on him, he might tip off his friends at the agency before we can get that video uploaded."

Dempsey turned. "I'm not sure I have any friends left at the agency," he said. Then under his breath, "I'm not sure I ever did." He pulled out his cell phone and tossed it to Chico. He turned and began to walk away again, still looking a bit too sure of himself.

"Wait." This time I was the one to raise my voice.

"What is it?" Dempsey said without turning around. "I'm starting to get tired of this. I don't really need another lecture."

I directed my comments toward Chico. "He gave up his phone too easily. I know Dempsey. If he's got one phone, he's got at least two more as backups. Why don't you see if you can find them?"

Chico almost smiled. Then he walked over to Dempsey, picked him up by his boots, and began to shake.

Chapter 42
THE PICKUP

THE NEXT SEVERAL MINUTES WERE a flurry of activity. Peng found Dempsey's laptop and helped Zack upload the videos to several different locations for safe-keeping until he could get the evidence to the president.

Zack took my cell phone from me and made several calls to people to come help clean up this mess. But his first call was to his family. I thought about listening in to see how a tough guy like Zack would handle this kind of conversation, but I decided I really didn't want to see Zack cry. I preferred to think of him as invincible.

Demetrius and Chico loaded up the prince and his guard, as well as two pilots they'd found inside the cockpit of the plane, and took them in Dempsey's van to some secret location that Zack had suggested they not even reveal to us. Zack asked them to drop him somewhere on the way.

The rest of us—Permelia, Hope, Jin, Peng, and I—got into my rented SUV and began the journey home.

About thirty minutes out of Wendover, I asked, "What day is it?"

"Friday," Hope said. Her hair looked wild and windswept, and she smelled like smoke-canister dust. I had a sudden urge to kiss her. "We've been gone less than a week, but it seems like a year."

"We're supposed to be returning the boys to their families today," I said. "The pick-up after that high adventure."

Hope's cheeks turned pale. "We can't face those families. Not after what happened to the boys in the woods."

"Don't worry. I'm sure Ron's got it all sorted out by now." But even as I said the words, I felt a nudge of concern. I didn't think Ron's injuries were major, but I'd left him on the road with three Scouts and a homemade crutch. I hoped they'd made it to a hospital.

"Can you grab that phone and dial Ron for me?" Tim's phone sat in the compartment between the two seats.

Hope dialed the number and handed me the phone.

Ron picked up. "I don't recognize this number," he said flatly.

"It belongs to Tim. He was the guy who picked me up in the convertible. Kind of a jerk, really. I took his phone."

I heard Ron breathe a sigh of relief. "I was getting ready to contact some of my Delta friends to come looking for you. You all right? How about Hope and the kids?"

I looked around me in the car and grinned widely. "We're all fine. How about you and the boys?"

"We are all good," Ron said. "Except maybe Eric. I think he really would eat a bathtub full of Easy Cheese if I let him. We're on our way back from the condo now, ready to arrive at the rendezvous point in approximately one hour."

"How's your foot?"

"The doc says it will be fine, but I'll be in a boot for a few weeks. Driving is a little dicey."

"You could have turned the wheel over to JR."

"I don't think I'm quite ready for that yet." Ron chuckled. "Hey, what's your ETA?"

"We're just coming into Salt Lake. Why?"

"I'm taking the boys to the pick-up point. Parents are going to start asking questions. I've phoned the bishop to meet us there and given him a heads-up, but I could really use another leader to help divide and conquer. If you and Peng could swing by for just a few minutes . . ."

"We'll be there," I said. "We'll need time to clean up a bit though. The boys need to tell their parents the truth, but I'd like to limit the details to what happened in the mountains. I'm sure the government would consider anything that happened after Peng and I left as highly confidential. Since you guys have been lounging in a condo with real showers for a couple of days, the other parents might be a bit suspicious if Peng and I show up smelling like the trail."

"Jin and I are coming too." Hope must have been able to piece together both sides of the conversation from what I'd been saying. "It would also be suspicious if one of the parents is missing."

"We'll see you in a few," I said to Ron. I could hear him yelling at JR to keep his hands away from the steering wheel as I hung up. I saw Peng looking at me expectantly in the rearview mirror. "They're fine." I met his eyes in the mirror. "As long as JR doesn't kill them all on the way home."

Peng smiled.

* * *

Peng and I took the rented SUV and parked around the corner from Ron's house. Hope, Jin, and Permelia would arrive with the rest of the parents and look pleased and surprised when they came to pick us up. Permelia had been practicing her lines as we left. I got the feeling she would overact, but I didn't think anyone would notice. It was Permelia, after all.

The boys were standing on the lawn as Peng and I rounded the corner. JR was gesturing with his hands, Eric was holding his sides laughing, and Joey seemed to be studying some sort of insect in the palm of his hands. For some reason, they all looked taller than I remembered.

"Hey, it's Peng," Eric shouted and pointed at us. Everyone stopped for a second to look, and then all three of the boys rushed to us, nearly bowling us over with their hugs and pats on the back. Everyone was talking at once, asking questions, telling stories, going off on random tangents. I couldn't make any sense of any of it. I just looked over at Ron, who was sitting on the grass with his real crutches and boot, and I grinned at him. He grinned back. These were a great bunch of boys, and they would make great men. I not only loved them, but I also really liked them. I liked them a lot. I couldn't wait to spend more time with them. I didn't think our Sunday meetings would ever be the same again. I turned my head and wiped my sleeve against my face. I was glad Zack wasn't around to see me cry.

"Incoming," Ron said as he pulled himself up on a crutch. "The first of the parents is arriving. Places, everyone. Don't screw this up. The bishop is going to call a meeting tomorrow, and we'll fill your parents in on all of the details. For now, they mainly need to know that you're safe."

The boys moved to sit on the lawn, still talking, still laughing. Peng flowed back with them as if part of a choreographed dance. It struck me how well he fit in.

I looked up to the heavens and voiced a silent *Thank you*.

Joey's mom parked her minivan, slid her short, squat body out of the seat, and scooted over to Joey with a mixture of furrowed brows and worried tsks. She licked her thumb and wiped at his face.

"My poor baby." She began examining him from head to toe. He still bore some of the scratches he'd received in our battle with Tiny, and I worried that our fragile cover story of Ron taking a fall and the boys having to work together to save him was quickly going to crumble under the light of scrutiny.

"You have scratches all over your head," she said. "Was it just awful?" She pulled Joey to her. "Tell me, was it awful?"

Joey pulled away from his mother and looked her in the eye. I saw his lip begin to quiver, and I thought the whole story was going to spill out right now. But the quiver turned into a wide smile. He glanced at the other boys sitting on the ground, watching him with anticipation. "It was awesome," he proclaimed. His smile grew even broader, and his eyes darted back and forth from the boys to his mother. "It was the most awesome experience of my life."

"Better than Disneyland," JR agreed.

Joey's mother blinked as if this was not the answer she had expected. "What happened to you?" She continued to rub at his face. "You look different."

"He found a pony," Eric said, and then all the boys looked at Joey's mother.

Joey began to laugh. And he couldn't stop. And then all the boys were laughing with him, so hard they couldn't talk, so hard I wondered if they would ever be able to regain their composure.

Joey's mother turned to Ron, a look of horror on her face.

Ron shrugged. "Sorry about that. They found my stash of Easy Cheese in the condo. I think they might be a little giddy."

Joey's mom turned back to Joey, the horrified look on her face becoming even more pronounced. "You ate processed food? You know how you get when you eat processed food."

For some reason, the boys found that funny as well, and they fell into another fit. To tell the truth, I had to check myself so I didn't join them.

The other parents began to arrive, and it wasn't long before Hope pulled up in our Hyundai. She looked around at the scene in front of her. The frivolity was beginning to subside, but the parents were taken by surprise at the enthusiastic hugs they were receiving from their normally subdued teenagers. There was an electricity in the air, and everyone seemed to feel it.

"I thought I told you not to bring them home damaged?" Hope said, looking at the boys and their fits of laughter.

It had been only a few minutes since I had seen her, but I gathered her into my arms and swept her in a circle. "What kind of fun would that be?"

Permelia had been carrying Jin, who quickly latched on to Peng's neck. I put Hope down, and they joined us in a large group hug.

I looked around at the other families and noticed we were not alone in our affection.

We were back, we were alive, and somehow, despite everything that had happened, we were better off than when we had left.

"This trip is so over," I said. "Let's go home."

Epilogue

"MATT, WAKE UP. I HEARD a noise." My eyes came open, and I rubbed at my ribs where Hope had nudged me to get my attention. I suspected she had been sharpening her elbows for just such an occasion.

I looked at the clock—2:00 a.m. The rustling noise moved down the hallway toward the stairs to the living room.

"It's just Peng. You know he likes to run at night. He'll be fine. Maybe it's time for us just to trust him and let go." As I said it, I knew those might be the two most difficult things a parent could ever do: trust and let go.

"I'd feel a lot more comfortable if you went with him. Please?"

It sounded like a mere request, but I knew that if I declined, I would be subject to more sharp elbows and likely a cold shoulder as well. I wiped the sleep out of my eyes and tried to forget about my eleven o'clock class in the morning and all the preparation I still needed to put into it.

"Thank you," Hope said, rubbing my back as I got up. "I know we need to let him live his life, but I'm not quite ready to let go. You're a great father."

I wasn't sure about that, but at least I was an obedient husband.

Peng was downstairs in the living area, dressed in shorts and a tank top, looking like he was waiting for me.

"She make you come down again?"

I nodded and yawned. "You know your mother."

Peng nodded back. "You don't have to come, you know. You could just sleep here on the couch. I won't tell her."

I shook my head and pulled on my running shoes. "She would know," I said. "Mothers always know."

Peng almost smiled. "I really like to run alone . . ."

"I know you do, Peng," I said, cutting him off. "And I trust you. I really do. But I think we need to respect—"

"Let me finish." It was Peng's turn to cut me off. "What I was saying is that I really like running alone—with you. Especially at night. It's my favorite part of the week."

This time I was speechless. Even with all the progress we'd made with Peng, it was rare for him to share any type of genuine emotion.

"You said you used to run at night in the mountains," he said. "I was thinking I'd like to try that before it gets too cold."

"I don't know," I replied, thinking that my window for preparing my class was quickly closing to nothing. "You remember the last time we were in the mountains?"

"I do." This time Peng did smile. "Every minute of it."

I thought about what Peng was asking and realized this might be one of those times I could look back on either with fondness or with regret. My adopted son wanted to spend time with me—the same son we'd worried we wouldn't ever have a connection with. I could call in a sub for my class if I had to. Ron was always a good fill-in. And he didn't need to prepare. He could just tell stories.

I wondered where I should take Peng, and I realized I knew the perfect place. "Okay," I said. "I think it's time for sunrise at Moose Lake."

"What's that?"

"Something a terrorist friend introduced me to. But telling you about it won't do it justice. You really need to have the experience."

"I'm ready," Peng said, heading for the door.

"Not quite. We're going to need some warmer clothes. And we'll need to pull the headlamps out of the camping gear. We're going to be running along the edge of a cliff, and your mother would never forgive me if you fell off."

Peng ran excitedly to gather the clothes and equipment, but as we once again began heading toward the door, I thought of one more thing. "Wait here a second. I need to get my watch."

Peng raised his eyebrows but didn't say anything.

"Your mother made me promise to wear it if I traveled anywhere outside of the ordinary," I said when I got back. I pushed the buttons that activated the tracking beacon.

Peng watched with interest. "Won't that wake somebody up and put them on alert?"

"Don't worry," I said. "It's just Demetrius and Chico. They've tracked me to Moose Lake before. It's one of their favorite things to do. Trust me."

"I don't think you want to make Chico mad. I saw him turn that guy upside down at the airfield."

"Chico's a big teddy bear," I said. "Besides, I miss those guys. This will give us an excuse to see them again."

"What if they're in the middle of something really important?"

"There's nothing more important than family and friends," I said. "Nothing else in this world."

Peng seemed satisfied. We picked up our gear, and he began unlocking the doors.

"Let me help you with those," I said. "Why do we have so many locks anyway?"

"Because you wanted to try to stop me from sneaking out," Peng said.

"Look how successful that was. Now you've got me sneaking out with you. Maybe we should get rid of some of these."

Peng started to laugh, and then he stopped and frowned.

"What?" I asked.

"I was just thinking. It won't be too many years before Jin will be a teenager."

We looked at each other in horror. "Let's keep the locks," we said together.

Hope appeared at the top of the stairs. "Where are you two going with all that gear?"

"Taking Peng for a run in the mountains."

Hope bit her lip. "Are you sure that's safe? I won't forgive you if you die out there."

"It's not about dying," I said. "It's about living." I smiled at her, and she relaxed and smiled back.

"Why do I feel like I'm missing out on something great?"

"Next time you can come too."

I opened the last lock, waved good-bye to my wife, and then Peng and I stepped out into the night. Together.

The End

About the Author

FRANK HOLDAWAY LIVES, WORKS, WRITES, and hikes in the foothills of the Wasatch mountains. He is blessed with a beautiful wife, two wonderful children, and a slightly warped sense of humor. He enjoys reading, eating tacos, and, most of all, watching characters come to life.